THE
DEVIL
ASPECT

OR

WHERE THE DEVIL HIDES:

*The strange truth behind the
occurences at Hrad Orlú Asylum
for the Criminally Insane*

CRAIG RUSSELL

CONSTABLE

CONSTABLE

First published in Great Britain in 2019 by Constable

1 3 5 7 9 10 8 6 4 2

A CIP catalogue record for this book
is available from the British Library.

ISBN 978-1-4721-2835-5 (hardback)
ISBN 978-1-4721-2834-8 (trade paperback)

Typeset in Times New Roman by TW Type, Cornwall
Printed and bound in Great Britain by Clays Ltd, Elcograf S.p.A.

Papers used by Constable are from well-managed forests and
other responsible sources

MIX
Paper from
responsible sources
FSC® C104740

Constable
An imprint of
Little, Brown Book Group
Carmelite House
50 Victoria Embankment
London EC4Y 0DZ

An Hachette UK Company
www.hachette.co.uk

www.littlebrown.co.uk

For my wife, Wendy

The heart of man is the place the devil dwells in;
I feel sometimes a hell within myself.

Thomas Browne, 1605–1682

PROLOGUE

he appearance of that voice, of that dark personality, was like some terrible black sun dawning, filling the castle's tower room with a shining darkness and sinking with malice deep into the dense, thick stone of its ancient walls. Despite the patient being securely fastened to the examination couch, Viktor felt strangely isolated, vulnerable. Afraid. What he was hearing didn't make sense. It could not be.

Viktor realized this voice was not simply some fragment of his patient's splintered personality. This was something else, something other. Something much worse.

'I can sense your fear,' said Mr Hobbs. 'I am attuned to the fear of men. It is the energy which renews me and you renew me now. You have sought me out, and now you have found me. You want to know what I think, what I feel. Well, let me tell you: when I killed them – when I killed all those people, did all those terrible things to them – I enjoyed every second of it. I did what I did because of the dark pleasures it brought. Their pain and their fear were like fine wines to me.

'I especially liked it when, at the end, they begged for their lives: when they did that – and they all did that, eventually – I would pretend to hesitate and see in their eyes the glimmer of a faint, final, desperate hope. I let them have that, for an instant, then I took it away. It was that – that extinguishing of their very last hope – that I savoured more than anything, more even than the extinguishing of their lives.

'You see, Dr Kosárek, it was at that moment that they would feel the presence of the Devil and beg God to come and deliver them from him. And it was at that moment that I made them see – that they finally realized – that God had been there all along.

'It was then they realized that the Devil is just God in his night attire.'

PART ONE

A PLACE WHERE EVIL IS BOUND

CHAPTER ONE

*I*n the late autumn of 1935, Dr Viktor Kosárek was a tall, lean man in his twenty-ninth year. He was handsome, but not that unexceptional handsomeness that most of the Bohemian race possess: there was a hint of ancient nobility about his long slender nose, high-angled cheekbones and hard, blue-green eyes beneath dark-arched eyebrows and raven-black hair. At an age where many still looked boyish, Viktor Kosárek's rather severe features made him look older than he actually was: a guised maturity and accidental authority that aided him in his work. As a psychiatrist, it was Viktor's professional duty to unfold inner secrets, to shine a light into the most shadowed, most protected corners of his patients' minds; and those patients would not release their closest-held secrets, deliver their darkest despairs and desires, into the hands of a mere boy.

It was night and it was raining – a chill rain that spoke of the seasons turning – when Viktor left his rented apartment for the last time. Because he had so much luggage and his provincial train was leaving from Masaryk Station on Hybernská Street rather than Prague main station, he had taken a taxi. Also because he had so much luggage – a large trunk and two heavy suitcases – and because he knew how difficult it could be to secure a porter, he had timed his arrival at the station with three-quarters of an hour to spare. It was just as well because, once paid, the dour taxi-driver simply deposited the luggage on the pavement outside the station's main entrance and drove off.

Viktor had hoped his friend, Filip Starosta, would have been there to see him off and to help with the luggage, but the increasingly unreliable Filip had called off at the last minute. It meant Viktor had no option but to leave his baggage where it was and go off in search of a porter, which took him a good ten minutes. He guessed that the absence of porting staff had something to do with the commotion inside the station – the urgent shouts and cries that Viktor could now hear but which were out of his sight. Eventually he secured a young station attendant of about sixteen in an oversized red kepi who, despite his slight build, swung the trunk and cases onto his porter's trolley with ease.

They were heading into the station when a Praga Alfa in police colours pulled up into the rank that Viktor's taxi had just vacated. Two uniformed officers leapt from the car and ran across their path and into the station.

'What's going on?' Viktor asked the boy porter, whose shoulders shrugged somewhere in his loosely fitted uniform jacket.

'I heard a lot of shouting,' he said. 'Just before you called me over. Didn't see what was going on, though.'

Following the boy and his luggage into the station, Viktor could see right away that some significant drama was unfolding. Over in a far corner of the concourse, a large crowd was clustering like iron filings drawn to a magnet, leaving the main hall almost empty. Viktor noticed that the two newly arrived policemen had joined a number of other officers trying to disperse the crowd.

Someone concealed by the cluster of people was shouting: a male voice. A woman, also hidden by the throng, screamed in terror.

'She's a demon!' yelled the man's voice, hidden by the curtain of onlookers. 'She's a demon sent by the Devil. Satan!' There was a pause then, in an urgent tone of frightened warning, 'He is here now – Satan is here! Satan is come amongst us!'

'Stay here . . .' Viktor ordered the porter. He walked briskly across the station hall and shouldered his way through to the front of the crowd, which had formed in a police-restrained semicircle. As he pushed through, he heard a woman whisper in dark excitement to her friend: 'Do you think it's really him? Do you think he's Leather Apron?'

Viktor could now see the source of the cries: a man and a woman. Both looked terrified: the woman because she was being held from behind by the man, who had a large kitchen knife to her throat; the man terrified for reasons known only to himself.

'She's a demon!' the man yelled again. 'A demon sent from hell! See how she burns!'

Viktor could see that the woman was well dressed and prosperous looking, while her captor wore a working man's garb of battered cap, collarless shirt, coarse serge jacket and bagged corduroy trousers. At first glance it was obvious they were not a couple and he suspected the woman had been seized at random. The wild, darting, wide-eyed gaze of the young man indicated to Viktor the existential terror of some schizophrenic episode.

A single police officer stood closer than his colleagues to the couple, his hand resting on his undrawn pistol. Keep it holstered, thought Viktor; don't add to his sense of threat. He pushed through the front rank of onlookers and was immediately restrained by two policemen, who seized him roughly.

'Get back!' a Slovak accent commanded. 'Why can't you ghouls—'

'I'm Dr Viktor Kosárek, of the Bohnice Asylum,' protested Viktor, wriggling to wrest his arms free from the policemen's restraint. 'I'm a clinical psychiatrist. I think I can be of help here.'

'Oh . . .' The Slovak nodded to the other officer and they both released their grip on Viktor. 'Is he one of yours? An escapee?'

'Not that I know of. Definitely not one of my patients. But wherever he's from, he's clearly in the midst of a psychotic episode. Paranoiac delusions. Schizophrenia.'

'Pavel!' The Slovak called over to the policeman who stood with his hand still resting on his gun holster. 'There's a head-case doctor here . . .'

'Send him over,' said the officer without taking his eyes from captor and captive.

'I need you to disperse this crowd,' Viktor said quietly to the Slovak policeman as he stepped from the throng. 'They're hemming him in. The more anxious he gets, the more threatened he feels, the greater danger the young lady is in.'

The Slovak nodded and, with renewed urgency and determination, he and his fellow officers pushed and cajoled the crowd into a retreat from the drama.

Viktor went over to the policeman the Slovak had addressed as Pavel.

'You the headshrinker?' asked the officer, without taking his eyes from the knifeman.

'Dr Viktor Kosárek. I'm an intern at the Bohnice Asylum . . . well, I *was* an intern at the Bohnice Asylum,' he corrected himself. 'I'm actually travelling to the Hrad Orlů Asylum for the Criminally Insane to take up a new post.'

'Thanks for the curriculum vitae, Doctor – but we do have a bit of an urgent situation on our hands here.' The sarcasm dropped from his tone. 'Wait a minute – Hrad Orlů? Isn't that where they've got the Devil's Six locked up? In that case, this should be right up your street. Can you help?'

'I'll do my best, but if he's seriously delusional, I don't know if I'll get through to him.'

'If you don't get through to him, then I'm afraid I'll have to.' The policeman gave his leather holster a tap.

Kosárek nodded and placed himself squarely in front of the woman and her captor. He looked directly into the woman's eyes first.

'Try not to be afraid,' he spoke to her quietly and evenly. 'I know this is very difficult, but, whatever you do, don't struggle or scream. I don't want him more emotionally aroused than he is at the moment. I need you to be brave for me. Do you understand?'

The woman, her eyes wide with terror, gave a small nod.

'Good,' said Viktor. He noted that the sharp edge of the knife creased the skin of her neck right above the jugular. It wouldn't take much – the smallest of movements – for her deranged captor to sever the vein. And if he did, within seconds she would be so far from the shore of life that there would be nothing anyone could do to save her.

He turned to her captor, looking over the woman's shoulder and again directly into his eyes. He was a young man, perhaps even a couple of years younger than Viktor. His eyes were no less wide and no less afraid than those of his captive, his gaze scanning the space around them, not focusing on, not even seeming to see, the now moved-back police and agitated crowd. Instead he seemed to be watching horrors unfold that were invisible to everyone else. It was something Viktor Kosárek had already seen many times in his brief career: the mad inhabiting a different dimension mentally, while remaining in this one physically.

'My name is Dr Kosárek.' Viktor's voice was again calm, even. 'I'm here to help you. I know you're afraid, but I'm going to do everything I can to help you. What is your name?'

'She is a demon!' cried the man.

'What is your name?' Viktor repeated.

'A fire demon. Can't you see? They are all around us. They feed off us. She's been sent here to feed off me. She's been sent by the Devil . . .'

The young man broke off and looked as if he had suddenly heard a sound, or smelled a strange odour. 'He is *here*,' he said in a forced, urgent whisper. 'The Devil is here, now, in this place. I *sense* him—'

'Your name,' said Kosárek quietly, kindly. 'Please tell me your name.'

The man with the knife looked confused, as if he couldn't understand why he was being distracted with such trifles. 'Šimon,' he said eventually. 'My name is Šimon.'

'Šimon, I need you to keep calm. Very calm.'

'Calm?' asked Šimon incredulously. 'You ask me to be calm? The Devil is among us. His demons are here. She is a demon. Don't you see them?'

'No, I'm afraid I don't. Where are they?'

Šimon cast his gaze like a searchlight over the marble floor of the railway station. 'Don't you *see*? Are you blind? They're everywhere.' He suddenly looked more afraid, more agitated, again seeing something that only he was witness to. 'The ground – the floor – it's *sweating* them. They ooze up out of the stone. Lava from the bowels of the Earth. Then they bubble and froth upwards until they take form. Like this one.' He tightened his grip on his captive, the hand with the knife twitching.

'Šimon,' said Viktor, 'don't you see you've got it all wrong? This woman is nothing but a woman. She's not a demon.'

'Are you mad? Can't you see? Don't you see the fire horns curling out from her head? The lava of her eyes? Her white-hot iron hooves? She is an elemental demon. A fire demon. I am so terribly burned from just touching her. I have to stop her. I have to stop them all. They are here to feed off us, to burn us all, to take us into the lake of fire where there will be no end to our torment.' He thought about his own words, then spoke with a sudden, but quiet and considered resolve. 'I've got it: I have to cut her head off . . . That's it, I have to cut her head clean off. It's the only way to kill a demon. The only way.'

The woman, who had been doing her best to follow Viktor's command and remain quiet, let out a desperate cry. Kosárek held up a calming hand to both captive and captor. He realized he was dealing with a delusional schizophrenic paranoia of massive dimension; that there might be no way of reaching Šimon's tortured mind before he killed his captive.

He cast a meaningful look in the direction of the police officer, who gave a small nod and quietly unbuttoned the flap on his leather holster.

'I assure you, Šimon, this woman is no demon,' said Viktor. 'You are unwell. You're unwell in a way that makes your senses deceive you. Close your eyes and take a breath.'

'It's the Devil who deceives. The Great Deceiver has blinded everyone but me. I am God's instrument. If I close my eyes, the Devil will sneak up on me and drag me to Hell.' He lowered his voice; sounded pained, afraid. 'I have seen the Great Deceiver. I have seen the Devil and looked into his face.' He gave a cry of terrible despair. 'He burned me with his eyes!'

'Šimon, please listen to me. Please try to understand. There is no Devil. All there is, all you're experiencing, is your mind. Your mind – everybody's mind – is like a great sea, a deep ocean. We all live our lives, every day, every one of us, sailing on the surface of that ocean. Do you understand me, Šimon?'

The madman nodded, but his eyes remained manic, terrified.

'But beneath each of us,' continued Viktor, 'are the great dark fathoms of our personal oceans. Sometimes frightening monsters live in those depths – great fears and terrible desires that can seem to take real form. I know these things because I work with them as a doctor all the time. What is happening to you, Šimon, is that there is a great storm in your ocean; everything has been stirred up and swirled around. All of those dark monsters from the deeps of your mind have been awoken and have burst through the surface. I want you to think about it. I want you to understand that everything that is frightening you at this moment, everything you think you see, is being created by your mind.'

'I am being deceived?' Šimon's voice became that of a frightened, lonely child.

'You're being deceived,' repeated Viktor. 'The woman you hold is an ordinary woman. The demon you think you hold is a demon of your imagination. The Devil you fear is nothing but a hidden aspect of your own mind. Please, Šimon, close your eyes—'

'I am being deceived—'

'Close them, Šimon. Close them and imagine the storm passing, the waters calming.'

'Deceived . . .' He closed his eyes.

'Let the lady go, Šimon. Please.'

'Deceived . . .' He let his arm fall from around the woman's shoulders. The hand that held the knife eased away from her throat.

'Move!' The policeman hissed the urgent command at the woman. 'To me, now!'

'Deceived . . .'

The woman ran, sobbing, across to the policeman, who ushered her beyond the police line; a woman from the crowd folded comforting arms around her.

'Please Šimon,' Viktor Kosárek said to the young man, who now stood alone with his eyes still closed, 'put the knife down.'

Šimon opened his eyes. He looked at the knife in his hand and again repeated: 'Deceived.' He looked up, his eyes plaintive; his hands, the knife still in one, held out beseechingly.

'It's all right,' said Viktor, taking a step towards him. 'I'll help you now.'

'I *was* deceived,' said Šimon, suddenly angry. 'The Great Deceiver, the Guiser, the Dark One – *he* deceived me.' He looked directly at Viktor and gave a small laugh. 'I didn't recognize you. Why didn't I recognize you? But I know who you are now.' Šimon's eyes became suddenly hard and full of hate. 'Now I know! Now I know who you are!'

It happened too fast for Viktor to react. Šimon launched himself at the young psychiatrist, the knife raised high and ready to strike.

Viktor froze and two sounds filled the space around him,

reverberating in the cavern of the station concourse: the deafening sound of the policeman's gunshot; and Šimon's screaming, as he lunged at the young doctor, of a single word.

'Devil!'

CHAPTER TWO

*t seemed to Viktor Kosárek that bureaucracy and the Bohemian mind were woven inseparably, one into the other. In every aspect of life, in every action taken, there seemed always to be one more form to be filled in, one more official to be encountered.

Viktor had telephoned his new employer from the kiosk in the police station in Benediktská Street. He told Professor Románek what had transpired in the railway station and how the police had needed him to fill out a report, then another, causing him to miss his train. He explained that his luggage was being held for him at the Masaryk Railway Station and that he would be on the first train the following morning, and that he was dreadfully sorry for the inconvenience.

'My dear boy,' Professor Románek had said, 'think nothing of it. You clearly saved that young woman's life. And the poor unfortunate at the centre of this tragedy – how is he?'

'Thank you for understanding . . .' Kosárek paused as a knot of uniforms bustled urgently and noisily down the corridor, past the kiosk, and out through the main door. 'He is in a serious condition,' he continued once the policemen had passed. 'It isn't yet clear whether he'll survive or not, unfortunately. The police officer aimed to kill, fearing for my life, but his bullet lost much of its force as it passed through the musculature of the upper arm and deflected off the scapular spine into the abdominal cavity. The young man was very lucky it missed vital organs but there has been massive internal bleeding. Only time will tell. If he does survive, then I've arranged for him to be admitted to the asylum infirmary at Bohnice as soon as he's sufficiently recovered.'

'A most distressing episode. I hope it hasn't soured your new beginning with us.'

'Not at all, Professor. I'm very much looking forward to working with you.' And he was: Professor Ondřej Románek was famed for his innovative, sometimes controversial, methods. Románek believed in using the latest technology and was credited with developing new and effective ways of treating the mind.

'I regret that I will not be able to meet you at the station in person.' The normally buoyant Románek suddenly sounded less cheerful. 'Herr Dr Hans Platner will pick you up. You'll remember meeting Dr Platner at the interviews; he's in charge of general medicine at Hrad Orlů. Hans is a fine physician and a good man, but can be a little *forceful* with his opinions. Please pay these no mind. I look forward to our meeting.'

'As do I.'

After he hung up, Viktor Kosárek puzzled about what to do with himself. He had given up his lodgings, having expected to have been by now safely invested in his new place of work and residence. He couldn't make up his mind whether he should call Filip Starosta, his friend and former contemporary at university, and ask if he could put him up for the night. But Filip had already let him down once: Viktor had arranged to spend the previous evening, his last in Prague before taking up his new post, with his friend, but at the last minute Filip had sent a telegram to say he could no longer make it nor see him off at the station. It had troubled Viktor: Filip was a young man of intense intelligence and equally intense passions, his increasingly erratic behaviour of late having caused Viktor concern. Perhaps it would be better, he thought, to try to find a hotel close to the station.

A parsimonious-looking old man, small, meagre and birdlike, was waiting to use the telephone, so Viktor vacated the kiosk while he tried to make up his mind about what to do. He was standing in the hallway outside the telephone kiosk, debating with himself, when another group of policemen, this time in plainclothes, trotted along the hall. They were led by a striking-looking man – tall, broad shouldered and sternly handsome – whom another officer addressed as Kapitán Smolák as they passed and headed out into the street. Viktor could hear the urgent revving of engines, the slamming of car doors, the screech of too-eager tyres slipping on damp cobbles.

An older uniformed policeman, heavily built, bristle headed, magnificently moustachioed, and with fleshy jowls that spilled over the top of his stiff-collared police tunic, came in through the entrance. His service cap was tucked under his arm and he read notes on a clipboard. His shoulder flashes indicated he held the rank of nadstrážmistr.

'What's going on?' Kosárek asked the master-sergeant.

'Police business,' the sergeant said dully and walked on into the body of the station.

'I heard . . .' said the old man who'd been waiting to use the telephone kiosk, speaking with the conspiratorial eagerness of someone who truly appreciated bad news. 'I heard them talking. They've found a body. Another body.'

'A murder?' asked Kosárek.

The old man nodded his bird head with grim glee. 'A woman's body, all cut up. Leather Apron has been busy again.'

CHAPTER THREE

*H*is father had been a butcher.

It perhaps wasn't odd that, given the scene confronting him, the trade of butcher came to Lukáš Smolák's mind; but it did strike him as strange that he thought of his father at a time like this. There again, it had always been to his father he had gone, rather than to his somewhat distant mother, whenever the tribulations of childhood had overwhelmed him, whenever he had been worried, confused or frightened. And these were emotions he felt in no small part now.

Despite possessing the large, muscular build his son had gone on to inherit, Smolák's father had been a gentle, kind man of quiet demeanour; someone who never seemed to become perturbed, no matter how grave or heated the situation. And the young Lukáš had never felt the sting of angry hand or word from his father. That was perhaps why Smolák, himself, had matured into a calm, equanimous man.

There had been one event, however, in Lukáš's memory of his father that had shaken him: an event so dissonant and dislocated from every other experience of his parent that he found it difficult to believe it had actually occurred. One day, when Lukáš had been nine or ten, he had after school been sent on an errand by his mother. She had asked him to go to his father's shop, which was in a low-roofed, whitewashed building near the church in the middle of the village, to collect a kilo of Ostravské sausages for the evening meal. Lukáš had done as he was bidden, but when he arrived, his father was not at his usual station behind the counter. Instead the door to the back rooms – the part of his father's butcher business the young Lukáš had never before seen – was open, and strange sounds were coming from some far part of the building.

When his calling for his father had gone unanswered, young Lukáš had tentatively made his way into the forbidden realm of the back shop. In the sudden dark and cool, he had found himself amongst pendant slabs of meat, trays of cuts and sausages. There had still been no sign of his father and he had ventured further, following the strange sounds: an urgent, shrill squealing.

Pushing open the door at the rear of the shop, Lukáš had stepped out and, blinking in the sun after the dark of the coldstore, found himself in a small rear courtyard. His father was there, his side turned to the boy whose arrival had gone unseen. The urgent squealing came from a small pig that his father held tight between leather-aproned knees. Lukáš had arrived in the courtyard just in time to see the heavy-headed mallet in his father's hand arc downwards. There was a sickening thud as the mallet collided with the piglet's head and the squealing was stilled. His father had dropped the mallet and taken a long-bladed knife from his apron pocket and drawn it swiftly across the throat and neck of the beast. Gouts of blood had pulsed slick onto the cobbles and into the drain, each pulse weaker than the last.

It had been then that his father had seen him. His hands on his son's shoulders, he had turned Lukáš from the sight of the dying pig and ushered him back into the coldstore. Hanging his blood-covered leather apron on the pantry door, his father had taken the sobbing Lukáš back through to the shop, had sat him down and had told him, gently and patiently, about the sad necessity of violence in life.

His father had been a butcher.

The thought had come to him here, in this room that had become a small encapsulation of hell. Kapitán Lukáš Smolák of the Prague City Police and son of a long-dead butcher, had been an investigator of murders for twenty years and had seen just about every act of violence that could be imagined. He had seen decapitations, burnings, shootings; heads pulped with rocks or steel bars, bodies ripped and stabbed. But the worst scenes he'd ever had to face had been the previous murders committed by the maniac all Prague knew as 'Leather Apron'.

But this – this latest hell – was unsurpassed.

The woman on the bed – and it was only from the fragments of clothing that her gender could be ascertained – had been butchered. There was no other word for it: whole parts of her anatomy had been excised and removed and the empty cauldron of her abdomen and thorax lay prised open, like the superstructure of a shipwreck, the white bone of her ribs gleaming through the gore. Sitting neatly piled on one corner of the bed, the slick grey-brown and pink coils of the victim's intestines had been set aside by her killer. On the floor at the foot of the bed sat a carefully placed china wash bowl. Equal care had been taken in arranging the contents of the bowl: the victim's kidneys and heart.

The head was turned in Smolák's direction, but even this gave no indication of gender or personality. The face had been removed and the lidless white orbs of the eyes stared at Smolák in emphatic accusation from red-raw flesh above a bright white, gleaming, lipless grin.

All of the horror was confined to the area of the bed, the covers of which were sodden with blood. There were no signs of struggle, of violence, anywhere else in the bedroom. If he were to turn his back to the bed and examine the room, the scene would be one of normality, except for the stain on the carpet by the door where the caretaker, who had been the first to find the body, had vomited.

Since then, Smolák had had to send several officers from the room to be sick out in the street below. Even with his years-long experience of murder, he himself found he could not look at the corpse for any length of time without his own gorge rising. The only person who seemed to be able to maintain professional dispassion was the small, almost-portly man dressed in a baggy suit and businesslike demeanour who bent over the remains, his tie thrown over his shoulder to prevent it dangling in blood. Magnifying loupe in hand, only Dr Václav Bartoš, the police medical examiner, focused himself on the detail, not the whole.

Smolák's subordinate, Detektiv-Seržant Mirek Novotný approached him. Novotný was an ambitious red-haired young officer whose expression was usually self-assured to the point of cockiness. There was no such expression today and Smolák noticed the freckles stood out more vividly on Novotný's paled face.

'You have something?' asked Smolák.

'We have, Kapitán. Old Leather Apron's been clumsy this time.'

'How so?' Smolák asked without taking his eyes off the carcass of bone and gore that had once, unimaginably, been a human being.

'We've got fresh fingerprints that don't belong to the victim. And over in the corner, there . . .' Novotný pointed to an area on the floor next to the bed. 'He's stepped in blood and left a partial footprint.'

Smolák frowned. 'That's not like him.' He leaned over to examine the print. It was clear enough, all right: half a print from a smooth-soled shoe or boot. A man's footprint, but on the small side. 'That's not like him at all. He's not sloppy. He's never made a mistake like this before. Same with the fingerprints.'

Novotný shrugged. 'Maybe he wants to get caught. Sometimes they do, these looneys – they feel guilt deep down or some nonsense like that and they want us to catch and punish them. Or they play stupid cat and mouse games.'

'Not this one. This particular craftsman enjoys his work too much. If this slip-up is deliberate, it's because he wants to taunt us. To show us we can't catch him. But I even doubt that.' He looked at the footprint again. 'It's a strange one all right. Anything else?'

'As you know there's no sign of forced entry,' said Novotný. 'According to the caretaker, he had to let her into her apartment three days ago, after she'd visited the market in the Lesser Town Square. She'd lost her keys, thought she'd dropped them.'

Smolák nodded thoughtfully. 'You think that the killer picked her pocket in the market?'

'It's a possibility. Explains how he got in. I thought I'd put a couple of boys on checking if anyone else was pickpocketed in the market that day.'

'And check out if any of the previous victims lost keys in the days leading up to their murders,' said Smolák. 'It's the kind of thing that may not have been mentioned or overlooked.'

Once Novotný was gone, Smolák turned back to the medical examiner who, having finished his examination, straightened himself from the corpse, pulling his tie back into position.

'She's been dead a day or more,' said Dr Bartoš. 'It's difficult to give a specific cause of death: there are too many incisions and too much missing, but she has had her throat cut. If that was the first wound, then mercifully it would have been instantly fatal. We can only hope it was and saved her from everything that followed. But one thing I can tell you with certainty is that it was all well done.'

'Well done?'

'If this is another murder by the so-called Leather Apron, then he's becoming more ambitious, and in so doing is displaying skill in dismemberment. There is nothing tentative at all about this knife work. Whoever did this knew exactly what he was doing and did it in a methodical manner.'

'A surgeon?'

'Not necessarily,' said Bartoš. 'It could be a surgeon, an anatomist, or simply a slaughterman or butcher. Anyway, I heard a rumour that you may already have your man.'

'What?' Smolák was confused.

'A Jewish butcher's apprentice, I heard. Grabbed a woman in the Masaryk rail station and threatened her with a knife before being shot by one of your boys.'

Smolák shook his head. 'He wasn't Jewish – I don't know where that idea came from. Anyway, that wasn't our man. Just some looney with a knife.'

'And you don't think *this* is the work of a madman?' Bartoš said incredulously, nodding towards the dismembered remains.

'Of course I do, but a different kind of madman. A different species. Whoever did this lives in our world, not lost in some fantasy realm. He's organized and – like you said – knows exactly what he's about. I just don't know what it was about this woman that caused him to single her out.' Smolák again cast his gaze around the expensively furnished bedroom. The apartment was over two floors in a grand apartment building which sat in a curving terrace of similar baroque buildings in Malá Strana. This was a wealthy part of town, which had been so traditionally a German neighbourhood it was also known as Prager Kleinseite. On his way through the apartment to the bedroom, Smolák had noticed a copy of the German-language daily *Prager Tagblatt* on the hall table and that almost all the books in the bookcase had been in German. The victim's name, he had then been told, was Maria Lehmann. German. The previous victims had also had Czech-German surnames, but Smolák had paid little heed to the coincidence, assumed it had been their profession as prostitutes, not their ethnic backgrounds, that had been the motive.

The last thing Smolák needed was a crazed killer with some kind of cultural agenda.

'Anyway,' said Václav Bartoš as he made for the door, 'I'll write up my report and have it sent over.' Just before leaving, he turned back to Smolák, frowning.

'Something else, Doctor?'

The police surgeon shrugged. 'An observation, perhaps. Something beyond my professional purview.'

'Believe me, Doctor. I'm grateful for any observation you'd care to make. This is the fourth such killing.'

'All this . . .' The doctor swept the scene on the bed with a gesture of his hand. 'All this is very familiar. About fifty years ago there was a series of similar murders in England. London. Like all Leather Apron's victims before this one, the killings were carried out in the streets or alleys. But there was one committed in the victim's room, and I have to tell you that the scene left behind was *very* similar to this. You've maybe heard of the case: it's become almost folkloric in England. The killer, who has never been caught, became known as Jack the Ripper.'

Smolák frowned, looking at the scene of horror but this time looking beyond it, to the other cases, to a chronology of murder and mutilation. 'So are you saying that I should be looking for an Englishman? And one who must now be aged between seventy and ninety?'

The doctor shook his head. 'Amongst those who know anything about it, Victorian London makes people think of three things: Queen Victoria, Charles Dickens, and Jack the Ripper. And not necessarily in that order. Like I say, this insane killer who subjected women to the most horrific terror and pain has become an almost romantic figure to the English: folkloric, like I said. Just as our own Jan Neruda was influenced by Charles Dickens, perhaps our Czech Leather Apron sees himself as the creative heir to Jack the Ripper. There are certainly many similarities to be considered.'

Smolák nodded. It had been something that had crossed his mind before, but he hadn't had the doctor's knowledge of the London crime scenes. 'The victims in London were common prostitutes, I believe. This victim – ' he nodded towards the rent flesh on the bed – 'was no prostitute. She was a wealthy young woman.'

The doctor shrugged again. 'Like I said, just an observation.'

'I'll look into it,' Smolák said. 'Thank you, Doctor.'

'There is one other thing that occurs to me,' Bartoš said before leaving the crime scene. 'There was a sighting of a suspect in the vicinity of one of the Ripper's murders. He was described as wearing a leather apron.'

* * *

It was after the doctor had left that Smolák saw it: a small glittering something that had rolled across floorboards and into the corner by the bed.

*O*ne advantage of the delay, he told himself, was that it was much more pleasant to make the trip in the daylight. Viktor Kosárek had that uniquely Czech love of country: a deep connection with its nature, landscape and culture, without feelings of trenchant nationalism – a commodity on which Czechoslovakia's Teutonic neighbour seemed to be cornering the market. After the events of the night before, it would be good to sit and watch through the window as the city yielded to nature.

It was another cold day, but flickering bright as the sun danced through the thin fingers and translucent red and gold of the broadleaved trees that lined the rail track. And beyond the autumn-gilded fringe were the pine forests, thick and emerald dark, rich with legend and myth; rippling over hills, crowding mountains, breaking for field, town and village. The dark heart of Europe.

But as he settled to the window's field-forest-meadow-forest rhythm, the face of the young man in the station intruded into his thoughts. Particularly the desperate expression of terror and hate as he had launched himself at Viktor, knife raised. And now he lay in a ward of the General University Hospital in Prague, occupying that dark land, the space between life and death.

For all his studies, for all the cases of delusion and paranoia he had observed or treated, Viktor Kosárek still could not place himself at the centre of a madman's universe; to experience the world through his eyes, twisted and chaotic and terrifying. What must it be like to fear for your life so? To see – to really *see* – demons and monsters and devils all around you?

And when the memory of a deranged stranger didn't detract from his appreciation of the passing countryside, another, more familiar face, came to mind. The last time he had seen Filip Starosta had been three nights before his departure from Prague.

Filip was a warm, affable, relaxed soul whose company Viktor enjoyed; Filip was a dark, fervid, obsessive personality whose company Viktor found too intense. Since their first meeting, Viktor had learned to enjoy the former, tolerate the latter. Filip Starosta, Viktor realized, was a paradox of personalities: something that would have stimulated Viktor in a case study, but which worried him in a friend. And that worry had become acute of late: Filip's periods of withdrawal from society, his sudden and intense dark passions, had increased in frequency and duration.

That Filip had not made good his promise to see Viktor off was a matter of concern. And now that Viktor would be distant from Filip, he worried that his friend would become even more adrift on dark, choleric seas.

He resolved to make regular trips back to the city to check on his friend. After all, Hrad Orlů wasn't really that far from Prague.

The compartment he travelled in was occupied by one other passenger, a pleasant-looking man in his fifties who had greeted him amiably in German when he had entered and sat down opposite Viktor, who noted with some dismay the eagerness in the man's eyes to start a conversation.

'Are you travelling to Mladá Boleslav?' Viktor's fellow traveller asked eventually – and redundantly: there were few stops of note before the train's final destination.

'I am,' said Viktor.

'Wonderful part of the country. What takes you there? If I may ask.'

'Work,' said Viktor, in the knowingly vain hope that his companion's curiosity would end there. He could tell from the man's accent that he was a foreigner, his German neither Bohemian or Austro-Bavarian. Somewhere further north in Germany, perhaps.

'I also,' said the German. 'What is it that you do?'

'I'm a doctor.'

'Ah,' said the German. 'So you have been in Prague for a visit? Beautiful city, truly beautiful. So rich in history.'

'No, I live – I lived – in Prague. I'm taking up a new appointment.'

'*Toi, toi, toi!*' said the German. 'Congratulations and good luck! I wish you well in your new job.'

Viktor smiled and thanked him. Despite his intrusion into Viktor's preferred solitude, the German's friendly demeanour and appearance made him difficult to dislike.

'Professor Gunnar Pedersen. From the University of Hamburg. Nice to meet you.' The German leaned forward and extended his hand.

'Dr Viktor Kosárek.' Viktor shook his hand and smiled resignedly. Full-scale conversation was now, he knew, inevitable.

'So are you taking up an appointment in the hospital? Or are you a family practitioner?'

'Neither,' said Viktor. 'I'm a psychiatrist. I'm taking up a post at Hrad Orlů Asylum.'

'Oh, I know it!' said Pedersen. 'You see, I'm a professor of archaeology at Hamburg University: I'm visiting the very area you're travelling to.' The German thought for a moment. 'Hrad Orlů Asylum – isn't that where they have confined those murderers? The Devil's Six?'

Viktor stifled a sigh. Ever since he had taken the appointment, everyone he told bombarded him with questions about the six notorious patients confined there. The most notorious in Central Europe.

'It's not a helpful name for them, and their crimes were totally unconnected, but yes, that's the place.'

'I would love to visit the castle some time,' said Pedersen. 'Nothing to do with its current use as an asylum, mind you: it's just that archaeologically it's a fascinating place.'

'Really? The castle only dates back to the early Middle Ages, as far as I know.'

'Ah but you're wrong. The current castle perhaps, but what lies beneath . . .' The German archaeologist wagged his finger in the air. 'What lies beneath is truly ancient. The castle of Hrad Orlů was built on the site of a Neolithic hill fort. Danubian or Linear Pottery Culture, we think. In fact, the outer wall of the castle follows the circle of the original Neolithic rondel. Do you know that when the current castle was built, there were no kitchens or proper accommodations? That it was originally never intended to be inhabited?'

'Then why did they build it?'

'It's one of the most solidly built fortresses in Bohemia, despite having no strategic importance. It was built as a great fastness not to keep anything out, but to keep something in. Something locked up for all time. Which is quite appropriate when you think of its current use.'

'Really?' Victor was intrigued despite himself. 'Who was confined there?'

'Not who, what,' said the German. 'There's a network of caves beneath the castle that were believed to be the mouth of Hell. The castle was built to seal it up. All nonsense, of course, but it's true the Neolithic site was founded on the entrance to a network of caves. Have you noticed how the castle seems fused into the rock? It's like Predjama Castle in Slovenia, where its fortitude as a stronghold comes as much from nature's as man's design. Do you know we really have no idea how long there has been human habitation there? That's what makes it so attractive to us archaeologists. All kinds of stuff has been dug up over the centuries, by farmers and villagers mainly, in the fields down beyond the village.'

'What kind of stuff?' asked Viktor.

Pedersen leaned forward, clearly pleased to have an audience. 'Ceramics mostly: pot shards, small pottery discs with holes drilled in the middle – there have been lots of those – and stone implements. Lots of ornamental glass beads too, but they are from a much later period. The more important pieces ended up in universities or museums in Prague and Vienna, of course. All from around the castle and area.'

'Really? I didn't know that.'

'Oh yes, yes – believe me, Dr Kosárek, your new workplace is a most important archaeological location. In fact, about fifty years ago your own Josef Ladislav Píč, the father of Czech archaeology himself, carried out an excavation in the forest close to the castle. He uncovered important pieces too: two pottery figurines of fat Mother Earth types similar to the Dolní Věstonice Venus or the Willendorf Venus. They're now in the České Muzeum in Prague. And, of course, long, long before that there was the discovery of the Bear Man, but no one knows what became of that.'

'The Bear Man?' asked Viktor.

'Carved out of bone, apparently – human bone some said, but I doubt that, more likely bear bone. It depicted a figure with the body of a heavy-set man and the shoulders and head of a bear. It was discovered about a hundred and fifty years ago but became lost. When it was first discovered, the local Hussite cleric denounced it as a representation of Satan, claiming it was connected to Jan of the Black Heart and all his goings-on – I take it you know all about Jan of the Black Heart?'

'I'm afraid I don't.'

'Oh.' Pedersen looked disappointed. Viktor was always amazed at how experts invariably expected others to be versed in their speciality – something he'd come across a lot in the medical field.

'Never mind,' said the German. 'Jan of the Black Heart was the erstwhile lord of the castle and really has nothing to do with the

Bear Man other than the figure being represented on the familial coat-of-arms. Anyway, some of the locals claimed that the Bear Man carving was a representation of Veles – you know, the part-man-part-bear lord of the underworld of Slavic tradition. But of course that's nonsense: the carving belonged to a time millennia before the Slavs arrived. However it seemed everyone agreed something dark and powerful adhered to the artefact.'

Viktor gave a start as a train travelling in the opposite direction thundered past the window. He waited until it had passed before asking, 'What do you mean "dark and powerful"?'

'Oh, you know, satanic worship, that kind of thing,' Pedersen waved his hand dismissively. 'Completely irrelevant and totally anachronistic. But when the Bear Man carving went missing, the Hussite priest accused the locals of stealing it and using it in Black Masses. That's where the whole connection to Jan of the Black Heart came into it all. There was even a rumour that František Rint got his hands on it – and that he hid it among the thousands of other human bones he used when he was creating his macabre skeleton art in the ossuary at the Church of All Saints in Sedlec in 1870. Personally, I think the truth is more prosaic: that the Bear Man is just lying gathering dust on a shelf in some museum storeroom somewhere.'

Viktor chatted with the archaeologist for the rest of the journey and became glad he'd been drawn out of his dark reflecting. The journey took just over an hour and, as they drew near the regional railhead at Mladá Boleslav, Pedersen stood up.

'I'm afraid I have to leave you now,' he said, smiling and extending his hand to Viktor. 'I have to supervise the unloading of my equipment. Perhaps I'll see you around.'

After the cheery German left him, Viktor sat quietly once more, watching through the window as Mladá Boleslav took form around him.

The station was a shadowed place, the tracks seeming to sink between two huge embankments as the train slowed to a halt. The city of Mladá Boleslav was the nearest major settlement to the castle of Hrad Orlů – Adlersburg as it was known in German.

Everything here had two names: Czech and German. That was the schism of personality that Viktor Kosárek had grown up with: a nation of multiple and overlapping identities. His nation's, his contemporaries', his own identity had always been *miscellaneous*. He had been brought up in a small town in Moravia, his mother a German, his father a Czech. In any other land, it would be the basis for a feeling of detachment or displacement. Not here. Here it was the norm. Of course, most people in the newly formed republic identified themselves as mainly one thing: Czech, Moravian, Silesian, Slovak, German, Polish, Ruthenian, Hungarian, Jew – but it was always less a definition and more the naming of the principal ingredient in a richly seasoned stew.

The Republic of Czechoslovakia may only have been seventeen years old, yet it was also, as Pedersen had pointed out, ancient: cast in primordial stone that constantly shifted and melted, melded and reformed. Bohemians particularly were like no other people who walked the Earth: for them everything was fluid, ever changing. Like immortals, they had watched with amused disinterest the petty passions of mortals: the swelling and shrinking of borders; the rising and falling of flags, of empires, of patriotisms and prejudices.

As someone who studied the architecture of minds as his profession, the split-personality of the land of his birth fascinated Viktor. He had heard it said so often that if you wanted to know what your mother tongue was, it was the one in which you dreamed. Viktor Kosárek dreamed in both Czech and German.

When he disembarked from the train at Mladá Boleslav, Viktor noticed a medium-height, slightly stocky man in his late forties, standing at the station entrance. He was wearing a dark-green hunting-style overcoat and a Tyrolean hat. Viktor recognized him right away as Dr Hans Platner, Professor Románek's deputy at the asylum. Platner grinned amiably, waved and came over to Kosárek, bringing a porter with him.

'I hope you had a pleasant journey, Dr Kosárek,' Platner said in German and shook Viktor's hand. 'Especially after what happened last night – Professor Románek told me all about it. Dreadful business. Simply dreadful. We should feel relieved that you got here without further incident.'

'Well, it was just as well I was there, I suppose.'

'Really? But you could have been injured or killed,' said the doctor emphatically. 'I'm sure the police would have dealt with him. But it does sound like you saved that unfortunate woman's life. It would perhaps be better if the young man succumbs to his wounds.'

'Why then there would be no opportunity for treatment and recovery . . .' Viktor was taken aback by the general physician's statement.

'If recovery could ever be achieved, Dr Kosárek,' said Platner. 'We are clearly talking about someone who is a chronic threat both to himself and to healthy society.' Viktor noticed a lapel pin in the collar of Platner's coat: a narrow red shield with highly stylized, ribbon-type lettering forming an interlocking S, D and P. Viktor had seen it before, during his interview in front of both Professor Románek and his deputy. Platner was a Sudeten German. The lapel pin indicated he was a member of the newly formed Sudetendeutsche Partei – the Sudeten German Party. As such, Platner would not be one to hold with ideas of richly seasoned ethnic stews: the Sudetendeutsche Partei, like their cousins over the border, held an uncompromisingly singular view of national identity.

There were nearly three and a half million Sudeten Germans in Czechoslovakia, the majority in Bohemia, Silesia and Moravia. The Sudetendeutsche Partei had just emerged from that year's elections as the largest party in both the Senate and Chamber of Deputies. The party had been funded by – and had close connections with – the National Socialists in neighbouring Germany and all they represented. The darkness through the trees, as Viktor thought of it.

'Oh dear,' said Platner, looking at Viktor's luggage as the porter wheeled it over to them. 'I rather think I'll struggle to get that into my car.' He slapped Viktor heartily on the shoulder. 'But we can try.'

Viktor cast his gaze over to the platform where the rest of the luggage was being decanted, hoping to catch sight of Pedersen, but there was no sign of the German archaeologist.

'Shall we?' Platner said and guided Viktor to a brand-new Opel P4 parked outside the station. Despite Platner's reservation, they managed to wrestle Viktor's two cases into the back seat. While the P4 had no boot, it did have a barred luggage rack above the rear fender, and they strapped Viktor's trunk to it.

'You are part-German, I believe you said in the interview,' said Platner with clumsy casualness as they drove. It was a pleasant autumn day and Viktor was filled with the excitement of starting his new post – he also remembered Professor Románek's telephone caution about Platner's outspoken views – and really hoped the car journey wasn't going to turn into a political discussion. There again, almost everything did, these days.

'At least half,' said Viktor. 'My mother was from Gnadlersdorf –
Hnanice in Czech. Do you know it?'

'Sadly not,' said Platner.

'It's only a small village. In Moravia – close to the Austrian border. My father was Czech, but his mother too was German. For that
matter, the surname Němec features a lot in my ancestry, which sug-
gests a German origin.'

'There you are!' Platner seemed pleased with Viktor's pedigree.
'Your surname, Kosárek – that means "reaper", doesn't it?'

Viktor nodded. 'Or "maker of scythes".'

'You should be re-christened, dear boy,' said Platner cheerily.
'Now, what would that be in German? Sensenmann, probably – but I
don't think patients in any hospital would want to be reminded of the
Grim Reaper. Or maybe Sensemann? Come to think of it, there was
a missionary in the eighteenth century called Sensemann. Gottlieb
Sensemann. He was Moravian-German too. Maybe Kosárek is a
Slavicization of Sensemann. Maybe you're even more German than
you think!' Platner beamed.

'It doesn't really matter,' said Viktor. 'These things don't define
who you are. In my opinion anyway.'

Platner didn't say anything, but watching his profile Viktor
noticed his smile had faded.

As they drove in temporary silence, the pine trees seemed to
crowd thicker, taller, darker against the edges of the road, which
snaked and writhed as if twisting to be free of the forest's tightening
grip.

As a psychiatrist, Viktor knew how anxieties and traumas
could become abstracted into weirdly specific fears, and had
once treated a neurotic patient who had developed extreme hylo-
phobia: a morbid fear of forests; of their depths, their darkness,
the shifting shadows within them. When treating the patient,
Viktor had recognized some of the same symptoms in himself;
but in Viktor's case that had been understandable, attributable to

a specific traumatic event. In Viktor's case, there had been his experience as a child.

Discovering what he had discovered among the trees.

It had been a lifetime ago. Viktor had been playing in the forest, which he was forbidden to do; but he had a quiet place, a secret place, a clearing among the trees where he had always played with his younger sister Ella. But, after Ella's accidental drowning a year before, Viktor had been forced to play there in solitary sadness. Ella had been his constant companion, sole playmate, and her death had torn a hole in his world: a great gaping emptiness that was still less than that which had been ripped into his mother's heart.

That day, when the sun had dappled the forest floor and made the shadows between the trees dance as if alive, Viktor had come into the clearing that had been Ella's and his secret place. It had been there and then that he had made his dark discovery.

His mother had been waiting for him. She had stared down at him with emphatically unseeing eyes, her face and hands unnaturally, lividly dark, as if she was already becoming another shadow among the trees, the creaking of the bough from which she hung the only sound in the crowding dark forest.

The discovery of his mother's suicide had left two indelible marks on the young Viktor Kosárek. The first was a vague, unfocused fear of being in forests. He could still see their beauty when he saw them from a distance, but felt something akin to claustrophobic panic when among their trees. The second mark it had left had been a determination to understand and cure mental illness; to assuage the great sadnesses that led people, people like his mother, to derangement and to end their own lives, or the lives of others.

It had led Viktor into medicine, into psychiatry; into accepting the post at Hrad Orlů Asylum for the Criminally Insane.

It was another twenty minutes to the castle, the last of which was a steep and winding climb through the forest-mantled flanks of the mountain on which the castle – now the asylum – sat dominating the small village below and the surrounding countryside. The first interview panel had been held at the Academy in Prague, but the second had been here, at the castle. And again, just as he had when he'd attended the interview, Viktor felt an intense awe, almost fear, as the road rose out of the treeline and the castle was exposed.

A massive, tooth-like monolith erupted up from the forest, and in turn the castle erupted from the monolithic crag. The building seemed fused into the rock, just as the archaeologist Pedersen had described it. A high, palisade-topped outer bailey wall was cornered with round towers: swellings that rose up and were capped with witch-hat roofs. One tower, where the walls came together at a more acute angle, arced more fully and rose higher than the others, giving the impression of the prow of a ship. Three large buildings clustered together, contained by the walls but rising above them. The largest and highest of these, the main keep, had a huge, dark, high-angled roof, terminated with needling spires that spiked the sky.

Deep in prehistory, like an axe blow by an angry primordial god, some geological event had split the crag on which the fortress stood, and the barbican was balanced on the smaller part, the castle on the main, connected by a stone bridge across the chasm.

Looking at the castle, at its imperious, aggressive thrust into the sky, Viktor understood why it was called Hrad Orlů. Adlersburg. The Castle of the Eagles.

They passed through the barbican, which had a manned gatehouse. An orderly waved at Platner from behind glass and the heavy oak castle gates swung themselves open as if pushed by unseen hands.

'Electric powered,' said Platner proudly.

They crossed the stone bridge that spanned the deep chasm and passed through another gatehouse, into the cobbled courtyard of the castle. As they did so, Viktor Kosárek got a feeling he hadn't had the last time he'd been here.

Despite it being a bright autumn day, he felt as if the castle had closed behind him, around him, over him, and he could not now escape its stone embrace.

CHAPTER SIX

While everything about the castle's exterior spoke louringly of the old and centuries past, everything about the asylum inside it spoke of modernism, of the urgency of progress, of a promised future.

The metre-thick walls and the arched doorways remained mediaeval, but had been painted with light colours: pastel shades of blue in one corridor, rose in another. Everywhere whitewash had been applied it had been tinted with warm tones.

When he had first visited the castle for his second interview, over a month before, Viktor had noticed the colour scheme and realized that it had been done for the benefit of the patients: a deliberate policy of avoiding clinical white walls, making the asylum interior seem a little less institutional; distracting attention from its intimidating architecture and the ineluctability of its confinement.

On that first visit, the colour scheme had brightened his walk to the interview, promising that the asylum directors shared at least some of Viktor's progressive ideas. For Viktor, mental illness was a sadness – *the Great Sadness*, as he thought of it – that brought with it fear and isolation. He had seen too many institutions devoted to the ideas of the last century and dedicated to confinement; too many patients abandoned to their lonely sadnesses. And too many patients confined in conditions that were barely humane. As far as Viktor was concerned, any attempt to banish sadness from the treatment environment was a good sign.

Although Hans Platner struck Viktor as a very different type of man in every way from Professor Románek, he obviously took great pride in the asylum and its modernity. As they walked through its corridors, Platner would pause here to show a particular treatment room, there to point out an instrument that was always *'nothing but the very latest thing'*.

Viktor already knew Platner was not a psychiatrist, but a general physician whose responsibility was the overall health and physical wellbeing of the asylum's patients. It was therefore no surprise that the hospital wing was the greatest object of Platner's pride, and – pointing out that Viktor hadn't had a full tour of the castle on his first visit – he suggested they make a small detour so he could show him the wing.

In the infirmary, the castle's heavy wooden interior doors had been removed and replaced with handle-less, spring-hinged hospital doors, each with a round window set into it at eye level. When his Sudeten German escort pushed open the door for him to enter, Viktor could see Platner's pride was not ill placed. The infirmary gleamed and sparkled, equipped with the very latest appliances and furnishings. There was a Roentgen room, a fully fitted-out operating theatre, three consultation rooms and five standard patient treatment rooms, all shown with pride by the Sudetener.

Everything was bright, clean and orderly – but Viktor noticed that the infirmary was also uncluttered by the presence of any patients. In Czech, Platner introduced Viktor to the two regular nurses, but switched back to German to address a doctor whom he introduced as Dr Krakl. Krakl was very tall, blond and angularly built, with that slight stoop that the over-tall tended to adopt. That, combined with his hooked nose and hooded eyes, gave him a predatory, hawk-like appearance. Viktor smiled and shook Krakl's hand, but felt an instant, instinctive dislike for the man. He also noticed that, above the collar of his lab coat, Krakl's tie was held in place by a Sudetendeutsche Partei pin identical to the one on Platner's lapel.

They left Krakl to his patientless duties and continued the tour. On first sight the only thing that marked out the infirmary as being different from any ordinary hospital, other than its restricted size, was the fact that it had a further three 'secure' rooms with extra restraints on the beds and rubber-sheathed padding on all edges and corners. There was also a laboratory and pharmacy and, to Viktor's surprise, a large, well-equipped gymnasium hall, unusual for an infirmary.

'My responsibility is prevention, as much as cure,' explained Platner. 'Those patients whose symptoms are under control, or are in the remission stage between psychotic episodes, are brought here once a week for physical therapy and exercise. *Mens sana in corpore sano.*'

'Very impressive,' said Viktor with genuine enthusiasm. 'Really, Herr Dr Platner – very impressive indeed.'

Platner beamed.

'And where will my treatment room be?' asked Viktor.

'Ah . . . For your narcoanalytic sessions? Or narcosynthesis, whatever you call it.' Platner infused his question with friendly scepticism. 'I believe you've been allocated a room in the old tower part of the castle. But Professor Románek knows better what specific arrangements have been put in place.'

As they made their way to the asylum director's office, Viktor and Platner passed a number of staff members. Again Viktor noticed that the nurses' white uniforms were understated, less formal than the usual, and the orderlies wore short stewards' jackets, again white, with black bow ties. The one commonality with the other asylums Viktor had worked in was the build of some of the orderlies: no matter how progressive the regime, burly men were sadly often essential in restraining patients.

They passed four arched doorways, two on either side of the hall, each filled with a heavy oak door. Again a new age overlaid itself on an old, like a film transfer. Each of the doors was secured with a traditional heavy bolt, but this arrangement had been augmented by a modern mortice deadbolt lock. In addition, Viktor noticed two small, grey metal boxes on each: one on the door near the edge, its partner on the jamb.

'These doors lead to the patients' quarters,' explained Platner. 'Each door leads to a ward, each ward has four patient quarters off it. Our current inmates either have a wing to themselves, or those who share a wing are separated by two empty suites. As you know, Professor Románek has a theory about "mental contagions", as he describes them, and likes to keep the patients out of each other's earshot wherever possible. You'll see later that the quarters are quite unlike any you're used to: more like private accommodations than asylum cells. There's another set of rooms on the other side of the castle meant to be an isolation suite, but it's currently being used as an equipment store. At the moment, only six units are occupied by patients and that will remain the case for a while. But the ultimate aim is to treat sixteen at a time.'

Viktor nodded. He knew from the experience of his first interview to be circumspect in referring to the castle's half-dozen patients as the 'Devil's Six'. The state, he knew, was investing a great deal of money and resources in devoting a single, impenetrable fortress to the confining of just six patients. Part of that commitment came from the desire to conceal them forever, to wipe the trauma of their crimes from the still-young republic's memory. And part of dispelling the mythology that had developed around them was never officially to refer to them, as the rest of the world did, as the Devil's Six.

Platner nodded towards the top of one of the doors. 'You'll notice these strange grey boxes: they have electric magnets in them that are switched on centrally from the porters' office. If anyone opens a door while the system is set, it breaks the magnetic contact and an alarm sounds in the office. All the very latest, my dear Dr Kosárek, all the *very* latest.'

They passed more doors. One stood open and revealed several staff members in whites working over stoves, the smell of cooking issuing out into the hall.

'The kitchens,' said Platner redundantly.

Next to the kitchens was a doorless arch, double the width of the others, opening out into a large dining hall populated with half a dozen tables. Viktor noticed the art on the walls of the dining hall was of the same style as that in the main corridors. Given the antiquity and historic importance of the castle, he would have expected time-darkened and faded portraits of Karel IV, long-dead local aristocrats, or old landscapes. Instead the walls were punctuated by large, framed screenprints of Blaue Reiter paintings. Viktor recognized pieces by Feininger, Klee, Macke, Kandinsky – all vibrant with bright colours and strong geometrics. He asked Platner about the choice of art, but the Sudetener shrugged.

'Nothing to do with me. Herr Professor Románek's choice.'

'It could pass for a café in the city,' said Viktor. The hall did look incongruously like a normal café – a simulation of a life now forever denied to the asylum's patients.

'The truth is many of the patients dine in their rooms, either by choice or necessity. But when they're stable enough we encourage them to socialize here. Except the charming Mr Skála, whom you'll meet later. We even serve beer and wine in moderation to those whose symptoms or medications don't contraindicate. And you're right, you would think that it's a restaurant or café, except for the tableware.'

'Tableware?'

'Bakelite. The beakers and cutlery are made from it. No glass or metal in the dining room for patients. The staff eat here too. Don't worry, we get to use proper cutlery – but every knife, fork and glass is checked in and out.'

The next halls they came to contained a well-equipped music room and art studio, but Platner made no comment as they passed. Viktor got the clear impression that the general physician didn't care for any therapy that he couldn't view as strictly practical and the results of which couldn't be immediately quantified.

They turned into another hall. Viktor could see that this hall stretched to the other side of the castle. It was completely blocked by a span of iron bars and gate, like those of a cage. Platner took his keys and unlocked the gate, which creaked as he held it open for Viktor.

'You'll get your own set of keys,' he said. 'This is the administrative wing and staff quarters. There is no patient accommodation here – well, there was for a while: the isolation suite I mentioned, but that's just used for equipment storage now.'

As soon as the gate clanged shut behind them and Platner locked it, Viktor became aware of the difference in tone in this hall: here, the castle became a castle again. The warm-toned whitewash hadn't been applied here and the paintings that hung on the wall were no longer the bright geometries of those in the patient wings. The walls were either naked, aged stone or dark wooden panels.

'I know,' said Platner with a grin. 'It's all very gothic – this is what the whole castle would have looked like originally. You get used to it.'

'I see,' said Viktor distractedly. He had stopped to look at a couple of the wooden panels, the frames of which had been elaborately carved. His attention was drawn to a frieze of spiralling and weaving ribbons carved out of the dark wood. He followed them to the top of the frame; at its centre was a carving of what he at first thought was a representation of a werewolf. The snaking ribbons came together at the top of the frame and projected outward to form a bust: the chest, shoulders and arms of a heavy-set man, from which jutted the head of a snarling beast. It wasn't a wolf after all, realized Viktor, it was a bear.

'The Bear Man . . .' he said to himself.

Dr Platner, who only now realized his escort was no longer at his side, turned back to him. 'Professor Románek is waiting for you, Dr Kosárek,' he said.

*H*e cursed the fog. All of Prague was wreathed in it, casting spectral auras around its streetlights and turning its architecture into a shadow play of looming, angular shapes in shades of grey and black. Fog was bad hunting weather for a policeman.

Kapitán Lukáš Smolák drove past the address they had listed for the suspect. Ideally, he would have parked across the road and watched from the car, waiting for their man to come home, but this quarter was the poorest and most run down in Prague, and this area was the poorest and most run down in the quarter. Even in a veil of fog, a smart new Praga Piccolo such as Smolák's – any car for that matter – would be conspicuously out of place. And given there was a second car right behind him, an Alfa filled with three uniformed officers, Smolák decided to park around the corner and walk back to where he could watch the apartment house's entrance from the shadows of a doorway across the street. When their man arrived, he explained to his subordinates, he would signal back to the corner with two flashes of his flashlight.

So now he waited, dressed in shadow and fog, for his suspect. The name that had been matched to the fingerprints found at the Prager Kleinseite murder scene was known to the police, known to Smolák. The prints had belonged to a small, crafty, devious type who – although his record had been for dishonesty rather than violence – could be an expert hand with an open razor or stiletto if the need arose.

There had been no doubt about the match with the murder-scene fingerprints; and they did belong to someone who had all the pick-pocketing skills to have removed Maria Lehmann's keys from her bag. Nevertheless, knowing the suspect, Smolák still found it difficult to connect him with the horror in Maria Lehmann's Prager Kleinseite apartment.

He should be here soon. Criminals, Smolák knew, were just as likely to be creatures of habit as anyone else, and there was every reason to believe that their suspect would turn up here, tonight, as was his usual custom.

The police already had a comprehensive dossier on their suspect: a man whose disregard for the law had brought him before justice with disheartening regularity. But there again, he belonged to an outsider group: someone marked from birth to be cast out, mistrusted, suspected. And when you suspected someone deeply enough, for long enough, they usually became worthy of your distrust.

The suspect in question, according to his dossier, had a relationship with a young prostitute of the same outsider background, and who worked somewhere nearby in the Žižkov quarter. Tonight, Wednesday, was her night off, and the man they were after – whom Smolák suspected of being her pimp as well as lover – would bring her back to the apartment they shared.

Standing in the chill dark shelter of the doorway, Smolák had smoked only three cigarettes when he saw two shadowed figures turn the corner into the ill-lit street. He had planned that they grab their man as he reached his apartment building, but the silhouetted couple were on his side of the street, not the apartment side. Perhaps it wasn't their man, thought Smolák.

As the couple approached arm-in-arm, their forms combining into a single lamp-lit silhouette, Smolák noticed that the young woman limped slightly as she walked. It was the limp of a lifelong cripple, rather than recent injury. That matched what Smolák knew of the prostitute. Now sure it was his target, Smolák snuffed out his half-smoked fourth cigarette and turned his back to the couple so they couldn't see his flashlight signal to the look-out on the corner. He sank back into the shadows of his sheltering doorway.

As the couple drew closer, Smolák could hear them talk in dark tones: no joy, no affection. To his ears the male voice was drawn tight with anxiety. Not the reputation the suspect had. The female voice seemed to be trying to soothe, to reassure.

In response to Smolák's signal, the Praga Alfa came around the other corner and into the ill-lit street at speed, the dazzle of its head-lights muted by the dense mist. But it was bright enough to light up the couple who froze wide-eyed for a moment, caught in its fog-smudged gleam. Smolák recognized his suspect, all right, but he was struck by the sudden, stark fright written in the small, dark man's face: a genuine, deep terror. It was something else that didn't sit right with Smolák: this was a man who was known to have no fear of the police, only contempt.

'Tobar!' he called the suspect's name as the Alfa pulled up beside them. He stepped out from the doorway and grasped him firmly, his fingers closing tight just above the smaller man's elbow.

Smolák was taken aback by the suspect's reaction. He screamed. A high-pitched scream of terror. His eyes wide and wild and unsee-ing. The small man snapped his arm free of Smolák's grasp and shoved the policeman violently. Despite Smolák's much bigger build, the unexpected force of the wiry man's sudden and desperate shove caught him off balance and he staggered backwards, his heels catch-ing on the step of the doorway he'd been hiding in and causing him to fall back against the door.

The suspect seized the advantage, turned in the direction he'd come from and sprinted off. While Smolák gathered himself, a uni-formed officer set off after the suspect. The girl, who hadn't moved, swung a kick at the officer's shins and he tumbled face first onto the grimy pavement.

'You!' Smolák called to another of the officers as he started to run after the suspect. 'Hold her. You two come with me!'

Moving quickly for such a big man, Smolák sprinted along the street. When he got to the corner he saw a ghost in the fog running towards where three streets intersected. The police captain knew that, like most of Prague's Old Town, this quarter was a maze of streets and alleys; if he lost sight of his quarry in the fog, he may never find him again.

Smolák and the two uniformed police officers sprinted after the suspect, the younger officer opening up a lead on the other two and closing the gap on their quarry. The fleeing man made the corner and disappeared around it. When Smolák and the other older officer reached the corner, the younger man was leaning against the wall, his hands clutching his face. Blood oozed between his fingers.

'The bastard cut me,' he said. 'He has a blade.'

Smolák looked along the mist-shrouded street but could see no sign of the fleeing criminal. He turned back to the injured man.

'I'm all right,' said the younger officer. 'It's not as bad as it looks. I pulled back and he just nicked me.' The other officer had folded his handkerchief into a pad and the younger man had it pressed to his face. He indicated the direction the fugitive had taken with a small nod of his head. 'There are only two ways for him to go up there, both dead ends. Unless he takes shelter in one of the buildings, we've got him.' The young officer straightened himself up but Smolák eased him back against the stonework.

'You stay here. We can deal with this.'

Smolák and the older strážmistr ran along the street at a trot, scanning doorways on both sides as they did. At the end of the street the road forked on either side of an apartment building, Smolák indicated one direction to the uniform man with a jut of his chin.

'Be careful,' he said. 'This time he might do some serious

damage.' Smolák pulled his service automatic from his coat pocket; the breathless older officer unholstered his.

'Don't take any chances,' said Smolák, 'but I want him alive if at all possible.'

The uniform nodded and headed down his allocated street, Smolák down his.

The street was dark, a curtain of thick mist hanging in the air, dulling the streetlights. As he ran, the cobbles beneath Smolák's feet were black-wet and frequently sleek with motor oil. His foot landed on a slippery patch and he skidded and slipped, eventually landing heavily on the cobbles. The fall winded him, forcing all the breath from him, and it took him a few panicked seconds to pull enough air into his screaming lungs.

Easing himself back to his feet, he cursed loudly. He'd injured his knee as well – not badly, but badly enough to slow him down. The fog shrank Smolák's universe to a tight sphere of awareness, three or four metres across. The rest of Prague, the rest of the world, seemed distant and improbable, as if this small bubble of existence was all there was. And his suspect wasn't in it.

He hoped that the fugitive had gone off in the other direction and the uniformed strážmistr had him cornered by now. But there had been no signal blasts of a police whistle. Damn it, he thought, the little bastard's got away.

It was as he was getting to his feet that he caught something out of the corner of his eye: the smallest of movements through the mist. Smolák didn't look in its direction; pretended not to have noticed anything. His suspect was to his left, pressing himself against the wall of the apartment building, seeking to hide behind the curtain of dense mist. It didn't make sense: right next to where he tried to hide, the black shadowed mouth of a deeply recessed doorway offered the fugitive infinitely better concealment. If he had hidden in the door-way's shadows, Smolák would never have seen him.

Smolák made a show of cursing as he stood up, examining where the material of his trousers had become stained with grit and grease from the cobbles.

He turned suddenly on his heel and took three purposeful steps towards the figure, switching on his flashlight. The small, wiry man stood pressed against the wall, dazzled. The blade of an open razor flashed bright and hard in the light of Smolák's torch.

'All right, Tobar . . .' Smolák took another two steps towards him, keeping the flashlight in the small man's eyes. 'It's time to go.'

The fugitive held his free hand up to shield his eyes and peered squinting into the light. He made vague, targetless slashing movements in the air with the razor.

'Stay back! Stay back or I'll cut you!'

'Don't be silly, Tobar,' said Smolák wearily. 'I'm armed. Drop the razor now. Let's go.'

'I'm not going anywhere. *He* sent you, didn't he? He's not going to have me. I'll die first. I'll kill you first.'

'Who?'

'You know who. You know damned well who.'

'I don't have time for this, Tobar,' said Smolák, taking another step towards him.

The small wiry man again let out a high, shrill, inhuman scream and, still dazzled by the flashlight, launched himself at Smolák, slashing furiously, blindly at the air.

The detective only just stepped aside in time, the razor slicing into the fabric of his heavy coat but missing flesh. As the momentum of his attack thrust the smaller man headlong, Smolák slashed sideways with his pistol, hitting his attacker with a vicious swipe of gunmetal against temple. The small man fell to the cobbles, dazed, and Smolák stamped a boot onto the hand that held the razor, grinding the fingers open.

As the stunned man lay motionless, his hand pinned to the cobbles by the policeman's boot, Smolák blew three sharp blasts on his whistle.

'You're losing your touch, Tobar.' Smolák looked down at the man at his feet. 'Why didn't you hide in the doorway? I wouldn't have seen you there.'

'The shadows.' The small man's voice was weak, cracked. 'It's in the shadows that he hides.'

Smolák was about to ask again 'who?' when he heard response blasts from two whistles and the sound of boots running on cobbles. The police Praga Alfa turned the corner and lit up Smolák and his quarry.

As he waited for them to arrive, he again looked down at the man at his feet who now began to stir from semi-consciousness, and wondered what had so terrified the tough little petty-crook.

Who was it that he thought had come out of the shadows to get him?

*P*rofessor Ondřej Románek was waiting for them in his office. Románek was a pleasant-looking, bearded man in his late fifties, not too tall but robustly built. His thinning, bright blond hair was darkened slightly by the hair oil that swept it back severely from a broad forehead. There was intelligence and kindness in the psychiatrist's face: it was the kind of country-doctor face one instinctively trusted, and Viktor imagined it gave him an advantage when gaining a patient's confidence.

It was an advantage Viktor lacked: the handsome severity of his features may have lent him authority, but when Viktor's patients first met him, and for some time until they got to know their young doctor, they seemed almost afraid of him.

Given the carefully understated choices of interior design and staff uniforms, Viktor was surprised to see Románek dressed in a calf-length lab coat. It was of the mandarin-collared style with a button-fastened flap along his shoulder. It covered his day clothes completely and gave him the look of a clinician or surgeon, rather than a psychiatrist.

'My dear Dr Kosárek!' Románek beamed at Viktor, came around his huge, Hungarian-style mahogany desk and shook hands with him, laying his other hand on the younger man's shoulder. He spoke to him in Czech. 'It is so good to see you again. I'm so sorry that I couldn't come and meet you off the train, but I had a meeting with the trustees. But I'm sure Herr Dr Platner has taken good care of you?'

'Indeed he has,' said Viktor, smiling. 'And it's a pleasure to be here.'

'Well, I have to say I'm relieved you've arrived, particularly after that dreadful episode in the station. All's well with you?'

Viktor told him it was, and repeated the account he'd given to Platner of the last known condition of Šimon, the young man who had been lost in another dimension, pursued by imagined demons and devils.

Románek's smile faded. 'I'm afraid I had a telephone call from Prague General, only a few minutes ago. They were phoning to inform you that the unfortunate young gentleman has, indeed, suc-cumbed to his wounds.'

'He died?' Viktor asked, taken aback.

'An hour ago, I'm afraid. Tragic business.'

'I telephoned just before I left and they said he was stable.' Again Viktor remembered the young man's staring eyes, lost in the terrors of his own Great Sadness. 'I thought he'd make it,' he said.

'It is unfortunate,' said Románek. 'If he was indeed this so-called "Leather Apron", it would have been an opportunity for the police to question him.'

'I seriously doubt that he was,' said Victor. 'There was nothing organized about his behaviour. He was just a poor soul adrift in schizophrenic mania. From what I gather about Leather Apron, he is a highly organized killer.'

'Well, anyway, why don't we get you settled in? As we discussed during your interview, we are a highly specialized unit here. Please, please do sit down.'

'And a very well-resourced one,' said Viktor as he sat. Platner remained standing. 'Dr Platner was kind enough to show me around. I must say there are a lot of facilities for only six patients. Not that I'm complaining – it's a dream for a physician.'

'Mmm,' said Románek. 'It's true we only have six patients here, but those six patients are the most notorious cases in Central Europe: individuals who have wrought terror and misery out of all proportion to their number; six psychotics who have committed the most outrageously barbaric acts. I do hope you're prepared for them: as we discussed in your interview, as a physician here, you will discuss mental states, desires and actions that the rest of mankind would deem unspeakable, unimaginable. It will become commonplace for you to talk casually about murder, rape, torture, necrophilia and cannibalism. I'm afraid our normality would appear both aberrant and abhorrent to anyone outside our little circle.'

'I understand,' said Viktor.

'Do you? Be warned, my dear Dr Kosárek: talking about such acts in the abstract makes it easy to forget that our patients really did commit them. Some of our charges here can seem deceptively normal – even quite charming. Your predecessor made that mistake and it nearly cost him his life. It *did* cost him an eye. Always remember that these patients are housed here because this is the most secure place that could be found for them, and because each of them must always – *always* – remain removed from society.'

Viktor nodded: he had been told all of this before, at his interview. The psychiatrist he was replacing, Dr Slavomír, had allowed a patient the use of a pencil and Slavomír had lost the use of an eye. It had been strongly stressed at the interview that Viktor should not accept the post unless he was prepared to accept the risks that came with it. It was not work for the naïve nor the weak at heart.

It had also been explained that there were currently only six patients in the Hrad Orlů Asylum, not just because they represented the most extreme forms of human madness and so the most secure location in Czechoslovakia had been sought for them. They had also been confined there specifically to be studied: their insanities measured and examined, dissected and analysed. The hope was that the scrutiny of such extreme cases might offer better treatment for lesser madnesses. Viktor's appointment was based on the theories he had put forward in a recent paper: like Románek's own theories, the ideas Viktor had proposed were seen as innovative to some, controversial to many.

'We stand at the forefront of psychiatric medicine,' Románek explained. 'Now that you're on board we'll split the psychiatric caseload between us. Most of this work will involve standard therapeutic protocols, but the situation we have here in Hrad Orlů offers us the opportunity to learn and understand some of the most challenging mental conditions. In exchange, because each of these patients is destined to live out all their days here, we do all we can to make them feel that the castle is their home.'

'What happens if we cure them?' asked Viktor.

Románek shook his head. 'Sadly, such sicknesses afflict more than the patients themselves. Were we, by some miraculous new treatment, to be able to heal their psychoses, they still couldn't be released. The crimes they have committed mean that there can never be any acceptance of them back in general society, nor forgiveness of the dreadful things they have done. Our function here is largely palliative rather than remedial, but it allows us a unique chance to develop new therapies and help others in the future. We may not be able to save these souls, but we might be able to save others from the same fate.'

Professor Románek paused for a moment. 'When we talked at your interviews, I was greatly impressed with your Devil Aspect hypothesis. The patients here at Hrad Orlů are cases of particularly florid psychoses, involving delusions that aren't just extremely elaborate but strangely cohesive in their internal logic. And there is a strange commonality to these psychoses. I take it you're familiar with the rumours circulating among the public of a grand conspiracy being carried out within these walls?'

'That the so-called Devil's Six is in fact just the one killer, a case of multiple identity disorder and we have only one patient here?' asked Viktor.

'Yes. I can understand how it has come about: these six patients had no contact with each other before coming to Hrad Orlů, and limited contact during their time here – yet when you look through the case notes, you'll see they share striking similarities. All claim they encountered some kind of demon, some kind of Devil-like elemental figure, who compelled them to commit their crimes. Whether this is simply a device constructed by the Ego to protect itself from blame, or truly your theory of the Devil Aspect given almost literal form, I'm sure you can see why I feel these cases would be ideal for your narcosynthesis therapy.'

Viktor nodded. 'Indeed I do.'

'You see, Dr Kosárek, this isn't the first time I've seen this kind of thing. Throughout my career in psychiatry, I've been aware of odd – ' He frowned as he struggled for the right word – 'odd *coincidences*. Similarities arising in cases that are totally unrelated – just like the six here. I've often wondered if some forms of madness are, well, *infectious*: a powerful but distorted way of thinking that can spread and overwhelm a susceptible mind.'

'Like a suppressed immune system?'

'Exactly. We see it all the time in physical medicine: groups of people exposed to a virus where some fall ill and others don't. Those who are susceptible to infection generally have a compromised immune system. So you see there's something of an intersecting of theories between us: if your hypothesis of the Devil Aspect is right, then the disease is already present – *omni*present in all of us – waiting for some trigger to bring it forth. We are all infected with the potential for madness and evil, but only fragile psychologies fall victim to the full-blown disease.

'I want you, Dr Kosárek, to explore your theory with our patients here. You will have the opportunity to put some of your ideas to the test – but I demand rigorous documentation and verification. The eyes of the psychiatric community are upon us, and their gaze is critical, to say the least.'

'You can rely on me,' said Viktor.

'If I didn't believe I could, you wouldn't be here.' Professor Románek's authoritarian tone was dressed in a country-doctor smile. 'You and I have sole charge of their psychiatric treatment. As you're by now well aware, Dr Platner here is responsible for all general health matters, including staff health.'

'So if you have a hangover, feel free to call,' Platner said, with a hearty slap on Viktor's back. 'But if you'll excuse me, I'll let you get on.' Then, in German, he said, 'I'm delighted you have joined us, Herr Dr *Sensemann*.'

After Platner left, Románek raised an eyebrow in question.

'The German form of my surname,' explained Viktor, smiling. 'Herr Dr Platner seems keen to establish my pedigree. But I'm afraid it really won't stand up to scrutiny.'

It was a light-hearted comment, but the asylum director didn't seem to take it so. For a moment Viktor worried that he had spoken with inappropriate levity about Románek's deputy.

'This is a difficult conversation to have on such short acquaintance,' said Románek, 'but I would strongly advise you to avoid all political discussions with Dr Platner. I've known Hans for a long time and we've been close friends as well as colleagues. Hans is a good man, but like so many other German-Bohemians felt very aggrieved by the land reform act. The results of the recent elections trouble me and I'm worried that we may be swept up in this madness that has taken hold over the border. Our little Austrian corporal, I very much fear, would be well suited to joining us here as patient number seven.'

'You think the Nazis are actually a threat to Czechoslovakia?'

'I think they're a threat to everyone – and we're nearest to hand. Our philosopher President Liberator has been very clear from the beginning on the danger he feels Hitler presents.' Románek picked up a cigarette case and offered it to Viktor, who took one. 'The Sudetendeutsche Partei is just the Nazis in regional dress. Dr

Platner's enthusiasm for the party is something of a problem for me. I think it best if politics are left outside the castle.'

'I'm sorry, Professor Románek, I didn't intend—'

'Oh don't worry, dear boy.' The cloud passed from Románek's expression. 'I know you didn't. I normally wouldn't have said anything, but these are difficult times. As a clinician of madness, it's difficult for me not to diagnose it when I see it in its collective form, as well as the individual. I apologize if I have embarrassed you with my frankness, but you strike me as someone who recognizes the *complexity* of our new little republic.'

Viktor nodded. He knew there were so many tugging at the fabric of Czechoslovakia's newly spun identity: Sudeteners like Dr Platner and his deputy Krakl with their Bohemian Germanism; Pan-Slavists; fervent Czechoslovak nationalists; Silesian Polish separatists; even Alfons Mucha with his beautifully painted myths of Slavic purity.

Románek shook his head as if irritated with himself. 'Do forgive an old man's paranoia.' He pressed a buzzer on his desk and a few moments later the door behind Viktor opened. He turned to see a tall, slim, dark-haired woman enter. She was wearing a black suit of skirt and jacket, a pale blue blouse and a sad, dark beauty that stunned Viktor.

'Ah, Miss Blochová. This is Dr Viktor Kosárek. Dr Kosárek, Miss Blochová here is our chief administrator.'

Viktor stood up and shook hands with her. Her hand was slender and soft in his; her smile was almost perfunctory, but Viktor noticed how the fullness of her lips was accentuated by crimson lipstick. Her hazel-coloured eyes were large, brightly intelligent; her hair ink-dark, full and glossy. As well as a potent attraction, Viktor had the most overpowering feeling that he knew her from somewhere, that he had met her before.

'You studied under my father,' she said.

'You're Josef Bloch's daughter?' Viktor was taken aback.

'Judita Blochová, yes.' Another smile, perhaps a little less perfunctory.

'Your father was a huge inspiration to me: every bit as big an influence as Dr Jung,' said Viktor. 'I knew Professor Bloch had a daughter – but I thought you were studying medicine.'

Some defence slid into place behind the intelligent eyes and the smile faded. 'I had to take a break in my studies. In the meantime, I'm very happy to be working with Professor Románek.'

'Of course, of course – as am I. It's a great opportunity.'

An awkward silence fell between them and Románek broke it. 'Miss Blochová can show you some of the equipment available to you for your sessions. I'm sure you will be very impressed: we have the latest recording device, the AEG K1 Magnetophon recorder, straight from this year's International Radio Exhibition in Berlin. It uses magnetic tape instead of wire,' Románek said with the same kind of pride Platner had displayed. 'Miss Blochová will also provide any secretarial support you need.'

The professor came over and placed his hand on Viktor's shoulder. 'But now, Dr Kosárek,' he said, smiling, 'I think it is time for you to step into the lions' den. Come and meet your new patients . . .'

*D*espite herself, Judita Blochová was strongly drawn to the new doctor. What confused her was the strange, unshakeable feeling that she knew Kosárek: that she had not just met him before, but had *known* him. He was certainly attractive: tall and handsome, if in a slightly imperious way. He was someone, she thought, who looked very much at home in the setting of a castle. In the setting of this castle.

Unlike Judita, Viktor Kosárek was someone who would never have to question his belonging, or have it called into question by others. The way things were, that was reason enough for her to resent him. But added to that was the fact he now occupied a role that should have fallen to her, if her studies and her career had gone to plan. But they hadn't gone to plan.

The only thing that spoke well for Kosárek had been the comments he had made about her father, his clear affection for his former mentor. She would phone her father tonight and ask what he remembered about his student.

In the meantime, she would treat Dr Kosárek with the appropriate professional courtesy and respect, but otherwise keep him at arm's length. Arm's length was fast becoming the measure of all relationships. That was the way of things now: everyone – every new contact, every encounter – had to be analysed, assessed as a threat.

Something that had always been there in her life without

dominating it – her Jewish heritage – now had come to overshadow her interaction with everyone around her. Everyone and everything had now to be seen as a potential threat.

And there were threats enough here already. Young Dr Kosárek seemed to have hit it off with Dr Platner: Platner was a Nazi, whatever they called themselves in Czechoslovakia, and there was no ambivalence about the Nazis' view of Jews. In all his professional dealings with Judita, Platner had been polite and courteous, even friendly, never giving any hint of anti-Semitic leanings, but they would be there – she knew they would be there.

There was no need to search for such leanings with Krakl, Platner's assistant: every time he encountered Judita, Krakl dressed his expression in disdain, and when he spoke to her his tone wore a weary impatience, invariably suggesting he was being forced to speak to someone whom he considered his inferior in every way. An inconvenience he tolerated because he knew somehow that it was a temporary situation.

There was a new landscape of identity now; a new map of ethnicity on which she could find no bearing. The irony was that Judita had always considered herself as part of a minority community: not as a Jewess, but as a German-Czech. German – High German, not the Mauscheldeutsch dialect of some Prague Jews – had always been her main language and her Czech was fluent, but not perfect. A further irony was that her German was tainted with a Czech accent. She, her father, her whole family had all identified with other German-Czechs, had seen German culture as *their* culture. Suddenly, that had all been taken away from her.

And there were the dreams that plagued her. Terrible dreams of horrors waiting for her, for her family, for all of her kind.

Every time she spoke to her father he would seek to reassure her, to tell her not to dwell on dark thoughts, reminding her of the dangers of such dwelling. She would struggle to get him to believe her fears were well founded; that it wasn't like before. That it wasn't like it had been when she had been studying medicine and had become overwhelmed by irrational and inexplicable anxieties, suspicions and fears. Her fears now were all too rational, all too explicable. Yet whenever he reassured her, there was one phrase Judita's father would studiously avoid: the description of a single event that informed almost all their conversations but went without direct mention.

Her breakdown.

Judita Blochová's nervous breakdown as a medical student had been all about threats imagined, enemies unseen. It had been a sickness from which she had recovered but which had, for all time, destroyed her credibility. So now – when the threats were real, the enemies in plain sight and the sickness dwelt in others, not her – no one would heed her warnings.

Everyone seemed blind to what was before their eyes: everyone could see the gradual accumulation of cruelties but not their clustering into some monstrous ultimate malice. They could see the clouds but not predict the storm.

The newspapers were full of the Nuremberg Race Laws the Germans had enacted the month before, forbidding all relationships between Jew and non-Jew; anti-Semitic restrictions on education, occupation and social interaction. It frustrated Judita that she could not persuade her own father of the threat imminent to all of their kind; of the slow and irreversible division of humanity.

So now Judita Blochová judged every acquaintance, every new encounter with a stranger as a potential threat. But she was attracted to Kosárek; and when they had met he had made no effort to hide that he was attracted to her. Didn't that mean that he was uninfected by the insanity around them?

Tonight. She would ask her father about Kosárek when she phoned him tonight.

*T*hey had spent two hours going through the six psychiatric case files of the patients. Professor Románek had a strangely mellifluous voice, a soothing tone that must have served him well when dealing with troubled patients. But when reading and commenting on patient histories, it had the odd effect of making him sound like a storyteller: as if each case was some kind of dark fairy tale. Given the horrific, almost surreal details of each case, it was easy to believe that such horror could only exist in the mind of an author, or a folk tale spun and embroidered over generations.

'You make these cases sound almost lyrical, folkloric, Professor,' said Viktor.

'I didn't realize I was lyricizing. There's nothing more prosaic than psychotic violence. But I've often considered how darkly creative we Czechs are – the higher incidence of both mental disorder and of musical, artistic and literary creativity than practically any of our neighbours in Europe. Maybe we have a deeper cultural Unconscious.'

Románek stood up, walked across to the window of his office and looked out over the nightscape of forest and gully below.

'Maybe that's why we're here, in this particular castle. We live in an ancient land, and nowhere is our land more ancient than in this place. The people who live down there in the village and in the fields and forests beyond – their roots go far back into the earliest days.

Theirs is the blood of the mothers and fathers of Europe: people who lived in this land long before the Celtic Boii, before the Germanic Suebi, and long, long before the Slavic Czechs. Believe it or not our little village has a history going back seven thousand years.'

'I know,' said Viktor. 'On the journey here I shared a compartment with a German archaeologist who told me all about the Neolithic hill fort the castle was built on. He said there's also a network of caves.'

'There's supposed to be, but whether there is or not, we have no access to them from the castle, despite what the locals believe.' Románek turned from the window, went across to the cabinet in the corner of his office and took out two thin-stemmed liqueur glasses. He placed them on the desk and filled them with cherry brandy from a decanter before handing a glass to Viktor.

'Maybe,' said Románek, 'with seven thousand years of a collective cultural Unconscious all around it, our little fortress here could not be better placed for exploring the folklores of deranged minds.' Románek sat down at his desk and closed over the final case file before raising his glass in a toast.

'Well, here's to you, young Viktor. Now that you've heard our six horror stories, do you regret your appointment? You could probably still make the last train to Prague, you know.'

'I didn't buy a return ticket.' Viktor smiled and raised his glass. 'In any case, I dealt with very violent patients with the most florid psychoses at Bohnice Asylum. Admittedly not as extreme as these patients – like you said, these cases are here because they're the most extreme in Europe. I knew that when I accepted the post.'

Románek smiled. 'Then let's drink up and go and meet your first patient.'

*K*apitán Lukáš Smolák was a man of measure: someone not quick to rush to judgement; someone who took his time to assess, to think things through, to weigh them up. Too often in his career he had seen other officers jump to a conclusion too quickly, then shape a theory to fit the conclusion, then shape an investigation to prove the theory.

That was why Smolák always took great care and all the time available to him to measure the facts, to look beyond the obvious.

The guilt of the small, dark man sitting in the centre of the inter-rogation room was so obvious, however, that it was difficult to see past it. After all, it was not the first time Smolák had sat in an inter-rogation room facing Tobar Bihari, and on almost all those previous occasions, Bihari had been guilty.

There was a desk set about four metres from where the accused sat, fastened to a stout oak chair which was in turn fastened to the floor. Two other police officers from the uniformed branch stood on either side of the restrained man, their tunics removed and hanging on the wall rack, their shirtsleeves rolled up past their elbows. The fruits of their labour were already blossoming vividly in the con-tused flesh of the bound suspect's face.

When Smolák had entered the room and sat behind the desk, the two policemen had stood to attention and saluted the plain-clothes kapitán. He read the file fully before taking a moment to study everything about the suspect: Tobar Bihari was small, dark in countenance and complexion and wiry in build. His suit was slightly too big for him and – despite the ambition of its tailor to make it look fashionable – was made of inferior material. There were many, Smolák knew, who would say that Tobar Bihari was himself made of inferior material: his ruffled hair was coal black and the ghost of a distant sun, a distant subcontinent and a distant time lingered in skin several tones darker than everyone else's in the room.

Tobar Bihari, as Smolák already knew, was a *cikán* – a gypsy. That simple fact in itself would have been enough to convince most police officers from Plzeňto Košice of his guilt. But Smolák knew that prejudice was the quickest path to a false conviction. Many cells in Pankrác and Ruzyně prisons were filled with dark-complexioned shadows in the stead of a paler truth left free.

Irrespective of his race, Bihari still looked guilty: there was an arrogant handsomeness to his face, but the course of his interrogation had caused the fine-structured features to swell, one cheek badly distended and the eye above it beginning to puff shut. Smolák disapproved of the mishandling of anyone in custody but said nothing to the officers about the prisoner's condition: Bihari had injured a uniformed policeman, had taken a blade to him, and there was an unspoken procedure to be followed in such cases. An unwritten message to be sent to others.

Smolák had arrested Bihari several times before. On each occasion, guilty or not, Bihari had maintained the same cockiness, the same arrogant defiance, that no beating could dislodge.

On each of their previous encounters, Smolák had found the gypsy to be mendacious and devious, dishonest to his core. Nevertheless, he grudgingly admired Bihari's resilience, strength of will and his courage. Where others saw only low cunning, Smolák had seen keen intelligence. It had occurred to the policeman more than once that if Bihari had lived a life free of prejudice and the grinding poverty of his kind, then he might have amounted to something significant.

But today Bihari was changed: stripped of his arrogance, his confidence, his defiance. Smolák knew it had nothing to do with the beating he had just received. He knew it didn't even have anything to do with the severity of the crime of which he was accused – a crime that would send him to the gallows.

Something else had broken the gypsy's will.

'I'll take it from here . . .' Smolák nodded to the door and the two uniformed officers gathered their tunics and left the interrogation room.

'You're in trouble, Tobar,' he said when he was left alone with his prisoner. 'Like no trouble you've ever been in before. You do realize that, don't you?'

Bihari cast dark eyes empty of resistance or hostility at Smolák. 'I know how much trouble I'm in. I know only too well how much danger I'm in. The thing is you don't. You think you know, but you don't. The trouble I'm in, the danger I'm in, don't come from you.'

'What do you mean?'

'You wouldn't understand,' the gypsy said bitterly. 'You have no way of understanding. You didn't see—'

'Didn't see what?'

'Skip it.' Bihari shook his head. 'Where's Tsora? Did you let her go?'

'She's along the corridor,' said Smolák. Tsora Mirga was the woman who had been with Bihari; the one who had tripped up the first policeman to pursue him. 'We have questions for her, too.'

'She has nothing to do with anything. She doesn't know nothing.'

'Then she'll be free to go. But she did interfere with an arrest.' Smolák thought back to the young woman they had arrested. Like Bihari, Tsora Mirga was a gypsy. When they had got both back to the station and he had seen her in the stark, uncompromising light of the reception hall, Smolák had been struck by her considerable dark beauty. Dressed in a form-hugging deep-blue suit, her figure and her looks jarred with the ugly corrective boot that encased her left foot.

'She's a cripple. Why can't you leave her be?'

'What's wrong with her foot?' asked Smolák.

'Her mother, when she was expecting Tsora, accidentally walked over a grave. Because of that Tsora was born with a club foot.'

'That's just superstition, Tobar.'

'It's what my people believe.' He gave a small, strange, bitter laugh. 'They also believe she's safe from the Devil. Her club foot means if he tries to follow her footprints, he won't be able to tell which direction she took.'

'It's your footprint I'm interested in. It led us straight to you. Why did you do it, Tobar?'

'Do what? I didn't do nothing, but you'll never believe that.'

Smolák sighed wearily. 'All right, Tobar, I can understand you killing the woman. Violence isn't your normal way, I know that, but if she disturbed you after you broke into her apartment and caught you stealing her stuff – well, I can see how things could get out of hand very quickly. She starts screaming; she even attacks you or tries to keep hold of you until help arrives. In the heat of the moment – in a situation like that – anything can happen. A struggle turns into a frenzy; you try to silence her screaming, a blow is misjudged or her footing is lost and then before you know it, a simple burglary turns into a murder. Or at least manslaughter. Now *that* I can understand. A sort of occupational hazard, one might say.' Smolák paused. 'But for you to do what you did to that woman. For you to butcher her like a steer in a slaughterhouse, to dig your hands into her insides and take out her organs. *That* I just don't understand.'

'I didn't do that.' Bihari's voice was flat, dead, but he closed his eyes, as if shutting something out. 'I didn't do none of it.'

Smolák, who'd in the past heard every form of denial for every kind of crime from Bihari, could tell the gypsy truly didn't care in the slightest if Smolák believed him or not. And that troubled the detective greatly. He was beginning to look past the obvious.

'Do you recognize it?' he asked, placing the small glass bead he had recovered from the murder scene on the desk. The gypsy strained to see it.

'What is it?'

Smolák picked it up from the desk and walked across to the prisoner. He held the bead in front of his face for him to see, rolling it between fingertips.

'I've never seen that before.' The gypsy's voice was still flat.

'You dropped it at the scene. Everyone missed it. I nearly missed it – but I didn't. I'll bet, when we've finished going through all your stuff, we'll find more like it. Even just one – one tiny glass bead to match this one – and we'll have enough to hang you.'

'You'll hang me anyway.' Still no emotion.

'Why do you admire the London ripper so much, Tobar? Why would a Hungarian gypsy in Czechoslovakia have an interest in fifty-odd-year-old murders in England?'

Bihari looked up at Smolák blankly. 'What are you talking about?'

'Jack the Ripper – the original Leather Apron – your great inspiration.' Smolák acted out wide-eyed pantomime awe, waving his hands vaguely in the air.

'I don't know what the hell you're talking about,' said Bihari. Again Smolák could see his prisoner couldn't care less if he believed him or not. He sighed.

'All right, let's keep this simple: why did you kill Frau Lehmann, Tobar? Let's get this over with quickly. There's no need for more unpleasantness with those two uniform boys waiting outside. No need for anyone to get all agitated and wound up. Just tell me you killed her, why you killed her, and why you killed all those other women. Maybe we can swing a madness plea and you'll be sent to an asylum. Spare you the rope.'

Bihari looked up at Smolák. His eyes were large, dark and empty. 'Hang me. I want you to hang me.'

'Why do you want to be hanged?'

'Because I can't live with it any more. I want to be free of it all. I want there to be blackness, nothing – instead of those pictures in my head, over and over again.'

'I understand that,' said Smolák. 'To have done such terrible things must be painful to bear. Why don't you tell me everything, from the start? Maybe it will help you.'

'You understand nothing. Your mind is too small. I didn't kill her. I didn't kill that woman and I didn't kill none of the others. I could maybe live with that.' The small, brave gypsy laughed. There was such bitterness, such pain in that laugh. 'I could live with that, but what I can't live with is *him*. The fact that *he* owns me. That *he* will come for me one day. And if *that* . . .' He nodded to the glass bead in Smolák's hand. 'If that truly belongs to him, then he'll come for that. And because you took it, he'll come for you too.'

'Who Tobar? Who is *he*? Who are you talking about?'

It was then that Smolák saw something he'd never seen before: Tobar Bihari started to weep.

'I saw him. I saw him and he saw me. He made me watch.'

'Who, Tobar? Who?'

'Beng. It was Beng who did it. It was Beng who killed her and made me watch while he did all those things to her.'

'Who is Beng, Tobar? Is he another member of your band? Did he come along on the burglary with you?'

Bihari shook his head. 'Beng isn't a person. Don't you see? Don't you understand? Beng is the name our people have for the darkest of the dark demons. Beng is the Roma name for the Devil.'

Smolák walked back to the desk. It was a contrivance to allow him to think through what Bihari had said. The gypsy was mad, he realized. Smolák cursed to himself: madman murderers were always the most complicated to process. They generated the most paperwork: psychiatric reports, conflicting expert opinions on competency, the statistics of madness . . . It would be easiest, he knew, if he could get a straightforward confession.

'You're saying you saw someone else kill Maria Lehmann?' Smolák retook his seat, placing the small glass bead back on the desk in front of him. 'That you were there, but you didn't kill her? Just sat back and watched someone else do all that to her?'

Tobar Bihari, sitting shackled to his chair, small, bruised and broken, stared at Smolák, his eyes growing wide with terror: he may have been looking at the detective but the gypsy was seeing someone else, somewhere else, some other time.

'It was Beng!' he yelled. 'I saw Beng do all that to her. It was Beng that made me watch.' He started to shake. Again, this was not the defiant Tobar Bihari that Smolák knew.

'All right, Tobar,' he said quietly. 'Why don't you tell me the story from the start? The absolute truth, as you see it. Start at the beginning and don't leave anything out.'

*I*n Professor Románek's storyteller style, each patient's case file was titled with a soubriquet. The first of the Devil's Six Viktor was to meet was 'the Vegetarian'.

The patient rooms in which Hedvika Valentová was confined were just as Platner had described: more like private accommodations than an asylum cell. Again there were calming, non-representational paintings on the walls, a comfortable armchair and sofa, a coffee table. Over by the barred castle window sat a writing bureau and chair. Viktor noticed that the bureau was naked of paper or writing implements, but its position offered a calming view of the deep, tree-dense gully below the castle and out over the surrounding countryside of the Central Bohemian plain. There were two doors off the main sitting room: one leading to the patient's bedroom, the other to a bathroom.

On first sight, and except for the cage of bars beyond the window and the absence of a kitchen, it looked like a small but perfectly normal apartment. It was only on closer inspection that Viktor noticed the paintings were fixed to the walls, rather than hung, and that every piece of furniture was unusually robust in construction and immovable, having been bolted into the stone floor. Even the glass in the window was infused with a fine steel mesh to prevent it being shattered into shards. There was nothing here that could be broken into a weapon and used to injure staff or patient.

The most disconcerting element in the room was the patient herself. Madness, even violent madness, could be contained in any vessel; there was no such thing as a lunatic type. But Viktor was struck by just how unlikely a vessel Hedvika Valentová was.

Mrs Valentová was a painfully thin, priggish-looking woman of about forty. The kind of woman you would pass on the street without noticing, she was dressed in an unexceptional skirt, blouse and cardigan and had the mien of a provincial schoolmistress. She looked hollow-cheeked and sunken-eyed in a way that suggested undernourishment rather than a natural tendency to leanness. Before they had entered the patient's quarters, Professor Románek had explained that Mrs Valentová's extremely particular attitude towards her diet presented 'difficulties'.

When they entered, Hedvika Valentová was sitting straight-backed and somewhat perched on the edge of the sofa, her posture almost birdlike, and Viktor found it unimaginable that this homely, unremarkable and slight woman had been enumerated as one of the Devil's Six.

She looked across to the two doctors as they entered before casting her eyes downwards to the floor, her hands fidgeting on her lap.

Professor Románek introduced Viktor and explained that he would be taking charge of her treatment from then on.

'What happened to Dr Slavomír?' she asked, seemingly perturbed, but in a small, quiet voice.

'Dr Slavomír is no longer with us,' explained Románek. 'You perhaps remember that. Dr Kosárek will take very good care of you. I assure you he really is one of the brightest young doctors in Czechoslovakia.'

'I'm looking forward to working with you,' said Viktor. 'I have new methods that will help us get to the bottom of your problems . . .' He went on to explain, in layman's terms, the principles and theories behind his sedative-aided hypnosis therapy. When he had finished, Mrs Valentová kept her gaze floorwards. She glanced up at Románek and a redness flushed up from her neck onto her cheeks.

'I should very much like to complain,' she said in awkward protest. It was clear she found asserting herself difficult. 'I should like to complain very much indeed.'

'About the treatment Dr Kosárek is proposing?' asked Románek.

'I don't care about that,' she said, her gaze returned to the floor. 'I don't need *treatment* – there's nothing wrong with me at all except the ill-humours that come with being fed poisons from flesh. If I were fed properly, if I were left alone to cook for myself, then my bad tempers would be gone. And it's my bad tempers you worry about, isn't it?'

'This again, Mrs Valentová?' Románek sounded vaguely irritated. 'We do everything we can to accommodate your dietary—'

'Lard,' she cut the professor off.

'I'm sorry?'

'There is no point in providing me with a vegetarian diet if those vegetables are cooked in animal fat. It's disgusting. I had to force empty my stomach twice today to be rid of it.'

'I will make enquiries,' said Románek, his patience restored. He stood up. 'Well, I must introduce Dr Kosárek to his other patients.'

'I look forward to talking to you further,' said Viktor. Mrs Valentová ignored him.

'I'm afraid you have your work cut out for you there,' said Románek, once they were outside in the ward hall. Viktor and his employer took back their belongings – the pens, pencils, coins and other loose items – that they had placed in the metal trays in the hall before entering Mrs Valentová's quarters.

'Do I really need to deposit everything here every time I go in to see her?' asked Viktor. 'She doesn't seem that much of a physical threat.'

Professor Románek turned to Viktor, his face uncharacteristically stern. 'I'm afraid, my dear Dr Kosárek, you are in danger of making the same misjudgement that your predecessor sadly made. You must never, ever go into that room with anything that could be used as a weapon.'

'It was she who stabbed Slavomír with the pencil?'

Románek nodded. 'She believed he looked at her lustfully. "With a desire for her flesh", as she put it. His eye offended her, so she put it out.'

'The eye was completely lost?'

'You could say that. By the time the warders were drawn by Dr Slavomír's screams and burst into the room, our rather prim 'Vegetarian', Mrs Valentová, had already snatched up Slavomír's eye and swallowed it.'

'I had this idea.' Tobar Bihari paused, then his eyes lit up with sudden realization. 'No – that wasn't it. I remember now, someone *gave* me this idea. A new way of scoring more for less risk. Now I see – now I get it – that must have been him! I didn't think about it until now – it must have been Beng what gave me the idea! He came out of the shadows that night and put the idea in my head! Oh God, it was him all along – don't you see?'

'Calm down, Tobar. Take a deep breath,' Smolák knew he had to keep him on course. Keep him from raving. 'What idea? And whose idea was it?'

Bihari took a moment to calm himself, but Smolák could sense the white electricity of fear course through the small man's frame. 'Well, I was in this bar in Vršovice, a *Skopčáci* place – German, you know? The landlord put me out as soon as he sussed me as a gypsy. He said he didn't want scum like me in his place. He was all big man about it, just because he had some of his Kraut friends to back him up. So I leave, but when I get outside this guy just appears out of the shadows. I get ready for a fight but this guy says he heard what happened and I shouldn't let Krauts talk to me that way. I should get my own back on them. I don't really know why this guy was in a German pub, 'cause he seemed to hate them. Anyway, he says he saw me get kicked out and came after me 'cause he knows about me – knows I'm *in the business*. We get talking and he says he has this secret for scoring big, him being *in the business* himself. But he don't look like no pickpocket or housebreaker I ever seen.'

'What did he look like?'

'He was tall, is all I can say for sure. Very tall and sort of gangly. He was wearing a long black coat what looked too big for him. It was dark outside and he had a hat pulled down over his face. But from what I could see, he looked like he needed a bath and a shave. His clothes weren't bad quality, but he looked like he'd been sleeping in them.'

'And did you get a name for him?'

Bihari frowned. 'I can't remember. Oh God – oh God it was him – that was Beng too. I should have known the way he just appeared out of the shadows.'

'Stay calm, Tobar. Tell me what he said.'

'He told me I'd been doing things all wrong – every time I picked a pocket or a purse, I was taking a big risk for little profit. No matter how good I was at it, he said, you're always rumbled by the mark maybe once every five or six times. And maybe once out of the five or six times you're rumbled, the police get you. That's why it's best to work in crowds: you can disappear quick and then move in on another mark. But it's risky enough, all right. So he tells me this idea: he says I'm good at the pickpocketing, and I know how to turn over a house or an apartment really quiet like. So why not be real choosy with marks? He says when you've been a pickpocket as long as I have, your fingers become your eyes in other people's coats and purses. You can tell what's in there and what's worth stealing. His big new idea was that I should leave everything in there: not take cash or wallets or purses. Instead, only take their keys. If your keys go missing but your purse or wallet is still there, you don't think you've been robbed. I mean, you'd reckon any thief would take your money, not *just* your keys. No, you wouldn't think you'd been robbed at all – you'd just think you'd lost your keys.'

'Until someone burgled your apartment,' suggested Smolák.

'That's right. He says most people don't look for their keys till they're at their door – so, once I have the keys, all I have to do is follow the mark home to see where they live. Then I wait till night or whenever it's empty, then do the place over. Just let myself in.'

'So you just followed this complete stranger's advice?' asked Smolák. He didn't believe a word of his story, but it troubled him that Bihari seemed genuinely convinced he was telling the truth.

Bihari nodded. 'I decided to hang around the Malostranské Náměstí on market days, when the square's full of rich Germans.'

'You targeted German-Czechs? Why? Have you got a particular grudge against them?'

'No . . .' Bihari shook his dark head slowly. 'No, it's got nothing to do with that. It's just that they're richer, most of them anyway. Got more stuff to steal. Anyway, while the market was on in the square and there were lots of people milling about, bumping into each other like – well, that's ideal pickpocket conditions. So, every market day I'd mingle with the shoppers in the Malá Strana market, even buy a few groceries, all the while on the look-out for likely marks – you know, the richest-looking ones. When I found one, I'd move in and lift their keys. When they left the market I'd follow them home. I'd wait while they got someone to let them in, or they sorted out spare keys. If they called a locksmith and got their locks changed right away, then I'd have to forget about the job, but they never did. I'd watch till they went to bed. When it was safe, I'd turn their place over. I done half a dozen jobs like that. Good haul every time. The best. And it was all so easy.'

'And that was how you ended up in Maria Lehmann's place?'

'I seen her in the town square market in Malostranské Náměstí. I could tell from the way she was dressed that she was loaded. I also saw she was on her own. She was at a vegetable stall choosing stuff and she had her handbag open, so I was able to get close enough to take her keys – there was a purse and other stuff but I only took her keys. Then I followed her around the market until she headed back to her apartment building, which turned out to be a fancy place in Sněmovní Street.

'I watched her, laughing to myself like, while she searched for her keys to get in the main street door. She even looked around at the ground to check if she'd dropped them. Eventually she pressed a bell and the caretaker opened the door and let her in. I just stood out of sight across the street and around the corner and watched.

'Of course, her getting in the building main door was one thing, but she didn't have no key for her apartment. So I waited to see if a locksmith arrived. If one did, then I'd have to give up: having a key to the building was no good if she had the lock on her apartment changed. But I was counting on the caretaker having spare keys to all the apartments. I waited an hour, then another. A prize like this was worth waiting for.'

'A prize?' interrupted Smolák. 'The woman you mean? Was she your prize?'

'The woman?' Bihari frowned, confused. 'I wasn't interested in her. I wasn't after no woman. But she was a rich German bitch – it was her stuff what interested me, not her.'

'If that's true, why didn't you steal anything? Except maybe the partner to this . . .' He pointed again to the small glass bead on the desk.

'I told you, I don't know nothing about that. Never seen it before. I didn't take nothing from the apartment because *he* was there.'

'Beng, you mean? Your gypsy Devil?'

'I know what you're thinking, but he *was* Beng, he *was* the Devil. No man could be that evil. No human being could do those things to another. I know you think I'm mad, or that I'm making it all up, but it's true. It's all true. And now that I think about it, it must've been him that night outside the pub in Vršovice.'

'Tell me what happened. Tell me what you remember.'

'I waited until after midnight, maybe nearer one. I didn't make my move until all the lights had been out for at least half an hour. Then I let myself in. Her apartment was over two floors: the top two floors of the apartment building. I knew the best stuff, the jewellery, would be in her bedroom, but I stuck to the downstairs rooms to start with – it's always risky going into a bedroom with someone sleeping in it. I reckoned I'd maybe find enough in the rest of the apartment without taking that extra risk. The secret, you see, isn't to grab everything, even if it is all valuable.

'I brought a small case with me – like a businessman's case. It wouldn't hold too much and anyway you don't want it weighed down. You know what you coppers are like: the sight of me in the middle of the night lugging a big heavy case about would draw you lot like flies to shit. The secret is only choose the best pieces. The other thing was I wanted to get out of there quick like. As soon as I stepped into that place I had got this real bad feeling.'

'What kind of bad feeling?'

'That there was someone else there. Some*thing* else there. You know, you're working away in the dark with only a dim flashlight to see with, and sometimes the shadows dance about, your eyes play tricks on you. You think the shadows move funny, but it's just the flashlight and your nerves. But in there – I don't know – I just got this feeling them shadows were moving. *Really* moving. And like I was being watched. You know – that feeling you get on the back of your neck.

'I was in the living room going through a desk-bureau-type thing and realized I'd hit the jackpot. Cash. There's no need for a fence when you hit a pile of cash like that. There was a thick bundle of hundreds, one of five hundreds and even a few thousand-koruna notes. As soon as I seen them, I knew I'd struck gold and I didn't need to take nothing else. The best score yet.'

'But the cash was still there in the bureau when the body was found. Why didn't you pocket it?' As soon as he asked the question, again Smolák saw something run through the small gypsy like a cold electric current: a fear so intense that its chill even touched the policeman.

'I thought I saw a shadow move and I turned round, real quick. And he was there. He was just standing there in the dark, like he had taken shape from the shadows, watching me.'

'Describe him to me.'

'He was Beng.' Bihari started to shake again, his thin wrists rattling the chains of his shackles. 'How do you describe the Devil?'

*L*ukáš Smolák came round from behind his desk and took a cigarette from his case, placed it between the gypsy's lips and lit it for him. Bihari drew on the cigarette hungrily. Because he was shackled to the chair and unable to hold the cigarette, the act of smoking demanded some concentration and he tilted his head back to keep the smoke from his eyes. It had the effect Smolák had wanted, relaxing Bihari and distracting him from his fear.

After a moment Smolák reached for the cigarette and Bihari nodded for him to remove it from his lips. He still hadn't stopped shaking, but the tremors had eased.

'Listen Tobar,' said Smolák, sitting on the edge of the desk. 'I don't know what you saw, or what you think you saw, but it wasn't the Devil. If there really was someone else in the apartment, your best way of saving your neck from the rope is to give me a description.'

Bihari nodded. 'He was tall. I couldn't see his clothes because he was wearing a leather apron over them and elbow-length leather gauntlets. The apron and the gauntlets were stained dark, some stains darker than the others. Some was black-brown, others red-brown. I could see they was all old stains where blood had soaked into the leather and dried. I could smell it off him: I could smell old blood and death off him.'

'His face, Tobar. Describe his face.'

The gypsy started to shake again. Worse this time. A tear found its way down a dark cheek. When he spoke, his voice was reduced to a terrified whisper. 'His face . . . His face was the Devil's face. Oh God help me! Oh please God help me!'

'What did his face look like?' Smolák demanded.

'I told you! It was the Devil's face. A long, dark grey face with a horrible grin of sharp teeth. Black horns coming out of his head. Like them masks the Germans wear around Christmastime.'

'*Perchtenmasken*?'

'Yes, them,' said Bihari. 'Like Krampus.'

'So he was wearing a mask?'

'A mask?' Bihari frowned. 'A mask – I don't know, maybe it was a mask. But I thought it was his face.'

'Then what happened?'

'I froze. I was so scared. I wanted to yell. I tried to scream, but nothing came out. I wanted to run, but I couldn't move. Then he came at me. He came out of the shadows but it was like the shadows moved with him. He pulled this knife out from beneath his apron: a big, long knife, like something you'd use to butcher animals. He stepped towards me and grabbed me by the throat. Through his gauntlets I could feel he had long, very thin, very hard fingers, like they was just bone. He was so strong and his grip was so tight I couldn't breathe. When I did get a little air it smelled of old blood, like death – that smell again from his leather gauntlets and apron. He looked at me – into me, into my head. He looked right into me and seen everything there is to me.' Bihari paused, for a moment trying to gather himself as the memory seized him. The shackles still rattled with the shaking of his thin wrists.

'He took the knife and pushed the point into my cheek, into the bottom eyelid just below my eye. I felt the blood in my eye, like tears. He said he might take my eyes as a memento. He said he collected such things.'

'Then what happened?'

'He let me go. He said that I should keep my eyes because he had something for them to see, for me to remember forever. I was to bear witness, he said. He told me we had work to do – *he* had work to do and I was to watch. We went up to the bedroom. We went up to where the woman was.'

'So you just went with him?'

'You don't understand.'

'Actually Tobar, I think I do. Tell me what happened.'

'You know what happened! You seen what happened. You seen what he did to that woman.' His head hung limp between shoulders that heaved with great sobs.

'So this man in the Devil mask – you're saying he's the killer, not you?' asked Smolák. 'Despite the fact that you admit you stole Maria Lehmann's keys and used them to break into her apartment, that there's no evidence whatsoever of anyone else having been in the apartment; that we found your fingerprints, no one else's.'

'My gloves. He made me take off my gloves. He made me touch things. He made me touch *her*. He made me stand by the bed.'

'The woman – Maria Lehmann – was she still alive at this point?'

'She was sleeping.'

'Go on . . .'

'Beng leaned towards me and started to whisper in my ear, saying all these terrible things.'

'What kind of things?'

'He told me that she was nothing but a *Fotze*. It's a German word. A bad word. You know what it means?'

'I know what *Fotze* means.'

'He told me she was a *Fotze* and she deserved everything that was happening to her. He told me what he was going to do to her, all the things I was going to have to watch. He said I was going to find out what it was like to capture a living soul, that's the way he put it; to watch their eyes as the life went from them. What it would smell like, taste like, feel like to cut her open, to take everything out of her.'

'And why was he doing this to her? Did he tell you that?'

'He said she would serve him after death.'

'What does that mean?'

'He said just like no one lives forever, no one dies forever. You come back, time and time again. But he said there's a place after death – a place of shadows between lives, he said. You spend longer there. He said he was gathering slaves – souls to serve him there.'

'And all this time you did nothing to stop him?'

Bihari's shoulders heaved as great shuddering sobs shook him. 'I tried – you've got to believe me I tried. I begged and begged him not to do it to her. He told me I could save her from it all – that he would leave her be and she could go on with her life. All I had to do was die in her place. He said that he would kill me quickly and wasn't interested in doing things to my body afterwards. My life was worthless, he said, but I could give it some meaning if I saved that woman.'

'But you didn't.'

More sobs. 'I couldn't. I was afraid. I didn't want to die. So he made me watch. He said that the price for my life was to watch him work.'

'You could have stopped him. Or at least tried to. You could have at least run away and raised the alarm.'

'I couldn't – I just couldn't. You don't understand – I was helpless. He had this, this *power* over me, like I was paralysed. And he *made* me watch. He said that's the only reason he had let me keep my eyes: so I could bear witness. He told me if I looked away or closed my eyes he would cut off my eyelids.'

'And so you watched?'

'He *made* me watch!' Bihari was now almost hysterical. 'God help me, Beng made me look! The Devil made me see!'

*T*here were different architectures to madness, Viktor knew. The 'Great Sadness' could take any of an infinite range of forms. Where a mind had broken or crumbled in one aspect, a scaffold would be hastily thrown up by the Unconscious, then slowly elaborated into a buttress or defensive wall. Some of these assembled structures, which we all had to some degree, could be sound enough: reinforced supports and protections to help us deal with emotional or psychic trauma.

Others, on the other hand, would embellish into grotesqueries; would become gross deformities of personality. Some would even accumulate into great dark palaces of madness that overwhelmed the mind: monstrous belvederes that shadowed and distorted the view in all directions.

Such architectures, Viktor realized, applied to all the cases confined in Hrad Orlů. Each of the Devil's Six had constructed a different madness around some ancient defect. Some more elaborate than others. All monumental.

And each had their case-note nickname. After his encounter with the Vegetarian – Mrs Valentová – Románek had introduced Viktor to each of the other five patients.

'The Woodcutter' was Pavel Zelený from Czech Silesia, whose occupation really had been that of a simple woodsman, but who had committed his atrocities with the tool of his trade: an axe. Viktor had been warned that Zelený was unpredictably violent and two orderlies had accompanied him and Románek into his quarters.

The next patient was more docile. Leoš Mládek, known by the epithet 'the Clown', was a slight, childlike man who seemed mild and innocuous, and who had previously been a successful circus performer touring Czechoslovakia, Hungary, Austria, Southern Germany and Poland.

The fourth of the Devil's Six was 'the Sciomancer', Professor Dominik Bartoš. A scientist of some note, who had carried out ground-breaking research in quantum physics, Bartoš's powerful intellect had become lost in a labyrinth of abstract and arcane ideas, resulting in an unshakeable delusion that he could commune with the dead.

'The Glass Collector' was Michal Macháček, an egomaniac whose renowned expertise on Bohemian glass had become a deadly fixation.

Each introductory meeting was brief, the patients compliant without being cooperative. The final introduction, however, required the most caution: Vojtěch Skála, the sixth of the Devil's Six.

'The Demon'.

Skála had a ward to himself, occupying Patient Suite Six, the furthest in its ward from the reinforced ward door and the main hall.

'He was originally kept in the isolation suite,' explained Románek as they prepared to enter Skála's accommodation. 'His is the most virulent and contagious form of madness and we keep him apart from the others as much as possible.'

Viktor nodded. He knew Vojtěch Skála was a man with a belief as powerful as that of the most committed churchman. But Skála's faith lay in what he saw as the power of pure evil. He believed evil to be the strongest force in the universe, and had acted out his fantasies of ultimate cruelty in the most horrific ways possible.

Skála's psychosis was the deepest and darkest of all the Devil's Six. And for exactly that reason, the monster in Patient Suite Six was

Viktor's greatest hope of reaching that which he sought to isolate in the Unconscious.

The Devil Aspect.

'Are you ready for this?' asked Professor Románek as they stood in the ward corridor.

'I am.'

Románek, dissatisfied with the eagerness of Viktor's response, placed his hand on his arm. 'Skála is no genius, but he has this unique way of getting into your head. And if he does, you'll never get him out. Of all the homicidally violent individuals locked up in these walls, Skála is by far the most dangerous. So I'll ask you again: are you ready for this?'

'Yes, Professor Románek, I'm ready.'

It was the most unscientific of feelings and Viktor silently censured himself for the feeling of it. As a psychiatrist he knew there was no such thing as Evil. In his short career Viktor had already worked with damaged, twisted and cruel minds, personalities empty of empathy for others; but Evil was a societal construct, and an outdated one at that. Yet, when he came face to face with Vojtěch Skála, Viktor had the unbidden impression of something more than madness inhabiting the room. It was the sense of some monumental wickedness.

Skála had been restrained in preparation for their visit. He was a huge man, his hair as black as Viktor's own and his features heavy, thick and brutal. The too-small eyes that watched the two psychiatrists enter were a malevolent glitter beneath a heavy brow ridge.

Despite being a new piece of hospital equipment, the chair to which Skála had been strapped looked strangely at home in the castle setting. Like some device of mediaeval torture, it was hewn from solid oak with steel bands and leather fastenings bolted into the wood. Small, rubber-hooped wheels under each chair leg allowed it to be pushed across the flagstones, the patient's feet ankle-strapped onto the footrest. A broad steel band, fastened with a slide bolt, spanned

Skála's chest and gave the odd impression of the breastplate of a knight's armour. Smaller steel cuffs fastened his wrists to the arm-rests, a padded restraint crossed the forehead and a series of sturdy leather straps bound his upper arms, denying all other movement.

Románek introduced Viktor, asking him to explain briefly to his patient the treatment he was proposing. Throughout, Skála sat silent, his small eyes fixed malevolently on the younger psychiatrist.

'Is there anything you'd like to ask me?' Viktor said when he had finished.

'You know the things I have done?' Skála's voice was quiet and slightly high-pitched. It was at complete odds with the physical pres-ence of the man, which made it all the more disturbing.

'I'm familiar with all the details of your case, Vojtěch.'

'You think I had to be mad to do them?'

'I think you have a disorder. I want to try to understand it.'

'I have raped, tortured, mutilated and cannibalized. Men, women, children, babies, animals. I have explored the capacity of just about every sentient species to feel fear and feel pain. And afterwards, I cut off their faces and wore them as masks so I could see what they saw and they could see what I saw. I showed them the truest, purest nature of Evil.' Skála grinned malevolently. 'And that, Dr Kosárek, is what you describe as a "disorder".'

'What would you call it?'

'My faith. My religion. My belief in an all-powerful evil.'

'Whatever you may think it is,' said Viktor, 'it's nothing more than psychosis. I want to get to the bottom of it and help you conquer it. I look forward to working with you.'

Skála sat, his large body immobile in the restraint chair, his face immobile in an expression of dull contempt.

'You're a very handsome man, Dr Kosárek,' he said as both psy-chiatrists rose to leave. Viktor said nothing.

'I'm sure you've been fully warned about me,' said Skála. 'That you have to be careful at all times. The thing of it is, you have to be lucky all the time, I only need to get lucky once. See my chance and take it. I look forward to working with you too, Dr Kosárek, because the very first chance I get I'm going to slice and peel that handsome face clean off your skull, while you're still alive, and wear it as a mask. Then everyone will say how handsome *I* look.' He laughed. 'Won't that be something?'

'If I may make a suggestion,' said Románek as he led Viktor from the patients' accommodations, 'it would be a good idea if you spent your free time away from the castle. The walks around here are truly beautiful, there's a pleasant inn down in the village, and Prague is close enough for you to visit on your days off.'

'I hadn't thought much about free time.'

'Then you should. In most institutions, there's at least some kind of spectrum of mental illness: some normality scattered throughout the abnormality. Here, well . . .' The professor sought the right words. 'Here all our cases are at the extreme end of that spectrum: madness in its most highly concentrated form. You'll discover some of your charges are people of considerable intelligence, with the ability to rationalize the irrational. They'll almost persuade you that you're the one with the skewed vision of reality, while they have some special insight into the truth of being – infect you with their delusions. Trust me, it's a good idea to take time away from this place – to reconnect with the real world and healthy minds regularly.'

'I am sure I'm grounded enough—'

'I'm speaking from personal experience,' Románek interrupted, uncharacteristically bluntly. 'Many years ago, I allowed one to get under my skin. I followed her down one path too many and became lost myself for a while. I started to question the truth of things.'

'What happened?'

'I was called away for a few weeks. And with that distance the spell was broken: I could see how her insanity had been more complex, more persuasive, more *convincing* than my sanity.'

'A patient here?' Viktor asked. A strange expression cast its shadow across Románek's face.

'No, not here. And she died a long time ago. Tuberculosis. Anyway, learn from me: examine closely the webs your patients here weave, but don't get so close that you become trapped in them. Take time to enjoy life among the sane. Do you have a girl?'

'Not now. There was someone, but . . .' Viktor left the thought hanging.

'Well, get yourself another.' Románek grinned, his habitual good humour restored, and slapped Viktor on the back. 'Enjoy life.'

Like the rest of the administrative wing, the office allocated to Viktor had been left in its original castle state, other than the electricity conduits and bulky heating pipes snaking along the stone walls. It was large, with two windows set into half-metre-thick stone. While the accommodation wing offered pleasant views over the gully, the winding road down to the village, and the patchwork of countryside beyond, the office windows looked out onto an ugly swelling of rock that sat like a kyphos on a hunchback at the rear of the castle. Viktor stood at his window thinking back to what Pedersen, the archaeologist he had met on the train, had said about the castle sitting on a network of caves. He imagined the spaces in the black, cold rock, dark and damp, filled with the air of a distant world and time.

'I've brought you some supplies.'

Viktor turned from the window to see Judita Blochová standing behind him, carrying a box filled with stationery materials.

'Sorry, I didn't mean to startle you,' she said. She smiled; with a little more warmth this time, Viktor thought. 'It's not much of a view, is it?'

'What? Oh, no – I suppose not. Here, let me take that.' Taking
the box and setting it on his desk, he waved a hand to indicate the
office around them. 'I have to admit I wasn't expecting anything this
grand.'

'You look at home in it,' she said. 'You have a – ' she thought
for a moment – 'a *dynastic* look. Anyway, if there's anything else I
can do, please tell me. I'll take you to the storeroom to pick out the
recording equipment and other stuff you'll need for these sessions
with the patients.'

'Thank you, Miss Blochová.'

She made no sign of leaving. 'May I ask you how you ended up
here, Dr Kosárek?'

'Professor Románek read my paper on the theoretical Devil
Aspect. In fact my interview turned out to be all about my theory.'

'I read something about it,' she said. 'You believe in the Devil,
is that right?' Her tone was neither mocking nor serious, and it took
Viktor a little off guard.

'As a matter of fact I do. I believe the Devil is responsible for all
the darkness and evil in society; all madness and violence in individual people. But the Devil I believe in is no supernatural being:
he is a natural force alive in us all – and most alive in the violently
insane. And because the Devil hides in the Id's Shadow Aspect, his
presence is often denied. That's why so many psychotic patients
cannot remember their violent actions.' Viktor again indicated their
surroundings with a gesture. 'And that's why I'm here. I believe I
know where the Devil hides, and that I have discovered a means of
reaching him and binding him.'

'And you think we all have this Devil Aspect?'

'I do. Just like Jung, I believe religions, myths and superstitions
all derive from shared archetypes. That we all have that part of ourselves that we seek to deny, yet which is where all our dreams and
nightmares come from, where our instincts and all human creativity
lives. And in there are all the shared archetypes and aspects that take

form in our cultures, in the stories we tell ourselves. Like stories about the Devil. The Devil isn't a being, he's just one of these universal ingredients. The Devil lives hidden in us all.'

'And you go hunting for him by using drug-aided hypnotherapy on murderers?' asked Judita.

'I'm convinced I can reach the Devil Aspect through narcosynthesis, yes. Using hypnotic drugs means I can strip away the Ego and reach deep into the Unconscious. Once there, I can guide the patient to confront his or her own Devil Aspect and excise it. Or at least confine it. A cure for violent psychoses. Surgery on the soul, if you like.'

Judita Blochová regarded him with an unsettlingly blank, frank stare. She was clearly thinking about what he had said.

'Maybe it would be best,' she said at last, 'if you left the Devil alone in his hiding place.'

'*D*o you have a moment?' Kapitán Lukáš Smolák stood filling the doorway of the police surgeon's office with his impressive bulk. Dr Bartoš, in contrast, sat small, portly and crumpled in a wrinkled dark suit at his desk, smoking. Smolák was surprised at the contrast between doctor and desk. Václav Bartoš had the ability to make any suit he wore look as if he'd slept in it, and there were the ghost trails of dripped cigarette ash on a lapel, yet his desk was immaculately ordered, files neatly stacked; pens, blotter, notepads all carefully arranged. Smolák wondered if the order of the desk, rather than the chaos of the man, expressed the true form of the physician's mind.

Bartoš, who had been bent over a file, sat upright and smiled. 'The interruption would be welcome. What can I do for you?'

'I know you're not a psychiatrist, Doctor.' Smolák accepted the chair but declined the cigarette Václav Bartoš offered. 'But you know we have a suspect in custody for the Leather Apron murders?'

'I do.'

'Well, he's told the wildest tale. I have a theory about it and I just wanted to get your opinion on it.'

Dr Bartoš leaned back in his chair and made an open-handed gesture.

Smolák ran through all that Bihari had told him: an account now being noted down by one of Smolák's subordinates as a formal statement. He told Bartoš about gypsy devils, about a man in a Perchten mask taking shape in the shadows, about Bihari's claims of impotence while under the thrall of a leather-aproned demon. He then put forward his own opinion on it all.

When Smolák finished, the small, untidy doctor sat thinking and smoking, two activities that seemed, in the police physician's case, to be indissolubly linked.

'I think you're most likely right,' he said eventually. 'I find it highly unlikely that this killer who's evaded capture for months simply decided to allow your suspect to witness him commit murder and then let him walk away. Like you, I think this "Beng", this Devil, is a story your deluded suspect told himself to deny responsibility for such horror.'

'I suppose it could have been someone else,' said Smolák. 'The same person he claims put the idea of taking keys in his head, but I find that highly unlikely.' He paused thoughtfully. 'The more I think about it, I'm sure it's Bihari – that he's some kind of split-personality killer.'

Bartoš frowned. 'You don't look happy to have got your man.'

'It's just that this kind of psychological case is almost impossible to explain to a panel of judges. They all think it's mumbo-jumbo.'

'I'd be surprised if it goes before a criminal court. Bihari will be committed to an asylum. But if you need to present evidence of split personality, then I suggest you get in touch with Professor Ondřej Románek, at Hrad Orlů Asylum. They're experts in that kind of thing.'

Smolák nodded. The gypsy, he had realized during the interrogation, was quite mad. Something murderous and monstrous was hiding inside Bihari. There had been no mysterious stranger sharing ideas about larceny, no masked gypsy demon. Just a nature Tobar Bihari denied dwelt in him.

There were some deeds so evil, so horrific, that the mind could only deal with them in the third person.

'Thanks Dr Bartoš. I appreciate your time.'

'Why did you ask for my opinion in particular?' asked Bartoš.

'Because you're a medical man. Because your insight has been useful before.'

'Not because you thought I might have some *personal* insight?'

'I see . . .' Smolák realized what the doctor was referring to. 'No, Dr Bartoš, I didn't ask your advice because of what happened with your brother.'

Bartoš nodded.

'Thanks again, Doctor.' Smolák left the physician to his files. But as he walked the corridors back to his own office, he wondered if his seeking out of Bartoš's opinion really did have something to do with the doctor's personal experiences. Another thought struck him: it had been odd that Bartoš had suggested Smolák get in touch with the asylum.

After all, that's where they had confined the doctor's insane brother.

PART TWO

THE CLOWN AND THE VEGETARIAN

For the first week, Viktor concentrated on familiarizing himself with his patients' case notes. He also had another meeting with Judita Blochová, who seemed to be becoming better disposed towards him.

As she had suggested, they met in the equipment store set up in an unoccupied patient suite. These rooms were broadly like the others yet subtly different. If anything, because of the suite's aspect, the rooms were brighter and the view cheerier, looking out over the deep green scar of the valley and the clustered geometry of white walls and red roofs in the village below. Beyond that, the tapestry of Central Bohemia's fields and forests unfolded in shades of emerald, jade and laurel. It was certainly a contrast to the view from Viktor's office.

But despite the comparative brightness and the soothing view, there was something about this particular suite that unsettled Viktor, and for some reason he again felt the castle's stone embrace close in on him.

'You feel it too?' Judita seemed to read Viktor's mind. 'This room gives me the creeps. I hate it if I have to come in at night to pick up secretarial supplies.'

Viktor nodded. 'It's strange. It's even more pleasant than the other accommodations – but it has, I don't know, a bad feel to it. Has it ever been used for a patient?'

'Professor Románek's original idea was to use it to isolate any patients undergoing extreme psychotic episodes. You know, the screamers, the ranters and the yellers. The other accommodations are more or less soundproof, and the six are kept pretty far apart from each other, but you know how determined some patients can be to be heard.' The pale smooth skin on her brow creased in a frown. 'It's the strangest thing – you know, the way a mad idea, a delusion, can spread like a virus. Professor Románek seems especially worried about it happening here.'

'So this was intended to be a sort of psychotic quarantine . . . ' Viktor nodded. While he wasn't entirely convinced by Románek's theory, the general idea made sense to him: existing madness compromising a patient's mental immune system and making them prone to delusional infection. 'I've seen cases where something similar has occurred. Not many, but a few. *Folie à deux* mainly. One case of Lasègue-Falret Syndrome or *folie en famille*. But I do think it's a rare thing for madness to be infectious.'

'That's where we disagree,' Judita said, her mood suddenly darkening. 'I don't know about *folie à deux*, but I see *folie à plusieurs* all around us. If you want to see a true case of the Madness of the Many, just look at what's happening in Germany – if that isn't a psychotic epidemic then I don't know what else to call it. Our own Doctors Platner and Krakl already seem infected.'

'Some believe that communism is the vaccine.'

Judita gave a small, scornful laugh. 'A vaccine that protects against the virus by killing the patient? Oh, I'm sorry – are you a communist? You look too aristocratic to be a communist.'

'No. But I'm a socialist. Any other time I'd be apolitical, but no one can afford to be apolitical these days.' He paused. 'Anyway, why is this a storeroom now?'

'It was hardly ever used for patient isolation. We only ever had one case in here: the charming Mr Skála, of whom you've no doubt had the pleasure.'

'The Demon? Briefly, yes.'

'When he was first admitted, he'd rave for hours on end like some demented preacher about how the Glory of the Devil was at hand. He'd rant endlessly about how the world is soon to be turned on its head, how the desolate one and layer-of-wastes was coming, and how we'll all be made to wear the mark of the Beast. All of that kind of nonsense. Unless, of course, the layer-of-wastes has a Charlie Chaplin moustache and the mark of the Beast is a swastika.' Judita shrugged. 'Skála's still effectively isolated now he's in his own ward wing. Professor Románek has him on a regular sedative, but he's still regarded as the most dangerous patient here. If you think of the others, that's saying something.'

'I know something about that,' said Viktor gloomily. 'He's promised to cut my face off and wear it as a mask.'

'That's our charming Mr Skála.'

'You've had contact with him?'

Judita shook her head. 'The strange thing about my job here is I get to know each patient intimately through transcribing their case notes, but I never meet them. They're all far too dangerous for non-medical staff to be exposed to them. Unfortunately, I'm non-medical.'

Viktor desperately wanted to ask Judita what calamity had prevented her completing her medical studies. But her defences had only just begun to come down and he didn't want to jeopardize her growing openness with him.

'Maybe you have the most objective view of them,' he said. 'The benefit of distance.'

'It makes their histories seem like fiction. Horror stories that keep me awake at night, but just stories. Maybe that's why I don't like coming in here.' She indicated the room around them. 'It brings me that little bit closer to the reality. Anyway, we're here to see you get fixed up with everything you need. Where are you going to conduct your sessions?'

'There is a room at the base of the main tower – the only tower room that's been renovated,' said Viktor.

'It's the only room in the tower you can get into. No one's ever been able to find an access to the rest of it. Maybe I'll tell you the story about that one day.' Judita smiled archly.

'Story?'

'Dark deeds and Devil worship in the Middle Ages. Long story.'

'I see,' said Viktor. 'I've already heard something of the castle's history. Maybe you can fill in the gaps some time. In the meantime, the professor told me that the tower room's perfect for my purposes. It's close enough to the accommodation wing to allow secure transfer of the patients, and it's been fitted out with a push-button electric bell system in case I need an orderly in a hurry.'

'And that's where you'll need the recorder. Have you seen them?' She led him over to where the cubes of three large, dark, metal-edged cases sat side by side. 'These are the K1 Magnetophons. I'll get an orderly to take one to the tower.'

'I know Professor Románek and Dr Platner are avowed technocrats, but are these Magnetophons really any good?'

'The sound's not fantastic, but good enough for what you're proposing, so long as the microphone is set centrally between you and your patient. Professor Románek uses one for his sessions and I can make out almost everything clearly enough to transcribe it. The only problem is you'll have to be closer to the patient than you'd maybe want.'

'That's not a problem,' said Viktor. 'They'll be sedated and on a restraint couch.'

'Well,' said Judita contemplatively, resting a pale, slim hand on one of the boxes, 'I'd say they're better than the vinyl cylinder recorders but not as good as the wire ones, in my opinion anyway. If you'd prefer one of those we have a couple in store.'

'No,' Viktor smiled. 'I don't want the professor to think I'm anti-progress. I'm keen to make a good impression.'

'You like Professor Románek, don't you?' Judita smiled.

'He cares about his patients. He sees all the evil they do as a sickness, not a measure of their true natures.'

'That's what you believe too?'

'Yes, I do. We can all become mentally ill the way we can all become physically ill. And we all do – to one degree or another, at one time or another. I believe psychiatry is at last waking up to this fact. Waking up very slowly. Did Professor Románek tell you about my views?'

'No. My father told me you were one of his best students, and that you cared deeply about your patients. He passes on his best wishes, by the way.'

'I meant what I said about your father being as big an influence on me as Dr Jung. I've fond memories of him,' said Viktor, smiling. There was an awkward silence and he realized that he had been staring at Judita, drinking in every detail of her: the intense dark eyes, the full lips, the flawless pale skin. 'Anyway . . .' he said clumsily.

'I'll go get a porter,' said Judita, and they set about organizing the other materials Viktor needed. Once everything had been arranged and a porter had taken the equipment down to the tower room, Viktor thanked Judita for her help and she made to leave.

'Miss Blochová . . .' Viktor called when she reached the door. She turned.

'There's a café in the village,' he said. 'It's not much, but I wondered if you'd like to take coffee with me there some time. You can tell me all about the castle's dark history.' He winced at his own clumsiness.

She stood at the door, silent for what seemed an eternal moment, her eyes full and dark and swallowing Viktor, her expression impossible to read.

'I think I'd like that,' she said at last with a smile. 'I have a day off at the end of the week . . .'

Viktor nodded and she left. Once she was gone and Viktor was alone in the room, his severely handsome face broke into a broad grin.

iktor held his first narcosynthesis session three days later. He chose to start with the patient whom all the staff considered to be the most biddable and least aggressive.

Leoš Mládek. The Clown.

Having helped set up his equipment, Viktor had become accustomed to the room allocated for the narcosynthesis sessions; but when he'd first set foot in it he'd felt a vague claustrophobic panic, again as if the castle walls had closed tighter on him.

Set into the base of the castle's main tower, the round, high-ceilinged room was accessed by a ramp, rather than steps, that steeply declined to a door one floor down from the patient accommodations. Viktor guessed the room had originally been a grain or food store, its two-metre-thick, curving, windowless walls keeping it a reasonably constant temperature in summer and winter. The ramp to the upper floor would have been installed to allow the easy transport of stored goods into the castle kitchens.

The heavy oak door, reinforced with iron panels, combined with the dense walls to make the room all but soundproof. Románek, knowing Viktor was determined to carry out the sessions alone with his patients, had insisted on the fitting of an alarm button. An orderly would always be on duty just outside the door.

'Heavily sedated or not,' the professor had warned, 'these are the most dangerous mental patients in Central Europe. I need to know that every precaution will be taken.'

At the centre of the room was a desk and a chair for Viktor and a reclining, sectional examination couch. The couch's three adjustable segments and armrests were covered with padded leather, as were the wrist and ankle restraints. Another condition imposed by Románek had been that, even with sedation, the patients must be restrained at all times.

For his narcoanalysis to work, the lighting had to be subdued, luring the patient's mind into an induced twilight, so Viktor had arranged for an angle-poise lamp to be placed on the desk, another set on the floor and its light cast up the wall to soften the mood of cold, harsh immurement.

The Clown, Leoš Mládek, was a small, slender man with a head that seemed too large for his body and pale blue eyes that seemed too large for his head. It was a disproportion that made him look younger than he was: more like a boy or a youth than a man in his mid-thirties. His black hair was short and oiled, severely parted in a sharp line of white scalp, giving the impression his hair was painted on. His face was very pale, the skin like a canvas awaiting paint. To Viktor's eyes, Leoš Mládek was already halfway to being Pierrot, even without make-up.

'What am I doing here?' Mládek asked, looking all around with large, confused eyes as he was led into the room and over to the examination couch by two orderlies. 'What is going to happen to me?'

'There's nothing to worry about, Leoš: we're going to have a talk, that's all.' Viktor opened the stainless-steel case that held a syringe and two glass vial bottles, each crimped with a rubber seal. 'I'm going to give you an injection to relax you and help you remember things a little more clearly.' Viktor punctured the first vial's rubber seal with the needle, drew the viscous liquid into the syringe and stepped across to his restrained patient. 'I promise you'll find this a pleasant, relaxing experience. I just need you to trust me.'

'But I don't *need* treatment.' There was desperation now in Mládek's tone. 'I'm not mad. I keep telling everyone that. I didn't do anything. It was Teuffel who should be here. It was Teuffel, the Harlequin, who did it all . . .'

Viktor found a vein with ease, blue beneath the almost translucent skin of his patient's forearm. Ignoring Mládek's increasingly desperate protestations, he eased the hypodermic needle into the vein. He nodded to the orderlies who left the room.

Viktor watched as the drugs began to work. Very soon his patient would begin to fall into his own consciousness, tumbling through the layers of his being. Mládek no longer tensed against the grip of the restraints; the urgency left his slender frame, soft voice and large eyes. As Viktor hoped, the former clown didn't lose consciousness or seem especially drowsy. It was simply as if all his fears and anxieties had evacuated his slight frame. With a loud clunk, Viktor turned the Magnetophon's dial and the brushed-steel spools started rotating.

'Are you Leoš Mládek?' Viktor asked.

Mládek nodded slowly, the large eyes emptily on Viktor.

'Please answer all my questions out loud so your response is recorded. Are you Leoš Mládek?' Viktor kept his tone quiet and relaxed. He knew the scopolamine would already be dissolving Leoš's will, his ability to steer his own thoughts without instruction.

'I am Leoš Mládek.'

'What do you do for a living?'

'I am a clown. Pierrot. I make people sad and I make them laugh.'

'Are you also Harlequin?' asked Viktor.

'No. I never play Harlequin. Only Pierrot.'

'You've never played Harlequin?'

'I've never played Harlequin.'

Viktor wrote a note in his notebook. 'Do you know where you are?'

'I'm in a madhouse,' said Mládek, without bitterness or ire. 'Locked up with lunatics.'

'Are you a lunatic?'

'No.'

A pause. Then Viktor said: 'Leoš, I want you to imagine yourself as a great sea. A wide and very deep ocean. I want you to imagine we are floating on that ocean. Can you see it?'

'An ocean.'

'The water is deep – very, very deep – but calm. I need you to imagine that beneath us, the ocean is filled with all the things, all the memories, all the events that have happened in your life. And swimming among them are all the versions of you there are or ever have been: Leoš the clown, Leoš the friend, Leoš the lover, Leoš the child. Can you imagine that? Can you see that?'

'A deep ocean.'

'Where we are now, where you know yourself to be, here in the castle, that's the surface. I want you to leave that behind and dive down into the water, deep into the memories. I want you to find the first moment, the first event, that led you to be brought here. The beginning of your story. Can you find it?'

There was a pause. Mládek closed his eyes. 'I've found it.'

'That's very good, Leoš. What event was it that started your journey to this place?'

'It was when he arrived.'

'When who arrived?'

'The Devil. It was the day the Devil arrived. The day Manfred Teuffel came to the circus.'

'When most people think about clowns, they just think of slapsticks and funny wigs.' Lying in the artificially twilit room in an artificially twilit state of consciousness, Leoš Mládek spoke quietly, a faint tone of drug-attenuated passion in his voice. 'That isn't what I am. Pierrot is a figure from Commedia dell'arte, from a time when the circus was truly the theatre of the people. To be Pierrot means to be an actor, not a buffoon; to have the skill of improvisation, to read your audience and channel their emotions. It's not a job: it's a calling – a grand tradition. When I am in the ring, I don't just *play* Pierrot, I *become* him. I *am* him.'

'And what led you to become Pierrot?' asked Viktor.

'People imagine I came from a circus family, that performing was in my blood. It wasn't like that at all. The circus called to me – Pierrot called to me.

'I was born to a reasonably well-off provincial family. My father was a country doctor in Doudlebsko and my mother had fulfilled any ambitions she might have had by becoming a country doctor's wife. You couldn't imagine any background duller or more bourgeois. It was decided before I left my crib that medicine was also where my career was to lie. I mean, what kind of parent predestines their infant to mediocrity?'

'Being a physician can be an important job, Leoš,' said Viktor. 'A doctor can make differences to people's lives, important differences.

I'm a doctor and I don't find anything mediocre about it. I hope to make an important difference in your life.'

'My father was never that kind of doctor,' said Mládek. 'He was a simple country general practitioner: a village repairman setting broken bones for farmers, applying poultices for croup, stitching and bandaging fieldworkers' injuries. Anything more serious and he was as useless as anyone else. He'd attend children with diseases he was impotent to cure. He'd stand and frown and occasionally take temperatures and shake his head with professional gravity. Then watch them die. That was his life and he wanted nothing more for himself and that was fair enough – but he also wanted nothing more for me. He saw me as his continuation – that I would qualify and join the practice, then take it over when my father retired. Presumably he thought my son would in turn take over from me. A horizonless continuum of mediocrity. But there was no way I could do that. I couldn't stand around and watch children die. Children . . .

'I didn't protest. I was a biddable child, then a compliant adolescent. I excelled at school, which seemed only to confirm to my father my suitability for the medical profession – that and my docility and lack of imagination.'

'What happened to change your path?' asked Viktor.

Even through the fog of sedation, a light shone in Mládek's large eyes. 'The circus. The circus happened. The circus came to the village. I was seventeen and it was Masopust, The Days of Fools. The first Masopust after the war – there hadn't been any during the hostilities. More importantly, it was the first Masopust of our new country free of Austro-Hungary. The name "Czechoslovakia" still felt new and strange in our mouths and in our ears and everyone was full of Austroslavic zeal – and I was full of the rising sap of adolescence. Everything felt new and fresh and nothing seemed impossible. We'd been given a country but felt we'd been given the whole world.

'Doudlebsko has as many Germans living in it as Czechs – more probably – and our village was no exception, but even they seemed more, well, *excited*. Having so many Germans also meant our Masopust had more than a little of their *Fasching* mixed into it and it always started with a Procession of Masks. I remembered those masks, that procession. I truly did feel they were driving out old spirits from the land.'

'What kind of masks, Leoš? German *Perchtenmasken*? The kind of masks that look like the Devil?'

'Yes.'

'Did they frighten you?'

'I was seventeen; I was beyond that.'

'But masks are important to you, aren't they?'

A frown formed on Mládek's pale brow. 'What do you mean?'

'You wear masks in your performance, don't you?'

'Pierrot doesn't wear masks . . .'

'But Harlequin does,' said Viktor.

'I never played Harlequin.'

'But even Pierrot wears a mask occasionally, doesn't he? The Black Mask. Pierrot sometimes wears the Black Mask to hide his emotions or conceal his identity, isn't that so?'

'Perhaps. In some traditions. But I never did. Harlequin wears a mask.'

'But so does Scaramouche, so does Pantalone, so does the Doctor – masks are a big part of the Commedia dell'arte tradition.'

'I never wore a mask. And I performed alone.'

'I see,' said Viktor. 'That puzzles me. You see, just like Jungian psychology, Commedia dell'arte is all about universal types. For the character of Pierrot to work, for him to make sense, depends on his interaction with other types: with Harlequin, with Columbine, with Scaramouche. Yet you say you performed alone. You claim until Manfred Teuffel joined the troupe there was no Harlequin. How can that be? How could there ever be Pierrot without Harlequin?'

'I did work with others. I worked with the audience. With the children. Pierrot shares the innocence and the mischief of children.

He's really just a child himself – full grown, but a child. The eternal child.'

'All right,' Viktor paused for a moment. 'Tell me more about Masopust, about the circus that came to town.'

'It was special that year,' said Mládek. 'After all the processions, all the dancing and the parties, there was the circus: a small troupe of Commedia dell'arte performers set up a tent in the meadow nearest the village. That was the first time I had ever seen Pierrot. He held all the village children in his thrall. If you had seen their little faces – they were mesmerized by him. I knew right there and then that that was what I wanted to do. Who I wanted to be.'

'So you decided to join the circus? How did your parents react to the news?'

'I didn't tell them. I was supposed to be going to Prague the following year to study medicine. I knew if I told them they'd find some way of stopping me. So I talked with the circus people and they said I could come with the troupe when it left. My sister tried to talk me out of it, but I'd never been so suddenly, perfectly, totally sure of anything. I left a letter with her for my parents. Not an apology – I had nothing to apologize for.

'That was the start of my career. I graduated from that troupe to a larger one, then another larger. Eventually the Circus Pelyněk recruited me. I became their biggest star – their biggest draw. We toured all over Europe. It took me more than ten years to get to the top of my profession, but once I was there, no one could touch me. I was so happy. Completely happy.' Even through the drugs, Mládek's tone and expression darkened. 'Then he came. Manfred Teuffel. Harlequin. As soon as he came, everything was ruined. He had everyone fooled, right from the start, but not me. I saw through his guise. I saw him for what he was.'

'The Devil?' asked Viktor.

'Don't you see that's why he came as Harlequin? The original Old French name *herlequin* means devil, demon. And *Teufel* in German means devil. He called himself Manfred Teuffel and he played Harlequin and no one could see he was the Devil. Except me.' Again, a deep swelling of emotion was lost beneath the suppressing blanket of the drugs. 'Everyone marvelled at his performances. Everyone loved him. But only I could see him for what he was. He was no great performer – he was a great *bewitcher*. Teuffel bewitched audiences. Especially the innocent, because that's the Devil's way. The children. He'd perform wearing the mask of Harlequin, as was tradition, but underneath he'd have his face painted as Pierrot – a deliberate insult to me. But the way he had his face painted was an outrage – a distortion and perversion of the Pierrot tradition. Pierrot is white-face, red pursed lips and black outlines, a single tear painted on his face. Teuffel did all of that, but it was twisted, contorted, demonic.

'He wore the two-coloured, long-nosed Harlequin mask. It meant no one could see what was painted underneath. But every now and then he'd go to the edge of the ring and lean into the crowd. He would say, "Gather around, dear children. Come closer and pay close heed, dear children. Come let me whisper secret knowledge to you." When they did, he'd rip away his mask and snarl at them, making them scream and cry in terror. Then he'd put the mask back on and go to another part of the audience and do the same. The children would gather to him eagerly, gleefully, wishing sudden fear on themselves. On each other. They relished the fright. That's the thing about children: they like to be frightened. Where Pierrot reflected their finest, gentlest emotions, Harlequin excited their coarsest and darkest.

'He became a huge draw. Bigger even than me. Harlequin displaced Pierrot. We toured throughout Central Europe – Austria, Hungary, Yugoslavia, Poland and Germany. Our show became a huge attraction and in every performance Harlequin appealed to the darkness in the children, ridiculed and defeated Pierrot. Humiliated him. Made him the laughing stock of the piece.

'I hated him for that. The whole troupe worshipped Teuffel as much as the audiences did. But I could see through him. I could see he was evil, that he was the Devil. Only I could see how he enjoyed frightening the children at every performance. How he *fed* off their fear.

'Word got to us that a small girl had gone missing in the last town we'd performed in. That was in Poland. The police stopped us on the road before we reached the border and searched all our trucks and cars. They didn't have any particular suspicion about us, but you know how everyone is naturally mistrustful of travelling people. In any case we were close to Těšín Silesia and the Poles were still touchy about the Seven Day War and Czechoslovaks in general. We were all questioned but no one knew anything about the little girl. No one could remember seeing her, but there were always so many children. So it was forgotten about – even I didn't think much of it at the time.

'But then it happened again, about six months later. Two children, a boy and a girl, this time in Bavaria. But we were back across the border before anyone made a connection with the circus. But now I knew – I knew it was Teuffel. I knew he had been feasting on the fear of little children.'

'Did you tell anyone that you thought Harlequin was taking children? Anyone in the circus?'

'They wouldn't have believed me.' Mládek paused, then through the drugs said with an earnestness that surprised Viktor: 'You have to understand – it's the nature of the Devil to disguise his presence. The truth is that the Devil comes into all of our lives, at least once, at one time or another. Everyone encounters him, but most don't know he's there. They blame the evil in others, or in themselves, for anything bad that happens to them. The truth is nobody really believes in him any more, which is his most powerful weapon.

'I needed to find proof. I needed to show Teuffel for who and what he was. We were performing in Ostrava – in Přívoz, the Moravian part. We pitched our tents on fields down by the River Oder. For two solid weeks we filled the marquee every night. The youngsters all loved the show – they loved me, Pierrot. But Teuffel – Harlequin – always spoiled it. He always distracted them from me by doing his scaring thing. They all screamed in fright – then begged him to do it again and again. As soon as Harlequin came in, they forgot all about me.

'There was one little girl in particular – she seemed obsessed with Harlequin and came to almost every performance. The first time she was there with her mother, after that she came alone. I guessed that she must have lived close to where we had pitched our tents. She could only have been about nine or ten and was an earnest little thing, all Silesian green eyes and brown curls. But when Harlequin ripped off his mask, no matter how many times she had seen it, she squealed in fright and delight, clapping her little hands.

'Teuffel usually paid her particular attention – focused on her more than the other children. But the last night she was there, he hadn't done the thing with his mask at all. He spent all the time ridiculing and humiliating Pierrot, ridiculing and humiliating me. That night, I didn't mind. I knew what he had planned for that poor little girl and I was happy his cruel attention was focused on me, not her.

'But he had it all planned. I found out later that, after she'd been to the show the first couple of times, Manfred Teuffel had arranged a general admission ticket for her to get in whenever she wanted.

'Anyway, that night he had ignored her and I could see the disappointment on her little face. But as he and I did our act, I saw underneath his Harlequin mask his face was painted as his usual corrupt, twisted parody of Pierrot.

'Suddenly, completely out of the blue, he went up to the little girl. I could see she was thrilled, her eyes all big and bright and excited. Then he ripped his mask off. She screamed. But not like before. I'll never forget that scream. This time there was no exquisiteness to her fear: it was raw, unadulterated terror. I don't know what she saw beneath that mask, but she ran from the tent and out into the night, still screaming. Teuffel quietly replaced his mask, which he kept on for the rest of the performance, turned back to me and continued with the show as if nothing had happened.

'But I knew, you see. I knew she was to be his next victim. He'd sampled her: taken a bite of her fear and it had enflamed his hunger. I knew Harlequin was going to feast on her. I had to find that little girl before Teuffel did. I didn't even have time to take my make-up off. I simply pulled an overcoat over my costume, put on a hat and ran out to find her.'

'And you did . . .'

'I found her where she'd been hiding in some bushes down by the Oder. But I was too late.' A tear found its way down Mládek's pale face. 'When I found her she was all still and quiet, lying broken in the dirt and the dark. Teuffel had been there – Harlequin had found her first.

'Others had been searching for her and before I had a chance to do anything, they found me there. With her. They attacked me and they would have killed me if the police hadn't arrived. They blamed me, you see. They didn't understand. They said it was I who'd killed her and the other children – they said I was some kind of monster. I tried to explain to them. I tried to get them to see it was Manfred Teuffel who was the real killer. That it was the Devil himself who had done it. But no one believed me, so they locked me up in this lunatic asylum.'

'All right, Leoš,' said Viktor. 'We're coming to the end of this session. I need you to come back to the surface of the ocean. Back to here and now.' He flicked open the buff file on the table and took out a printed paper leaflet, headed 'Circus Pelyněk'. He took it over to Mládek and held it in front of him to see.

'Can you tell me what this is, Leoš?'

'It's a flyer for the circus. An advertisement.'

'Yes it is. Can you tell me what you see on the cover?'

He nodded, his too-large blue eyes focused on the leaflet. 'I see me as Pierrot and Manfred Teuffel as Harlequin. The circus's two biggest draws.'

'Look again, Leoš. Look carefully. See what it says? It says *you* are the sole clown in the circus. The greatest clown in Europe. Do you see the photographs? This . . .' Viktor pointed to the first image, 'is you as Pierrot. But *this* . . .' He pointed to the second image. 'Can you tell me who this is, Leoš?'

'That's him. That's Teuffel. Teuffel dressed up as Harlequin.'

'No it's not, Leoš,' Viktor said emphatically. 'That's you. There never was any Manfred Teuffel. *You* are Harlequin and *you* are Pierrot. You played both parts. You always have. It's always been just you.'

'It's not true.' Despite the drugs, he shook his head vehemently. 'They tried to tell me that before. They said it when they arrested me – they said *I* did all that to that poor girl. To the other children. They all believed the Devil's lies.'

'But look, Leoš. I see it myself. I see you are both clowns. Leoš Mládek as Pierrot *and* Leoš Mládek as Harlequin. It was you who frightened the children. It really was Pierrot beneath the mask of Harlequin. It was another part of you who was Harlequin.'

He shook the too-large head wearily, the drugs now pulling him towards sleep. 'You're wrong,' he said quietly. 'The Devil is deceiving you, just like he deceived all the others . . .'

*I*t was a bright, chill late morning as they walked together down the forest path that led from the castle. Autumn was protesting its coming end in a blaze of colour in the broad-leaved trees, while the pines stood in dark, ageless silence. As they had walked, the thin veil of clouds had torn apart into frayed shreds and the sun now turned the autumn leaves to embers. Viktor felt they were removed from everything: from the castle, from the events around them. It was a timeless, contextless moment and he sensed Judita, too, felt removed from her worries.

They made small talk, Viktor easing his way into the detail of Judita's life. They talked about Professor Bloch: Viktor's experience of him as a mentor, Judita's experience of him as a father. They talked of their lives before the castle, about friendships and family, about ambitions and hopes, Viktor cautious not to intrude on that part of Judita's history that had diverted her from her medical studies. Then, for a while, they walked in contented, comfortable silence. As they did, Viktor was aware how easy she had become around him, so quickly. How easy he felt around her.

'Isn't it beautiful?' she asked eventually, breathing deep and taking in the forest around them.

Viktor smiled. 'Yes it is. Although I always feel a little uneasy in forests.'

'Really?' She turned to him, surprised. 'Why?'

'I don't know. Probably something very Jungian – you know, how forests are like the Unconscious, deep and dark and full of secrets.' Viktor felt relaxed with Judita, but not relaxed enough to tell her his own forest secret: a twelve-year-old's discovery of a mother's suicide in the woods; of how, even now, shifting shadows between trees could awaken a memory of a hanging, lifeless body, its face darkened. Of how his future as a psychiatrist had been determined by that discovery. 'The truth is I'm glad to get out of the castle for a while,' he said instead. 'Professor Románek was right, it does get to you if you don't reconnect with the world outside.'

'Ondřej Románek said that?' Judita again looked surprised.

'Yes, why?'

'Oh, nothing. It's just he doesn't seem to take his own advice too much. He spends almost all his time in the asylum. And he has a habit of disappearing into his study for hours on end.'

'Really?'

'Oh yes. And he gives strict orders not to be disturbed. Poor man.'

'Why poor man?'

'All he has is his work. A widower, you see. No children. He was apparently devoted to his wife – but she died comparatively young, I believe. I don't really know that much about it. To be honest I don't really know that much about Professor Románek: he's one of those people you think you have a measure of at first meeting, but he's a very deep character indeed. And don't let his cheery disposition fool you – he's subject to very dark moods every now and then. That's why he locks himself away.'

'His wife died, you say?'

'Yes.'

'She didn't die of tuberculosis, by any chance?'

Judita stopped and turned to Viktor. 'How do you know that?'

He held her in his gaze, considering telling her how Románek described almost becoming lost in a patient's madness. But it hadn't been a patient; it had been a wife. 'I think Dr Platner mentioned something of the sort,' he said instead.

It took them half an hour to reach the village. A pretty place without being exceptional, it looked much as it would have two centuries before. Czechoslovakia was full of villages and small towns like this – at the very heart of Europe, yet insulated from it by a smothering blanket of forest, tradition and parochialism. Everyone here would know everyone else: the families in the village, as Románek had pointed out, would have lived here generation after generation since before recorded time. It filled him with a vague cultural claustrophobia which made him yearn for the noise and bustle of Prague, for the anonymous faces of strangers. He felt that way, he knew, because he had come from a village just like this one. On another edge of the country, but just like it.

The four or five other people in the café watched Viktor and Judita enter, staring at them with the blank curiosity of villagers: no hostility as such, but no welcome. Viktor was aware they watched Judita more; he couldn't decide if it was her striking looks that attracted their attention, or if they sensed that extra dimension to her otherness. He was a stranger in the village; Judita was a stranger in her own land.

'It's a lovely day,' Viktor said to her, 'even if it's a little chilly. Shall we sit outside?'

She nodded and they went out to a table near the door. It afforded them a view along the village's main street and up the forested gully through which they had just descended. Above it all, the castle loomed dark, forbidding and dominant, the hump of black rock sitting on its shoulder. Viktor again felt a claustrophobic flutter; a sense of the castle's ineluctability, as if he were forever condemned to live either within its walls or within its shadow.

The café's owner, a robust, friendly man in his fifties and sporting a handlebar moustache, came out, smiled at them both and took their order for coffee. When he came back out he brought a plate of *koláče* cakes. Viktor protested that he hadn't ordered them, but the proprietor smiled.

'On the house,' he said. Viktor was always amazed at how dialect and accent changed so dramatically this close to Prague. 'You folks from the castle?'

Viktor said they were and introduced himself and Judita.

'You have to excuse the regulars staring – we don't get such beautiful guests usually,' he made a small bow to Judita. 'And any strangers we do get tend to be from Hrad Orlů, and I'm ashamed to admit my neighbours are more than a little mistrustful of anyone to do with the castle. You know, with all the crazies being locked up there. And then there's the whole history of the place of course.'

'The history?'

'I'll explain,' said Judita. 'It's a long story.'

'It is a long story indeed,' said the café owner. 'And I leave you to tell it. Well, you enjoy your coffee and cake. And please remember you're welcome here any time.' He again gave a small bow and left.

'How did your session with Leoš Mládek go?' asked Judita, pulling her coat collar up before sipping at her coffee.

'I made a start, let's put it that way. You'll hear when you get the tapes. All I could get to was the surface personality – the gentle Pierrot clown who believes himself innocent of any wrongdoing, who refuses to accept that he allowed his personality to take two different forms. The person I really want to talk to is Harlequin – or Manfred Teuffel as Mládek has named that part of his personality.'

'You think you'll find your "Devil Aspect" there?'

'If I do, and if I can remove it from Mládek, then there's a chance I can cure him. Evict Manfred Teuffel and allow Leoš Mládek to take sole occupancy.'

'Sounds more like mediaeval exorcism than twentieth-century psychiatry.'

'Maybe that's all mediaeval exorcism was: the recognition of the

Devil Aspect. But recognition without understanding or empathy. Something we're still guilty of today.'

'I can see you as a Middle Ages witchfinder, somehow,' she said archly. 'Maybe it's fate you ended up at this castle particularly.'

'Oh? Between yours and the waiter's cryptic references, my curiosity is spiked. You promised to tell me the tower room's dark history.'

'Do you know what the locals here call the castle?'

He smiled and leaned forward, resting his elbows on the table. 'Enlighten me.'

'Hrad Čarodějek.'

'Really?' Viktor looked up the valley at the dominating structure on the mountain. 'Why the Castle of the Witches?'

'Dark deeds and the dark arts. And a man with a dark, dark heart.' She sipped at her coffee, watching Viktor teasingly. 'The usual story is that everywhere Christianity went, the local Slavic paganism had to be wiped out,' she said when she replaced her cup in its saucer. 'Occasionally with the sword and the execution pyre. The aristocracy was at the forefront of it – the establishment of the Christian church was another means of subjugating the locals and cementing the powerbase of the nobility. And, of course, the old fertility superstitions were branded as witchcraft. Anyone who adhered to them risked being burned at the stake or throttled.'

'You seem to know a lot about it.'

'History interests me. It helps me understand the present. And, of course, good simple country folk weren't at all averse to burning the odd Jew back then as well. Truth is the Czechs were never much for witch hunts, other than old Boblig up in Northern Moravia, and that was more to do with Catholic Austria suppressing Czech Protestants through false charges. Witch-hunting was only brought in to Bohemia in the sixteenth century. By the Germans. Like I said, history helps me understand the present.'

'So that was why it was known as the Castle of the Witches?'

Viktor asked enthusiastically, steering Judita back to her story and away from her dark thoughts of the here and now. 'Because there were a lot of pagans in the area?'

'No, not at all. It was a very different story here. The local aristo was no pillar of community and faith. He was quite the other thing, by all accounts. Known locally as Jan Černé Srdce – Jan of the Black Heart.'

'Oh yes. Professor Románek mentioned him – as did an archae-ologist I met on the train. But all I know is he was once lord of the castle.' He grinned at her, taking in her dark beauty. 'I sense a tale of dastardly deeds about to unfold.'

'You have no idea . . .' said Judita. 'The legend still hangs over the castle, like the innkeeper said. Jan of the Black Heart was the son of the local duke; not the first-born, he had two older brothers. It's said that Black Heart was so inherently evil, ambitious and ruthless that he sold his soul to the Devil when he was still a boy. His brothers both died before they could ascend to the dukedom. One drowned while swimming in the small lake behind the village – the other died in a hunting accident in the forest.' She nodded up towards the castle. 'You see, this wasn't the family seat – it was their hunting castle. Both deaths were attributed in hindsight to the involvement of the Devil, but the truth was that Jan had been present – the only witness, in fact – to both misadventures. Anyway, when he became the local duke, he spent more time here than at the main castle, where his wife and children lived, practically prisoners and practically abandoned.'

'So why did the demonic duke prefer here?'

'It's remote enough today, but back then it was completely iso-lated. It was particularly wild around here and therefore provided excellent hunting. They say he ruled this valley and beyond like an absolute monarch. Absolute power and absolute corruption. Everyone feared and secretly hated him. All kinds of rumours were spread and they have become so embroidered over the years that they're now local legend. Suffice it to say that the locals never venture near the castle. Almost all the orderly, maintenance and catering staff travel in from Mladá Boleslav and board in the castle for five-day shifts.'

'Legends usually have some foundation in truth,' said Viktor.

'Oh, he was a bad boy, all right. Jan of the Black Heart was supposed to have practised the dark arts in the castle, gathering witches and warlocks from all over Bohemia. It's claimed he succeeded in summoning up Černobog – The Black God – the Devil of Slavic myth – or Veles, the Dark Lord of the Underworld. There were tales of Black Masses in the forest or in the castle, all that kind of thing. Whatever the truth or otherwise about that, one thing is true: he abducted and murdered women and girls from the local villages. Scores of them. Maybe more than a hundred.'

'Why is that particularly credible?'

'It's part of the historical record. The king sent a commission to investigate and it was found to be true. No trial, of course. If Jan of the Black Heart had been an ordinary peasant, he would have been publicly hanged or broken on a wheel for his crimes. Instead he was immured in the castle: common punishment back then for delinquent aristocracy. Instead of prison or execution, they'd be walled into a sealed room with just a slit left for food and water to be handed in. They'd live like that for years, sometimes decades. Depending on which version of the legend you believe, the servant assigned to tend to the immured Jan of the Black Heart was either a deaf mute or had had his ears stopped with molten lead and his tongue cut out.'

'Whatever for?' asked Viktor.

'It was believed that Jan of the Black Heart could talk anyone into doing his bidding, persuade the most pious to turn to Satan. Some claim that he wasn't the Devil's disciple at all, but actually the Devil himself – that Jan Černé Srdce is really Jan Černobog – and it's really Satan who's bound for all time in the castle. In any case, the servant had to be deaf, literally, to his beggings to be set free.' Judita drew closer to Viktor, lowering her voice in mock-conspiratorial tones. 'Maybe you've heard old Jan of the Black Heart

– you know, when you're practising your own dark arts during your sessions in the tower. They say he was immured in a room in that particular tower because it has the thickest walls, but no one has ever been able to find it.'

'I can't say I've heard him,' said Viktor. 'I've enough real demons to exorcize as it is.'

'Maybe you should listen out for him. One legend says he can be heard at night beating his fists dully on the stone and calling for his master, Satan, to free him.' She put on a face of mock-realization. 'Perhaps it's you who'll release him: maybe Jan of the Black Heart is the Devil Aspect you've been looking for. Or maybe he'll come looking for you – another story says the master stonemason who constructed the sealed room was a warlock and the nobleman's partner in depravity. And that he created a concealed door and passageway into the network of caves in the mountain beneath the castle. According to this version, the malevolent ghost of Jan still resides in the sealed tower room but, whenever there's a full moon, it makes its way through tunnel and cave and out into the forest in search of victims to slate his bloodlust.' She grinned mischievously, a dark eyebrow arching. There was both a delicacy and a strength to Judita Blochová and Viktor found himself captivated by her.

'The archaeologist I met on the train said the caverns and tunnels beneath the castle are supposed to be the mouth of Hell and the castle was built to seal it. Did you know about that?'

Judita laughed. 'Yes, I've heard that one too. The other name the locals have for the castle is Pekelná Brána – Hell's Gate. The tower was probably built with thicker walls as a defensive battlement. But depending on which story you believe, Hrad Orlů was either built as a hunting castle or as a plug on the mouth to Hell. Either way it wasn't a strategic post, and never intended to face assault. But the tower would make an ideal prison.'

'You said there was something about the treatment room? The grain store?' asked Viktor.

'Aha,' said Judita, arching an eyebrow. 'Maybe it was intended to be a grain store, but Jan of the Black Heart is said to have used it for a variety of purposes – all of them dark. The legend is he *entertained* guests in there, presumably because the walls stifled any screams. And, of course, it's another place the locals say was used for his Black Masses and summonings of the Devil. And now you're doing your own Devil-summoning in the very same room.'

'I think you've been transcribing too many case histories.' Viktor laughed, but as he looked past Judita and up towards the castle, he again had that feeling of dark captivity. 'Maybe we should start heading back . . .'

CHAPTER FIVE

*T*here had been no confession. There would be no confession.

Smolák had interrogated Tobar Bihari half a dozen times and the gypsy's story remained the same. Or at least it had the first three or four times; after that Bihari seemed to withdraw into himself. Smolák's questions would go unanswered, not because Bihari avoided them, more that he hadn't heard them. He would sit silent and staring, as if looking at some distant point in space, in time, or both. No amount of cajoling or entreaty, inducement or threat could entice him from whatever space in his mind he had retreated to.

With each interrogation, with each passing day, less of Tobar Bihari inhabited this world or the body that moved within it. He was no longer handcuffed or shackled to the chair during his interrogations: the small gypsy went where he was led, sat when guided to the chair, stood when taken by the elbow.

Smolák bitterly accepted that there was nothing now between his suspect and the madhouse. He would never be able to get Bihari to give details about the other women he had murdered. A search of the rooms the gypsy shared with the club-footed prostitute yielded no bloodstained leather apron, no razor-edged murder weapon, no glass bead to match the one Smolák had found.

Watching his suspect sink deeper into mute, motionless madness, Smolák asked Dr Bartoš to sit in on one of his interrogations of Bihari and offer his professional opinion of the suspect's mental state.

'As I've already recommended, Kapitán,' said Bartoš, once another fruitless session with Bihari had concluded and he and Smolák stood smoking in the corridor. 'You really should bring in a proper psychiatric expert. I'm not competent—'

'An opinion, Doctor. All I'm asking for is your informed opinion. I'm at a loss with Bihari. He doesn't act like someone who's guilty; he doesn't act like someone who's innocent. Sometimes it's like he doesn't know I'm in the room with him.'

'Or more correctly, he's not in the room with you,' said Bartoš. 'Do you notice the way he only moves when given a gentle push? Or only sits when physically placed in the chair? It's called waxy flexibility – a precursor to full-blown catatonia. From what I've seen – and I repeat I'm no expert – he's exhibiting oneirophrenia, dreaming while awake. He'll soon stop talking, stop moving, stop reacting to stimuli. Like I say, complete catatonia.'

'What do you think caused it?'

The small police doctor brushed some spilled cigarette ash from the front of his crumpled suit. 'He's in extreme shock. Shock at having come face to face with the Devil, even if that Devil is some monstrous part of himself, the Devil within. Or maybe there really was someone with him that night – someone who turned out to be Leather Apron and whose will was much greater, much more dominant than Bihari's. But I'm telling you, you *must* get a psychiatrist involved now. It's your only chance to find out if Bihari really is your Leather Apron or not.'

'All right, Doctor, I'll phone this Professor Románek and see if he can help.'

They were both still standing in the hallway when the door opened. Bihari, small and blank faced, was dwarfed by the uniformed policeman who held him by the elbow, steering him out of the interrogation room and down the corridor towards the cells.

Smolák and Bartoš watched in silence until prisoner and escort had turned the corner at the hall's end.

'I'd make that call sooner rather than later,' said Bartoš, 'before he withdraws from this world completely.'

Smolák was about to answer when there was the sound of yelling from around the hall corner. Smolák was already running before he recognized the voice as Bihari's. Dr Bartoš ran behind him.

When he turned the corner, Smolák came face to face with Bihari. His larger escort was slumped on the floor, stunned. It was clear his nose was broken. A bloody smear on the cream and green paint showed where the guard's face had been slammed into the station wall.

Smolák froze and held an arm out to halt the progress of Dr Bartoš.

'Get back around the corner,' said Smolák in a low, even voice.

'But—'

'Do it now, Doctor,' said Smolák, without turning or taking his eyes off Tobar Bihari, or the service automatic he had taken from the police officer at his feet.

'Tobar . . .' Smolák now held his hand up to the gypsy. 'Tobar, you're only going to get yourself into more trouble. Give me the gun.'

Bihari responded by raising his aim to Smolák's face. 'Stay where you are,' he said, and the calmness of his voice and the certainty of his actions disturbed Smolák. Bihari no longer seemed frightened, nor did he have the dull, sleepwalker passivity he had shown in recent interrogations. Smolák wondered if both had been an act; if this was the calculating, organized mind behind a string of brutal, but carefully calculated murders.

Mentally measuring the distance between himself and Bihari, Smolák did a desperate calculation on how quickly he could close the space and how many bullets he would take in the effort.

'Stay where you are,' Bihari said again. 'I don't want to hurt you. I don't want to hurt anyone.'

'Then give me the gun, Tobar.'

'You'll get your gun back, but first I want you to make me a promise.'

'Tobar, I can't do deals—'

'I didn't say I want a deal. There's nothing I can ask for, nothing you can offer me. I didn't ask for no deal, I'm asking for a promise. A promise from you.'

'What kind of promise?'

'I can't live with him in my head. I want you to understand that. He's in my head and the things he did are in my head and I can't live with it no more.'

Smolák heard the sound of other officers, probably alerted by Dr Bartoš, running towards them.

'Give me the gun, Tobar. Now!'

'Make me your promise.'

'What promise?'

'He's the Devil, you see,' said Bihari, almost matter-of-factly. 'He's Beng the Devil and he has to be stopped. I want you to promise me that you'll stop him.'

'I promise,' said Smolák.

'Thank you,' said Bihari.

The sound of the shot was deafening in the confines of the police station hall. Every muscle in Smolák's body instinctively tensed for the bullet's impact. But there was none. Instead there was a plume of blood, bone and brain from the back of the small gypsy's skull. The underside of his jaw was black-grey with the powder burns where he had jammed the muzzle of the gun and pulled the trigger.

Smolák watched as the small man folded up like a collapsing table and fell lifeless to the ground. The end of a small man, a small life.

As the uniformed officers crowded around Smolák and Dr Bartoš bent down to examine Bihari's body where it had fallen, a dark crimson halo oozing onto the stone floor around the shattered head, the police kapitán tried to work out whether what he had heard had been a confession. Or not.

*T*he day darkened around them as they climbed the path towards the castle. Clouds began to cluster around the witch-hat roofs and spires of the asylum, casting the gully into sudden and chill shadow.

By the time they reached the halfway point, the sky had turned darker yet, blue-grey, heavy and threatening. When the threat was fulfilled, it was with vehemence: the torrential rain a sudden, rattling assault on the leaves around them and soaking through their coats within minutes.

'Come with me!' Judita grabbed Viktor by the wrist and pulled him towards a narrow track that led off the main path.

'Where?'

'Never mind, just come,' she insisted. 'Somewhere dry.'

He followed her at a trot, her slender, rain-cool fingers still wrapped around his wrist. The trees closed in dark and tight around the track and Viktor felt that old claustrophobic feeling, that strange, dull dread, settle on him.

'Come on!' urged Judita, smiling, as she sensed his reticence and tugged eagerly at his wrist. Viktor followed, still puzzled what shelter could possibly be offered in the middle of the forest. After about sixty metres, the trees suddenly gave way to a clearing, about twenty metres square. At its heart, elevated on a rocky outcrop, was an ornate, deep-roofed and hip-gabled wooden building, intricate carvings traced around all its edges and dark timber pillars. Its wood was stained and oiled almost black, and in the rain and gloom it loomed like a lurking forest spirit. A narrow witch-hat spire thrust skyward, tipped with an orb from which rose an Orthodox cross, double sparred with a crooked footrest.

An old Slavic forest chapel.

From the style and the carving, Viktor guessed it had stood in this spot since the Middle Ages. It was a sequestered, even secretive, location for a place of worship but, given Bohemia's history of shifting religious and political affiliations, that wasn't particularly surprising. What did surprise Viktor was that, despite its age, the chapel was in excellent condition; someone from the village obviously still maintaining it.

Judita pulled him towards it. 'Come on,' she commanded.

They huddled in the shallow portico. Viktor pulled back the portal bar and pushed at the heavy oak door; despite there being no obvious sign of a lock, the door didn't budge.

'I've tried to see inside before,' said Judita, 'but the door's solid. I'm guessing there's some kind of hidden trigger lock. But the awning will keep us dry.'

They stood in silence, watching steel rods of rain thunder into the dense, dark green forest around them. There was a strange beauty to a rainstorm in the forest, and they were both content simply to watch nature at work from the shelter of the portico. Viktor was surprised at how relaxed he felt, despite his habitual unease in forests. It must be being here with Judita, he thought.

'I was right about forests,' said Viktor. 'They have all kinds of secrets hidden in them. How did you know about this place?'

'I often take walks in the woods. Like you said, you need to get away from the castle. I heard there was an old chapel between the castle and the village so I decided to find where it was. It must have been here for hundreds of years.'

Viktor took in the structure around them. Dark and heavy, it was at once perfectly at home in the forest, yet jarringly out of place. 'Maybe this was where your Jan of the Black Heart held his rituals . . .' He grinned and leaned towards her in mock menace. It was an innocent gesture that brought their faces close, kissing close.

'The rain's easing,' Judita said awkwardly. 'We should head back before it gets heavy again.'

Viktor kept his eyes on hers. 'I suppose we should.'

Judita started to move out into the open when she stopped, something on the portico's wooden pillar catching her attention. She moved closer to examine it, frowning and running her thumb over the wood.

'That's odd,' she said, 'I haven't seen that before.'

'What is it?' asked Viktor.

'Something carved into the wood.'

Viktor laughed. 'The whole chapel is covered in carvings.'

'No, look.' She moved to one side, allowing Viktor to lean in to examine it.

'I see . . .' he said. 'Some kind of writing – carved into it with a knife.'

'What kind of writing is that? It's not Latin or Cyrillic script. Is that Glagolitic?'

'That's exactly what it is,' said Viktor. The characters had been carved into the ancient timber with great care, meticulously outlining the graceful curves and angles of the ancient alphabet. There were four lines of characters etched into the dark wood. 'That's weird . . .'

'What?'

'To find Glagolitic characters carved into a building like this, you'd expect them to be centuries old. But this is comparatively fresh. Look . . .'

Judita examined the carving again and shrugged. 'You're right. I'm sure it wasn't there the last time I was here. It looks like we have a vandal at work.'

'Well, he's a pretty sophisticated vandal if he carves his graffiti in Old Church Slavonic. I wonder what it means . . .' Viktor took a notebook and pen from his pocket and noted the characters down. 'The friend I told you about – Filip Starosta – he studied this kind of thing. When I see him again I'll ask him if he can translate it.'

CHAPTER SEVEN

$\mathscr{V}$iktor spent the following week carrying out ordinary interviews, without the use of the drug cocktail, with each of the patients. It was his way of getting to know them on the surface of their psychoses in preparation for the narcosynthesis sessions, where he would be able to delve deeper into the dark folds of each mind's complexities.

Oddly, Leoš Mládek seemed almost no different when interviewed without the drug, offering exactly the same account of events. Viktor decided that in the next session he would have to use a more powerful dose to bypass Mládek's surface personality and talk directly with Harlequin. There, perhaps, he would find the Devil Aspect in concrete form, and prove his theory.

Viktor's non-narcotic interviews with the others yielded mixed results. Despite the commonality of violent madness, they were as disparate a group of individuals as you were likely to encounter. Even their attitude towards their sicknesses and confinement varied. Some, like Leoš Mládek or the simple woodcutter Pavel Zelený, seemed genuinely bemused by their internment, the accusations against them, or their diagnoses of madness. They were the so-called egodystonic cases, where the crimes they had committed were so alien to their personalities that they rejected responsibility for them.

Others, like the prim and proper Hedvika Valentová or the glass-collecting Michal Macháček, seemed to feel that their confinement was a gross overreaction to what had been their under-standable, even justifiable, acts of violence. Like so many of the mad, they had adjusted their expectations of the world to become consistent with their delusions; to fit with their insanity. These were the egosyntonic patients – their treatment made especially difficult because they conceived their abnormality to be the norm: they saw those around them as the deviant and deranged, while they them-selves maintained a measured, explicable logic.

Vojtěch Skála, however, was a completely different matter. Even restrained and subdued by sedatives, Skála could only be interviewed in a restraint chair or straitjacket and with two orderlies on hand. Viktor was struck by the mass-murderer's magnetism, the air around him seeming charged with a dark, potent electricity. It brought to Viktor's mind what Judita had said about Skála being quarantined from the other patients lest he infect them with the power of his delu-sions. Professor Románek had since explained that the duty orderlies attending Skála were rotated more regularly than with other patients.

'Whatever you do,' Romànek had cautioned Viktor, 'make sure it is you who gets inside Skála's mind, and not the other way around.'

During his first full interview with Viktor, Skála relished recounting his misdeeds; at every opportunity singing a paean in praise of the commission of evil. While denying none of his acts – indeed rejoicing in them – he did, like so many of the patients, reject his diagnosis of insanity.

He was, he declared, not mad, simply bad.

Twice that week Viktor phoned Filip; both times there was no answer and he started to worry even more about his friend. Added to which was the Glagolitic script cut into the forest chapel's post that Viktor had copied down in his notebook. If anyone could translate it, it would be Filip.

Professor Románek talked regularly with Viktor, but later in that first week withdrew into his rooms, with instructions he wasn't to be disturbed. It was exactly as Judita had described, and everyone except Viktor seemed to accept Románek's withdrawal as something normal.

Once he had interviewed all his patients, Viktor prepared a time-table for narcoanalysis sessions and drew the narcotics he needed from the pharmacy, the administration of which was a duty that fell on Dr Krakl. Viktor struggled to conceal his instinctive antipathy towards Krakl, and as he got to know Platner's assistant better, the instinctive antipathy became a reasoned dislike.

Krakl seemed perpetually suspicious of Viktor and interrogated every request for sodium amytal, sodium pentothal, phenobarbital or scopolamine, but disguised his inquisition as professional inter-est in Viktor's methods. The disguise was at its thinnest when he demanded to know why Viktor could possibly have need of the highly poisonous picrotoxin.

'Narcoanalysis is a new and developing therapy,' explained Viktor, hiding his irritation. 'I'm mixing sodium amytal with other barbiturates in small, calculated doses. But each patient metabolizes differently, reacts differently. In the unlikely case of barbiturate overdose, picrotoxin is the most powerful antidote.'

Krakl said nothing for a moment, a lab-coated vulture holding Viktor in his assessing dead-eyed gaze.

'What do you believe you can achieve through this therapy?' the Sudetener asked eventually. 'Remission? Cure?'

'I know of course that none of these patients will ever go back into the world, but I can at least try to help them find peace.'

'Peace? You really think these monsters deserve peace after all they've done?'

Viktor shook his head in disbelief. 'They aren't responsible for what they did, can't you see that? They're sick, and it's our sworn duty as physicians to do all we can to help them. And I believe if I can reach the Devil Aspect in each patient and make it totally subject to the Ego, then the patient's aberrances will cease. It's surgery on the Unconscious: the excision of a psychic tumour.'

Krakl smiled a twisted vulture smile that stopped just short of a sneer. 'These people are deformed, hideously deformed, but in a way you can't see. Just as no amount of surgery can repair a hunchback or restore a congenitally missing limb, these people have a hidden deformity that cannot be cured.'

'I find that a strange position for a physician,' said Viktor. 'Are you saying we shouldn't try to cure the sick?'

'A physician's duty is remediation. Sometimes that remediation is societal, rather than individual.' Krakl tilted his head back to accentuate his looking down on Viktor. 'And sometimes a doctor's function is preventative, rather than curative. We need to ensure that a greater percentage of the population is healthy in both mind and body. The greatest threat to human evolution is degeneration. If we don't permit the physically and mentally degenerate to breed, if we remove them from society, then society benefits. We all benefit.'

'So you believe the answer is eugenics?' Viktor asked, incredulously.

'The best cure for imperfection is for there to be no imperfections in the first place.'

Viktor shook his head. 'I'm sorry, Dr Krakl, I'm afraid I wouldn't much care to live in your perfect world.' He gathered up his pharmacological supplies. 'In the meantime, I'm going to continue to do my best for my patients. For their sake *and* for society's sake.'

iktor's sessions with Leoš Mládek had led nowhere, either in isolating the Clown's specific psychosis or taking Viktor closer to proving his Devil Aspect theory. He had allowed Mládek his clown make-up, hoping it might unlock something hidden deep in his Unconscious. At least that was the professional reason; on a personal level Viktor felt sorry for the inoffensive, gentle personality that was confused by his confinement for crimes of which he truly believed himself innocent. In many ways Mládek was right: innocent Pierrot was condemned for the crimes committed by malevolent Harlequin.

Victor hoped his next narcosynthesis session would yield more fruit. Hedvika Valentová. The Vegetarian.

Having met with some resistance from the nursing staff over the evening timing of his sessions, Viktor explained he wanted to synchronize the drug therapy with the patient's natural circadian rhythms. To convince the mind it was entering a twilight sleep, he explained, the body had to believe it also.

It was therefore two hours after the evening meal that Madame Valentová was brought into the converted tower granary. Again Viktor got the impression of some priggish provincial schoolmistress: her too-thin frame dressed entirely in grey; skirt, blouse, cardigan and stockings all drab, shapeless and unfashionable. He was concerned to see she had, if anything, lost more weight since he'd first encountered her.

Even premedicated with sedative, Hedvika Valentová looked around with mistrust, particularly at Viktor, as she was brought in. She would only allow the female nurse to assist her onto the couch and, when she insisted that it was indecent for her to be alone and 'recumbent' with a man, Viktor allowed that the couch be adjusted slightly so Madame Valentová was in more of a seated position.

Again to assuage his patient's suspicions as the restraints were fastened on her, Viktor told the nurse to remain in the room until after he had administered the scopolamine combination and Valentová was fully under its influence. Eventually, the stiffness eased from her posture and Hedvika Valentová's Ego, the helmsman of her consciousness, released control. Soon Viktor was able to direct her thoughts in whatever direction he chose.

After a few minutes of easing her into the depths of her own mind, beyond the ten years she had spent confined in asylums, Viktor asked her to find a moment that defined who Hedvika Valentová really was.

'I want you to go to the first moment your troubles began,' he said. 'To be an observer and see yourself as others saw you. Find that moment, then move us both there.'

She closed her eyes as instructed; there was a silence. As his patient travelled through internal time and space, he examined her profile. It was strange; everything about her face was in proportion, there was no deformity or abnormality of feature, other than the hollow-cheeked and sunken-eyed ravages of malnutrition. She could not be described as ugly; yet she could not be described as attractive. Hedvika Valentová, Viktor realized, could not be described as anything. Hers was a face you would never notice; a face you would forget as soon as you turned from it.

Her internal journey completed, she spoke. 'I am there.'

'Where are you?'

'I'm at a party. A birthday party.'

'A party for you?'

She shook her head. 'For one of the other girls in my class. She's pretty and rich. Her father is somebody important in the Škoda factory. She didn't invite me to the party to start with, I know that, but I think Mamma has said something to her mother.'

'Are you close to your mother?' asked Viktor.

'Yes. "We have to look after each other," my mother always says. "It's just the two of us and we have to look after each other".'

'You have no brothers or sisters?'

'No brothers or sisters. No friends. My father died when I was a baby and all I have is my mother.' Valentová spoke now with the voice of a child.

'Are you a happy girl, Hedvika?'

'No. I'm not happy. I've never been happy. I'm so lonely. My mother does everything she can to help, but I'm always alone. No one notices me.' Her voice began to break, thirty-year-old pain biting fresh.

'Hedvika, I need you to step outside yourself. Remember what I said about being an observer, remaining detached. Stay in the time of the party, but I need you to see yourself as others would see you. I want you to describe events as if you're watching them, not living them. Do you understand?'

'I understand,' she said, an adult again.

'Describe yourself, the girl you see.'

'A little girl who was invisible. A little girl who was meant to be alone.'

'Why do you say that? Why were you meant to be alone?'

'I was plain. I was shy. It wasn't that I was bullied or teased – in a way that would have been better, at least that would have meant I'd been noticed. I simply went unnoticed. If people did notice me, they thought I was odd. I *was* odd. The solitary confinement of my childhood made me odd, I think. But all I wanted was to be noticed.'

'Tell me about the party.'

'Mamma made me a dress. The most beautiful thing I'd ever seen: all pink silk and lace. "You look so pretty," she said when I put it on and, for once, I believed her. I stood in front of the mirror and felt so happy. So very, very happy. I imagined all the things the other girls would say about my dress. All the fun we'd have. All the new friends I'd make. This was going to be the day everything changed.'

'What happened at the party?' asked Viktor.

'Nothing. The dress made no difference. No one noticed me, no one spoke to me. I gave my present to Markéta, the girl whose party it was, and she said thanks and smiled but didn't speak to me for the rest of the day. She wasn't being cruel; she wasn't being rude. She simply forgot I was there unless I was right in front of her. That's the way it was with everyone. No one even noticed my dress. I realized that the dress was pretty but there was no one in it. I started to think maybe I didn't exist at all. That I was just a story I was telling myself. Everyone played party games but forgot I was there. Then Markéta got her present from her parents: a puppy. It was a beautiful little thing. Everyone got to hold it.'

'Did you hold it?'

'For a while. I loved that puppy. I wished and wished that I could have one just like it. I thought that maybe dogs, unlike people, would notice me, would love me no matter what I looked like. But when Markéta called the puppy back it went to her. I stroked it and spoke softly to it and begged it to stay, but it just wriggled and struggled to get away and back to Markéta.

'Everyone went back to having fun, to laughing and playing and hugging each other, hugging themselves with the joy of being children and being happy. I just sat there and watched. It's been like that ever since.'

'But something happened at the party, didn't it? At the end?'

'I wanted to leave but Mamma kept saying to go and play with the other children. But eventually even she forgot about me, getting into talk with the other mothers. I got to hold the puppy once more, but then it started struggling again, wanting to be away from me, to be with the others, to go to all the laughing and excitement. So I let it go again. I sat at the bottom of the garden on my own and watched them all. It was a hot, sunny, bright day. People don't realize it, but that's when loneliness is sharpest, when it cuts deepest: when the sun shines and everything is bright and warm.

'Then, suddenly, Markéta started crying, howling. Her face was all twisted up and red. I tell you something, she didn't look so pretty then. Everyone else was crying too, running around.'

'What was wrong?'

'They'd lost the puppy. It must have wandered off while they were playing because no one was paying it attention. That wouldn't have happened if it had stayed with me. I wouldn't have ignored it. I would have looked after it.

'Everybody searched for the puppy, but couldn't find it. Then they all started to say I was the last person seen with it, but I told them it had gone back to Markéta, to where they were all playing without me. But they just stared at me, at my dress.

'They found the puppy in the bushes at the bottom of the garden. It was horrible. What had happened to it. It must have been a wild animal, a fox or a bird of prey or something. If you'd seen the poor thing.

'Markéta started screaming when they found it. Then she started screaming at me. She said I'd killed it. They all started saying I'd killed it, but I hadn't. All I'd done was cuddle it. But even my mother stared at me funny – all shocked and sad and worried.

'Markéta's parents said they were going to talk to the school, to the police even. But I hadn't done anything. I couldn't have done *that* to that poor little thing. Anyway, I told them, where's the blood? Why is my dress all bright and clean? My hands too. When I got home, my mother told me to go straight to my room and change out of the dress, but I wanted to look at myself in the mirror again. I wanted to look at my dress and pretend I was pretty and to be happy again.'

'And were you?'

'No. When I looked in the mirror the dress was as pretty as ever. But then I saw the reflection of my face. I must have started to scream, because my mother came bursting into the room.

'There, in the mirror, above my pretty dress, I had no face. No eyes, no mouth, no nose, just smooth skin without any features. A blank empty mask of flesh.' She turned drug-vague eyes to Viktor. 'Do you understand? I could now see what everyone else saw when they looked at me. I could now see that I was nothing. And when I looked again I saw someone had ruined my dress. Someone had covered it in blood. I saw my reflection without a face and a pretty dress all ruined with blood.'

'So what happened then, Hedvika?'

'That was when they sent me to the special school.'

*T*he store was a lot grander than he imagined it would be. It was situated in the ground floor of a large Secese – the uniquely Czech version of Art Nouveau – building on the corner of Křemencová Street. The name above the store, Petráš Sklo a Skleněná Bižuterie, was in gold letters, again in the Art Nouveau style. It was a theme continued by the gracefully sinuous lines and mouldings of the stonework.

As the name suggested, the windows of the Petráš shop were filled, but without clutter, with glass items of all types, functions and sizes: from vases to jewellery, from drinking glasses and decanters to lamps and paperweights. Everything was stylishly designed and – as he saw when he leaned in to examine the prices written in tiny black ink – very expensive.

When he entered, the woman at the cashier's desk wore an expression of predictably arrogant disdain as she watched him approach. She was in her early forties, slim, poised, dark and elegant, clearly setting the tone for the establishment. Her black hair was severely brushed and tied back and her eyes were made up darkly, her lips crimson. When he drew close he could see her eyes were striking: a bright, pale-emerald colour that seemed to pierce him. The thought occurred to him that she had perhaps been recruited because of the lustre of those eyes, the perfect complement to the wares sold there.

She was dressed entirely in black with a satin blouse with a high mandarin collar. The colour, he realized, had been chosen to empha-size and not distract from the iridescent sparkle of the elaborate Art Deco necklace that clustered tight around her throat and fanned out across the silk of her blouse. A network of white gold chains and clasps held together both the geometry of the piece and the lozenges of iridescent emerald, green and turquoise glass.

It was a sample on display and she was, he realized, as much mannequin as sales assistant.

'I'm here to see the owner, I'm assuming that's Mr Petráš,' he said bluntly and held out his bronze criminal police disc. He found himself resenting her shop-girl arrogance – and the fact that he was strongly attracted to her. 'I'm Kapitán Lukáš Smolák of the criminal commissariat.'

'What's this about?' she asked, still aloof. Still distractingly attractive.

Smolák sighed wearily. 'I'll discuss that with the owner. Where do I find him?'

The assistant pointed across the salesroom to a door over on the far wall. 'Those are the offices. Wait in there.'

'I haven't got time . . .' he started to say, but she had already turned to serve a middle-aged woman dressed in furs, switching to German to address her.

Smolák crossed the sales hall. Glazed display counters sat like glittering islands in a sea of white marble, their cases full of beau-tifully crafted glass items. The onyx-faced pillars and the walls were fringed with classical cornicing. Smolák guessed that a police kapitán's salary wouldn't extend to the prices charged here, and the three other saleswomen, each behind a counter and each dressed in a similar style to the first, were clearly of the same opinion and paid him no attention as he passed.

He knocked on the door and when there was no response he stepped into the office. It was empty except for a large desk with trays piled with paperwork. A half-full crystal ashtray was the only evidence of the store's stock-in-trade. Compared to the grandeur of the sales hall, this was a highly practical and unadorned space. Smolák sat down in the chair facing the desk and waited.

He turned and rose as the door opened, but it was the attractive sales assistant and he sat down again.

'I thought you were going to get the owner,' he said, injecting impatience into his tone. The dark-haired woman moved behind the desk and sat in the leather chair.

'I *am* the owner,' she said. 'I am Anna Petrášová.'

'Oh, I see,' said Smolák. 'I'm sorry, I—'

'What can I do for you, Kapitán?' she cut him off. He wasn't sure if her brusqueness was because she sensed and was irritated by his attraction to her, or simply because she had a dislike of police-men. He had found that, generally, people tended to have a dislike of policemen. He reached inside his coat pocket and removed a hand-kerchief, which he carefully unfolded on the desk top. In its centre was a glass bead, about the size of a pea. It seemed to contain a tiny white rosebud at its heart.

Madame Petrášová took a jeweller's loupe from a drawer and put it to her eye, then picked up the piece and examined it, rolling it between her crimson-nailed fingertips. She removed the eyepiece and placed the glass bead back on the handkerchief.

'Not one of ours,' she said dismissively. 'In any case, we have had no items of any kind stolen recently.'

'That's not why I'm here, Madame Petrášová. I need to know where this piece of glass came from.'

She shrugged. 'It's difficult to tell. The craftsmanship's not exceptional for Bohemian glass. Could come from anywhere.'

'I'd be obliged if you could help,' pressed Smolák. 'This is no simple theft investigation. It really is an important matter.'

'How so, if I may ask?'

'A woman was found murdered. This bead was found close to the body and it matches nothing the woman owned.'

Anna Petrášová's bright emerald eyes widened. The detached composure slipped a little from her demeanour. 'Leather Apron? That poor woman butchered in the Prager Kleinseite? I thought you had someone for that. I read that he killed himself while in your custody.'

'I'm afraid I can't comment on that, Madame Petrášová. All I can say is that this is a most important matter.'

She regarded him for a moment, assessing him, then leaned forward and picked the bead up again, examining it even more closely.

'I've never seen this particular design before, although it could be domestic – I mean Bohemian glass. *Could* be Gablonz. There again, a huge proportion of Bohemian glass comes from there. Some manufacturers from Gablonz moved to the German Rhineland, so it could even be from there. Rhinestones, the foreigners call the facet-cut pieces, even though it is just a German-produced version of Gablonz glass.' She shrugged. 'But it could be from Bohemia, Germany, France, Poland, Russia – anywhere. I'm sorry I can't help you more,' she said, and Smolák could see she genuinely was. She placed the bead back in the handkerchief and he folded it carefully before putting it back in his pocket.

'Thank you for your time, anyway,' said Smolák resignedly as he stood.

Remaining seated, Anna Petrášová frowned, as if a thought had just occurred to her. 'There is one person who might be able to help you – if you're desperate enough, I suppose,' she said. 'He's an expert on Bohemian glass. An obsessive expert, one could say.'

'Oh I'm desperate enough – who?'

'Michal Macháček. No one knows more about Bohemian glass. He has – *had* – one of the largest and most comprehensive collections in the world.'

'Where do I find him?'

'You don't know?' Anna Petrášová looked genuinely taken aback. 'Oh, well, I suppose all that *unpleasantness* happened in Plzeň, not

Prague. Believe me, Kapitán Smolák, you'll have no trouble in find-ing this particular Bohemian glass expert.'

'And why's that?' Smolák tried not to sound impatient.

'Michal Macháček,' she said, holding the policeman in her bright emerald gaze, 'is one of the Devil's Six, locked up in Hrad Orlů Asylum for the Criminally Insane.'

$\mathcal{V}$iktor smoked a cigarette in silence, his patient sedately semi-recumbent, her habitual tension completely gone from her body. The subdued bloom from the angle-poise lamp seemed only to emphasize the insulating, impenetrable substance of the castle tower. He again felt the asylum's stone embrace and for a moment found it difficult to imagine the dark brooding forests and dusk-velvet plains beyond its walls.

Hedvika Valentová had committed horrific crimes, seemingly devoid of compassion or empathy, but she had also been a sad, lonely child: a plain and shy little girl twirling in a pretty dress in front of a mirror, waiting to go to a party and full of expectations never to be fulfilled.

But something worse had happened to Valentová: something Viktor could not reach, even with his patient in the drug-induced twilight state.

She had been sent to a school for disturbed children: a place about which there had, in hushed professional circles, been dark rumours. Valentová had been there for three years and there were lacunae in her memory of that time. Whatever had happened in those memory-less shadows, it was so bad it refused to be brought into the light of recall. He had tried to break into that dark experience, coming at it from every angle. None had succeeded.

'What happened after you were released from the school?' he

asked, having resolved to return to her school experiences in some future session.

'I went back to Mamma. She took care of me, but it was never the same again. She was always watching me, always making sure she knew where I was and what I was doing. She'd aged while I was away – aged far, far more than just three years. I spent the next two years at the ordinary school, then went to work in the glassworks.'

'Did you have any boyfriends in that time? I mean before you got married?'

'I never got the attention that the pretty girls got. There were other girls who weren't so pretty, but still got attention because they were bold with boys, but I didn't want to be that kind of girl. I was too meek, too shy. In any case, everyone knew I'd been in that place, that school for crazy children. Everyone thought I was odd.'

'But you wanted to be married?'

'I very much wanted to be married. I was so afraid of being alone. Of being lonely for the rest of my life. But I knew no one would ever ask me. I knew I'd never get the kind of man I really wanted. There was a chance that I wouldn't get any man, would never get married at all. However, I may have been plain, but I was also very practical. So I made up my mind that I would be exceptional in some other way.'

'And in what way did you choose to be exceptional?' asked Viktor.

'Cooking. I determined to become the best cook in our district. In the city, in the region. I cooked meat dishes – pork mainly – soups, desserts, breads and cakes, everything.'

'Meat dishes? I thought you were a strict vegetarian?'

'I wasn't back then. That was before I realized how filthy, how disgusting, flesh is. Back then, it was my meat dishes that were most popular. And most of all my pork dishes. I cooked the pork so that it flaked from the knife and melted on the tongue. I could make the coarsest raw flesh into the finest cooked meat.

'I had excelled in nothing else, but now I excelled in that. All men are interested in is flesh; all they want is flesh. So I decided the best way for me to win a man was to serve the tastiest, most delicate flesh. What they didn't desire from my body, they would desire from my table.

'I cooked for myself and Mamma to start with, until I was sure I was getting it perfect. Mamma would tell me how wonderful my food was, what a great cook I was becoming. Then I would take lunches in a hot-kettle for the other girls in the glassworks. Then they noticed me. My face was forgettable, but they remembered the taste of my cooking. After a while I was offered a job in the glassworks canteen. Even the bosses, who'd normally go to a restaurant, started to eat in the canteen. Bring customers too.'

'And that's how you found your husband?'

A memory stung her through the drugs. 'Mamma died in the spring of that year and, without the only person who had ever cared for me, I found myself completely alone. I had that great fear that I would disappear, would cease to exist without anyone to notice me. I dreaded looking in the mirror and seeing myself without a face again. But then there was Mořic. Mořic used to buy pieces from our jewellery department and often came into the canteen. He eventually asked me out.'

'He asked you to marry him?'

'Yes. He asked me because of my cooking. Or at least in part. I think he perhaps thought, mistakenly, that I also had some money left to me by Mamma. I think his sister maybe put the idea in his head. So when Mořic Valenta asked me to marry him, I said yes. Even though I was nineteen and he was forty; even though he was fat and short and ugly, I said yes.'

'So you married. Was he in love with you?'

Again the scopolamine and amytal failed to mute completely her emotional responses; she laughed bitterly. 'Love? What has love got to do with marriage? What has love got to do with anything? You don't understand; nobody understands what it's like to be truly lonely. Everybody feels it sometime, but what they experience is a passing infection, like a cold. The loneliness I experienced as a child, as a young woman, was a cancer.

'Mořic Valenta knew what it was like to be lonely, unnoticed. Mořic and I married to save each other from loneliness, but all that happened was that we were lonely together. Mořic became a bitter, spiteful little man – always critical, always pointing out my flaws. I tell you something, he loved my cooking, couldn't get enough of it. But did he ever say? Did he ever praise me for it? Never.

'You ask me if he loved me – I tell you what he loved: he loved my *kulajda* and *bramboračka* soups, my *svíčková*, my *karbanátek*. And most of all, although he never said it to me, he loved my *vepřo knedlo zelo* – yes, the true object of Mořic Valenta's desire was a plate of my roast pork, dumplings and sauerkraut.'

'There was no affection between you?'

'None. He would belittle me at every opportunity: tell me how ugly and boring I was; what a mouse I was. How he could have done so much better. "You're no Adina Mandlová or Anny Ondra," he would say. He would say things like that because he knew I thought film actresses were immoral, or maybe because he knew that I was secretly envious of their looks. Of course, I never had the courage to answer him back and say, "Well, you're no Karel Lamač yourself".'

'And you? How did you feel towards your husband?'

'I felt nothing. He was an easy man to feel nothing about. But he had a good business,' she said, as if that offered balance. 'He was a traveller specializing in glass jewellery and made a good living from it. That's why he would be in the factory sometimes. Diamond-cut crystals and glass beads with tiny porcelain flowers in them. Necklaces, earrings, bracelets. After we got married he insisted I give up work. We lived in a large apartment in the centre of Mladá Boleslav, and he kept all his stock in a safe in the pantry. He would go on the road for a week at a time, travelling around the whole republic. He had this little Jawa motorcycle and he used to strap his sample case to the back and pull this leather motorcycle helmet and goggles onto his fat little head. The helmet was too tight and made him look ridiculous, like a fat little pig balanced on his Jawa. Off he'd go, wobbling down the street, and I'd be glad to see the back of him.'

'You enjoyed these breaks from him?'

'I didn't get that much of a break. His older sister, Jitka, would come and stay at least one night every time he was away. "To keep an eye on me", she would say. Between them they never let me forget that I'd had to spend time in that special place, "the mental school", they'd both call it. Jitka was a vicious, spiteful, bitter witch of a woman. Fat like Mořic. Same plump pig face. She used to take every opportunity to praise her darling brother and demean me. And me, well, I was too meek to protest. The thing is I knew that they both enjoyed my cooking – that was why Jitka visited so often. Not that either of them ever praised a single meal I made.'

'All right, Hedvika,' said Viktor. 'I need you to find a specific time. I want you to take us both to the day of your arrest. Can you remember how it started?'

'Oh, *that* day?'

'That day,' said Viktor. 'Can we go there?'

She was quiet for a moment. Viktor found it strange how patients always needed time to locate a specific memory. It wasn't as if they were riffling through mental files to find it, more as though they really were making a journey through their own internal space, navigating a universe only they occupied.

'It started in the kitchen,' she said at last. 'All my days started, remained and ended in the kitchen. Mořic was away but due back and his sister was coming over for lunch, so I was up early preparing dumplings. I felt strange that day. I don't know why, but I was determined to make the very best meal I had ever made: to force Jitka – and Mořic if he came back in time – to admit finally what a great cook I was.

'For some reason I'd hardly slept that night, and the next morning, when I got up early, I felt strange.' She frowned. 'No, it wasn't me who felt strange, it was the world that felt strange. Like the light was different, you know? Like everything was the same – the apartment, the street outside, the back yard through the kitchen window – but it had all been moved to a different planet, under a different sun that made different shadows. So strange. And then he came into the kitchen.'

'Mořic?'

'No.'

'Who came into the kitchen, Hedvika?'

'An angel. A man. He was both and he was neither. He was the most beautiful thing I had ever seen. He was naked and perfect. His body, his face.'

'Didn't it strike you as strange that a naked man suddenly appeared in your kitchen?'

'No, no – you don't understand. This was no ordinary man. He was beautiful and he was an angel. His skin was like bronze, his hair the brightest gold, and there was a glow all around him, as if the air was sparkling. He was more than a beautiful angel, don't you see? He was *the* Most Beautiful Angel. The Fallen One.'

'Satan? You're saying that the Devil revealed himself to you in an apartment kitchen in Mladá Boleslav?'

'That's exactly what I'm saying. He spoke to me, but his lips made no sound. His words just *appeared* in my head. He explained it all to me. He stood there in the room but not *belonging* to it, as if he had been projected there from some other dimension. His beauty was dazzling and he waited till I adjusted to it, then he told me about the puppy.

'He said it had been he who'd done that to that poor little thing. He showed me what had happened – put the memory in my head. It had been he who'd made them send me to that school. He said that he couldn't be sorry and he didn't care about forgiveness, but he was there to make it up to me.'

'And how was he going to do that?'

'By giving me mastery over all food, over men's appetites. Making me the greatest cook in history. Making it so that everyone would remember exactly who Hedvika Valentová was. Without speaking, with the words and images put straight into my head, he explained all about food to me. How food was *his* medium, how the Devil had all the best recipes. In an instant he had placed the whole history of cooking in my mind. The whole philosophy of it. How each meal is a gift and a covenant and an expression. How dead flesh is resurrected and how the flesh is transcended and becomes the purest communicable joy. About mouths and tongues and minds and memories.

'Then he told me how I could improve my *vepřo knedlo zelo*. He told me how I could make roast pork that would become legendary – the Devil's recipe – a dish my husband and sister-in-law would never forget. He put the recipe in my head and it was perfect. So completely perfect. It would take me longer than usual because the pork needed to be slow-cooked at a lower temperature and for longer than even I usually did. So I set about preparing the meat, selecting the very best cuts and getting the rosemary marinade ready.'

The room fell silent for a moment, except for the sound of the K1 Magnetophon spools turning, and Hedvika Valentová's smooth, easy breathing.

'I worked all morning on it, imagining how Jitka and Mořic would react, how – despite themselves – they wouldn't be able to conceal their delight. How they'd be forced to praise me.

'Jitka came for lunch as arranged. She asked where Mořic was and I said that he would be back later. "Why is his Jawa still here?" she asked. I told her he decided to leave his motorcycle at home and take the train. I could see her looking at me suspiciously, but there again, she never looked at me any other way. "Just as well I'm here to keep an eye on you then," she said.'

'So you served lunch?' asked Viktor.

'I served lunch. I started with home-made *jelito* – the blood sausage the Germans call *Grützwurst* – for which the Beautiful Angel had given me a recipe.

'I mixed blood, finely chopped liver and flour with marjoram, cumin and pepper. The Angel said I should serve it cooled and thinly sliced as a starter, followed by the *vepřo knedlo zelo.*'

'And the Devil – this bright angel – stayed with you all day?' asked Viktor.

'He was there all day: sometimes his brightness would hurt my eyes. At other times the glow around him would change colour, but he was always beautiful.'

'Weren't you afraid of him?'

'There were some times when he would change. His brightness would become darkness. But it was like no other darkness. A shining darkness that flooded the kitchen and soaked the colour and light out of everything. But that would only last for an instant.

'After the *jelito* starter I served the main course. I tell you, that *vepřo knedlo zelo* was the best I'd ever made. The roast pork was perfect. All the courses were perfect. I could see that Jitka thought the same, even if she said nothing. I watched her eat. She was a little fat pig just like her brother and she ate with so much enthusiasm that the gravy dribbled down her chin. I could see it in her eyes: that this was the best meal she'd ever eaten, the sheer joy of its taste. But, being Jitka, she was still determined not to say anything, to hide her enjoyment as much as possible.'

'And the Devil? Was the Devil there in the room while you ate?'

'He was! Oh, how he was! He lit the room with his brightness. The Angel sat at the other end of the table, watching us and laughing at Jitka. He glowed bronze and red and gold and was so beautiful and bright it hurt to look at him. He told me in my mind that he could see us and I could see him, but Jitka couldn't. He told me that he was pleased with what I had done with his recipe.

'Jitka ate every last morsel. She dipped bread to soak up the last of the gravy, even took the dumplings I had left on my plate. After we were finished, she still didn't say how good the food had been. She was still too mean and petty to admit it. But she did ask me where I had got the pork from.'

'And you told her?' asked Viktor.

'Oh yes, I told her. How the Beautiful Angel laughed when I told her! His laughter rang in my head but of course Jitka couldn't hear him and she started screaming and screaming, more like a squeal, too frightened even to get up from the table.'

'She was screaming because you told her that she'd been eating her brother?' asked Viktor. 'That you had murdered, butchered and then cooked him?'

'I told her how he'd really come home the night before and how the Beautiful Angel had instructed me, that morning, to go up while he was still sleeping and cut his throat with my filleting knife. He had told me to take a basin to catch the blood for making the *jelito* sausages. He'd also explained that I would have to cut out a length of intestine and clean it out to use for the sausage casing.

'While the Angel ran through the recipe, Mořic had lain shaking and twitching as the blood came in spurts into the basin. It was good, thick, fatty blood, perfect for making *jelito* sausages. How the Angel and I had laughed! Once Mořic stopped twitching, the Beautiful Angel had explained very carefully and clearly exactly how I was to butcher him for meat: how to extract the most succulent cuts. It was all very interesting, you know – really fascinating – and I tried to explain some of the more interesting technical points to Jitka over lunch, but she wouldn't listen. She just screamed and screamed.

'The neighbours must have heard Jitka squealing like that and knocked on the apartment door but I ignored them. They must have called the police after that. In the meantime, the Beautiful Angel sang to me. Such beautiful songs. When the police finally arrived, they found what was left of Mořic in the bathtub.'

'What about Jitka?'

'When the police found me in the kitchen, I had Jitka's head in a pan, simmering away with some salt, cracked pepper, marjoram and parsley. For broth, you know.'

Viktor didn't respond. Again the room became empty of noise other than the low whirr of the tape recorder and the measured breathing of his sedated patient. His hand rested on her case notes, which included scene-of-crime photographs and police statements. Included there were statements from bewildered neighbours and others who spoke of Mořic Valenta as an attentive, loving and demonstrative husband who had cared deeply for his emotionally fragile wife; and of his sister Jitka, who had been devoted to her sister-in-law for the happiness she had brought her brother.

'Have you seen Satan since?' Viktor asked eventually.

'Oh yes, yes – many times. As a matter of fact he's here now. In this room. The Beautiful Angel is standing in this room in all his glory.'

Viktor felt a thrill; perhaps now he would make direct contact with what he'd been seeking: the Devil Aspect within Valentová's Unconscious. 'May I speak with him?'

'No,' said Hedvika, frowning. 'You may not. He will not commune with you.'

'Where is he?'

'Don't you know?' said Valentová. 'Can't you tell? He's standing right behind you. The Devil is at your shoulder . . .'

*T*he weather had turned colder and the damp warmth of food and its consumers steamed the thick-glazed window beside his table. Everything about this place was thick or dense or robust: it was a place of pebbled glass and dark wood, of solid stone and solid tradition. In one form or another, it had probably been an inn for two centuries or more.

It had not been easy to find an establishment in Prague that catered to his special needs. In a city and a land where pork was the most common staple, finding a restaurant with anything on the menu to keep him sustained had been a challenge. It probably would have made more sense for him to eat at home, to prepare his own food, but he had neither the time nor the inclination to spend what few free moments he had to himself boiling lentils.

So, years ago, he had found this place and now they knew him here. It had become his regular place for a glass and a plate. Every station-sergeant in the City of Prague Police knew that if they wanted to reach Kapitán Lukáš Smolák when he was neither at the station nor at home, then the Café U Hipodromu should be their first port of call.

Why it was called the U Hipodromu was beyond Smolák's ken, interest or curiosity. In this close-packed quarter of Prague's ancient heart, he couldn't imagine there ever having been any kind of race-course or arena here. Maybe the naming was recent and a foible of the current owners, who had hand-painted the blue horse motif on the sign above the door; maybe, on the other hand, the name was more ancient than the inn that had preceded the café, more ancient than the Old Town, and had been handed down from some distant time of first settlement.

That's the thing about this country, Smolák thought as he idly stirred his vegetable stew: the old and the past is always there, no matter how much we try to grab the new and the future.

Now he sat over his meal, bound round by deep, ancient walls to separate him from the city beyond. Smolák was tired, his mood gloomy. Since Bihari's suicide in the police station, he had slept little, and when he did sleep the small gypsy had come to haunt his dreams. Everyone else, except himself and perhaps Dr Bartoš, seemed convinced that Bihari's last utterances had amounted to a confession: that the Devil who he couldn't get out of his head was the part of Bihari that had killed and mutilated those women.

All were agreed: the gypsy had killed the Devil, killed Leather Apron, when he had killed himself.

Yet Smolák was unconvinced. As he sat alone at his usual table by the pebble-glassed, condensation-misted window, looking out at the ghost of Prague's Old Town, Smolák wondered if his inaction and indecision meant that the city was being left to the real Leather Apron. Sitting there within the thick-walled café, he felt a guilt that somewhere out there a monster, a devil in human form, could still be walking the streets, taking his time to select his next victim.

Smolák's choleric mood had not been lightened any by his brief phone conversation, before he left his office, with the chief quack at the Hrad Orlů Asylum for the Criminally Insane. Professor Románek, who to start with had sounded a reasonable, friendly sort, had become very sniffy about letting Smolák visit his patient, Michal Macháček, whom the beautiful Anna Petrášová had described as the leading expert on Bohemian glass.

Smolák soon realized that Románek's reticence had stemmed

from a suspicion that the police kapitán had perhaps wanted to quiz Macháček about further crimes for which he may have been a suspect. Smolák had reassured Románek that it was Macháček's expertise in glass, not in torture and murder, that interested him. It had been agreed that Smolák could visit in four days' time. The delay, Románek had explained, was that for the policeman to get anything intelligible from Macháček required the easily agitated patient being made comfortable with the idea of a visit. Added to which, he was actually the patient of Románek's colleague, Dr Viktor Kosárek, and was about to undergo revolutionary treatment, something about drug-aided deep-therapy sessions that might leave him disoriented for a couple of days. Despite Smolák's insistence that this was a matter of urgency, Románek remained amiably, politely obstinate.

Smolák had said nothing to Románek about his other reason for visiting the asylum: to get a posthumous psychiatric diagnosis on Tobar Bihari. Maybe the experts up there could offer an opinion on whether the gypsy had been battling a personal demon, or really had lived in fear of someone else's. Dr Bartoš had been right: he should have sought their help earlier.

He sipped at his stew. It was good but perhaps too heavily seasoned. Marta, the chief cook and mother of the U Hipodromu's owner, had always seemed to believe that the lack of meat in Smolák's diet had to be compensated for by a heavy hand with herbs, salt and pepper. Outside the city had darkened, and when Smolák wiped the condensation from the window with his sleeve, all he saw were the reflections of himself and the café's interior.

Lukáš Smolák was never too comfortable with his own reflection. He was a handsome enough man, slightly heavily built, strong featured and with an open, honest face. But he had always felt there was something of the lie in the way he looked, perhaps because there was an ordinariness, a predictable simplicity, even a dullness to his appearance. And if there was one thing Smolák knew about himself, it was that he was anything but simple and ordinary.

It had, however, served Smolák well: many suspects had given themselves away by underestimating the keen intelligence behind the detective's pleasantly pedestrian appearance.

The image of the rich and beautiful businesswoman, Anna Petrášová, suddenly came unbidden into his mind. There again, her face had come unbidden into his mind several times since he had met her. As he sat eating his meal and sipping his beer, he wondered idly what she'd seen when she'd looked at Smolák. Had she seen her polish and sophistication reflected in his coarseness and simplicity? Had his been the pleasant enough but eminently forgettable face of a dullard policeman?

He tried to dismiss her image but it persisted. He would never see her again, he knew that. And, even if he did, even if he summoned the nerve to go back to the store and ask her to have a drink or a meal with him, or to visit the cinema or a show, would she laugh at him? At his coarseness? Smolák found himself becoming angry at an imagined encounter. It would never happen. He would never see the beautiful Anna Petrášová again.

It was the strangest thing. Without looking up from his stew, as soon as he heard the unseen heavy oak outer door slam shut, when he heard the urgent trotting of feet up the stone steps and through the low-vaulted arch of the café, Smolák knew they were coming for him. That bad news was coming for him.

When he looked up, he saw it was Mirek Novotný, one of the duty detectives, accompanied by two uniformed policemen.

CHAPTER TWELVE

*or someone who dealt day in, day out with the vagaries
of the human mind, Viktor Kosárek always surprised
himself at how unacquainted he seemed to be with his own psychology. He had planned to buy a car to make trips to and from Prague
easier, but had been too busy settling into his new job to do anything
about it. So his return journey to Prague had been on the train. It
had not once occurred to him that arriving back into the main hall of
Masaryk Station would bring back the distressing memory of a desperate schizophrenic fighting imagined demons. A lost soul whose
great sadness had been ended by policeman's bullet not physician's
remedy.

More than a memory of the threat to his own safety, Viktor was
struck by the realization that this railway station, now cleaned of any
trace of the event, had been the scene of a great professional failure.
The restored normality of the station hall did little to assuage the
feeling and, on his way out, he happened to pass the teenage porter
in his oversized uniform and kepi, who exchanged a look of grim
recognition with him.

Maybe Viktor had not given it any thought on the journey because
he had travelled with such a sense of mission. Blind to the scenery
beyond the train's windows, Viktor's thoughts had been focused
on tracking down his friend, Filip Starosta – or what dread facts
he might discover about Filip's condition. Viktor had tried to reach

him by telephone several more times, with no success. Knowing his friend was subject both to dark, deep depressions and wild, uncontrolled bouts of mania, Viktor's unease now sat on the cusp of alarm: fear that his friend may have done something to injure himself.

He took a taxi from the station directly to Filip's apartment, which sat on the top floor of a once-grand Secese-styled tenement on the easternmost edge of the Old Town. The elegantly wrought-iron and coloured glass Art Deco elevator, he knew, had not worked reliably for years, so he headed straight to the stairwell and the five-flight ascent to Filip's flat. As he made his way up, his footfalls on stone steps resonated in the stairwell and he was relieved to hear the sliding back of a door bolt above him, his approach having clearly stirred Filip, whose apartment was the only destination for anyone on the final flight of stairs.

But when he reached the top landing he was surprised to see a plain, black-haired young woman standing framed in the doorway, the glass-edged sound of a crying baby stabbing out from somewhere deep in the apartment and echoing urgently in the stairwell.

Viktor removed his hat and introduced himself, telling the young woman he was looking for Filip Starosta.

'Oh, he was the last tenant,' she said distractedly, clearly pulled by the continuing urgent wails of her unseen child. 'Wait a minute . . .' She disappeared into the apartment, leaving Viktor at the open door. When she reappeared she held a baby, now quiescent, in the crook of her left arm. 'We never met him – he had cleared his stuff out weeks before we moved in, but we found this.' She held out a slip of paper to Viktor. 'I guessed it was a forwarding address, you know, for mail and stuff. He left it behind, anyway. Maybe you can find him there.'

Viktor stared at the slip of paper, confused for a moment. Then, when he had memorized the address, he held the slip to the young mother for her to take back.

'You can keep it,' she said. 'Nothing ever comes here for him. And you're the only person to come looking for him since we moved in. I don't think anyone will ask now.'

'Why?' Viktor asked. 'When did you move in?'

'About two months ago. Nearer three.'

'Two months?' Viktor was taken aback when he realized that for three, maybe four months, his friend hadn't invited him to his apartment and they had always met in town. Why would he have been so secretive about his move?

He paused and frowned thoughtfully, then remembered something. 'But I have a phone number,' he protested. 'For this address . . .'

'No phone here.' The young mother had a broad, East Slavic face and her accent was tinged with something. Maybe Ruthenian, thought Viktor. Both her broad face and voice were now also tinged with something else: a growing suspicion of the stranger at her door. She glanced past him and down the stairwell, then behind her into the apartment.

Viktor felt annoyed that his presence provoked mistrust, but when he thought about it he realized that ever since the Leather Apron murders had started the Prague papers had been full of cautions about strangers. He smiled, quickly apologized for disturbing her, thanked her for her help, and headed back down to the street.

There was no way it could ever have been described as a move up in the world. Viktor found the address the woman had given him for Filip in a dark courtyard of broken cobbles in Vršovice, southeast of the Old Town. It wasn't a good part of town, the grandeur of some of the buildings diminished and tarnished by having to sit cheek-by-jowl with metal works and factories.

All the apartments in the smoke- and soot-darkened Art Nouveau tenements huddled around this particular courtyard seemed occupied, but nevertheless there was the faintest hint of desuetude to the place: a promise of imminent abandonment. There was a motorcycle and a car parked in one corner of the courtyard, both were old and rusting and looked as if self-propelled locomotion was long beyond them.

It took Viktor an age to find the number given on the slip of paper, and he could see no one around to ask. He was about to knock on a door and seek help when he saw a passageway between the tenements; a grimy enamelled plate in the wall promised that numbers 71 and 73 lay that way. The passageway was long and dark and smelled of boiled cabbages from one of the apartments that had a side door onto it. He was surprised to see the passage open out into another courtyard of sorts. Number 73 turned out not to be a tenement apartment at all but, like its neighbour, some kind of former coach house that had been converted inexpensively and inexpertly for habitation.

An older man, elbows resting on the stone sill as he leant out of a second-floor window of one of the overlooking apartment buildings, smoked his pipe and watched with little interest as Viktor crossed the courtyard.

When he answered the door, Filip's expression was one of surprise at seeing his friend standing there – perhaps unwelcome surprise, thought Viktor. He guessed that his own expression was probably one of shock: Filip Starosta was thin, pale and gaunt, his blond hair dishevelled; he wore an open-necked shirt in want of a wash and his jaw was in want of two days' shave. The suit he wore was creased and bagged. Filip had always been a smart dresser – not flashy, but stylish – and it was his sartorial as much as physical decline that worried Viktor.

'My God, man,' said Viktor. 'What has happened to you?'

'Happened?' Filip stared blankly at him with blue eyes less bright than those Viktor remembered. 'Nothing has happened to me. Nothing ever happens to me.'

'Can I come in?'

Again Filip's gaze was empty for a moment. 'Sure,' he said, and stood to one side to allow Viktor admission.

The courtyard coach house had been converted into one large room, with a kitchen at one end, the main living area at the other. There were steps up to a gallery with a bed. Two doors, both closed, led off the main living area. Viktor was relieved to see that, while untidy, the apartment was clean and had a certain touch of Filip's old style about it. There were books everywhere: the walls were hidden by stacked bookcases, a dining table was heaped with them, and Filip had to move a pile from the leather chair in the corner to allow Viktor to sit.

'What's happened to you?' Viktor asked again. 'And don't tell me nothing. It's obvious something's wrong. And why didn't you tell me you'd moved? I've been worried sick.'

Filip shrugged. 'Nothing to worry about. I lost my job at the university, that's all. You know me and my big mouth. My big opinions. I had to adjust to my new circumstances . . .' He waved a hand vaguely to indicate his current accommodations. 'I suppose I didn't want to tell you until I had something sorted out, job-wise. A bit embarrassed, I suppose.' He sat down on the battered leather sofa opposite.

'God, Filip, I'm sorry to hear that. What are you going to do?'

'I'm doing it. I'm writing. I've written two plays and I've sent them to František Langer at the City Theatre – he's not got back to me yet but I'm really hopeful. They're the first in a cycle of surrealist plays about ancient Slavic gods living in the modern world, here in Prague. If the City Theatre is happy to produce crappy plays about mechanical men, then my pieces should sail through . . .' There was a touch of Filip's old enthusiasm now, sitting paradoxically with his dullness. 'And that's not all, I'm writing a book.'

'A book. What kind of book?'

Some fire seemed to reignite in Filip's eyes. 'A big book, an important book. The definitive and most comprehensive-to-date history of Bohemian myth and legend. The whole West Slavic pantheon and every folk story that's woven into our consciousness. I'm telling you, Viktor, it's going to be noticed; I'm going to be noticed.'

'And how do you pay your way in the meantime? For this?' It was Viktor's turn to indicate their surroundings.

'My allowance,' Filip said. 'The advantage of having a rich father who has no time for you and replaces contact with cash. It's not much, but it's enough to keep me going in the meantime.'

'Listen, Filip, I have to ask this. Have you been using any type of narcotics? Whatever ails you, they will only make it worse.'

Filip snorted. 'Do I look like a drug fiend to you, old friend? I thought you would have known me better than that.' Then, emphatically, as if humouring Viktor, 'No – I am not taking narcotics. My sunny disposition is down to me and me alone.'

They sat and talked. Every now and then Filip would fall into a dark, sullen silence and Viktor would have to coax him out of it. Viktor felt a little relieved to see his friend alive and relatively well, but it concerned him that he was using his professional skills to draw Filip out of himself. At other times, Filip became unduly animated and loquacious – pacing the small space of the apartment and gesturing wildly as he discussed his ambitions. It seemed that talking about his writing and its focus, Bohemian myth and legend, animated Filip most. Even that vitality troubled Viktor, who could see in it seeds of monomania. And that wasn't all that worried him: he recalled his conversation with Románek about the relationship between the Unconscious and myth and legend; it occurred to Viktor that in writing some vaguely grand work about West Slavic mythology, his friend was perhaps exploring the mythology of his own inner landscape, chasing his own demons.

'I would have thought my work would be of special interest to you. You see, there are three foundations to ancient Bohemian beliefs,' said Filip, suddenly animated again. 'The first is dualism: everything belongs to the Light or to the Shadows. The Light ruled over by Svarog the Bright and the Shadows by Chernobog the Dark and by Morana, the goddess of night, winter and death. The second is the realm of elemental spirits: gods and demons that spring from the forces of nature. The third is the cult of death, where the dead inhabit the Other World, governed over by Veles and entered through caves.' He shook his head in wonder. 'Doesn't it all make sense to you, Viktor? I mean, as a Jungian and all that? Isn't it really all just the same as you believe?'

'There are similarities,' said Viktor. He could see the fire in Filip's eyes and it again troubled him. 'And we believe the reasons gods and demons have the same form across cultures is because they spring from shared archetypes. Anyway, it sounds like you have found a subject that excites you.'

'Oh, I have. I have.'

After a while Filip disappeared into the kitchen and came back with two glasses and a bottle of Becherovka. Viktor noticed that the glasses were particularly fine: violet, green and blue iridescent glass twisting up the stems to the bell-shaped, frosted bowls.

'These are new,' Viktor said, turning the stem of his glass between his fingertips. 'Never seen them before.'

Filip shrugged. 'A gift. From a lady admirer who knows about such things.' He filled the glasses and sat opposite Viktor. They sat and talked and drank; as they drank, Viktor noticed that his friend downed two glasses to his one.

Eventually, clearly warmed by the liquor, Filip started to ask Viktor about his life, about his new job. Viktor answered in general terms, without discussing specific patients. He then remembered the note he had scribbled down while in the portico of the forest chapel. He described the church to Filip, as well as the freshness of the carving cut into its ancient timber.

'I reckon it's Glagolitic script. Old Church Slavonic, maybe.'

'Let's have a look,' said Filip, holding out his hand. After Viktor handed him the note, Filip found a notebook and began transcribing.

Viktor noticed he needed no recourse to reference books, despite being surrounded by them.

'Now this is interesting . . .' Filip tore his translation out of his notebook and handed it to Viktor along with the original.

Viktor read the translation and, for some reason, he felt it chill deep into him.

Here am I and I here stay,
for this is where Evil resides.
Here am I and I here stay,
for this is where the Devil hides.

*S*ometimes homes mirrored their owners. That was certainly the case here. As Smolák stood in the elegant hallway – fighting back the emotions stirred in him by the idea of seeing Anna Petrášová once more, of her imminent and unavoidable presence – he could sense the touch of her cool elegance all around him. He wanted the moment to last, to feel her touch, sense her unseen personality, before having to confront her in person.

Her home was much as he had expected, except he had somehow imagined her in an apartment closer to her city-centre business premises. Instead, Anna Petrášová lived in a large villa overlooking a garden square in Bubeneč, across the Vltava and in the north of the city.

There was a lot about her living environment that reminded him of her working one: reminiscences of the sales hall of the Petráš Sklo a Skleněná Bižuterie. The pillars and floor were of the same polished marble and onyx; the same cool décor on the walls: bright, unpatterned, so not to detract from the bold geometries and colours of the Modernist and Supremacist paintings that hung on them.

And, of course, there was glass: radiant swirls and vivid violets, greens and blues in slim-necked vases and the open mouths of dishes and bowls. In the hallway stood what Smolák thought to be the most beautiful piece of the glassmaker's craft he had ever seen: a meter-and-a-half-high vase crafted in uranium glass. It had a menacingly

organic look to it, with tendril-like flutes rising up from the bul-
bous base and swirling around the slender neck, before fusing with it
again just before it opened out into an abstractly flower-like mouth.
The sculpting of the glass in itself inspired awe, but what most drew
the policeman's attention to it were the iridescent colours: peacock
hues that seemed almost to shimmer and glow.

Being here, his summoning to this place, seemed unreal. And it
took a lot to give Kapitán Lukáš Smolák a sense of unreality these
days. Policemen, particularly murder detectives, see aspects of life
that most others are blind to. He was used to navigating situations
that would seem to others surreal, bizarre. And in a profession where
all coincidences are treated as suspect, he had nevertheless seen
countless cases of inexplicable chance and happenstance.

Yet, as he stood in Anna Petrášová's hall, dreading coming face
to face with her, and staring in deliberate wonder at the motionless writhing of an iridescent glass vase, the ground under his feet
seemed that little less sure.

This coincidence – this was a coincidence too far, even for
Smolák.

'Kapitán?' asked Mirek Novotný, Smolák's youthful and aggres-
sively ambitious subordinate, who had collected him from the Café
U Hipodromu and now stood beside him in the cool, silent, marble
hallway.

'Where?' asked Smolák.

'The bedroom.' Novotný held out a hand to indicate the stair.

Smolák led the way up the curving staircase to the landing.
The sound of voices told him which of the three bedrooms was his
destination. The voices, he discovered on entering the room, were
those of the medical examiner, Dr Bartoš, and a uniformed police
under-officer.

And she was in there. Anna Petrášová was in there.

She lay on the bed, watching him with heavy-lidded eyes. He
found himself wishing himself back downstairs, standing in the

hallway admiring the vase: a place of calm, elegance, taste. What confronted Smolák in this room was chaos, horror, anguish. And a face he knew.

It was Anna Petrášová's face that was the greatest horror. It was perfect. Untouched. Still beautiful. Her make-up was as carefully applied and unsmudged as when he had last seen her, the hair brushed and clasped back from her perfectly proportioned features. Her crimson lips were slightly parted to expose a little of her white, perfect teeth. Her face was flawless, intact and uninjured; unstained by blood.

But everything else, everything below the neck, was rent flesh, gore and bone.

He had prepared for it on the drive to her house, knowing what waited for him. He had prevaricated in the hallway downstairs, steeling himself against the shock that awaited him, but it hit him anyway. He felt sick, was aware of the urgent throb of his pulse in his temples, found the image of her swirled and shuddered a little.

Václav Bartoš was already there, studying what was left of the victim. He turned and nodded to Smolák. 'So our little gypsy friend was innocent after all,' he said.

'Or he was working with a partner who has decided to carry on their business,' said Smolák.

'Her name is Anna Petrášová,' said Novotný. 'She owns an upmarket glass store in the Nové Město.'

'I know,' said Smolák.

'You know?'

'I know. Her name, her business. I know her.'

'You *know* the victim?'

'That's what I said. I talked to her two days ago at her store.'

'Two days ago?'

Smolák turned to Novotný, his expression dark. 'Yes, two days ago. Am I going to have to repeat everything I say?'

Novotný shook his head, his lips pursed contemplatively. 'No –
no, Kapitán. It's just that it's, well, quite a—'

'Coincidence?'

'Well yes. What were you talking to her about?' asked Novotný.

Smolák held the younger man in his gaze. If Novotný felt uncomfortable under his superior's scrutiny, he didn't show it. He was just
doing his job. Except he was doing his job on Smolák: checking what
his boss's connection with the victim had been; what the nature of
their relationship was. When he had last seen her alive.

'The glass bead,' said Smolák. 'The one found at the last murder scene. I took it to her for an opinion. She couldn't help with
it but referred me on to Michal Macháček, who would be a better
expert. Unfortunately he's locked up in Hrad Orlů Asylum for the
Criminally Insane, but I've arranged to interview him.'

Dr Bartoš, who had been bent over the butchered carcass of the
murdered woman, half turned and spoke over his shoulder. 'You're
going to Hrad Orlů?'

'I was. Or at least I will be. This new murder means I'll have to
postpone it a few days.'

Václav Bartoš nodded dully, a thought clearly fading from his
mind, then turned back to his work. Smolák knew about the medical
examiner's brother, a scandal that, though nothing to do with Bartoš
directly, had nearly ruined his career by association. A scandal that
ended with Dr Bartoš's brother, an eminent scientist, being branded
as one of the Devil's Six and confined in the remote asylum.

'This changes things,' said Novotný. 'Leather Apron has murdered someone who was connected to the investigation into his
murders.'

'Only tangentially connected. And, like you said: probably a
coincidence. But it's a hell of a coincidence.'

'And you went to see her about that glass bead you found at the
Prager Kleinseite scene?'

Smolák nodded. He still watched Novotný's face; he could almost have sworn his subordinate had emphasized the *you* in 'the glass bead *you* found'. Smolák had found the glass bead all right, and he had found it after all the other officers who'd been at the scene before him had missed it. Another coincidence.

He knew that Novotný would not seriously regard him as a suspect, but he also knew that the young officer was fiercely ambitious. Despite his fresh-faced youthfulness, there was a calculated hardness about him. Ruthlessness, even. Novotný knew only too well that suspicion was a stain to darken one man's career, lighten another's. These were times of uncertainty, where the future constantly changed shape; times such as these tended to bring out cold opportunism in the ambitious and the young.

One thing was certain, Smolák would have to pull himself together. He could do nothing to allow his junior officer to suspect that he was unduly or especially disturbed by this murder scene, that he had been strongly attracted to the victim. That he had been thinking about her ever since he met her. He even convinced himself that his racing heart was not because of his connection to the victim, but because of the blood. So much blood.

No matter how often you were faced with it, how experienced you were as a policeman, the sight of blood excited an instinctive, visceral response. The pale grey satin bedsheets were sodden dark and sticky. The walls of her bedroom had been decorated in white, again to emphasize the artworks hung on them. Now they emphasized the art of her murderer: great plumes of arterial spray arced across them. And there was something else standing out stark against the pristine white. Daubed in hand-smeared blood on the wall above the bed was a single word. *FOTZE.*

'Do you think our suspect is German?' asked Novotný. 'Or wants us to believe he's German?'

Smolák shook his head. He remembered how during his interrogation Bihari had claimed that 'Beng', the demon the petty thief claimed had forced him to watch his butchery, had used the German swearword to describe Mara Lehmann. 'Do you know what the word means?' he asked Novotný.

'Of course. It means cunt. It's a sexual slur against the victim.'

'It's more than that. He's saying it in German. He's saying she was a German cunt. All of the victims so far have been partly or fully of Bohemian German blood. Except for some reason he got it wrong this time. Petrášová isn't a German name. Unless she was married?' He turned questioningly to the uniformed under-officer.

'Not that I'm aware, Kapitán. She lived here alone, according to the neighbours. I've got men questioning them all now to see what further information we can get.'

'Anybody so far see anyone visiting?' asked Novotný, glancing at Smolák. 'Any male visitors?'

'None so far. She was a particularly private person, apparently.'

'What have you got, Doctor?' Smolák asked Bartoš.

'She's been comprehensively eviscerated. That much you can see for yourself. This time he's taken body parts with him when he left the scene. And I have to say it adds to what I said before about the Jack the Ripper *homage*: the vagina and uterus have been completely removed, just as in the London murders.'

'So he really is copying the English killer . . .' Smolák spoke as much to himself as the others. At that point, a young uniformed policeman came in, clutching a handful of papers, and spoke to the under-officer, who in turn came over to Smolák and the others.

'We've spoken to the neighbours and we also found her identity papers in a bureau downstairs.' The under-officer held out an identity card, which Smolák took and examined.

'Damn . . .' Smolák handed the card on to Novotný. 'Her papers say she's originally German-Czech from Silesia. Her maiden name was Anna Dietrich.'

'According to what my man has found out from the neighbours,' said the under-officer, 'she married into the Petráš family but she was widowed. Her husband died about four or five years ago and left her the business.'

'So maybe our killer has an agenda after all,' Novotný said to Smolák. 'You had no idea she was German-Czech?'

Smolák glowered at him. 'If I had known that, I would have stated so right at the start, Detektiv-Seržant Novotný. I only met the woman once, and for less than twenty minutes, to discuss non-personal matters.'

'Of course, Kapitán. I'm sorry.' Novotný apologized, but he had achieved his aim: Smolák could see the surprise in the expressions of both the young uniformed policeman and the under-officer. A rumour had been born.

'There's something else,' said the under-officer. 'Something you need to see. Outside.'

The young uniformed policeman led the under-officer, Smolák, Novotný and Dr Bartoš out through the front entrance and around the side of the villa. There he shone his flashlight onto the whitewashed wall.

'He must have done this on his way away from the scene,' said the young policeman. 'I'm guessing that this is the victim's blood again.'

'Damn it to hell,' said Smolák. 'That's all we need: yet another political angle.'

'It's not political,' said Bartoš. 'Or at least, that's my opinion. It's another part of the killer's *homage*. Almost exactly the same message was daubed on a wall at one of the Jack the Ripper crime scenes in London. It's just that here, now, it has a deeper political significance.'

Smolák sighed, reading the blood-smeared message again. Like the obscenity on the bedroom wall, it was in German.

Die Juden müssen getadelt werden.

The Jews must be blamed.

PART THREE

THE GLASS COLLECTOR AND THE WOODCUTTER

CHAPTER ONE

*A*fter the liquor, Viktor hadn't wanted anything more to drink, and he was aware the part of town they were in was not the safest. Indeed, it was with dark dismay that he remembered that two earlier victims of the so-called Leather Apron killer had been found within a few streets of his friend's new lodgings.

But he noticed that Filip's mood had lightened: he had become more relaxed, clearly warmed by the alcohol in his system, and there was an easing of the twitchy nervous energy that had seemed in turns to stimulate and enervate him. Viktor wanted him to stay relaxed so he could find out more about his friend's current mental state. So, when Filip insisted they go out and visit a local pub, he relented.

The irony struck Viktor that he was, in an odd way, applying the same methodology to his friend that he applied to his narcosynthesis patients. In this case, it was beer and Becherovka, rather than scopolamine and sodium amytal, that he was allowing to calm his subject and open up his inner thoughts.

It was already dark by the time they headed out of Filip's lodgings. The long dark coat that Filip put on was one that Viktor recognized: when his friend had bought it, it had looked stylish and expensive, fitting Filip perfectly. Now it seemed to hang loose on his frame and looked shabby and bagged from neglect. Filip's hat too was battered looking, and he pulled it low over his eyes as if concealing them from his friend, from the world.

They left through the back door, entering a small, dark square yard that Filip's apartment shared with its neighbour. The ancient lock rattled loosely in the door as he locked it but, instead of pocketing the key, Filip bent down and lifted a loose flagstone next to the door, placing the key under it.

'I'm always losing things,' he said as explanation. 'Specially if I've had a couple.'

A faint muslin mist of fine rain hung damp and chill in the night air, and Viktor was glad that the pub turned out to be only three blocks distant. Vršovice was a clustered warren of narrow, long streets of once-elegant tenements and the deep gullies of high-walled intersecting alleys, all broken up with workshops, factories and storage yards.

Whatever it had once been, the quarter was now resolutely working class and predominantly Czech, with pockets of Czech-German. While rural Sudeten Germans were referred to as *Skopčáci*, hillbillies, here in Prague, the legacy of the Austro-Hungarian Empire had been that the Germans tended to form the elite. In the working-class Vršovice quarter, that had been diluted, but still meant German collars tended to be a lighter shade of blue: workshop managers, factory foremen and skilled workers.

Viktor was surprised to see the bar Filip took him to had a German name. It was down in a cellar reached by steep steps, with just the arced tops of the windows above pavement level, like a hippopotamus's eyes peering above water. Inside, the pub was bustling and hot, the air fumed with beer-breath and damp coats. Most of the clientele looked to Viktor like workers, others looking decidedly more shady, and he heard as much German as Czech as he and Filip wove their way to the bar. It did Viktor's sense of unease no good that, as they did so, his smart and expensive clothes – collar and tie, suit, hat and coat – seemed to draw attention.

Viktor ordered a beer for each of them and resolved to make his drink last, but Filip leaned in and added two *jablkovicas* to the order. A table cleared in the corner and Filip carried his beer and apple brandy over to it, indicating with a jerk of his head that Viktor should follow with his drinks.

As they sat and drank and talked, Viktor tried to get more information from Filip about his dismissal from the university, and whether he had grounds to appeal. Filip was unforthcoming with details, even evasive, and Viktor got the impression that it had taken more than his sacking to derail him so drastically.

'Elena and I broke up,' he admitted eventually, with a shrug of feigned nonchalance.

'I'm sorry to hear that,' said Viktor. 'She was a nice girl. She was good for you.'

'No she wasn't. She was a bitch. A cunt. And, worse than that, she was a German cunt,' said Filip suddenly and unpredictably venomously, so loudly that two men at the neighbouring table turned in his direction. Viktor, shocked at his friend's vehemence, smiled a nervous apology at them and they turned back to their drinks.

'They're all bitches. All women,' Filip continued, his expression darkening again. 'They lie and cheat and fuck around behind your back – but they still want to keep you in the palm of their hand. They think they can do anything they want. But I tell you something, that fellow who's cutting them up – you know, the one they call Leather Apron – he's making them think twice all right. Maybe a homicidal maniac is the only one who's got the true measure of the female kind.'

'For Christ's sake, Filip, you don't mean that.'

'Don't I?' He looked his friend in the eye defiantly. Then just as suddenly the rage and the defiance evaporated and his shoulders sagged. 'Of course I don't. I don't know what's wrong with me. I get so – so *angry* all the time these days. Angry with everyone, even people I care about, like you. That's what got me sacked.' The shoulders sagged even more and he looked at Viktor almost meekly.

'Truth is, there's no chance of an appeal getting me my job back at the Charles or any other university. I hit Ferentz, the head of my department.'

'Hit him?'

Filip nodded. 'And I didn't hold back – knocked two teeth out. They sacked me on the spot and called the police. I spent four days in the cells but eventually old Ferentz relented and dropped the charges so long as I never darken the university's corridors again. Fair enough, I suppose.'

'Christ, Filip,' Viktor shook his head. 'And is that why Elena left you?'

'God no. She pissed off long before that. We were *politically incompatible*, you could say. And I was naïve – I thought it was possible to trust a German. I was doubly naïve thinking I could trust a woman. You know how Elena was from up north, Liberec – how all her folks were German-Czechs? But they were supposed to be the good and loyal kind – moderates and members of the Czech-German Social Democratic Workers' Party. Against joining Germany, but for self-rule in a federal Czechoslovakia and all that guff, you know? But good old Elena reverted to type – all for Konrad Henlein and the Sudeten German Party. Stupid bitch couldn't see it. She couldn't see it at all. No matter how often I tried to explain it to her, she couldn't see what these Kraut bastards are going to do.' Filip had started to rant, his mood heating up again. Viktor became more and more uneasy, aware that many of the conversations around them were taking place in German. 'Ten years from now – no, five, or even less – this little republic of ours will be gone. I told her, I did; I told her that she, Henlein, the lot of them won't have a pot to piss in then because that little Austrian egomaniac Hitler will run this as a fucking province.'

'All right, Filip, keep it down . . .' Viktor was now aware that the men at the next table, the two who had turned before and a third companion, had stopped talking and were exchanging meaningful looks.

'What? Can't two friends have a conversation? Can't two friends discuss politics?' Again said too loudly, as if to the audience around them rather than to Viktor.

Viktor leaned forward, resting his elbows on the table and talking quietly and calmly. 'Of course they can. But there's a time and a place. And at a time like this, this isn't the place. Nowadays politics is something to talk about with care, Filip, and not in public.'

'Balls to that,' said Filip, raising his voice again. 'They need to hear. Everyone needs to hear. They need to know what that little Austrian pig-fucker and his Sudeten poodles are going to lead us to.'

At that, one of the men at the table next to them said something to his companions and all three stood up abruptly and crowded around Viktor and Filip. They all had the empty-eyed, hostile blankness of men on the verge of violence. Filip jumped to his feet.

'What?' he shouted. 'What the fuck do you want?' He tossed what was left of his beer onto the pub's stone floor and brandished the empty glass in front of the face of the largest of the men. Filip's lack of fear and clear willingness to use a weapon caused the large man to pause, then take a step back. Viktor took advantage of his hesitation and stepped between them.

'All right, gentlemen,' said Viktor, holding up his hands and employing the same calming tone he used professionally with potentially violent patients. 'My friend here is just upset and has had a little too much to drink. That's all. I'm going to take him home now, so he won't bother you any more. I apologize for the trouble.' He reached into his pocket and placed a crumpled bunch of five koruna notes and a handful of heller coins on the table. 'Please, buy yourselves a drink. We'll be leaving now.'

He turned to Filip, whose face was still filled with defiant anger, and placed his hands on his friend's shoulders. He spoke in a hushed tone but firmly. 'For God's sake Filip, are you trying to get us killed?

Walk away now. I'll take you home.' Viktor took the empty beer jug from his hand and placed it on the table, gathering up his coat and hat. Filip still glared at the three men over Viktor's shoulder but allowed himself to be steered towards the door.

'*Gute Nacht, die Damen . . .*' Filip called to the men as Viktor guided him backwards towards the door.

When they were out on the street, Filip roughly shook himself free of Viktor's grasp. 'I don't need your help. Did I ask for your help? Who do you think you are, searching me out and sticking your nose into my business? I didn't ask you for anything. I'm not one of your looney patients. I'm not one of your nut-jobs.'

'No you're not, Filip,' said Viktor. 'You're my friend. You're my friend and I'm worried about you. And what worries me most is that you knew that was a German pub. You chose to go in there to start trouble deliberately, didn't you? You're out of control, man.'

Some of the tension eased from Filip's frame, but he still seemed agitated. 'Let me go home, Viktor. Leave me alone with my life and you get back to yours. Get back to your career and your future. Don't you see you should steer clear of me? I'm trouble, I know that. I seem to bring chaos down on all around me. That's why I've stayed out of your way. If only you knew—' Filip cut his own thought short.

'If I knew what?' Viktor turned to Filip. In the streetlight he looked even more pallid, less substantial, as though he was a ghost, the shade of his friend. As if he wasn't really there.

'Skip it,' said Filip. 'We used to joke that we were different sides of the same coin, you and I. We're not. We're different coins, different currencies, struck from different metals. You're a good sort, I'm a bad sort; that's all there is to it. You can't stop what's going to become of me, but if you hang around me it could mess up what you could become. Your future. You have to let me go.'

'You're my friend, Filip, that's not how it works. I'm not going—'

Viktor didn't get a chance to finish what he was saying. They had just reached where the tenements gave way to a road junction when three men stepped out from around the corner of the building and into the pool of white light from the streetlamp.

CHAPTER TWO

'*S*o when are you going to Hrad Orlů Asylum?'

'What?' Smolák turned to Dr Bartoš, who sat small and dark in the passenger seat beside him, the question diverting the kapitán's attention from the road. He had agreed to drive the police surgeon home after they had concluded their discussions at the station. Now that reports were filed, statements cross-referenced, the flash-bulb horror of scene-of-crime photographs developed and processed, both men were weary from the twin narcotics of a long workday and the emotional draining that, inevitably, no matter how used to it you were, followed yet another exposure to violent death.

'I asked when you're going to Hrad Orlů. I thought, if you didn't mind, I would come with you.'

'But why?' asked Smolák.

'Oh come now, Kapitán,' reproached Bartoš wearily. 'You know only too well that that's where they locked up Dominik. I dare say everyone in the Prague Municipal Police knows all about my brother being one of the Devil's Six.'

'Yes,' said Smolák. 'I know. That's why you want to go?'

'I've never been. To see him, I mean. I thought – if you're going up there – you could perhaps help me arrange it. And I'd appreciate the company travelling. Stupid, I know, but I feel apprehensive about seeing him again. It's been five years, but every time I've thought about visiting Dominik . . .' The police surgeon sighed in the dark.

'I suppose I've always felt that facing my brother also means facing up to what he did.'

'I understand,' said Smolák. He knew, of course, about Dominik Bartoš, the brilliant physicist turned murderer, brother of Václav Bartoš. As the doctor had said, just about everybody in the Prague Municipal Police knew. Some, Smolák included, had even speculated that Dr Bartoš had chosen the career of police surgeon to confront murder and try to understand the crimes committed by his brother.

'I'm happy to see if I can arrange something for you,' said Smolák. 'And I'd be glad of the company driving there.'

Their compact agreed, both men fell into silence. Prague and the night slid past the windows of Smolák's Praga Piccolo as an expressionist geometry of streetlight, baroque silhouette and angular shadow. Eventually they reached Bartoš's apartment building.

'Would you care for a schnapps?' asked Bartoš after he got out, leaning in to Smolák's window.

'No thanks, Doctor. It's been a long day.' It was the truth and Smolák could see the equally weary Bartoš, who had clearly made the invitation out of politeness, was relieved.

'Then we'll talk soon. Thanks for the lift.' The doctor paused for a moment. 'What we saw tonight. What he did to that woman – all the extra symbolism that he's added . . .'

'Yes?'

'It's an escalation. He's delivering a message in pieces. He's clearly inspired by Jack the Ripper, but I fear he's inspired by more than his deeds, more than the methods he used.'

'What do you mean?'

'I get the feeling he's emulating Jack the Ripper's fame. He wants to become not only *as* famous as the London murderer, but *more* famous. He wants his fame to spread wider and endure longer. And you know what that means.'

'That there'll be more victims than there were in London. That he won't stop. He will go on and on until we catch him.'

Bartoš nodded. 'When we're at the Hrad Orlů, I strongly rec-
ommend you ask the experts there what they think about Leather
Apron. Goodnight, Kapitán.'

'Goodnight, Doctor.'

Smolák watched the small, untidy police surgeon disappear into
his apartment building. He liked Bartoš, but it disturbed him that
the brother of such a notorious multiple murderer had himself such a
profound understanding of a killer's mind.

iktor didn't have time to recognize them as the three German-Czechs from the bar; he did not even register the blow from the man he had suddenly found himself facing. All he knew was that he was on his side on wet, greasy cobbles. He gathered enough composure to roll sideways as a work boot swung viciously at his head, missing its target of his face but glancing painfully off the scalp at his temple. Viktor lay stunned, vulnerable to a better-aimed kick. None came. When he came fully to himself he could hear yelling. Loud, ranting, barely human yelling. Mad yelling. Asylum yelling.

He got to his feet and saw the reason he hadn't been kicked again. His attacker was leaning against the wall of the tenement, his face bleached of colour, and clutching his right forearm. The material of his jacket sleeve bloomed black-red in the streetlight. His two friends were trying to get to him, but Filip stood between them and the injured man. Something long and bright in his hand flashed malevolently in the lamplight. Every time one of them made a move towards their friend, Filip slashed at the air in front of their faces with the long-bladed knife. And all the time he screamed and yelled and laughed maniacally at them, showering vile, foul-mouthed insults on them; challenging them, insulting their masculinity, their ethnicity; mocking their cowardice; threatening what he was going to do to them. What he would do to their women if he found them.

Viktor could see that the anger had left the men: they clearly realized they were dealing with something much worse, much more dangerous and much more out of their control than the street fight they had been prepared for. The ambushers had become the ambushed and their faces wore the uncomprehending fear of those unaccustomed to coming face to face with insanity. Viktor ran across to Filip.

'Let them pass,' he yelled. Filip spun around and glared at Viktor, the long-bladed knife now pointed at him.

'Let them get their friend and go,' said Viktor, more calmly. 'They've got the point.'

Filip turned back to them, glaring. Then he indicated their wounded comrade with a jerk of his head. After a moment's hesitation, the two men ran across to the injured man and ushered him away, back down the street in the direction of the pub.

'We'd better get out of here,' said Filip. 'Even though they started it, the bastards'll probably call the police.'

Viktor said nothing, but started to follow Filip to his coach-house apartment.

'No,' said Filip, weary but emphatic. 'Time's come for us to go our own ways. Don't you see that? To do what each of us has to do.'

'But Filip, you need help. I don't know what's happened to—'

'You'd better get out of here too. Those Krauts could be back at any time with more chums, or the police. If you hurry, you might make the last train.'

With that, without any other kind of farewell, Filip Starosta walked quickly into the misty dark of the Prague night, around the corner and out of sight. And, Viktor knew, out of his life.

Finding himself alone in the empty street, Viktor felt suddenly exposed and vulnerable. He picked his hat up from the ground, straightened and dusted down his overcoat, and made his quick-paced way in the other direction to where the railway station lay.

*I*t was after four in the morning by the time Lukáš Smolák returned to his apartment. He resolved to get a couple of hours' sleep before returning to the office, but as he lay in bed the images from the evening before played out relentlessly and mercilessly across the screen of his mind. Never before had a murder seemed so immediate, so personal. He found himself resenting the dead woman for the way she had, with the briefest of contacts, impressed herself so deeply upon him. Why was that? What had it been about Anna Petrášová that had got so much under his skin?

Lying on the bed, he smoked for a while, his limbs leaden but his chest fluttering, his restless inertia keeping beyond his reach the sleep he so desperately needed. He tried to block out the images that continued to plague him. A trick he often used at times like this was to think back to his childhood, to the happy times he spent with his father, fishing in the river that crookedly underlined their village on the map, or walking together through the dapple and mottle of sun and shadow in the dense woods to its north. After a while, his refuge of distant childhood soothed him enough for sleep to claim him.

And Lukáš Smolák dreamed.

The world, and everything in it, was big. Unlike true childhood, where the proportions of things are accepted for what they are,

Smolák the adult dreamed himself Lukáš the child, a boy of ten, and his smallness troubled him. He felt tiny, weak, defenceless. Even the landscape he dreamed of – the reconstructed topography of a remembered childhood into which he so often escaped – carried a menace. Everything he saw was sharped with hard edges and granular textures: every detail so impossibly stark and clear that he felt his retinas itch in protest.

He was running through the village, which remained as he remembered it, except he was aware of the overwhelming size of the buildings and the harsh, eye-hurting clarity with which he saw them. The sky above the village was altered: the clouds boiled and scudded across the sharp-etched horizon with unnatural speed, their dark bubbling forms tinged with carmine red.

The man-turned-boy Lukáš knew his mission: his mother had commanded him to go to his father's shop, to collect a kilo of *ostravské* sausages for the evening meal. She had done so in German, her native tongue, which she habitually did whenever possible in an effort to invest the language in her son's young mind. She had done so since he had been a baby.

And throughout Lukáš's childhood, German had also been the language of admonishment, of punishment.

Lukáš Smolák ran through the village, past the church, the red onion-domed steeple of which seemed to loom larger, higher and sharper than he remembered, like a blood-swollen needle piercing the sky. He reached the low-roofed, whitewashed building that was his father's butcher business and entered to find the front shop empty. Once more, just as he had been on that undreamed day thirty years before, he was pulled towards the door that led to the back rooms, the forbidden reaches of his father's business, drawn by the strange, shrill sounds coming from beyond.

As they had in remembered reality, his calls of 'Papa?' went unanswered, and he stepped through the dream-enlarged, black gape of the door to the back shop and meat store. Again Lukáš felt his skin prickle in the sudden dark and cold, as he stood surrounded by darkly pendant carcasses and trays of cuts and sausages.

He followed the urgent, shrill squealing.

As he stepped out into the rear courtyard, Lukáš Smolák found himself suddenly restored to the full proportions of adulthood. Again his father was there, his side turned to him. For a moment Smolák found it strange to occupy this space with his father and for them both suddenly to be the same age. His father turned and smiled at him – a warm smile – while the creature between his knees struggled and writhed.

'I'm so glad you're here,' said his father. 'You can help me with my work . . .'

Smolák smiled as he looked down at the animal to be slaughtered. It was no piglet, but Anna Petrášová. Naked, screaming, her beautiful but terrified face turned to Smolák beseechingly, entreating him to help her.

His father raised the heavy-headed mallet in his free hand, ready to arc it down and stun his victim.

'No!' yelled Smolák. 'Stop!'

His father stayed his hand but frowned, confused. 'Why?'

'You mustn't damage her head,' said Smolák. 'Her face must remain intact.'

'Oh, of course . . .' His father nodded. 'It's good that you're here. It's important that we do it right.' He nodded towards the meat-store door. 'You'll find all you need in there.'

Smolák went back into the cold store. This time, however, he seemed to notice more the hanging carcasses and trays of cuts, or see them more clearly. All the flesh was human. What he had assumed were pig carcasses became clearly those of women, breasts pendant and askew on either side of sliced-open, eviscerated and prised-apart abdomens. In one of the trays sat the faceless, red-raw head of Maria Lehmann, the Prager Kleinseite victim, staring at him in blank accusation with the glossy white globes of lidless eyes.

Smolák went through to the pantry and found what he was looking for, that which his father had told him to fetch. That which he needed.

He lifted the large filleting knife from a drawer and eased closed the pantry door to remove what was hanging there on its hook, waiting for him.

He took the leather apron – one just like his father's – from its hook and put it on before heading back out to the rear courtyard, butcher knife in hand.

To where Anna Petrášová waited for him.

CHAPTER FIVE

His relief at being back in the Hrad Orlů Asylum surprised Viktor. After the events in Prague, the castle's
stone embrace was no longer purely oppressive; there was a sense
of safety, of a dense, warm comfort within it. And when he saw her
again for the first time in two days, Viktor realized just how much
Judita had to do with that feeling.

'So what are you going to do?' she asked him as they sat alone
drinking coffee together in the ersatz café-cosmopolitanism of the
asylum's canteen.

'Do? There's nothing I can do,' he said. 'Filip is my friend but he
won't listen to me. I'm a psychiatrist but he isn't my patient – and I
don't know if even then I would have clinical grounds to intervene.'
He shrugged gloomily. 'I'm afraid that after what happened in the
street, I'm going to have to follow his advice and steer clear of him.'

'Street?' Judita frowned. 'What happened in the street?'

Viktor sighed. He had resolved not to discuss the experience
with anyone. He had thought himself lucky to bear no mark from the
punch that had stunned him or from the inexpert kick to his temple:
no bruises to explain away to Románek or colleagues. But Judita
seemed to be the only person in whom he could confide. So he told
her about the incident in the pub and what followed. About the knife.
About Filip's unpredictable, violent combustibility.

'Filip has no anchor any more,' said Viktor when he had finished telling her about the fight in the street. 'He was involved with a girl, Elena Kreusel. A really nice girl, and she was a stabilizing influence on him, but that's all fallen apart too. I'm gone, his job at the university's gone, Elena's gone. Filip is rudderless and he's not the kind of man who can plot his own course.'

'It sounds like he's beyond your help'

Viktor looked suddenly sad. 'Even if there was something I could do. In any case, I just can't afford to be dragged into that kind of mess. Filip is on the edge. I think he has depressive mania, and clearly has a problem with impulse control, but that doesn't make him mad. And it certainly doesn't excuse him responsibility for his actions. Like I say, I can't control him as a friend, I have no grounds to manage him as a patient – and I'm too far away here to babysit him. I have to think of myself, of my career. Does that sound selfish?'

'No, it just sounds sensible,' Judita said firmly. 'But from what I know of you, you'll fret. You'll worry about him.'

'I can't help that.'

'Is there something else you're not telling me?' asked Judita, reading his darkened expression. Viktor held her gaze for a moment. There *was* something more: a vague, dark suspicion about Filip to which Viktor didn't want to give utterance; a suspicion he didn't want to acknowledge to himself.

He shook his head. 'I'm just tired,' he said, 'and upset.'

A gloomy silence fell between them for a while. Then Viktor said, 'Oh there was one thing – Filip was able to translate that carving.'

'Oh?'

He handed her the slip of paper with the translation. Judita read it out loud. *'Here am I and I here stay, for this is where Evil resides. Here am I and I here stay, for this is where the Devil hides.'* She gave a small laugh. 'There, see? I told you: Jan of the Black Heart is alive and well and domiciled here in the castle. He sneaks out at night with his penknife to whittle messages into churches. Just to let the locals know he's still in the black magic business.'

'Don't you find it just that little bit, well, odd? Creepy even?'

Judita shrugged. 'It's probably just some local youth trying to frighten the village.'

'A local youth who can write in Glagolitic? And expects his peers to be able to read it?'

'So what do you think, man of science?' She smiled. Archly. Beautifully. 'That there are forest demons out there? Or it really is the handiwork of Jan of the Black Heart?'

'I'm more concerned about the demons we've got in here. That it's a reference to the castle.'

'That's silly – the carving can't possibly be connected to a patient here. There's no way an inmate could be sneaking out into the woods.'

'Perhaps not. But read it again – you could interpret it a completely different way: that the "Devil" is one of the patients, and that "here I'll stay" isn't about rejoicing in evil, but guarding it, keeping it locked up. Maybe even waiting for an opportunity to destroy it.'

'What?' Judita smiled sceptically. 'One of the staff?'

Viktor shrugged. 'Or maybe a relative of a victim. Someone connected to either a patient or their crimes in some way. It could be, you know.'

'No. It doesn't make sense,' said Judita. 'Why so cryptic? And as you pointed out yourself, why in Old Church Slavonic? We're both educated people, yet you had to get your expert friend to translate it.'

'I suppose you're right.' He smiled. 'But it *is* odd.'

'I thought odd was the norm for you. For all of us here.' She sipped her coffee. 'By the way, I've got all your sessions transcribed to date – never mind cryptic graffiti, *that* gives me the creeps. Who's up next?'

'I've had sessions with Mládek, Valentová, Zelený and Bartoš. And of course I've yet to have my first session with the charming Vojtěch Skála, which will be fun, I'm sure – added to all of which

I really wanted to do follow-ups with the Clown, Leoš Mládek, and especially with Hedvika Valentová – to see if I could get her to manifest her satanic "beautiful angel".'

'You think the Devil Aspect would reveal itself in so obvious a way? It does seem a little, well, *literal.*'

'I know what you mean, but Valentová isn't a particularly imaginative or creative thinker. Even the imagery of her psychosis is literal: the flavours of the flesh she cooks and the gratification it gives others is a pretty blunt metaphor for the concept of flesh in the sexual or moral sense. Her vegetarianism is an obvious analogue for her sexual abstinence. Freudianism at its bluntest and crudest, I'm afraid. Anyway, that'll have to wait for the moment: I'm preparing the so-called Glass Collector, Michal Macháček, for a police interview in two days' time. According to Professor Románek, the police are seeking the benefit of Macháček's specific expertise on glass.'

'Didn't you hear?' said Judita. 'That's been put back at least a few days. There's been another Leather Apron murder in Prague, so the detective who—'

'Another murder?' Viktor interrupted her.

'Yes. A business woman. Someone quite important.'

'When did it take place?'

'Two nights ago. What's wrong?'

Viktor shook his head. 'Nothing.'

But the same unspoken, dark suspicion clouded in his mind again. He recalled Filip's strange, malevolently agitated state; how quickly he had turned violent; his venomous misogyny. Most of all, he remembered the streetlamp flash on a deadly looking knife.

'So the interview is cancelled?' he asked eventually.

'No – not cancelled, just postponed. According to Professor Románek, the Prague detective's still keen to talk with Macháček. This most recent victim was involved in the glass trade, apparently. But the police have stressed they're not talking to Macháček because he's a suspect in anything – it's just his expertise they're after.'

Viktor nodded, but another image came into his mind: the Bohemian drinking glasses, so ornate and elegantly carved and so out of place in Filip's apartment.

CHAPTER SIX

*A*s he was guided into the tower room for his narcohypnosis session, Michal Macháček looked as unlikely a killer, as unlikely a maniac, as Hedvika Valentová or Leoš Mládek had. A small, bustling, fussy-looking man in rimless glasses, Macháček was fleshy to the point of being fat, his skull bald, high-domed and broad, almost egg-shaped, edged with a short-trimmed band of black hair.

Viktor's main impression of the Glass Collector was that of a fidgety, almost pathological impatience. As he was brought into the treatment room, the small man seemed impatient with the inconvenience of his confinement; impatient with Viktor, impatient with the orderlies.

Impatient with the unacceptably slow turning of the Earth.

It was the kind of intense, relentless exasperation that Viktor recognized as a symptom of megalomania or narcissistic complex: an egomaniacal sense of entitlement; a belief that the world and the universe beyond it revolved around him; that everyone and everything in that universe was there exclusively to serve his needs.

For Viktor's purposes, it was the strongest kind of will to overcome: a morbidly engorged Ego that stood like a burly doorman guarding the doors to the Unconscious. The whole point of the narcosynthesis sessions was to overcome the Ego, to subject the will of the patient to the will of the physician and throw wide those doors.

For this session, Viktor increased the dose of hypnotics.

The effect was like watching the peeling of an onion as layer after delaminated layer of Macháček's personality was shed. First was the physical restlessness, the fidgeting fingers stilling; then the tensions in his expression, his eyes. Macháček's characteristic, continuous impatience fell from him and the small balding man seemed, for the first time in Viktor's presence, somewhat at peace. The scale of the transformation was striking, like watching paraldehyde take effect on an epileptic patient. He decided to allow Macháček a few moments of peace before delving into his mind.

While he waited, Viktor once more took in the grain storeroom around them. The ceiling was high-vaulted, an interlacing of arcs and beams of the same centuries-old wood as the single door. The walls arced around him, dense and heavy, the ripples and creases in the thin skin of plaster telling of a history beyond: a stone history of damage and repair, of ancient perpends, bonds and ties. Perhaps there was, hidden in that history, a doorway filled in to immure an aristocratic monster.

Perhaps also, as local legend had it, there was yet another secret door, but this one to set free the same monster. That, he realized, had become the function of this room now; his function too: the letting loose of monsters.

Macháček made no protest as Viktor administered the second injection, the power of his will ebbing, or perhaps simply because the Glass Collector was content to remain free of his habitual impatience and restlessness. After a while, Viktor pressed the clunking Bakelite knob of the Magnetophon recorder and began the session, asking all the preliminary questions, guiding Macháček through his early life, his training as an accountant. Even with the level of sedatives and hypnotics that Viktor had applied, Macháček still aggrandized, conflated and confabulated, exaggerating his achievements and his own importance in every context he had passed through.

On a couple of occasions he even challenged Viktor's right to ask such questions. But as the drug cocktail took greater effect and stripped yet more layers from the small man's huge Ego, Macháček became more compliant.

As bidden, he told Viktor his story.

'I worked as an accountant for the Plzeň City Council,' he explained. 'I was, without doubt, the most important and efficient employee in the department. In fact, I should have been made head of the department right away – the mayor himself all but told me that. No one was as dedicated as I. No one had the same eye for detail. Nor the same single-minded commitment to their employer. As I'm sure you can imagine, I had many lovers, but I was so steadfastly dedicated to my work that I never made the commitment to marry any of them.'

'So why didn't you continue to work there?' Viktor was aware that, even with the increased dose of hypnotics, he was going to have to steer the course of the session with a firmer hand than usual. Macháček's exaggerations of his own importance made it difficult to set sail for the true deep channels of his mind, and not drift onto the shallows and reefs of his Ego. 'Why did you give it all up to collect glass?'

'I always collected glass – Bohemian glass mainly, and some Italian – ever since I was a boy. I used to read up about it from an early age. My parents were very wealthy – important people, my family – and when my mother died, shortly after my father, I inherited enough money, a small fortune, to collect full time. But I very soon became so successful in trading in pieces that I could live off that income alone.'

Another exaggeration. Viktor knew from the files that Macháček's background had been most definitely of a *bourgeoisie* that was *petite* rather than *grande* or *haute*; and while his inheritance had been reasonable, it had not been on the scale he suggested. It was true, however, that he had become a leading authority on everything to do with Bohemian glass and its history. Viktor knew that a singular expertise could be the one advantage of monomaniacal focus.

Macháček had also inherited his parents' large but somewhat dilapidated villa in Táborská Street, near Plzeň's railway marshalling yards. According to his case files, the villa had three floors, a huge cellar and an attic. Once he became sole occupant of the family home, he had fitted out the top floor and the attic to contain his glass collection. As his collecting became increasingly obsessive, he had also converted, and heavily secured, the cellar to house his most precious pieces: those he wanted no one else to see or enjoy.

'I see,' said Viktor. 'And your collection was highly regarded, I believe. One of the best in Bohemia.'

'Not one of the best – *the* best. So many beautiful pieces.'

'But what about the Kalbáč collection? Wasn't that as extensive?'

'Never.' Macháček's protestation was stripped of its passion and vehemence by the drugs. 'Nowhere near.'

'But you knew Kalbáč?'

'Anton Kalbáč was a smug, arrogant swine,' said Macháček. His Ego was still there – weakened, but still there. Still obfuscating and obscuring. Still trying to dominate its universe. Viktor considered whether he could risk another injection to boost the effect of the already heavy drug cocktail.

'He claimed to have the largest and widest collection of old Bohemian glass in Europe,' Macháček continued. 'It was a lie. A damned lie. I had much more than he had, much more. He had pieces by Friedrich Winter, for which I envied him, that much is true, but I had several original pieces by Georg Schwanhardt, worth much more in historical and financial value. I even had an intaglio-engraved glass panel by the master himself, the great Caspar Lehmann, who started as gem cutter to Emperor Rudolf the Second. Practically priceless – the idiot who sold it to me had no idea of its true value. I tell you, I ran rings around that yokel. Anyway, I also had a much more extensive range of hyalith glass. Where Anton Kalbáč got the nerve to claim his collection was better than mine I could never guess.'

'But you did have a dispute with him? I mean a dispute over the ownership of a particular item. The so-called Devil Goblet?'

'I did. But I got it. I took it from under Kalbáč's nose.'

'Tell me about the Devil Goblet.'

'The Devil's Goblet, not the Devil Goblet,' Macháček corrected Viktor. 'It's the most incredible example of the glassmaker's craft. No, not craft, art. It's seventeenth century and is an example of the use of iridescent uranium glass long before anyone else used it. The glass seems to be alive: writhing and twisting around the stem. And the bowl – so many colours, so many patterns. If you look long enough they swirl and change. I tell you, I have stared at that piece for hours on end, sinking into the glass, seeing deeper, seeing it change and move. I swear I have seen faces in that bowl. It was crafted by Karl-Heinz Kleinfelder. You know how they say a great composer lives on through his music, that his personality persists in it? Or a great painter lives on in his canvases long after his death? Well, it's like that with the Devil's Goblet. Kleinfelder lives on in the glass he crafted.'

'You say there is a story about that, don't you? About Kleinfelder and the Devil's Goblet. You say there's a legend behind it.'

'Yes there is. But, I tell you, having spent hour upon hour studying the piece, I believe it. I believe the legend to be true. I saw the truth in the glass.'

'And what is the legend?' asked Viktor, already knowing the answer.

'Like the better-known Schwanhardt, Karl-Heinz Kleinfelder was an apprentice to the great Caspar Lehmann. He worked for him for twenty years and became almost the equal of his master, but could never quite match him.

'Remember we are talking about a time when the emperor himself was said to dabble in alchemy and the occult. It's said that Kleinfelder was a friend of Jiří Bareš, the famous alchemist, and worked with him to create a new form of glass with almost magical qualities. But that wasn't enough for Kleinfelder: he was so jealous of Lehmann's skills that it's said he summoned up Satan himself to help him fashion the most striking, perfect piece of glassware.

'Some say that the glass was made by melting down the ancient glass beads known as the Tears of Perun – Perun is the old Slavic god of thunder and he was supposed to have created the first glass when he dropped a lightning bolt into a sand pit. After the Tears of Perun had been melted down, the Devil was supposed to have mixed hellfire into the glass, giving those reds and umbers in it a unique and hypnotizing quality.

'But there was to be another ingredient in it – the most important ingredient of all – an ingredient that would make the goblet the most exceptional piece of glass ever made. The Devil said he would only tell Kleinfelder what the secret ingredient was after the goblet was completed.

'Kleinfelder was so obsessed with creating the goblet that he promised the Devil his immortal soul. He did so gladly. In return Satan said that he would not claim Kleinfelder's soul for as long as the Devil's Goblet remained unbroken and intact. According to the legend, the Devil came to Kleinfelder's workshop at midnight to work with him, melting the glass with his breath and moulding and twisting it with his talons, and all the while promising the glass-maker that when the first rays of morning light shone through the window, he would see and wonder at the completed goblet. And he did. The Devil's Goblet was ready as the dawn broke and it was magnificent. Kleinfelder was overwhelmed with the piece, but could tell there was still something missing from it.'

'What was missing?' asked Viktor.

For a moment Macháček lay still on the couch, his eyes gazing upwards to the vaulted ceiling. The only sound was the quiet turning of the Magnetophon's reels and once more Viktor felt confined: shut in with an encapsulated madness.

'It is part of historical record that Kleinfelder was found dead sitting at his workbench that same morning,' Macháček eventually continued. 'His hair had turned white and his dead eyes were fixed on the completed Devil's Goblet that sat in all its glory on the bench before him. They said that his heart had given out, but I know the truth.

'You see, at the exact moment that the sun started to rise above the horizon and its rays began to penetrate the goblet's glass, the Devil had added that most special, most magical final ingredient he had promised Kleinfelder. To give the Devil's Goblet that writhing, twisting, tormented element for which it is famous, Satan trapped Kleinfelder's soul in the glass. He remains there to this day, confined and screaming inside its crystal prison for nearly three hundred years. And he will remain there until the Devil's Goblet is broken. But if it ever does shatter, then, of course, the Devil will come to claim Kleinfelder's soul.'

'I see,' said Viktor. 'You became obsessed with this legend – would you agree?'

'Obsessed? No. But when you look into the glass of the Devil's Goblet, as I have for countless hours, you believe the legend. I told you I could see a face in the goblet – well, I swear to you now that's whose face I saw: Karl-Heinz Kleinfelder's. I saw with my own eyes his spirit trapped in there, his essence, screaming in the glass. Like I said, people say a great composer or artist lives on through his work. That was Kleinfelder's fate, but literally, not figuratively. A living death – sleepless, endless, screaming – locked inside his own diabolical masterwork.'

Viktor paused for a moment. Again the quiet turning of tape reels filled the thick-walled silence.

'And where did you hear this legend?' he asked eventually.

'Where? Why everyone knows the legend of Kleinfelder and the Devil. It's part of glassmaking mythology.'

'The strange thing is,' said Viktor without accusation, 'that I can find no record of such a tale. Indeed, I can find no record of such an apprentice to Caspar Lehmann. In fact, you seem to be the only one who knows the legend.'

'That's nonsense, everybody knows it.' Macháček's protest was passionless beneath the cloud of sedative and hypnotic. Viktor sensed his patient slipping towards sleep.

'I see,' said Viktor. 'Would you not agree that this legend is really a metaphor for your rivalry with Anton Kalbáč? That you would have sold your soul to surpass him? To surpass his collection?'

'No. That's not it at all.' Again, without the drugs, the protestation would have been more vehement. 'I already had surpassed him.'

'But you agree you murdered Kalbáč? You accept your responsibility for his death?'

'I do. He deserved everything he got.'

'Tell me what happened.'

'He started a suit against me: claimed I had stolen the Devil's Goblet from his collection.'

'And had you?'

'I took what was mine by right. When I got the notice of the lawsuit I contacted him and asked him to come and discuss the matter. I gave him to believe I was going to return the goblet to him. He was a big man – arrogant with it and always throwing his weight about – so he clearly thought there was no danger in coming to see me. No danger from me. When he arrived, I told Kalbáč that I was truly sorry and I didn't want any trouble. I said I wanted to make things right: I would return the goblet straight away and he could take any other piece from my collection – any one he wanted, so long as he dropped the lawsuit.

'I had a particularly splendid Slovak Tokaj wine and I poured him a couple of glasses and that warmed him up a little. Arrogant swine thought he'd bettered me, humiliated me, and I let him go on thinking that. I begged him for forgiveness; told him that I had pieces that rivalled the Devil's Goblet and he could have one of them. I told him the legend and explained that I had other glass that was said to contain trapped souls. Priceless pieces, my best pieces. I explained they were kept in the basement. I told him he would never have seen any glassware, apart from the Devil's Goblet, to compare with the pieces I had down there.'

'So he went with you?'

'He did. I genuinely did want to see his reaction to my collection, in the display cases.'

'And how did he react?'

'He was overwhelmed. He was awestruck. Then he went mad – started shouting at me, yelling wildly, telling me I was insane and that he was going to fetch the police. But the poison I'd put in the Tokaj was already working on him. He didn't make it halfway up the cellar stairs.'

'He died?'

'Not there and then. I put him in the enamel bath I had in the cellar for preparing my other pieces. I stripped him and tied him up tightly so he couldn't move. Then I fastened the mould over his head. I'd learned that earlier with the other pieces: if they could move they thrashed about and created bubbles in the molten glass.' He paused, matter-of-factly. 'You know, that was my hubris: using Anton Kalbáč for a piece. If I hadn't used someone I knew and could be connected to, then I would still be building my collection today.'

'I see,' said Viktor. He glanced through the photographs the police had taken in Macháček's cellar. There had been a furnace and all that an amateur glassmaker could need. A display case contained what looked like clumsily crafted, thick-stemmed vases, except each was topped with a sealed globe, not a bowl. Twelve of them. In each of eleven bowls, encapsulated in the glass, was a young woman's head. One woman abducted and murdered each year for eleven years. Macháček had used his glass-collecting trips to snatch victims from different parts of the country and bring their bodies back to Plzeň in the trunk of his car. No one had connected the disappearances.

Even the oldest of the eleven female heads showed limited decomposition, encapsulated in airtight glass. The twelfth head was that of a man. Anton Kalbáč.

When Viktor looked up from the notes his patient was asleep. He tried rousing him but Macháček was lost to the drugs and would be incapable of stirring for several hours. It had been, Viktor knew, a risk he had taken by administering such a heavy dose. There was nothing for it but to end the session. He noted down the time, then clunked off the tape recorder.

It happened when Viktor turned his back on his patient and crossed to the grain store's door to summon in the orderlies to remove Macháček to his quarters.

'*Do you still seek me, Doctor?*'

The voice came from behind Viktor, from Macháček, but it wasn't his voice. It was deep, much deeper than the Glass Collector's, and resonated in the wall-gripped air of the session room.

And it spoke in English.

Viktor spun around, stung. 'What did you say?'

No answer. Macháček was still asleep, or feigned sleep. Viktor crossed over to his patient and shook him roughly by the shoulders.

'What did you just say?' Viktor asked.

The Glass Collector stirred a little but failed to break the surface of wakefulness.

After the orderlies came and removed his patient, Viktor stood still and silent in the middle of the grain store treatment room, as if trying to catch the echo of the strange voice he had heard from Macháček.

And the more he thought about it – about the absurdity of an unexceptional accountant from Plzeň turned exceptional sex-murderer calling out to him in altered tones and a foreign language – the more he convinced himself that he had misheard it.

If only he hadn't switched off the recorder.

*S*ince his first visit with Judita, Viktor had been aware that the thick-walled and low-roofed inn in the village must have been centuries old. Each time they entered the main door, Viktor had had to stoop a little to avoid the heavy, ornately carved dark oak lintel above the door. But until today, he had never noticed the carving: a highly stylized representation of the forest, where leaves and branches weaved and interlocked in a pattern. Carved at the centre was the figure of a thick-set man, heavily cloaked and peasant booted. The head of the figure wasn't human, but that of a bear, turned sideways to reveal its profile. It was the same motif, Viktor realized, as the carving on the wooden panel in the castle's accommodation wing; except here its treatment and styling was rougher, more bucolic.

They entered and took a seat at the window. Again there was only a handful of other customers in the café, but this time they paid scarce attention to Viktor and Judita. In communities like these, Viktor guessed, being ignored was as close as you got to acceptance.

The grandly moustachioed innkeeper smiled and wished them both a hearty '*dobrou chuť*' as he served them their meal.

Viktor and Judita had made the walk down through the woods four times now, each time dining at the village inn and each time breaking their journey at the forest chapel on their way back to the castle. The ease that had grown between them had become an intimacy and they both knew they were on the verge of becoming lovers. But Viktor was aware he had to take his time: Judita, despite her openness and clear affection for him, remained fragile.

Today, as they sat by the window that remained filled with the view of the inescapable, constant castle, he noticed that she was pale, and that her eyes were shadowed and heavy lidded. But when he expressed his concern she dismissed it with a wave of her slim fingers.

'I didn't sleep well last night, that's all. Anyway, we were talking about your patient. Are you sure you heard him speak with this other voice?' she asked once the innkeeper had left them to their meal. Viktor and Judita habitually spoke in German when they were alone.

Viktor frowned. 'Truth is I don't know what I heard. It was definitely Macháček speaking, but his voice was so altered – and I could have sworn he spoke in English, but that doesn't make any sense. He was unconscious at the time so it could simply be somniloquy – a random and nonsensical utterance while sleeping. I just wish I hadn't switched off the recorder.'

'But it's clearly shaken you up.'

'To be honest, I'm worried that I'm exhibiting research bias: maybe I just want to believe I heard some discrete and separate part of Macháček speaking – the Devil Aspect part – when it's much more likely that he was simply muttering in his sleep.' He shook his head. 'It's just that it was so . . . *different*.'

'Isn't that quite common in sleep-talking? That a person's voice can be completely altered?'

Viktor shrugged. 'You're right, of course. Like I say, I'm probably giving it too much significance.'

'Are you planning more sessions with him? Macháček, I mean.'

'I have to get him ready for the police, so yes. But I've also got to select other candidates for my sessions. I'm beginning to despair that I'll ever find proof of my theory. I've scheduled a session with

Pavel Zelený – the Woodcutter, as Professor Románek calls him in his case file.'

Judita nodded between mouthfuls. 'And that's exactly what he is. Or was. His job, I mean: a forester on some estate. In Czech Silesia, I think.'

'I know,' said Viktor. 'I've been through the file.'

'Terrible story.'

'Aren't they all? Sometimes I think I should have become an obstetrician. Dealing with life and light instead of darkness and death. Bringing life into the world.'

Judita rested her knife and fork on her plate and leaned back in her chair, raising her eyebrow in an expression of mock seriousness, as if studying Viktor for the first time.

'I don't know . . . You'd have to soften your look a little.'

'My look?'

'A little less formal. A little less . . .' she made a show of struggling for the right word, '. . . *severe*. You'd frighten the babies. Their mothers too, probably.'

'Thanks,' he said glumly. 'I'll work on my bedside manner.'

An older woman carrying a basket of vegetables came into the inn, passing close to Viktor and Judita's table. Like the others, she paid scant attention to them, but when Viktor greeted her she didn't reply, regarding them both with something suspended between indifference and contempt. Wordlessly, she took her basket of produce through the archway and into the kitchens.

The innkeeper had witnessed the exchange, or lack of it, as he came over to clear their plates. 'That's old Růžena bringing in the last vegetables of the season,' he explained. 'She has the best vegetable garden in the village, but she's better at cultivating parsnips and marrows than friendships. I apologize if she seemed rude.'

'Is she like that with everyone?' asked Judita.

The innkeeper shrugged. 'I suppose she is. But like most of the people here, she's not happy about the Castle of the Witches being used for – well, what it's used for. You know, the Devil's Six being kept up there and all. Me, I couldn't care less, but you know how people are. Especially country people. They imagine things. Exaggerate them.'

'What on earth do they think we do up there?' asked Judita.

'Oh, there are different rumours in the village about the castle. All kinds of wild speculations about what goes on up there. Crazy experiments, that kind of thing. I don't want to offend anyone's politics – I don't know where you folks stand and it's none of my business – but this is a very traditional Czech village and there's a lot of talk that Hrad Orlů is a hotbed of Sudetener Nazis who carry out experiments on their Czech patients.' The innkeeper smiled beneath the impressive moustache and shook his head in a clumsy attempt to defuse the statement. 'But the rumour that gets most people worked up is that one of the mad killers up there has found the way out through Jan of the Black Heart's secret passageway. I don't know if you know of it, but there's an old wooden chapel in the forest above the village.'

Judita was clearly about to say that they knew it – knew it well – but Viktor cut her off, placing his hand over hers and giving a light squeeze.

'What about the chapel?' he asked.

'There are local legends about that place too. That Jan of the Black Heart used it for rituals and ceremonies. Black Masses, that kind of thing. But it's also said that an underground tunnel leads all the way down from the castle through the network of caves and into the chapel – either coming up into a secret trapdoor in the chapel itself or somewhere close by. Jan of the Black Heart was said to have used it during his supposed confinement – that all the time he was meant to be walled up in the castle he was secretly escaping at night and continuing to kill women and girls. It's all nonsense, of course: the chapel and the whole area around it have been searched over and over again over the years, but no one's been able to find

any secret entry to a tunnel.' The innkeeper shrugged burly shoulders. 'Anyway, forget old Růžena. She never speaks to strangers and
barely speaks to me, daft old bat. Enjoy your meal.'

After they had eaten, Viktor and Judita walked around the small
kidney-shaped lake – more like a large pond – that arced behind the
village. As they followed the path's curve, Viktor noticed the old
woman Růžena back at the village's edge, standing watching them
across the dark mirror of water, as if in silent accusation. Eventually,
empty basket looped over her arm, she turned and headed off in the
other direction.

It was a cheerless day under a grey sky, the sun a pale platter
behind muslin, and Viktor found himself wishing they hadn't come
this way. The path around the water's edge was narrow and the forest
next to it seemed particularly dense and dark, as if the trees were
jostling in menacing advance on the lake and village.

He felt strangely unnerved by the forest's inexorable presence, his
eyes drawn into the dark spaces between the crowded trunks. He tried
to put his unease down to the reading of the patient case notes he had
done in preparation for his session with the Woodcutter, scheduled
for that evening. The truth was, he knew, that there was something
about the lake and the crowding trees that reminded him of a place in
his childhood. Of a place and a day. Of Čertovo Jezero – Devil's Lake
– in the far west of the country, where the Bohemian Forest crowded
in on the lake in the same way. And of the day his sister had drowned.
He turned and looked into the shadows of the forest, half expecting to
see his mother's darkening face as she hung from a bough.

'You all right?' Judita seemed to sense his unease.

'Sorry,' he smiled. 'I was thinking about work. Maybe we should
head back.'

As they made their way through the forest trail back to the castle,
Judita looped her arm through Viktor's, resting her other hand on his

forearm and leaning into him. It was a relaxed, casual expression of her affection, her closeness to him, and it pleased him; he had been anxious about being the one to make the first moves in progressing their relationship.

'Shall we go and see the forest chapel?' she asked, her tone girlishly impulsive. There was something about her cheer that emphasized the darkness about her eyes, the paler than normal complexion. 'See if we can find Jan of the Black Heart's secret underground shortcut back to the castle.'

'Sure,' he said, after a moment's hesitation.

She led him by the hand, as she had done the first time they had been there, when they had rushed to the hidden chapel through the rain. The dark-leafed fingers of the bushes and trees seemed to reach out into the path, as if to grasp at them as they passed. Again Viktor felt that strange sense of oppressive unease, as if he had to escape the forest.

The trees gave way and revealed once more the clearing and the dark-hewn wooden chapel. Judita led Viktor into the shadow of the porch. He was taken by surprise when she pulled him to her, her body close and warm against his, and kissed him eagerly, urgently. He felt himself lost: sweetly, happily lost; but something about her urgency disturbed him.

'I want to be with you,' he said eventually. 'I want us to be together.'

'You are with me. We are together,' she said, kissing him again. 'We're together here, now. We're happy now.'

'I'm talking about beyond now. I'm talking about tomorrow, the future. I want us to be together.'

'There is no tomorrow.' She pulled back from him, the smile fading from her lips. 'We have no future. There is no future for us to have. Don't you see we have to live for now, Viktor? Like never before, people are going to have to live for now. We've got to seize this moment and any others we can grab. This isn't the time for us – for anyone – to look ahead, to make plans.'

'Why? Because of what's happening in Germany? The political situation?'

'What is happening around us isn't a "political situation", Viktor. And it isn't just happening in Germany, it's happening here: the beginning of something monstrous. A terrible storm that's going to wreck everything in its path.' She placed her hand on his cheek, her fingers slim and light and cool. 'The future you imagine for us will be part of the wreckage.'

'How can you be sure?'

'It's there for all to see, if only they look.' She frowned, her expression distrait. 'I have such terrible dreams, Viktor. That's why I hardly got any sleep last night. Such awful nightmares.'

He took hold of her shoulders and brought his face close to hers. 'What kind of nightmares?'

'Dreams of the dead. Dark shapes like shadows in the night, all moving silently, like ghosts. Huge, countless crowds of them. Somehow I know they are people who don't realize that they are already dead. People like me.'

'What do you mean people like you?'

'Jews, Viktor. Thousands of them. Jews like me.'

*T*he store was closed and there was no word of when it would open again. It seemed that with Anna Petrášová's murder her business had ended with her life. Despite having lost her husband, Madame Petrášová had not contemplated the possibility of her own premature death and had made no provisions for it. Her lawyer was apparently struggling to put all the relevant paperwork together and find some kind of workable disposition for the store.

It was to her lawyer that Smolák turned when trying to locate business associates or friends who could offer him any kind of insight into her habits and personality. As a murder detective, it was Lukáš Smolák's job to get to know the dead: learn their routines, quirks and foibles. Uncover in death the secrets they had kept in life. His head was full of close acquaintance with people who had never met him in life.

It was a familiarity with death that meant, unlike Anna Petrášová, Lukáš Smolák had no problem grasping his own mortality.

Her lawyer was Franz Schneider, a quietly-spoken Prague-German in his late fifties. He headed a medium-sized legal practice from offices in Řeznická Street, near Charles Square in the Nové Město. When Smolák visited Schneider, the lawyer wasn't able to provide much information, despite his clear desire to be helpful. Madame Petrášová had been a very private person and her business or legal dealings had had no other dimension to them. A difficult woman to get to know, the lawyer had admitted.

Maybe Schneider hadn't got to know his client well, but something about how he talked about her led Smolák to suspect the nondescript middle-aged lawyer had perhaps been a little in love with her. Smolák could understand that: he hadn't got to know Anna Petrášová well either, but she still haunted him.

Schneider was, however, able to give Smolák the names and addresses of the three shop assistants who worked with her. He also had a set of keys, should the detective need entry to the store.

Smolák recognized Magda Tůmová as one of the sales assistants he had passed when crossing the sales floor of Petráš Sklo a Skleněná Bižuterie. She had the same fine bone structure as her employer, but her beauty was that little bit inferior. As he had thought at the time, Anna Petrášová had hired her staff for their ornamental value as much as their sales ability.

Magda, whose name and address had been supplied by Anna Petrášová's lawyer, was at home in an apartment she shared with two girlfriends, both of whom were at work when Smolák called. When she answered the door she kept the chain fastened and Smolák was only able to gain admittance once he had shown her his police disc. She was clearly still shaken by her employer's murder and looked lost, cast adrift from her routine of work.

'Oh, I remember you,' she said when he stepped into the flat. 'You came to the store to talk to Madame. Just before . . .' Her eyes fell.

'That's right,' said Smolák. 'I don't want to distress you further, but it's important that I ask you some questions.'

'Of course,' said Magda, and guided him through to the living room.

Magda, freed from the black uniform of the Křemencová Street store, was dressed in a pale blue blouse, cardigan, and Marlene Dietrich-style, wide-legged jacquard trousers, her hair no longer fastened back but hanging loose in auburn waves over her shoulders. The cosmopolitanism and expense of her clothes jarred a little with the faint twang of a rural Moravian accent, which she did her best to conceal as she offered Smolák coffee.

'I'll do anything I can,' she said once she brought the coffee through and sat opposite Smolák. 'Poor Madame Petrášová. She was so good to us girls. Strict, but very kind as well.'

Smolák ran through all the usual questions, but, like with the lawyer, it became clear that Anna Petrášová had zealously guarded her personal life when around her staff. So zealously that Smolák wondered what the businesswoman may have been hiding. He had come across that so often in his career: people who led seemingly straightforward lives and guarded their privacy usually had something they were keeping in the shadows.

'What about male friends? Her husband died five years ago. Did she ever mention anyone she may have been involved with? Or did you ever see her with any man?'

'No, never. That doesn't mean she didn't have lovers,' said Magda. 'I know she was old and that, but men seemed to go for her. Even younger men. She never once flirted with a male customer – she was usually quite, well, aloof, snooty with them, but I think that was an act. It was part of her sex appeal, I suppose. I've lost count of how many times a man came into the store for an ashtray and left with a full decanter and glasses set. Then, after all that formality and aloofness, she would wink at us as we wrapped up some poor guy's purchases to show us she'd pulled it off again.'

'But there was no one she seemed to be especially friendly towards?'

Magda shook her head. 'It's sad, but for all her wealth and beauty, I think poor Madame Petrášová was lonely. Sad. You see, her husband's death had hit her hard. It was a long time before I'd started work for her, but that's what I'd heard. And she didn't seem to be interested in men.'

'I see.' Smolák sighed. Usually, if he worried away enough at the edge of an investigation, a thread would eventually come loose and he could start to unravel it.

'She liked you, you know.'

'Sorry?'

'Madame Petrášová – she liked you. That's why I remember about you coming to the store. After you went – I don't know, I could just tell. She seemed different.'

The statement hit Smolák like a blow to the chest. It was at the same time something he wanted to hear and something he wished he hadn't heard.

'How different?' he asked.

'I don't know, little things. You can tell. Women can pick up that kind of thing from other women. I just knew she liked you.'

'Are you sure it wasn't something to do with what I had been talking to her about? I brought in a glass bead to get her opinion on it. Could it have been something about that that caused her to seem different?'

Magda laughed. The first time she had smiled or laughed or shown any levity of spirit since he had arrived. 'I'm sure. You men don't have much in the way of intuition, do you? I could tell that Madame liked you.' The levity evaporated. 'Poor Madame, she deserved some happiness.'

They sat in gloomy silence for a moment, drinking their coffees. Suddenly, the electric shock of an idea seemed to jolt Magda.

'There was something . . . You asked if there was anything unusual. I've just remembered.'

'What?'

'It's maybe nothing at all.'

'Magda,' urged Smolák. 'Please.'

'A man came in to look at glass jewellery. He didn't look like he could afford it, but he wanted to see what we had in the way of glass beads. I'd forgotten all about him . . .'

'And Madame Petrášová served him?'

'No, that's the thing. She didn't have anything to do with him, wouldn't have known he'd been in. I served him. I showed him the beads but he didn't seem to be paying much attention to them, or to me. He kept looking over at Madame. All the time. I was beginning to get annoyed with him.'

'When was this?'

'It was the day you came to visit her. In fact, it was about an hour or so after you left.'

'Did he buy anything? The beads?'

'No. I was in the middle of showing him a set when he turned on his heel without a word and walked out of the shop.'

'And you say this was *after* I had spoken to Madame Petrášová?'

'It was.'

'What did he look like? Can you give me a description?'

'That's the thing. I remember he never looked me in the eye all the time I served him. He was tall and was wearing this black coat that was all creased and dusty. He looked like he hadn't shaved for a couple of days at least, but I couldn't see much of his face because he had this battered wide-brimmed black hat pulled down almost over his eyes. I remember thinking at the time, "How can he see what I'm showing him?". But now that I think back on it, he didn't want me to see his face.'

'Did it occur to you at the time that he was up to no good?'

'What, like a robber? Maybe a little. But he was too calm. He spoke in this quiet voice, deep and cultured, that didn't seem to fit with his clothes. Although they had maybe been expensive when they'd been bought.'

'Did he speak in Czech or German?'

'Czech, but he maybe had a faint German accent. But I can't be sure.'

'Did Madame Petrášová see him?'

'No, she was busy with another customer. I was going to mention him to her afterwards, but the store got so busy and I forgot. He had been staring at her all that time but I don't think she ever knew he'd been there. I should have told her . . .' A look of horror crossed Magda's face. 'Do you think that was him? If I had said something to her about him – oh God, do you think if I'd mentioned him I could have saved her?'

'No Magda,' said Smolák soothingly but firmly. 'There no reason to believe that he was involved with her murder. And, even if he was, you mentioning him wouldn't have made a difference. There's nothing you could have done.'

'Honestly?'

'Honestly, Magda,' said Smolák.

But as he left her in her apartment, Smolák's stomach churned with the same dark speculations of what could have been, how things could have turned out differently. That, and the fact that Magda's description of the man in the store matched perfectly with Tobar Bihari's description of the man who came out of the shadows to give him the idea of using stolen keys to break into Maria Lehmann's apartment.

That was where Smolák's darkest speculation lay: that Bihari had been telling the truth. That there really had been someone else there.

And that Smolák now had, for what it was worth, a description of Leather Apron.

*A*s they drew near the castle's gatehouse, Viktor and Judita, who had held hands all the way up the trail, released their hold and allowed a space to open up between them. It wasn't a conscious thing for either of them and they certainly hadn't discussed keeping their relationship secret, but some instinct advised caution. Once in the castle and out of sight of others, they kissed. But when Viktor made to move away, she grasped his forearm with surprising strength.

'When you've finished your session tonight, come to my room.' Her expression was fiercely earnest, but otherwise difficult to read.

'All right,' said Viktor. He was about to say something more, but Judita turned abruptly and headed purposefully towards the staff quarters.

Viktor decided to check in with Professor Románek before his session with Pavel Zelený, the simple forestry worker, to update him on his progress, or lack of it, so far. His route took him past the castle's kitchens and dining hall; as he approached them, three burly white-jacketed orderlies ran past him. Simultaneously, he heard a piercing female scream come from the dining hall, and Viktor too burst into a sprint.

He swung around and into the dining hall right behind the orderlies. Small, bald, corpulent Michal Macháček sat huddled in a corner, cradling something unseen in bloodstained hands. Across the hall a young female nurse was standing, both hands held to her cheek, bright blood streaming between the fingers and down her forearms. The orderlies barrelled across the dining room, colliding with chairs and sending them flying, before all three fell on Macháček and wrestled him face-down on to the ground, pinioning his arms to the floor. A broken glass tumbler, slick with blood, rolled from his grasp, and he screamed as he struggled unsuccessfully to retrieve it.

Seeing that Macháček was under control, Viktor rushed over to the nurse. He recognized her as Gita Horáková, a slim, dark-haired girl of about twenty whom he had noticed before for her prettiness. Despite his urging, she refused to take her hands away from her face. When he did succeed in easing her shaking fingers from her cheek, he understood her reticence. The relief of the pressure resulted in gouts of bright blood pulsing over her hands and his from an ugly, ragged gash that ran from her cheek close to her right eye and down deep into the risorius muscle. Viktor could see the bone-white gleam of her zygomatic arch through the blood and ripped flesh. He knew right away that the wound would heal bulkily and leave a disfiguring scar; and the damage to her zygomaticus and risorius would leave her with a crooked smile for the rest of her life. If she ever did smile again.

He took a clean handkerchief from his pocket and folded it into a pad, instructing the terrified nurse to press it to the wound.

'I'm going to take you to the infirmary,' he said with firm but gentle authority. 'We'll get you fixed up there.' He called over his shoulders to where the orderlies had Macháček pinioned. 'Patient secured?'

'Yes, Doctor,' the chief orderly called over, his hefty knee jammed into the small of the patient's back. Macháček whimpered piteously, not out of fear or pain, but out of desperation to reclaim his trophy, his gaze still fixed on the glass that lay shattered and beyond his reach. Viktor could see a pool of blood like a halo around his outstretched hand. He'd clearly also injured himself with the glass.

'Then get him into a restraint jacket and back to his quarters,' said Viktor. 'Give him fifty milligrams of sodium amytal, wait sixty seconds, then give him a second dose of fifty milligrams. When he's quiet, take him to the infirmary.'

Viktor put his arm around the shoulders of the nurse, his other hand ensuring she kept pressure on the wound, and steered her out of the hall and towards the infirmary. He could feel the quiver of her shock as they walked and he worried that she might faint. She wept now, trying to restrain her sobs and the movement of her mouth.

'What happened?' he asked.

'I don't know. He was quiet. I brought him into the dining hall and he sat down no trouble at all. We haven't had any trouble with him since he was sent here. I went to get him a drink and when I came back he had that glass. I have no idea where it came from. I mean, only staff get glasses, and they're all supposed to be accounted for.' She started to shake more. 'But I don't know if it was one of our glasses. It looked different.'

'We're nearly there,' said Viktor soothingly. 'Not far to the infirmary now.'

'He was just sitting there, cradling the glass in his hands and staring at it, staring *into* it, like he could see something else there. I told him he had to give me the glass and he looked at me as if I were crazy. Then when I tried to take it from him . . .' She broke down further and Viktor was aware that he was now having to carry much of her weight, her legs giving beneath her.

They burst through the doors and into the infirmary to be faced by two other nurses and Dr Platner. All three rushed forward and took charge of the injured nurse from Viktor. Krakl emerged from a side room and ordered the nurses to take their colleague into the treatment room and onto a hospital cot.

Viktor stood in the hall with Platner and explained what had happened.

'We'll take care of her. I'll stitch the wound myself,' said Platner.

He nodded to Viktor's jacket and shirt. 'You'd better go and get your-self cleaned up.'

Viktor looked down and saw a large, dark bloom of blood blotted into his shirt, tie and the lapel and shoulder of his jacket. He stared at it dumbly for a moment.

'Are you all right?' asked Platner.

Viktor pulled himself together. 'I'm fine,' he said, shaking his head in disbelief. 'Professor Románek is right, sometimes you forget just how sick, just how dangerous, our patients are.'

'That's where we differ,' said Platner, his expression serious. 'I never do.'

*V*iktor watched the pink-tinged water in the white-enamelled basin swirl around the steel ring of the drain. He scooped up cold water from the running tap and palmed his face with it, rubbing the back of his neck.

Viktor had been shocked by the Glass Collector's actions. Despite his crimes, Michal Macháček had never before shown violence to a member of the medical or care staff. There would have to be an investigation about how a piece of glassware that should have been accounted for fell into the hands of a patient. There would also be questions about what event or action could have triggered the change in Macháček.

Towelling his face and neck dry, he put on a clean shirt and tie. The soiled ones were beyond remedy, but he had folded his suit jacket up, binding it with string in a brown paper package, and intended to see if there was any magic to be worked on it by the hospital laundry. He looked at himself in the mirror above the washbasin and combed his thick black hair back from his broad brow. As he did so, he could see the same tiredness, the same dark shadows under the eyes, that he had seen in Judita earlier in the day.

Maybe, he thought, it was this place. Maybe it was being locked up with madness, held in the ineluctable stone embrace of the castle and smothered by the blankets of forest around it that sucked the vitality out of you. Yet Judita felt safe here, that the real madness lay outside, beyond the enfoldments of stone and forest.

In any case, Viktor had a job to do here. A quest to fulfil. This place, and the monstrous minds captive within it, was the only environment that could allow him to fulfil that quest.

He decided to visit the infirmary before he started his narcosynthesis session with Pavel Zelený, the so-called Woodcutter. Platner was off duty by the time Viktor arrived but his unsmiling assistant, Krakl, was there.

'I thought I would see how Nurse Horáková is doing,' said Viktor. 'May I see her?'

Krakl shrugged. 'This way.' He led Viktor along the infirmary corridor. 'We've sedated her. Herr Dr Platner cleaned and stitched the wound. Made a damned fine job of it too. She was making such a fuss about her looks. Stupid woman. So frivolous.'

'Frivolous?'

'Six inches lower and it would have been her carotid or jugular that got severed. She wouldn't be worrying about her looks then.'

Viktor was about to say something, but they had turned off the corridor into one of the treatment rooms. The lights had been dimmed and the young nurse lay on the bed, quiet but not asleep, her gaze fixed on some point on the ceiling. A thick cotton pad, held in place by gauze and bandages, covered the wound, but Viktor could see her cheek was distended and swollen. Bruising had set in and was emphasized by the violet iodine staining on her skin showing from beneath the edges of the dressing.

She turned and smiled sleepily when she saw Viktor. The swelling of the cheek immobilized one side of her mouth and made her smile lopsided, twisted. Viktor wondered how much movement she would get back eventually. He took her hand and asked her how she was.

'I'm fine,' she said. She thanked Viktor for all he had done, and he replied by saying that she should thank Dr Platner instead: that Dr Krakl had told him what a good job he had done.

She looked past Viktor to Krakl and her eyes filled with something cold for a moment.

'Dr Platner was very kind,' she said. 'Do you think I'll be badly scarred?'

Viktor ignored Krakl's sigh behind him. 'You'll have a scar, but I wouldn't worry too much about it. Dr Platner's skill will have minimized it and you'll probably be able to disguise it with make-up.' He smiled to conceal the falsehood: he had seen the wound. 'You just rest and get better.'

'Thank you again,' she said. 'I don't know what I'd have done if you hadn't—'

'It was nothing. You get some sleep now.'

Viktor followed Krakl back out into the corridor and said goodbye, explaining he had a narcosynthesis session arranged.

'We never had any trouble with him before.'

'What?' Viktor turned to Krakl.

'Michal Macháček – he never gave us any trouble before.'

'I know, but as Professor Románek has pointed out so many times, you can never let your guard down. There isn't a patient in here who isn't unpredictable and potentially lethally dangerous.'

Krakl shrugged. 'All I know is that we never had trouble with Macháček until your so-called narcosynthesis session with him.'

Viktor shook his head disbelievingly. 'You're implying that this attack was the result of the treatment? Or maybe even my clinical mismanagement of a patient?'

'All I'm saying is that it is reasonable to suggest that something about these *sessions* may have triggered his violent behaviour. That you maybe unlocked some aggression that had otherwise remained contained.'

'With respect, Dr Krakl, that reveals a profound lack of understanding of how these sessions work. Of that whole aspect of psychiatry and psychology.'

'Oh I understand it, all right.' There was now open contempt in Krakl's voice. 'Treatment for the untreatable. A whole thesaurus of jargon for conditions when one word suffices: "madness". Cod philosophy and pseudoscience to over-complicate a simple fact of nature: that occasionally people are born defective. Some with physical defect, others with mental defect. And, of course, there's always a sekel to be made out of these theories – and that's why the father of your psychology, Freud, is a Jew. Psychology isn't just a pseudoscience, it's a Jewish money-making racket, and that makes it doubly dangerous.'

'Well, if you believe all of that, why in God's name do you work in an asylum, man? And incidentally, I'm a Jungian psychologist, not a Freudian – not that Sigmund Freud being Jewish has a damned thing to do with anything.'

'I work here because I'm needed. I work here because we have to keep the mad from the sane. Confine them – or at least confine them until a better solution is found.'

'And Dr Platner shares these views?'

'They're my views. What Dr Platner believes is a matter for him. What *I* believe is that the hocus-pocus you indulge in during these sessions has no positive benefit. In fact, I believe the sessions are potentially harmful and that there will be more incidents like this attack if you don't stop them.'

Viktor looked at the tall, thin, bent, hawk-like figure of Krakl, suppressing the urge to grab him and smash his fist into his face. If this was the 'master race', he thought, then God help us all.

'I haven't time to listen to this nonsense,' he said instead, turning his back to Krakl and heading out of the infirmary. 'I have more hocus-pocus to perform.'

*V*iktor arrived in the tower's session room early, setting up his equipment before sitting quietly for a moment, gathering himself and easing his own mind before delving deep into the mind of another. He was doubly rattled, he knew that: the assault on the nurse had shaken him and brought home Románek's warnings; but Krakl had riled him too.

The truth was that Viktor *was* uneasy that Macháček's violent behaviour might have had something to do with the session. What if the voice he had heard really had been some hidden aspect that Viktor had unwittingly released? Added to that was the churning in the gut he felt every time he thought about Krakl and his views; about Judita's fears of persecution, the nightmares of slaughter and devastation that haunted her; about how Krakl seemed to give those insubstantial fears real form.

He sat alone in the circular, dense-walled and high-vaulted room and thought of these things. For some reason another even greater madness from centuries before came to mind. A legendary madness that had been confined, hidden somewhere behind these walls. Instead of bringing him peace, his isolation in the castle's tower room and the pattern of his thoughts stirred something else in Viktor.

He was, he realized, for some reason he couldn't pin down, truly afraid.

* * *

There was a knock at the door and when he answered it, Viktor found Professor Románek standing in the castle hallway, frowning perturbedly.

'I just wanted to thank you for your swift actions,' Románek said. 'A most unfortunate incident and a terrible lapse of security.'

'Please, come in, Professor.'

Románek stepped into the converted granary and took in the circular walls, the examination couch and desk at its centre, the cubes, reels and cables of the recording equipment. 'I'll only keep you a minute,' he said. 'I just wanted to thank you for helping that poor girl. And for taking charge of the situation.'

'It was nothing,' said Viktor. He could tell that wasn't the real reason for Románek's visit. 'Have you worked out how he got the glass from the kitchens?'

Románek's frown deepened. 'That's the thing – from the fragments we gathered up, it wasn't an item from the canteen or kitchens. It was some kind of blue-green glass – more decorative than functional. It's beginning to look as if Macháček had it with him: had it hidden on his person and brought it into the canteen. Like I said, a terrible lapse of security.'

'But where would he have got it if it didn't belong to the canteen?'

'That's what's puzzling us.' Románek paused for a moment. 'Dr Kosárek, do you think there was anything about Macháček's narco-synthesis treatment that could have triggered this episode?'

Viktor suppressed a sigh: the real reason for Románek's visit, and the same suspicion that Krakl had voiced less diplomatically.

'Absolutely not, Professor,' Viktor said firmly. 'In fact, these sessions should soothe, not inflame the psychoses of the patients. I'm afraid Macháček's violence is as great a shock to me as it is to you. What about this policeman who wants to interview Macháček?'

'I'll deal with that,' said Románek. 'It will have to be cancelled. Or at least postponed. You have another session this evening?'

'Yes,' said Viktor, 'with Pavel Zelený, the Silesian.'

Románek regarded Viktor for a long moment. 'Very well then. Thank you again, Dr Kosárek.'

*P*avel Zelený was a simple woodsman of limited intellect from Silesian Moravia. Viktor knew little about Czech Silesia, other than that Sigmund Freud had been born there. It wasn't a place he had had call to visit and he often found it difficult to follow the Lach dialect in which many Silesians spoke. Zelený's case notes, and the brief, non-drug-mediated conversation Viktor had already had with him, suggested that – though he tended to lapse into Lach – he could speak standard Czech to a reasonable degree. The case notes also advised, however, that the Silesian's intelligence was on the lower limit of normal, and that he had never learned to read or write.

When Zelený was brought in, he was wearing a neat white shirt and suit trousers, obviously supplied by the hospital. He was a large, solidly conformed man, clean shaven, although his strong jaw was blued by the evening ghost of a beard.

As it had been the first time Viktor met him, the Woodcutter's appearance was strangely disconcerting: dressed in nondescript city clothes, there was nothing about the man to suggest that this was a rural manual labourer, other than his clearly athletic build. Indeed, Zelený's face was handsome and well proportioned, his green eyes bright and suggesting an intelligence that the case notes assured was not there.

The forestry worker had been mildly sedated already and did

not resist when guided over to the adjustable couch and fastened in, but Viktor noted that this time four orderlies had accompanied the patient. Unlike Macháček, Zelený had attacked staff in the past, and the man's physical strength combined with his emotional volatility had marked him as a patient with whom special care had to be taken.

Once Zelený was secured, Viktor administered the cocktail of sedatives and waited for them to take effect. Once they did, he switched on the K1 Magnetophon and began the session.

The drugs seemed to dissolve Zelený's will particularly quickly, as if its fabric was woven from lighter thread than the other patients', and he responded to Viktor's questions without protest or resistance. His voice was surprisingly soft for such a big man and, as expected, he spoke with a strong accent, his Czech sprinkled through with Silesian and Polish inflections and dialect.

Once Viktor had led the Woodsman into the depths of his own mind, Pavel Zelený told his story.

'We were happy. Me an' my wife, we were happy. Šarlota was a pretty lass, a strong lass, and she was happy with me. The two of us, well we were like two sides of the same coin, if you know what I mean. For four years we was like that. Four happy years.'

'What happened to change things?' asked Viktor.

'The kids – twin boys – came along and everything was suddenly all different. But it had started to change even before that. She became sly. Secretive. And she didn't want to lie with me as much as we had to start with. When we were first married, like.'

'Did she say why?'

'Šarlota blamed the forest. She said it frightened her. Not just what might be hidden in it, but the forest itself. I laughed at that – I've lived and worked in forests all my life. We had a cottage through my work, an estate house. It was a nice enough place, but it was deep in the forest. She worried about when the kids would have to go to school, because the cottage was three kilometres from the village.

The nearest other house was the estate manager's, and even that was over a kilometre away.'

'So it was the isolation, the being lonely that got to her?' asked Viktor.

'I suppose. But she said it different. She said it was the forest. That it scared her – and that she had started to see things in the dark between the trees. She said the shadows was alive – that they was full of ghosts, spirits. She said she had been told as a child about all the demons and fairies and wood-witches that lived in the forest. I tried to explain to her that it was just the way the light changed and moved between the trees. But she didn't accept that: she said the forest was full of things we didn't understand. But there wasn't nothing I could do to calm her down. We couldn't leave the forest: it was my job. My work was among the trees.'

'What about you? From what you're saying you didn't believe in forest spirits?' asked Viktor.

'I didn't say that. That's what I told Šarlota – that I didn't believe in them – but like I said, all my life I've lived in the woods. You have to live and work in the forest to understand its ways.'

'Its ways?'

'The forest is alive. I don't mean just the trees and the mosses and the plants and the animals – they're all just parts of it, like fingers or hair or skin are parts of us – I mean the *forest*. It's a great spreading mind that stretches out and is filled with shadows and light. And more than that – it *dreams*. It dreams all kinds of things. Good things. And bad things.'

'And forest spirits?'

Zelený nodded a sluggish affirmation, the movement of his head slowed by the drugs in his system. 'They're all part of the dreaming. You see, the forest's dreaming and people's dreaming – it's like they get all mixed up and tangled. Like the roots of a new tree weaving its way between the roots of an old tree and getting all tangled up in them, you know? If you stay in the forest long enough, you start to dream its dreams. You start to see the demons and the angels and the spirits in the shadows between the trees. I think that's what started to happen to Šarlota. I think she started to see the spirits without understanding them.'

'So you think she was having hallucinations – I mean, seeing things that weren't there?'

'Oh they were there all right. They're real all right. They play tricks on you like. There's the Ten-kdo-číhá-vzadu – the He-Who-Hides-Behind – what watches you and walks right behind you in your footsteps but hides behind a tree as soon as you turn. And the region where we lived is the home of the forest giant Krakonoš – what the Germans call Rübezahl – and then there's the male wood spirits what's called the Leši, and the female Viła wood-witches. Or there's the black demon Čert, and of course great Veles himself, the spirit of the forest . . . The forest is their home because they are dreamed by the forest.'

'But you told your wife none of this?'

'It would only have frightened her more. I thought she'd get used to it in time. When you live for a long time in the forest, you get used to the spirits. I guess she did get used to them, after all.' Zelený sighed, his sadness attenuated by the sedatives. 'Šarlota changed. Changed again, I mean. This time it was a big change. She stopped complaining about the forest. In fact she started to go for walks in it all the time. Take the kiddies with her, like. But she didn't want to know about me no more. She didn't want me near her.' Zelený paused to think of the right expression. 'She didn't want me to do no *husbandly duties.*'

'She offered no reason for this?' asked Viktor.

'No. Just that she was tired. But I knew. I knew the truth. She was lying with another. Someone else was being husband to her.'

'How could that be? You said you lived remotely.'

'She met someone in the woods. I worked out that she had a forest lover – or that she had a lover coming to her when I was in the forest working. And there were other signs.' Again Zelený nodded dully through the drugs, affirming to himself his conclusion. 'The children started to look at me odd. They never wanted to talk to me or spend time with me. And the three of them – my wife and the children – would go off into the woods more and more often.

'And the children, the twins – one Sunday when I wasn't working, they was playing out at the back of the cottage. They didn't know I could hear them, but I did. I heard them. I heard them all right.'

'What were they saying?'

'That's the thing – I don't know what they was saying. I couldn't understand anything they said. They were talking – whispering really, like they wanted no one to hear them – in this strange language, nothin' like no language I'd ever heard before.'

'German?'

Zelený shook his head. 'I don't speak German but I know it when I hear it. This wasn't no German. It wasn't no German or Czech or Polish or Russian. It wasn't any language of ordinary men. The words were strange, not like words at all but more like purrs and clicks and growls. It wasn't human talk, know what I mean? It wasn't no language of this world. I knew then something had to be done. That I had to find proof.

'But it wasn't easy. The estate I worked for made me work hard, so hard. I had a quota to fill every day before the manager came with the horse team to start hauling the timber back to the yard. It meant I was away from first light when the forest was just coming to life and I couldn't keep an eye on them. But there was this one day when the sky was so full of a coming storm it was almost black, so the manager says to me that he's brought forward the pick-up. It meant that I arrived home that little bit earlier. But instead of going straight back to the cottage, I slipped off the trail and into the forest and hid in bushes where I could see everything what was going on. I'd catch them all right. And I did. I saw him.'

'Whom did you see?'

'I heard them first – from inside the cottage. The sound of my wife – *my* wife – moaning like a whore, while all the time the children were playing outside. After a while he came out. The Grey Man. He was tall, taller and thinner than any human man could ever be, and he was all grey. He came out of the cottage and I could see he wasn't human. He had a long, sharp nose and his mouth was huge and like it was smiling, but it wasn't: it was just twisted that way 'cause he had so many teeth – a hundred or more. Long, sharp teeth like needles. Everything 'bout him was sharp, not just his teeth: his face was all angles; his eyes were hard and sharp like diamonds. And he didn't take the path, but went straight back into the forest, into the deepest part of it. Where it was all dense and dark, like. He just sort of dissolved into the shadows, like he had melted. But I'd seen him long enough to recognize who he was. I knew who the Grey Man was. I knew that all right.'

'So who did you think he was?' asked Viktor.

Zelený dropped his voice almost to a whisper. 'I *knew* who he was – he was Kostěj the Deathless, you see. You know him? The immortal evil demon of the woods. I knew then that my wife was a wood-witch and a demon's whore. Then it all made sense, you see? Then I understood it all. Šarlota was a demon's whore all right, but maybe more than that. There's this swamp demoness; she seduces men and steals children so she can replace them with her own. She's the one what's called Divoženka. Then I seen it. I seen it all for what it was – Šarlota was Divoženka the swamp demon whore and stealer of children; that she had been going into the forest to bathe in filthy swamp water and fuck with Kostěj. And the children? I knew now for a fact that they wasn't mine: my children were dead and Šarlota had replaced them with *odmieńce* – change-lings. They was the spawn of Kostěj and the language I had heard them speaking was *forest* language. It was the talk of tree demons and underground spirits.'

'And you believed all this, Pavel?' asked Viktor. 'Do you still believe it?'

'Of course I do. It's all true. Why would I have done what I done if it hadn't been all true?'

'But this Grey Man you saw,' said Viktor, 'don't you see he couldn't have been Kostěj the Deathless? Kostěj the Deathless is just an old Slavic myth. He's not real. Nor are *odmieńce* changelings or Divoženka a swamp demon. It's all just superstition. Fairy stories.'

'Oh but he is real. And the myths are real. That's how I knew what to do. You see, I couldn't kill Kostěj because he truly is deathless. He keeps his death locked up far, far away from his body. You know the story – a long, long time ago, Kostěj travelled to the magical island of Buyan. His death is hidden in the form of a silver pin, hidden inside an egg, inside a duck, inside a hare, inside an iron chest buried under the magical Green Oak. And as long as the pin of his Death is hidden away, no one – not you, not me, not nobody – can kill Kostěj. And he has the gift of bringing others what are dead back to life: he breathes into the mouths of the dead and makes them live again, but without their souls. So that's why I had to do it the way I did. It wasn't a pleasant job, but I knew I had to do it.'

'You mean killing your wife and children with your axe? Hacking them to death?' asked Viktor.

'Yes,' he said matter-of-factly. 'But it was much more than that. And anyway, they wasn't my children and wife, they wasn't my family. They was a demon family – Kostěj's *odmieńce* bastards and their witch dam. And killing them with an axe wasn't enough, don't you see? If Kostěj found them, he would breathe into their mouths and bring them back to soulless life.'

Viktor referred to the case notes again. Again there were police photographs, but he found it difficult to look at them with professional dispassion. He found it difficult to look at them at all.

'You do see why I had to do it the way I done it, don't you?' asked Zelený. I had to chop their bodies up into really small pieces so I could scatter them through the forest. You see, I had to make it difficult for Kostěj to bring them back. And of course I had to find special hiding places for the heads. It was easy with the children, because their heads was so small.'

Viktor sighed. Suddenly he felt weighed down by the onerous banality of Zelený's madness and crimes. And by the absurdity of his own quest to find the so-called Devil Aspect. There was nothing more in this simple, unlettered woodsman than a vulgar and sordid madness, a crude paranoid delusion that had resulted in the butchery of his wife and children. There was no splitting of the personality, no elaborate facet to be exposed. No proof of his Devil Aspect theory.

For a moment there was only the sound in the room of the measured turning of the recorder's reels.

Zelený seemed content to remain still, his vague eyes on Viktor without question or impatience. Viktor made a sudden decision and snatched up the hypodermic and recharged it with a fresh dose of sedatives, confirming out loud the size of dose for the benefit of the tape.

'What?' asked Zelený.

'Nothing Pavel,' said Viktor. 'I was talking to the machine. I'm going to give you another injection, it'll relax you more, but it might make you a little more sleepy, so try to stay awake.'

'All right.'

Viktor waited a few minutes for the additional narcotics to take effect. Zelený was now in a limbo of consciousness, neither asleep nor awake.

'I want to talk to the Grey Man,' said Viktor. He could feel his heart beating faster in his chest: the increased dose was at the limit of what he dared administer, perhaps even beyond. He knew he was taking risks with his patient's life in pursuit of his theory. 'I want to talk with Kostěj the Deathless,' he said urgently. 'Are you there? Are you asleep inside Pavel Zelený?'

There was nothing.

'Kostěj? Are you there?'

Still the turning of the spools was the only sound in the room. Viktor noticed that Zelený's breathing was becoming quieter, shallower, the interval between breaths longer. The signs of dangerous hypoventilation. And of sedative overdose.

'Pavel? Pavel can you hear me?'

No reply.

'Pavel?'

The patient's breathing was now barely audible and Viktor could see only the slightest movement in the broad chest. He cursed his impatience and carelessness in administering the extra dose.

Sensing his patient was now in dangerous respiratory depression, Viktor fumbled with the syringe, searching with his free hand in the tin container for an ampule of the picrotoxin antidote. It slipped from his fingers and rolled across the table top. He made a grab for it but missed and the ampule rolled off the table.

When he went around to pick it up, he found the glass had broken on the floor, the fluid contents spilled as a viscous, glossy teardrop on the grey flagstones. He cursed. It was the only dose of antidote he had brought with him. He rushed over to his patient and shook his shoulders: Zelený was inert in his grasp.

'Pavel?' He shook him again. When he got no response he tried a sternal rub, pinching and twisting the skin on his patient's chest for a pain reaction. There was none: Zelený remained inert, his eyes closed, his breathing barely perceptible. Viktor ran back to his desk. He would hit the buzzer to summon an orderly to fetch more picrotoxin.

There was a great, shuddering gasping of breath behind him. Viktor turned and saw Zelený had regained consciousness: full, vital consciousness. The Woodcutter's eyes, which had offered the false promise of intelligence, seemed now to fulfil it. They were fixed on Viktor.

Viktor stood confused for a moment. That Zelený, with so much sedative in his system, had regained consciousness was unlikely; that he had regained it so fully, so lucidly, so intently was practically impossible.

'Are you all right, Pavel?'

Zelený didn't answer for a moment, but watched Viktor with his bright green, penetratingly intelligent eyes.

The patient's voice, when it did come, was totally altered. Deep, resonant, commanding, it turned the circular room of the castle's former grain store into an amphitheatre.

'You may call me Mr Hobbs,' it said, in deeply tonal English.

'You've never talked about your brother, Dr Bartoš.' Smolák offered the police surgeon a cigarette, which he took. The detective lit it, then one for himself. 'Not that it's anyone else's concern.'

'It isn't,' said Bartoš, bluntly. Sitting small and crumpled across the desk from Smolák, he looked around the detective's office. On the third floor of the Prague Police presidium, it was a self-consciously working environment: cluttered with files, law books, police manuals; but devoid of personal items or the slightest hint of the individual who occupied it.

The office had only one window, but it was large and there were no overshadowing buildings opposite to mitigate the daylight's brightness. When he had first moved into the office, Smolák had repositioned his desk so it sat directly in front of the window, allowing him to sit with his back to the daylight, which cast Smolák in partial shadow, but shining into the faces of visitors, such as Dr Bartoš.

It was a trick he had learned from stories about Emperor Karel IV, who had his audience throne set between two high, bright windows in his otherwise dark audience chamber at Karlštejn Castle. It set the emperor in unreadable shadow while his vassals stood before him in stark brightness.

Plain daylight, as both emperor and detective had learned, was the hardest place to hide a lie.

'But I suppose everyone speculates about it,' said Bartoš eventually, resignedly. 'That I do this work because of my brother and what he did.'

'Do you?'

'No.' The small, crumpled doctor gave a tight, bitter laugh, then took a contemplative pull on his cigarette. The smoke coiled blue, grey and silver in the cold winter daylight. 'We deal with murder and murderers every day. We see the banal reality of homicide, where almost every killing is within uneducated and lower intelligence groups. Drunkards and criminals mainly. There is no great lesson to be learned there about what motivated my brother to commit the crimes he did. Dominik's crimes – the murders he committed – were exceptional. But that was because *everything* about him was exceptional: his mind, his ambition, his madness. If I had truly wanted to unravel that mystery, I would have become a psychiatrist, not a police surgeon.'

'You had no clue? No suspicions about his mental state?' asked Smolák.

A great sadness swept across the physician's face. 'My brother was the most gentle human being I have ever known. For Dominik, this world, this universe, was brim-full of wonder. The wonders that we can see and the wonders yet to be revealed. That's why he became a scientist: to uncover more *wonder*.

'As a physicist, he devoted his life to understanding the hidden mechanics of the universe. The so-called quantum realm, where absolutely everything we know, everything we hold true about reality is turned on its head. Obviously, as a doctor I've got a scientific background myself, but even I don't understand that stuff. It's an upside-down, counter-intuitive world that demands a robust sanity if you're going to explore it. I suppose Dominik's sanity just wasn't robust enough. Somewhere in there, he found the wonder he sought all right, but it turned out to be some dark, dark wonder. Too dark for his mind to deal with. He'd been looking for reason and science, but he found madness and magic instead. The things he started to believe . . .'

Smolák nodded slowly. 'You do know he wasn't responsible for his actions, don't you? That he was at the mercy of his insanity?'

'I do.' He seemed to think about it for a moment. 'Yes, I do.'

'Yet you've never visited him until now.'

'I suppose I still blamed him, somehow. What he did was so monstrous, so horrific. Even knowing how unlike Dominik it would be to harm another living soul, and having heard all the proof of his madness, I guess I still blame him.'

'But you want to see him now?'

'When I heard you were going to the asylum—'

'I'm afraid the visit's been postponed even further,' said Smolák. 'The patient I want to talk to has apparently attacked a member of the nursing staff.'

'But you're still going?' Bartoš frowned.

'Next week. If you still want to come.'

'I do.'

There was a pause. Václav Bartoš smoked contemplatively for a moment. 'I saw the police artist's impression of your suspect,' he said eventually. 'The one you got from the shop-girl's description.'

'I got it into the *Lidové Noviny* and the *Prager Tagblatt*. Most of the other papers took it too. A damned lot of good it'll do,' said Smolák. 'A tall unshaven man in a shabby black coat and hat.'

'I think it may even do some harm,' said Bartoš.

'Oh, how so?'

'Mythology. Like you I don't think anyone could identify someone from that illustration. A shave and a change of outfit is all your killer needs – and he's probably done that already if he's seen the impression. But it really is like the London Jack the Ripper case all over again. People lose sight of the reality of a maniac ripping women apart and romanticize him, mythologize him. That's what happened in London and I fear that's what's happening here. The problem with that description and the impression drawn from it is that when people look in the papers they see a ghost, not a man. A faceless ghoul that has more to do with folklore than reality.'

'And you think that is counter-productive?' asked Smolák.

'I think it allows the public to enjoy the thrill of a story without the fear of the reality. The reality is too much to bear, so they detach themselves from it. That's maybe how all myths were born.'

For a moment, Smolák watched the grainy blue-grey ciga-rette-smoke ghost of his own breath coil and drift in the sunlight. 'Dr Bartoš, do you remember the conversation we had about Tobar Bihari, when I asked you if you believed madness can take on its own form? That someone who is insane could act homicidally and not be aware of it?'

'I do. But Bihari is dead and the murders continue. And if you have my brother in mind, that wasn't the case.'

'No, no – I'm talking broadly,' said Smolák. 'You agreed that there is such a thing as a truly split personality.'

Dr Bartoš shrugged. 'Like I said when we discussed the possibil-ity with your gypsy suspect, I've read of such cases.'

'And it's possible that one identity is totally unaware of what the other is doing? Even committing murder?'

'Again, in the cases I've heard about, that is by no means uncom-mon. In many instances the division of personality happens so that one splintered part is free to act out deepest desires without any other aspect knowing about it. Free from the inhibition and guilt that would otherwise accompany such behaviour.'

'So what on earth could cause that to happen to someone?' asked Smolák. 'Would they be born that way? A child growing up with two or more people inside?'

'Again, I think you should ask the experts when we visit the asy-lum, but my understanding is that it is an event, some childhood trauma that usually causes the personality to split. Very often, peo-ple have some deep, dark secret in their lives that they don't know about, simply because it's been *allocated* to another identity. They don't have to face up to what happened to them, or what they did, because it happened to someone else. It's just that their mind has invented that someone else.'

Smolák shook his head in wonder. 'So, take our Leather Apron killer – there's a chance he commits these murders and can't remember them?'

Bartoš pondered a moment. 'I don't think that Leather Apron is likely to be that type of case. I think he knows exactly who he is and what his mission is. But, technically, yes, I suppose it's possible. But you should hope that it isn't the case.'

'Why so?'

'Any murderer will usually do everything to hide his crimes from others: destroy evidence, cover up traces,' said Bartoš. 'In the kind of case you're talking about, the *others* the killer hides his crimes from includes himself. He will actively hide the evidence from the other part or parts of his personality. Remember that we're not talking about one person. We're talking about one *body* but two or more personalities. Each acts independently, and most of the time in mutual ignorance.'

'But there must be some evidence, surely,' said Smolák. 'Some *trace* left. Like a fingerprint left in the mind.'

'What kind of trace are you thinking of?'

Smolák paused for a moment. 'Dreams,' he said decisively. 'Do you think it's possible for a suppressed memory of a crime to manifest itself in a dream?'

'A dream?' Bartoš considered it, then nodded. 'Yes. In fact, that would be the most likely form for it to take.'

CHAPTER SIXTEEN

*T*he first thing Viktor did was to glance over at the recording device: he was relieved to see the tape spools still turning, the microphone connected and sitting poised on the desk. Everything that was happening was being recorded.

He took a deep breath. 'Who are you?' he asked.

'I told you,' the voice said in English. 'You may call me Mr Hobbs.'

'My English . . .' Viktor struggled with the foreign words, his racing mind dealing with the absurdity of a simple, illiterate Silesian woodsman having a better command of the language. 'My English, it is not so good. Where did you learn English?'

'I learned it many years ago. I spoke it as my native tongue for a long, long while. I speak many languages – wearing each like a coat for a season of being. If you struggle with English, I can speak to you in French, German, Czech, Polish, Russian . . .'

Viktor stared at his fully awake, fully alert patient. This was impossible. What was happening made absolutely no sense whatsoever. Absurd. He glanced again at the Magnetophon: the spools reassured him once more with their slow turning.

'Would you prefer if I spoke Czech or German?' asked Zelený in the latter. Viktor noted that his patient spoke it perfectly and without accent.

'German is fine,' said Viktor. 'Are you Kostěj the Deathless?'

'Kostěj the Deathless?' Zelený's laugh was hearty; disturbingly resonant in the treatment room. 'I heard you earlier, trying to summon up ancient demons. You sounded more like a witch-doctor than a physician of the human mind. As you said yourself, Kostěj is a myth.' He paused for a moment, his handsome face sharing a smile and a thoughtful frown. 'But in a way, I suppose that is what I am. I share a lot with Kostěj, inasmuch as I am deathless.'

'Pavel,' said Viktor, 'I need you to explain how it is you can speak so many languages. How did you learn them? Why is your voice so altered?'

Viktor's patient shook his head. 'I'm not Pavel Zelený. But you've guessed that already. I'm something else. Something quite *other*. Something beyond your understanding. And I know what I know because I have been around for a very, very long time. Much longer than this oafish woodcutter through whom I speak. I have seen such things – such great horror and terror. Things you are incapable of imagining.'

'*Who* are you?' Viktor heard something tight and shrill edge into his own voice and fought to compose himself.

'I told you twice now. You may call me Mr Hobbs.'

'I mean *what* are you?'

'That, my dear Dr Kosárek, is something you already know but don't dare to allow yourself to believe.' Zelený looked at the thick, blue-white painted walls of the ancient grain store, then up into the wooden vaults above him. 'The greatest danger in seeking out the Devil, my dear doctor, is that you might find him.'

'Are you saying you are the Devil?' asked Viktor, his heart racing.

'I am saying that you embarked on your journey of discovery without sufficient consideration. You set out in search of something that lives inside the mad, inside the sane; inside others and, of course, inside yourself. But you didn't take the time to consider what you might discover.'

'And what have I discovered?'

'You have discovered me.'

'The crimes Zelený committed – the murders of his wife and children – were you there?' asked Viktor. 'Was it you who killed them?'

'The woodcutter's wife went into the dark spaces of the forest. She sought out demons and spirits and elementals in those dark spaces. She went in hunt of that which frightened her most. That is what became her undoing. She found what she was looking for. She found me. And now, my dear Viktor, you stand in exactly the same dark spaces. You have arrived. You are now lost in the forest of the mind. You should take care that it doesn't become your undoing.'

'Can you show me the way?'

'To the light?' The patient on the couch smiled handsomely, malevolently. 'Now what use would I have for light? That's not where either of us wants to go, is it? But I will lead you, fear not. Come with me, my dear Dr Kosárek, and I will lead you into a darkness beyond your imagination. But that must wait till later. I must go now.'

'Why?' asked Viktor. 'Why must you go?'

'Your patient is dying from the overdose you gave him. But don't worry, we will talk again.'

With that, Viktor's patient closed his eyes.

'Pavel?'

Once more Zelený became unresponsive. His respiration again dangerously depressed. Viktor jabbed the emergency buzzer and two orderlies burst in.

'Get me picrotoxin from the pharmacy,' Viktor shouted. 'Three ampules. Now!'

As the ringing footfalls of an orderly running along the stone-flagged hallways towards the pharmacy faded, Viktor stood over his patient, trying to get him to respond to pain stimuli. Pavel Zelený lay unresponsive, paling, fading from life.

So this, Viktor thought to himself, is where the Devil hides.

On the edge of death.

CHAPTER SEVENTEEN

*T*he ghost of the session haunted the encircling chamber of the converted grain store. Viktor found it disconcerting to hear his own voice echo in the space, only to be disturbed even more by the deep tones of 'Mr Hobbs' resonating.

When the recording reached its end, Viktor turned the Magnetophon's clunky Bakelite playback dial to the 'off' position. He stood in the room with Professor Románek, Dr Platner and Judita, who was to transcribe the recording after they discussed it.

'But this is impossible.' Professor Románek stared at the now-empty treatment couch. 'You say this – I mean what he said to start with – was good English? I don't speak the language at all.'

'From what I could tell,' said Viktor. 'I barely speak it myself. But it did sound, well, *assured*. But how a simple and supposedly illiterate woodcutter from Silesia could establish *any* knowledge of foreign languages is beyond me.'

'And it's not just foreign languages,' said Platner, his face unreadable as, like Románek, he stared at the empty couch, as if it would yield an answer. 'His German too. Did you notice his German? It was cultured, educated. Perhaps even a little antiquated. Could it be that Zelený is not who he claims to be?'

'I don't understand . . .' said Románek.

Platner turned to Viktor. 'Do you believe that what we just heard on that recording is the voice of your so-called Devil Aspect in Zelený's mind?'

'I don't know.' Viktor frowned. The truth was that after the elation of discovery, doubts had begun to creep into his mind. 'But I believe it is. Whatever it was we've just heard, it's something significant.'

'Let's for a moment accept you're right. Whether it is the Devil Aspect or some other element, some hidden dimension to Zelený's personality – everything it knows, every skill it has, *must* still be Zelený's. The so-called "Mr Hobbs" cannot know or do anything that Zelený can't know or do.'

'I suppose so, yes.'

Platner turned back to Professor Románek. 'Then that's what I mean. What we heard on the tape is the product of Zelený's mind. So Zelený *must* know how to speak English and German fluently. He cannot simply be the unlettered country bumpkin he pretends to be.'

'Then who is he?' asked Románek.

Platner shrugged. 'I don't know. But remember the terrible crimes he has committed. Perhaps he has committed terrible crimes before and sought refuge, went into hiding, under an assumed identity. It could be that Dr Kosárek here is right – or at least right in part. Maybe Zelený – or whatever his real name is – has murdered before. Maybe he is an educated, cultured, but insane man who has hidden in the identity of a simple woodcutter.'

'I don't think that likely . . .' said Viktor.

'Don't you?' Platner looked surprised. 'I would have thought you of all people would recognize the possibility. I'm not just saying that Zelený, or whatever his real name is, has simply gone into hiding from the police or justice, but he's gone into hiding from himself. Maybe he suffers from hysterical amnesia and truly doesn't know or remember who he used to be.'

Viktor nodded thoughtfully. 'A fugue state – it could be. Yes, in fact, it's the only explanation that makes sense. Dr Platner's right when he says that any aspect of Zelený's mind, including the Devil

Aspect, can only be just that: an aspect of his mind. It can't know more than Zelený knows.'

'Have you spoken to Zelený about what he said?' asked Románek.

'I did,' said Viktor. 'When I managed to counteract the effects of the sedatives and bring him around fully. I even played him part of the tape. He doesn't remember any of it. And he swears blind that the voice isn't his, has nothing to do with him. He became very agitated – seemed genuinely afraid of it.'

'Maybe he's afraid of facing up to something he has hidden deep inside,' said Platner. 'Some secret past or identity, or some deep-buried misdeeds.'

'But we have his records,' said Románek. 'We know where and when he was born.'

'Does he have parents or siblings who could identify him?' asked Judita.

Viktor referred to the file. 'No. No surviving relatives. And of course his wife and children are gone too. There's only his foreman and a couple of other workmates – but they've only known him since he started work in the forest. And his wife didn't know him much longer before that.'

'So it *is* possible that maybe there's another member of the Zelený family chopped up and buried in the woods,' said Judita. 'Let's face it, he doesn't have the look of a simple woodman. Maybe he encountered the real Pavel Zelený somewhere before he took up his appointment in the estate forest.'

'Then killed him and took his place?' Viktor's tone was sceptical. 'It all seems very far-fetched.'

'No more far-fetched,' said Platner, 'than an illiterate forester speaking Goethe's German and fluent English . . .'

'So what do we do?' asked Viktor.

It was Professor Románek who answered. 'Continue your sessions with him. See if you can coax this "Mr Hobbs" identity out of him again. In the meantime, we have this detective from the Prague

Municipal Police coming to interview Michal Macháček next week. I think it'd be a good idea if we discussed Zelený's case with him – see if they are looking for anyone who matches his description. Someone who has been on the run for the last ten years.'

Viktor nodded. They all stood in silence for a moment, still haunted by the strangeness of what they had heard. The circular tower room around them seemed ageless, timeless.

'Well, Dr Kosárek,' said Románek eventually, 'whether it's your theoretical Devil Aspect or not, one thing is for sure: you've certainly unlocked something dark.'

CHAPTER EIGHTEEN

*I*t was that night, after the Zelený session, that Judita and Viktor first made love.

He went to her room when he finished work, as she had invited him to do that morning. When he did, he found she had prepared a small supper for them both. Technically, it was forbidden for staff to have or prepare food in their quarters, but Judita had bought some cold cuts of meat, cheese, bread and a bottle of wine from the inn-keeper in the village.

The edge of their initial awkwardness softened with the wine and their talk, as they fell once more into the swift ease that had developed so quickly between them: the feeling they had known each other for lifetimes rather than weeks.

The awkwardness returned when Viktor drew Judita towards him and kissed her. She returned his kisses with a passion close to vehemence and their lovemaking was sudden and urgent. Viktor became lost in Judita's beauty and passion, but something about the almost desperate eagerness with which she made love troubled him, as if she were clinging desperately to the vitality of the act, to the moment. To life.

Afterwards they lay in Judita's bed and smoked, their talk loose and unsteered. They discussed what had happened with Zelený, and Judita could tell Viktor was still disturbed by it.

'It was so damned strange,' he said. 'I still can't make sense of it. But there again, psychiatry is all about dealing with the strange, I suppose.'

'You know something I've never asked you?' said Judita, suddenly bright. 'I've never asked you why you became a psychiatrist?'

'Why?' Viktor shrugged. 'It was the specialty I . . . I don't know . . . I just drifted towards I suppose. It was where my interests lay.'

She leaned over him and shook her head, smiling. 'I may not have known you long, but I know you well enough to know that you're not someone to drift into a career – to drift into anything. Everything you do – I don't know – it's *purposeful*. So tell me, Dr Kosárek, what's the real reason? Why did you decide to spend your life delving into madness and the darkest recesses of the human psyche? I bet there's some deep, dark secret . . .' The teasing jocularity dropped from her tone when she saw his expression cloud. 'Sorry,' she said, 'I shouldn't pry . . .'

Viktor shook his head. 'It's all right. The truth is I don't dwell on it much but I know exactly why I became a psychiatrist; I can pin it down to an exact event when I was twelve years old. My mother, you see – she suffered from depression. The greatest of the great sadnesses. Eventually she committed suicide. She hanged herself and it was I who found her.'

Judita sat up in the bed, gathering a sheet to cover her breasts. 'Oh God, Viktor, I'm sorry. I shouldn't have been so—'

'It's all right.' He smiled sadly. 'It was a long time ago, but I suppose I've always been obsessed with trying to understand the place she occupied – the nature of the mental state that drove her to kill herself. I mean, I understand why she did it, in a way, with what happened to my sister.'

'Your sister?'

'I had a younger sister. She died in an accident when she was seven. Drowned. My mother blamed herself and the guilt and the grief became too much for her.'

'Oh God, Viktor, I . . . I don't know what to say. I'm so sorry. I shouldn't have joked about—'

'It's all right.' His soft smile looked misplaced in his handsomely severe features, a stranger lost in an unfamiliar landscape. 'I've come to terms with it, I suppose.'

'Does my father know?' she asked.

'He knows some of it. As does Dr Jung. The first thing they both asked me was why I was interested in psychiatry and psychoanalysis. Dr Jung told me that psychiatry is all about answering the question that is each individual mind. He said that the hardest question to answer is your own. I guess he was right.'

There was a silence for a while, Judita wrapping her arms around his arm and resting her head on his shoulder. After a while they found their awkward way back to talking idly about their day, but he could tell Judita felt bad about dragging up painful memories. Eventually she brought up problems she was having with Krakl, the general medicine deputy, who was becoming even less restrained in expressing his anti-Semitism.

'Do you want me to talk to Professor Románek about him?' asked Viktor.

'There's nothing Románek can do,' said Judita. 'Everyone is frightened of these people. No one wants to make enemies of them in case they end up on top – in case what's happening in Germany happens here and the likes of Krakl end up with the whip hand. Which they will.'

'I'm not afraid of Krakl or his kind. I'll talk to him.'

Judita let go of his arm and shook her head vigorously. 'No – no, don't do that. It'll only make things worse.'

'We can't just let Krakl—'

'Don't get involved.' Judita cut Viktor off. 'Whether you're ready to accept it yet or not, the only thing left to do now is to get out of Czechoslovakia – to get out of Europe. It's the only hope.'

Viktor gave a small, surprised laugh. 'You can't be serious.'

'Can't I? Why shouldn't we leave the asylum to the lunatics?' She waved her hand vaguely to indicate the oppressive weight of the castle walls, and the imagined walls beyond them. 'Platner, Krakl and all their Sudeten chums see Hitler as some kind of saviour. Some kind of racial protector. Trust me, when the Nazis come marching into Czechoslovakia, Platner and Krakl will be there waving their little swastika flags with all their other *Skopčáci* chums.'

The Czech slur for Germans sounded odd in Judita's mouth. As always, she and Viktor had conversed in German. Encapsulated in that linguistic jarring, Viktor heard Judita's frustration and confusion; the shifting of the ground beneath her. Brought up to think of herself as a Bohemian German, she was now cut adrift from that identity. Despite all his reassurances, Viktor could see that she had a very real point.

'When we were at the forest chapel,' she said, 'I told you that there is no future for us. That we have to live just for this moment. Well, I had a dream last night – the strangest dream. It's been in my head all day and thinking about it has made me change my mind.' She turned to him, resting her weight on one elbow. Like an artist sketching an assured line, Viktor traced with his finger the outline of her upper arm and shoulder. Her skin felt soft and smooth under his touch.

'Another nightmare?' he asked, concerned.

She frowned. 'It was and it wasn't. It was frightening in its way, I suppose, but not like the other dreams. It was more *strange* than anything – and you know I've had so many strange dreams recently – but it showed me that I have to get out of Europe.'

'What was the dream?'

'When I was a girl, we used to go to Vienna in the summer. Back then I had no idea why we went every year, but I know now it was to do with my father's work. A seminar or symposium, I suppose. Because I remember that Dr Freud was often there. And Dr Jung. I didn't know who they were then, of course, or how they were connected to my father, but he told me later. I was just happy to go to Vienna – to see the people all elegantly dressed and visit the zoo and the shops and the cafés.'

'And this was the time you dreamt about?' asked Viktor. 'About when you went to Vienna as a child?'

'Yes. But things were different – you know, the way things are always different or odd in dreams but you just accept the differences as normal. In this dream everything was almost exactly the same as I remember it: I wore my favourite summer dress, white with blue flowers, and my favourite blue sandals. But that's where the dream changed things: in the dream my sandals – and my feet – were all dirty from walking in the gutters. My father's shoes were the same: all soiled from the gutter.'

'The gutter?'

'Yes. Every time we passed someone on the pavement, Dr Freud, my mother, my father and I had to step into the gutter to let them pass. But not Dr Jung – Dr Jung stayed on the pavement. I asked my mother why we had to do that and she said, "Why, child, it's because we're Jews. It's our place." Then she just smiled at me that way adults do when children ask a naïve question – you know, when they ask something obvious.'

Viktor smiled at her and pushed back from her face a coiled strand of dark hair. 'Given the anxieties you've expressed recently – and all of that rubbish you're having to put up with from Krakl – it's not a difficult dream to analyse.'

'No, no – there was more to it than that. Eventually we stopped stepping on and off the pavement to let others pass and simply stayed in the gutter. And all the time no one behaved as if it were in the least bit strange. We just started to walk in the gutter – to *follow* the gutter – and, as we did, more and more people joined us. All Jews. Eventually we found our way out of Vienna, and suddenly we were surrounded by trees. A forest. No one questioned why there was still a gutter for us to walk in. There was no pavement any more, just the gutter running straight and unbending into the heart of the forest. Eventually we reached a clearing and the gutter opened out into a huge square of brick and flagstone, filled with rainwater and waste.

And Jews. It was so strange. The acceptance of it all, I mean: we just stood there, mute and unmoving; no one made the slightest effort to step out and onto the forest floor – to run away from what waited for us.'

'What waited for you?' asked Viktor.

Judita frowned again. 'I didn't know for sure, but I can guess. Whatever it was, I knew it was bad, but we all just stood about waiting for it. I asked my mother where we were and she said in that same calm, patronizing tone she had used before that we had arrived. That we were now where we had always been meant to be. Where our journey had been destined to end from the start. It was then that the sky went dark with black clouds. Then I woke up.' She turned to him and held his face in her hands, her fingers cool on his cheeks. When she spoke he sensed some of the desperate urgency that had driven her lovemaking. 'Will you come?'

'Come? Come where?'

'Away. Out of Europe. America.'

He laughed uncertainly, uneasily. 'I have my work . . .'

'You could get work in America. You could get funding for your research there – and I bet more easily than here. If the Nazis take over here, European psychiatry will be dead. You know that – you know they believe psychiatry and psychology is all a Jewish sham. Believe me, if these bastards take over, the treatment of mental disorders will be handed over to slaughtermen. If we went to America, I could find work too. We would be free of all this – all this *madness.*' She let the hands slip from his face, having read his expression. 'Sorry,' she said, turning her face away. 'We've really only just met. And my problem isn't yours.'

He took her by the shoulders and turned her back to face him. 'It's not that. It isn't that at all. It's just that I don't know if I believe things here are going to be as bad as you think they will. I think we should wait and see.'

'By then it could be too late,' she said dispiritedly. 'I could find myself in that forest clearing for real. I know why I dreamt that, you see. I know what the clearing in the forest meant: the pogroms. That's what they used to do: take the Jews into the forests and kill them there, leaving them for the birds and the animals to pick over their bones. That's what was waiting for us in the dream. That's what they're going to do to us again.'

'Listen, Judita, let's just give it until I've finished my work here with these case studies. If things still look bad, then I promise I'll get you and your father out of here. I swear it. All right?'

She nodded. 'All right,' she said, but there was something dull and shadowed in her eyes.

CHAPTER NINETEEN

*G*iven the highly unusual nature of the previous session, Professor Románek insisted he sit in on the next time Viktor used hypnotic drugs on Pavel Zelený. To start with Viktor protested, explaining that for narcosynthesis to work effectively, there had to be only two Egos present: the dominant Ego of the interrogator and the dominated and drug-diminished Ego of the interrogated.

'You have my word that I'll stay quiet and sit back from you and your patient,' said Románek with his calming, country-doctor tone. 'I promise I won't interfere. If I have any questions or points to make I'll hand you a note, but otherwise be assured I'll just be an observer. I hope you understand why I feel the need to be there, Dr Kosárek: what I heard on that recording was confusing – quite disturbing really. I just want to be there to hear "Mr Hobbs" explain his presence, his existence, in such an unlikely host.'

Despite making a show of his reluctance, the truth was that Viktor found the idea of having his mentor sit in on the session strangely reassuring. While he had meant all he said about preferring to be alone with his patient during sessions, for some inexplicable reason Viktor found himself dreading the return of Mr Hobbs, and he took some comfort from the idea of having Románek in the room.

He knew from the last session that Mr Hobbs lay in the most shadowed, hardest-to-reach depths of the forester's consciousness.

So, first making sure that he had a sufficient supply of the picrotoxin antidote to hand, Viktor applied the same heavy dosage of scopolamine and sodium amytal he had before.

This time, Pavel Zelený seemed more agitated as the orderlies strapped him into the restraints, and Viktor found himself wondering if his patient, despite denying any memory of him, also dreaded the return of Mr Hobbs. Eventually the tension eased from the forester's body as the drug cocktail worked its way through his system.

Switching on the slow turning of the Magnetophon's reels, and with Professor Románek sitting in the shadows behind him, Viktor spoke to his patient in simple Czech and guided him back into the remotest geography of his own mind. Zelený responded dully and sluggishly, movements of body and mind lead-weighted by the volume of sedatives in his system. At each turn he protested that he wanted to sleep.

'You need to stay awake, Pavel. We need to talk and you need to be awake. Do you remember the time before you came to work at the estate forest?' asked Viktor.

'What do you mean?'

'Where did you learn to speak English, Pavel? Or German? You must have learned them somewhere, some time, even if you can't recall learning them. So I want to ask you about the past. Maybe a past you can't remember, things your mind is hiding from you. I want to ask you about the time before you went to work in the estate forest.'

'I don't speak no English. German neither. If you think I can then it's you that makes no sense. If you believe that then it's you that's mad. Why would you think I speak German or English?'

'Because you spoke them the other night – we discussed this before, remember? When I came to your room and told you about how you had changed after I'd given you the injection; how you spoke to me in German. English first, but because I couldn't understand it, you switched to German.'

'I don't speak no German.'

'But you did. I was here and I heard you speak it. And that means you must have learned it somewhere at some time.'

'If I spoke it the other night, why can't I remember speaking it? Why can't I speak it now?'

'You don't remember because you were narcotized – I mean, because you were sleepy because of the medicine, like you are just now. So answer my question: what do you remember about the time before you started work in the estate forest? Tell me about your life before you met your wife.'

'Šarlota?'

'Yes, your wife, Šarlota. What did you do before you met her?'

'Šarlota? Is Šarlota here?'

Viktor wrapped a deep breath around his impatience. 'Don't you remember, Pavel? Šarlota is dead. You killed your wife and your children.'

Through the drugs, Zelený shook his head in annoyance, as if Viktor had said something stupid. 'I know she's dead. Of course I know that. And I know I killed her, and why – because she became a whore to Kostěj the Deathless. But is she here?'

'How can she be here if she's dead?'

Viktor's question provoked another irritated shake of the head. 'This place is special,' Zelený almost whispered. 'That's all. There's more here than the living. There's more here than madness.' He closed his eyes and his breathing shallowed.

'Stay awake Pavel.' Viktor spoke firmly, resolutely. 'I know you want to go to sleep, but you have to answer my questions. Then you can go to sleep, but not before. I need to reach into the dark that lies before the events we've talked about. It's a darkness that only you can light up. Start by remembering the time before you went to work in the estate forest. Before you met Šarlota.'

'I worked in another forest. And before that another forest. I've always been in the forest. Worked in it, lived in it. I never learned to read and write in my own language – and I definitely didn't learn no other languages. I learned other things though. Plenty of other things. I learned about trees. About the seasons. About the changing of the forest. Them's the things I learned. Them's the things I remember. I don't remember nothing else.'

'Maybe you're forcing yourself not to remember,' insisted Viktor. 'Maybe you had another life before, some life that your mind has forced you to forget because something terrible happened. That kind of forgetting is something that happens more often than you'd think. I know this is difficult to accept, to understand, but I think that there's a chance you are not Pavel Zelený. That Pavel Zelený is someone whose life and identity you took over.'

'That's nonsense.' The woodcutter's vehemence was again muted by the drugs in his system. 'You sayin' I'm not me but someone else? That's just stupid. How could someone think they was someone they wasn't? I know who I am. I know who I am and what I did and why I did it.'

'Then tell me about further back in your past. Tell me about when you were a child,' said Viktor. 'Where did you grow up?'

Zelený repeated the scant facts listed in his case file. What he gave was an outline of a life: a sketch, not a portrait. He listed the route-points on the journey his life had taken without describing the details, the scenery, the unexpected stops on the way. What he gave as a biography matched what was officially known about him. No more, no less.

'All right,' said Viktor. 'Remember how I talked about the ocean inside you? How deep it is and how it contains every version of you there is or ever has been? I want you to sink deeper into that ocean — deeper than we've ever gone. I want us to go deep and dark and find versions of you perhaps you didn't know existed. I want to find the most secret form of you: the one that exists down there, hidden from everyone else.'

There was a pause. Then Zelený said, 'Who you're looking for don't live there.'

'What do you mean?'

'Him. The one that you want. He don't live down there. He don't live in me.'

Viktor paused, keeping his gaze on his patient and resisting the temptation to glance over his shoulder at Professor Románek. He had learned from the last session with Zelený that what he sought lay in that darkest of regions: the black darkness that lay on the brink of death itself. To find the Devil Aspect, to prove his theory about the dark architecture of madness, he would have to take his patient to mortality's edge. The Woodcutter would inhabit that dark region for the shortest of times, before yielding to the pull of the drugs and sleep. Or, if Viktor misjudged it, death.

He would have to find what he was after in that moment before he applied the picrotoxin antidote.

And all the while he was aware of Professor Románek sitting behind him, patient and silent, but judging. What judgement was being politely made about Viktor's capabilities? Was the kindly but demanding asylum director now regretting his appointment?

'I want to speak with Mr Hobbs,' Victor asked with sudden resolve and in German. 'I want to speak to the person I spoke to before.'

'I don't understand what you're saying,' said Zelený.

Viktor repeated his question in Czech.

'I don't know no Hobbs,' said Zelený, his voice leaden and a frown failing to form completely on his broad brow. 'You asked me 'bout him before. I didn't say them things you say I did. Like I told you, I don't speak no German.'

'Then who was it spoke to me, Pavel? If it wasn't you, and if there is no Mr Hobbs in you, then who was it?'

'Maybe it's him that lives here,' said Zelený absently.

'Who?'

'Him that lives here. That lives in this place. Like I said, the one you're lookin' for don't live inside me. He lives here, in this place. He's here now. He's here in the room. Listenin' to us.'

Viktor cast a glance over his shoulder at his superior.

'You mean Professor Románek?' He turned back to his patient. 'He's just here to listen. And he wasn't here the other night.'

'No. Not him.'

'Then who are you talking about, Pavel? There's no one else in here with us.'

'Oh yes there is. There's another here. Another far darker.' Zelený's warning tone was dulled by his deepening narcosis, the oncoming dark wave slowing his speech further. 'I can sense him. Someone bad. Someone locked up in the walls, but not like me. Not like the others. He's been around for a long, long time. He's like the Grey Man. Maybe he *is* the Grey Man. Maybe he's Kostěj the Deathless after all.'

'Is that who I spoke with the other night, Pavel? Is that who spoke through you?'

'I told you: no one spoke through me. Don't you understand? He's *here*. Him that wears the mask. He's in this place. Part of this place. He's held in these walls. He's . . .' Zelený's voice faded; his eyes slowly closed.

'Pavel?' Viktor crossed to his patient and shook him.

'What?' Zelený's response was mumbled. His eyes only half opened.

'Stay awake, Pavel. Sleep is a different place and we can't find the truth there.'

'The truth?'

'Inside you lies the truth. And I think the only person who can tell us where to find it is Mr Hobbs.' Viktor tried to keep the desperation from his voice for the sake of both his patient and his silent audience in the shadows. 'Is it Mr Hobbs who you think lives here? Is he who you meant when you talked about another in the room? Pavel?'

Zelený mumbled incoherently. All that filled the silence was his breathing and the turning of the recorder's spools. Eventually it was just the spools, Zelený's breathing becoming less audible, less frequent, more fragile.

Viktor looked into the shadows to where Románek sat, his face hidden in shadow. 'I'm sorry, it's useless, Professor,' said Viktor. 'His respiration is becoming dangerously suppressed: I'll have to administer a dose of picrotoxin to bring him out of it.'

Viktor pressed the buzzer to summon the orderlies to come in and take Zelený back to his accommodation. While he waited for them to arrive, he charged his syringe from a vial of picrotoxin. He went over to his patient and slapped proud a vein on his restrained forearm, easing the needle under the skin.

'Oh,' said Viktor when he saw it. There was no fear. No concern.

It didn't occur to Viktor to be afraid; that his patient, so heavily sedated and sinking deeper through unconsciousness to the edge of death, should represent any danger. Nor did it occur to him that it had been exactly there, on the very edge of death, that he had last encountered Mr Hobbs.

So when he saw that the leather cuff restraint on Zelený's right arm had not been properly secured, the only thought that struck Viktor was that it was strange he hadn't noticed it when administering the original dose of hypnotics.

Again Zelený's sudden and complete wakefulness didn't make sense: there hadn't been enough time for the picrotoxin to take effect. As soon as Viktor had removed the needle from his patient's vein, Zelený's right arm shot up and Viktor felt the vice of the woodcutter's powerful hand close on his throat. The syringe, rubber tourniquet and metal tray fell from Viktor's hands and clattered onto the stone floor as he grabbed at Zelený's wrist, trying to wrench his hand from his throat.

His panic grew as he felt the unyielding muscle and solid girth of the forester's wrist and forearm. He looked down at his patient. The handsome face was twisted in an expression of fury and his eyes were open and ablaze with a dark, inhuman fire. The broad, powerful fingers tightened on Viktor's throat and neck, making it impossible for him to draw a breath. But all Viktor could focus on was his patient's eyes: inhuman eyes filled with a cold, dark, fathomless fire.

Somewhere a few metres behind him and a universe away, he heard Professor Románek shouting and the sound of his tubular metal chair falling to the flagstones.

With his unyielding grip still fastened on his throat, Zelený pulled Viktor's face close to his, pressing his mouth to the psychiatrist's ear.

'You thought you could parade me in front of your master,' he hissed into Viktor's ear. He again spoke in German, and again his voice was altered. Viktor realized through his terror that once more Hobbs had emerged from death's shadow. 'You thought you could reveal me to another like some cheap conjurer pulling a rabbit from a hat. You still don't understand my nature, do you? You don't understand that my revealing is always for a purpose. You don't understand the danger in showing me disrespect.'

Viktor became aware of other hands on him, trying to pull him back, wrest him free from the patient's grip. He realized it was Professor Románek and two white-jacketed orderlies. Yet he was still held fast, no air reaching his screaming lungs.

'I will return,' the voice hissed in Viktor's ear. 'I will return and show you the truth and you will be blinded by it. I will show you such horror and fear that you will be burned by its beauty and its clarity.'

Viktor became aware of a huddle of more orderlies around him, prising the iron grip of Zelený's fingers from his throat. Suddenly he was free and desperately tore air from the room to fill his lungs.

The orderlies had unfastened Zelený from the couch and wrestled him to the floor, forcing him into a restraint jacket. But Viktor could see that there was no fight left in the patient, that Hobbs had left him and he had returned to a state of semi-consciousness, suspended between the effects of sedative and stimulant. Whoever or whatever was behind the voice hissed into Viktor's ear, it was no longer present.

As Victor gasped for air, Románek took him by the shoulders and steered him back to his chair, loosening his tie and shirt collar. 'Are you all right?' he asked.

'Did you hear?' asked Viktor desperately, his eyes wild. 'Did you hear him? Did you hear Mr Hobbs?'

PART FOUR

THE SCIOMANCER AND
THE BONE CHURCH

he following week, on a day that was as cold and grey as wet slate, Kapitán Lukáš Smolák made the journey from Prague to the asylum at Hrad Orlů. Whenever he left the capital and travelled into the countryside, which he seldom did, he always felt he was travelling back in time. The village that sat as a red-roofed cluster in the valley below the castle looked, like so many Bohemian provincial settlements, as if the nineteenth century had made little mark on it, and the twentieth century none.

Václav Bartoš sat in the passenger seat of Smolák's Praga Piccolo and, despite the joylessness of the day and the bleak metronomic rhythm of the single wiper on the broad windscreen, the two men chatted amiably as they made the journey. Smolák was surprised at his own volubility: he had never been a 'talky' person, as he described it. But there was something about the police surgeon's relaxed but occasionally blunt manner that inspired the detective's confidence.

Their talk ranged across a variety of subjects, but he was grateful that Bartoš made no reference to Anna Petrášová's murder, almost as if the doctor had sensed Smolák's attachment to the victim and that this trip out of the city was a chance to remove himself, albeit temporarily, from the relentlessly close examination of her brutal murder.

Similarly, Smolák did not discuss with Bartoš the doctor's reason for making the trip with him: the brother who sat confined within the asylum's walls. But as they made their winding way up from the village towards the castle, the police doctor's easy chat faded into dark silence.

Smolák, who was used to his bronze police disc opening all doors, was surprised at the amount of checking and double-checking of his credentials before they were allowed to cross the bridge and park in the main courtyard of the castle.

Two men waited for them on the massive, hewn-stone steps that led up to the vast arch of the castle's main entrance. One was middle-aged and dressed in a white, shoulder-fastened, calf-length physician's dustcoat that gave him more the look of a surgeon than psychiatrist. He had a kindly face and gentle demeanour and introduced himself as Professor Ondřej Románek, the institution's director. Next to Románek was another, younger man, whom the professor introduced as Dr Viktor Kosárek.

'One of the most promising talents in modern psychiatry,' Románek assured his visitors.

The first thing that struck Smolák was the way the younger doctor looked so much at home in a castle setting: Viktor Kosárek was tall, lean and handsome but had a severe aristocratic bearing. It was easy to imagine an armour-gauntleted Kosárek standing on the same steps five hundred years earlier. Románek, on the other hand and despite his authority, looked completely out of place.

But something else struck Smolák about the two physicians: the way they stared at his travelling companion, as if taken aback on seeing him.

'Oh, excuse me, this is Dr Václav Bartoš,' Smolák explained. 'He's our police surgeon and I believe you've given permission for him to visit his brother, who's a patient here.'

'Remarkable . . .' Professor Románek stared at Bartoš for a moment longer before suddenly gathering himself. 'Sorry, do excuse me . . .'

'I quite understand,' said Bartoš, and it was clear that he did.

Whatever had startled the asylum physicians was clearly not the mystery to Dr Bartoš that it was to Smolák. 'May I see my brother?'

'Certainly,' Románek smiled amiably. 'Of course, of course. Please gentlemen, do follow me.'

As they were led through its corridors, Smolák was struck by how the asylum didn't feel much like a mental institution at all. Románek showed them into his office. As Smolák took a seat opposite Viktor Kosárek, he noticed purplish-blue bruising on the physician's throat and neck.

'An unguarded moment with a patient,' Viktor explained, his hand moving self-consciously to his throat. 'My own stupid fault. These things tend to happen despite our best efforts, which is why your visit with Michal Macháček had to be delayed. I'm afraid he made rather a mess of a young nurse's face.'

'But he's fit to be interviewed now?' asked Smolák.

'Yes,' said Viktor. 'But please understand there's no guarantee that he'll be lucid. Like many of our patients he can at times seem perfectly normal, at other times delusional and raving. You want to ask him about glassware, I believe?'

'I do.' Smolák volunteered nothing more.

'Then that should provide a focus for him.'

'May I see him now?'

It was Professor Románek who answered. 'We've arranged for Dr Bartoš to meet with his brother in the canteen. Kapitán Smolák, I hope you understand that because of the recent incident in which Mr Macháček injured that poor nurse, your interview with him will have to take place in a secure environment and with orderlies on hand.'

Smolák nodded.

Románek rose and indicated they should follow him. 'You know, Kapitán, you should spend some time chatting with Dr Kosárek here. He really is a leading expert on darker psychologies. Exactly the kind of psychology that is behind these terrible atrocities in Prague. I think you'd find his input most helpful.'

'If there's anything I can do . . .' said Viktor.

'I'd appreciate that,' said Smolák. 'If I'm honest, that's part of my reason for coming to Hrad Orlů. I have to admit I'm struggling to understand the mentality of the Leather Apron killer.'

'Dr Kosárek is doing some trailblazing work,' said Professor Románek. As they walked along the hallway to where a gate divided the administration and staff quarters from the secure patient accommodation, he outlined Viktor's theory of the Devil Aspect. 'Perhaps it's best if Dr Kosárek explains the details himself.'

Reluctantly, Viktor began explaining his Devil Aspect hypothesis; as he did so, he sensed the policeman's scepticism. Václav Bartoš, on the other hand, seemed very keen – agitated almost – to find out more about Viktor's theories.

'Have you undertaken such a narcosynthesis session with my brother?' asked Bartoš.

'Not yet. None of my sessions with him thus far have been narcotic aided.'

'But it is your intention to perform one with him?'

'Yes.'

'Do you think – I mean, is there a chance that you could cure him?'

Viktor considered his answer for a moment. 'I have two roles here: as a scientific researcher and as a therapeutic psychiatrist. My aim is both to learn and to cure. However, as I'm sure you'll appreciate, your brother suffers from a particularly elaborate and deep psychosis. Perhaps hope of an improvement is more realizable than hope of a cure.'

'The strange thing is,' said Dr Bartoš, 'in many ways my brother's research was similar to yours: the scientific measurement of the immensurable, the intangible. Dominik lost his way, I'm afraid.' He paused for a moment. 'Dr Kosárek, would it be at all possible for me to sit in on your narcosynthesis session with my brother?'

'I'm afraid that wouldn't be—' Viktor cut himself off. He looked at the small police physician in his crumpled suit. 'I suppose it might be possible. But only because you're a medical professional. You do understand that, if I do allow you in, you must remain out of sight of your brother at all times and have absolutely no interaction with him. You can't speak at all.'

'I just want to listen,' said Bartoš.

Professor Románek and Viktor led Bartoš and Smolák to a dining hall almost stage-set as a Prague café. An orderly waited with a small, dark-haired man who sat impassively at one of the tables.

In that instant, Lukáš Smolák understood why the two psychiatrists had been taken aback when they first set eyes on Dr Bartoš. In his dress, in his posture, in his demeanour, the man sitting at the table was the opposite of Václav Bartoš: he was neat in dress, his hair immaculately combed, his posture poised, even a little rigid. But, disconcertingly, Dominik Bartoš's face was practically identical to that of his police surgeon brother. The policeman Smolák noticed two notable exceptions to the brothers' similitude: Dominik's cheek was creased by a deep, ugly scar, and his right hand missed its small finger.

'Twins,' explained Václav Bartoš at Smolák's side, sensing the detective's surprise. 'I'm the older brother by two minutes. Sorry, I didn't think to mention it.'

Professor Románek guided Dr Bartoš over to the table where his brother sat looking up at him impassively, with no sign of recognition. The two brothers sat opposite each other, imperfect reflections, one of the other.

'If you'll follow me, Kapitán,' said Viktor. 'Michal Macháček is waiting for you in our secure room.'

'I'd no idea they were twins,' Smolák said as he followed the aristocratic-looking psychiatrist along the hall. 'I knew about Dr Bartoš's brother – that he'd gone mad and was locked up here as one of the so-called Devil's Six – but I had no idea that he was his mirror image. Václav Bartoš is a good man; it's so sad to see how his brother ended up.'

'Dominik Bartoš was a good man too, by all accounts,' said Viktor. 'Good people become mentally ill just as much as bad people. And they aren't responsible for the crimes they commit – they inhabit a different world, a world of hallucination and delusional beliefs.'

'Is that what happened with Bartoš?'

'We call him the Sciomancer.' Viktor smiled wryly. 'Professor Románek is very *lyrical* with how he titles case files. Do you know what sciomancy is?'

Smolák shook his head.

'The ancient belief you can gain knowledge by communing with the dead. Professor Bartoš was a gifted scientist, but his delusions made him believe, well, in magic. Ah, here we are . . .'

Viktor indicated that they had reached the door he wanted. Like the other doors off the hall, it was made of heavy oak, but had been strengthened with steel plates and had two prison-cell-type locks. From his pocket he took a heavy bunch of keys, secured to his belt by a chatelaine, and unlocked the door.

'Please go in. I'll leave you to it. There's an orderly in there for your safety.'

Smolák thanked Viktor and stepped into the room. It was windowless and the walls were painted bright white, unlike the rest of the castle. A stark caged bulb in a bulkhead fitting flooded it with an uncompromising light. At the centre of the room was a table and two chairs, also painted white. A small, balding, fleshy man who looked as if he would present no danger to anyone was sitting at the table. Behind him, like a burly waiter waiting to be summoned to take an order, a white-jacketed, black-tied orderly stood against the wall.

Smolák sat opposite Michal Macháček and introduced himself and informed him of the nature of his business.

'Well, you have come to the right person,' beamed Macháček. 'I am Europe's leading expert on glass. Probably the world's.'

'Quite.' Smolák took his handkerchief from his pocket, placed it centrally on the table and unfolded it to reveal the glass bead. 'Can you tell me where this came from?'

Macháček reached out to pick it up and the orderly stepped forward. Smolák gave a small shake of his head and the orderly retook his position at the wall. The small bald man rolled the bead between his fingers, examining it closely.

'I don't have a loupe here. They won't allow me one.'

Smolák smiled and took a jeweller's eye loupe from his pocket and placed it on the table. 'I thought as much.'

'May I keep it?' the glass collector asked enthusiastically.

Smolák looked over Macháček's shoulder at the orderly, who shook his head.

'I'm afraid they won't allow that.'

Macháček sighed and picked up the eyepiece and examined the bead.

'I've been given to believe it could be Gablonz glass,' said Smolák when Macháček didn't say anything.

'Who told you that?' he asked.

'Anna Petrášová. It was she who recommended I ask you about the bead.'

'Ah yes, Madame Petrášová – I know her through her business. She advised you well,' said Macháček, removing the loupe from his eye. He still held the bead in his other hand, rolling it between his fingertips. 'When she told you to consult me, that is. Her opinion of the bead's provenance is nonsense.'

'It's not Gablonz glass?'

'It's not Bohemian glass at all. It's an imitation of it, but not manufactured here.'

'So where was it made?'

'I should say it was made in Sun Tavern Fields: Cutthroat Lane, probably.' He said the name of the street in English.

'England?'

'London. Ratcliff – it was an area in the East End of London.' He leaned back in his chair, his tone self-important. 'These were manufactured in huge quantities, most not even to this quality. You see, there were a lot of Jewish immigrants in the East End of London at the time, mostly from Poland and the Bohemian Lands of Austro-Hungary. Many had worked in the glass industry here before emigrating. All kinds of ramshackle workshops were set up among the slums and sweatshops of East London, all mass-manufacturing cheap copies of Gablonz glass – worse than German Rhinestone copies. This is a much better example, but still very much inferior to the real thing.'

Smolák thought about what Macháček had said. In the material he had read about the Jack the Ripper case, at least two suspects had been Central European Jews. One had been Jan Pizer, arrested solely because of the nickname by which he had been known: Leather Apron.

'How old would you say it is?' Smolák asked.

The small balding man shrugged his narrow shoulders. 'Difficult to say. These things were made for cheap costume jewellery or as beadwork to decorate women's dresses. The fashion for them passed and all the workshops shut down, replaced by big factories making windows.' Again he rolled the bead between his fleshy fingertips and pursed his lips. 'I'd say anywhere between fifty to a hundred years old. Victorian.'

'This place—'

'Ratcliff,' reminded Macháček.

'Ratcliff – is it anywhere near Whitechapel?'

'My expertise is in glass, Kapitán Smolák. Not the geography of the British Isles.'

After the session with the Glass Collector, Smolák was escorted by Viktor Kosárek to a staff lounge, where he could wait for Dr Bartoš to conclude his visit with his brother. Kosárek sat opposite him, long legs crossed and his coffee cup balanced on the arm of his leather chair. There was, as throughout the castle, a certain grandness to the room, and Smolák noted again that a certain grandness also adhered to the psychiatrist. He toyed with the idea of asking Kosárek if he had any kind of noble background.

Instead, the detective discussed the Leather Apron case with his host, outlining all that had happened with Tobar Bihari, the gypsy who had blown his own brains out rather than live with the memories seared into them.

Viktor Kosárek listened in silence. Then, when Smolák had finished his story, said: 'It does sound like the gypsy was describing some monstrous part of his own personality, rather than another individual present at the scene of the crime. You're right to suspect that he simply abstracted the dark and violent part of his own psyche into a demonic figure – something he saw as being separate from himself. It was a logical conclusion to draw.'

'Dr Bartoš's conclusion more than mine.'

'But as a theory it's rather confounded by this new murder, which the gypsy couldn't have committed.'

'And we have a description of a suspect, for what it's worth, which isn't much. Have you seen it? We put it in the papers.'

'I'm afraid I haven't,' said Viktor.

Smolák unfolded a square of paper he took from his jacket pocket and handed it to Viktor.

As he looked at the artist's impression, Viktor felt his pulse quicken. The hat and coat, the general build, matched Filip. It couldn't be, he told himself. It just couldn't be. Yet the image of the man the police were looking for dovetailed perfectly with the suspicions Viktor had already had about his friend. He knew he had to tell Smolák. He had to tell him that his friend dressed like that. That his friend had been behaving erratically, had expressed hatred of women and his admiration for Leather Apron.

'It's not much to go on, is it?' he said casually, and handed the picture back to the detective.

'No, it's not,' sighed Smolák. 'Could I call on you for advice as more evidence comes to light?'

'Certainly. I'm happy to do everything I can to help catch this killer.'

'In the meantime, even if it's not Tobar Bihari, could it still be that the killer doesn't know he's the killer? A split-personality thing?'

'The "split-personality thing" is something I deal with all the time. That's why the Devil's Six are the subject of my research. Each places the blame for their actions, either by commission or compulsion, on a demonic figure they see as separate from themselves.'

'So Leather Apron might not know he's Leather Apron, if you know what I mean?' said Smolák.

'Possibly. It's rare for a personality to divide completely into separate, self-contained identities, but the cases we have here prove that it does happen. But if your killer is such a case, it makes your job much more difficult . . .'

'Dr Bartoš said as much. He also suggested that in such cases there's usually been some childhood or other trauma to cause the split.'

'He's right. Only one discrete part of the personality, operating independently, carries not just the pain of remembering the trauma, but all the consequent aberrant behaviours. In your case, murders.'

Viktor paused for a moment. *Tell him about Filip*, the thought screamed in his head. *Tell him Filip Starosta could be Leather Apron. No, I need time. I need to think it through.*

'Listen, Kapitán Smolák,' he said. 'I wasn't keen to let Dr Bartoš sit in on my session with his brother, but now that he is, maybe it's an idea for you to sit in as well. As one of the Devil's Six, Dominik Bartoš is a perfect example of someone who has abstracted a part of his personality into a separate, autonomous demonic figure

– much like you thought could be the case with your gypsy suspect. Although Professor Bartoš does take full and personal responsibility for his actions.'

'And you think that's the case with our killer?'

'I think it could be.' *Tell him about Filip.* 'We all have a part of ourselves – the Id – an element in our deep Unconscious that's impulsive, volatile and potentially violent. It's the impulses of the Id that our Egos keep in check. And within the Id, I believe there is an element that is the coalescence of all our ideas – individually and collectively – of evil.'

'Your Devil Aspect?'

'Exactly,' said Viktor. 'Our whole concept of the Devil – personally, culturally, psychically – lies in this aspect, which is why I gave it that name. We all have it, we all fall victim to its power at times, but our Egos keep its excesses in check. But in some cases of severe derangement, the Devil Aspect splits away and takes on an independent life of its own – even taking physical form in the eyes of the patient, who sees it as an irresistible controlling external force. It makes it easier, you see, if you can blame your worst excesses on someone or something else.'

'Like the gypsy, Bihari,' said Smolák.

'It's also what lies behind Professor Bartoš's crimes. And if Leather Apron isn't your gypsy and is still on the loose, then yes, it could be the case with him. And it could be history repeating itself.'

'What do you mean?' asked Smolák.

'If your murderer really does take inspiration from an earlier killer, the one in England fifty-odd years ago, the irony is that original killer could himself have been suffering from the same state. Jack the Ripper may have been some unsuspecting soul's own Devil Aspect.'

Smolák sighed. 'A killer hiding from himself.'

'Possibly,' said Viktor. *Tell him about Filip. TELL him.* 'But you may find he will eventually leave clues to lead you to him.'

'I have to ask this,' said Smolák, 'no matter how unlikely it sounds: is there *any* way a patient here could get out without you knowing?'

Before Viktor could answer, the door opened and Václav Bartoš walked in. Both could see the police surgeon was upset.

'When will you be carrying out your session with my brother?' he asked Viktor Kosárek.

'Tonight,' said the psychiatrist. 'An hour after the patients have their evening meal.'

'What was this place?' asked Václav Bartoš as he and Lukáš Smolák stood looking around the tower: at its dense walls, into the high dark wooden vaults of its ceiling, at the secure examination couch and the large dark leather-clad, met-al-edged block and brushed steel spools of the K1 Magnetophon recorder. Viktor recognized the same claustrophobic unease he him-self had felt when first setting foot in the room.

'A grain store, originally,' he said. 'But the legendary Jan of the Black Heart was supposed to be immured in the tower. If he was, his remains must still be here, somewhere. I've never found any door or other way into the rest of the tower – there are only two narrow arrowslits right at the top, both inaccessible from either inside or outside. And I'm guessing that the back wall of this room abuts directly onto the solid rock of the crag behind the castle.'

'But you've looked?' asked Smolák. 'For a way in or out?'

'I've looked. There's none I can see.'

'You're sure? Given some of the cases you've got in here and the nature of these Leather Apron killings in Prague, I think you can understand—'

'I'm sure,' Viktor interrupted the policeman. 'In any case, it's a long way to Prague from here when you have no money, food or even a coat.'

'Unless you have a friend, an accomplice, on the outside,' said Smolák.

'We're very remote here, and the locals shun the castle because of its history and its current use.' Viktor smiled patiently, but thought of a rhyme, carved in aged wood and Glagolitic on the forest chapel, of legends of a castle built as a stopper in the mouth of Hell, and of a village rumour about caves and hidden tunnels. 'Anyway, I'm afraid I'm going to have to ask you gentlemen to take your places.' He indicated where two collapsible metal chairs had been set against the wall.

'When the lights are dimmed you'll be in shadow and out of Dominik's sight. I must ask you to remain silent: it's essential he's unaware of any presence other than mine. This is particularly true for you, Dr Bartoš. If your brother knew you were here, he'd want to connect with you, not me, while under the influence of the hypnotics.'

'I understand,' said the police physician.

Viktor waited until they were seated before turning on the angle-poise lamps. He took the moment to still his anxiety about withholding from Smolák what he knew about Filip. After all, so far his suspicions were based on gut instincts and coincidences. The artist's impression the policeman showed him could have been anyone who owned a dark coat and hat.

He nodded to the orderly by the door, who switched off the main lights and went out into the corridor to fetch the patient.

The ritual followed its usual course: the orderlies guided the compliant Dominik Bartoš to the examination couch and fastened him in, Viktor administered the sedative and hypnotic drugs, sat down while they took effect, then switched on the Magnetophon recorder.

This time, however, he had reduced the potency of the drug cocktail. He wanted to make the Sciomancer compliant, to open up his internal story. But Viktor was also aware of his audience and felt strangely possessive of his techniques. If Bartoš were to manifest some spectacular, personalized form of Devil Aspect, as Zelený had in the form of 'Mr Hobbs', Viktor wanted it to be under his exclusive control and view.

When he spoke to answer Viktor's questions, Dominik Bartoš was quiet and unhurried: as efficient and precise in speech as he was in movement and dress. He confirmed his name, where he was born and details of his early life, speaking with drug-vague fondness of a childhood shared with a loved and loving twin brother.

'Do you know why you're here? In this asylum?' asked Viktor.

'Because of my experiments. Because of the subjects I used to formulate my theory of transdimensional resonances.'

'The people you murdered, you mean?'

'My quantum travellers. The Dark Shifters I sent to the other dimension.'

'But you accept you killed them? That they're dead?'

'Dead?' The former scientist frowned thoughtfully. 'But that's the question: are they really dead or merely shifted?'

Viktor paused. 'You were a scientist?'

'A quantum physicist, yes. And I *am* a scientist – I remain an investigator of the universe, of its mechanics. You can't chain curiosity, Doctor. The inquiring mind does not wither in confinement, it merely adjusts its scope of inquiry to a smaller segment of the universe. That's what I do here.'

'And you came up with this theory of transdimensional resonance. Perhaps later you can explain that to me in layman's terms.'

'But you're not a layman, Dr Kosárek,' said Dominik. 'You are a scientist in a field that, one day, will be indissolubly linked with mine. One day the quantum mechanics of the brain will be recognized – the superpositions, the entanglements, the multidimensional infinity of the human mind.'

'The beginning, Professor,' Viktor urged gently. The reduced dosage meant he wasn't as fully in control of his patient as he would like. 'Let's go back to when it all started.'

'When *what* all started?'

'Your belief in sciomancy. When the visions began,' said Viktor. 'When the killings started.'

'*I* suppose it all began when I left Charles University,' said Bartoš. 'They tried to say it was some kind of breakdown caused by overwork, but it wasn't. It was frustration: I simply couldn't resolve the problems in my theory. I'd get this, this *itch* in my head, like a grain of grit lodged in my brain. I knew the answer lay within my grasp – tantalizingly so – but I just didn't know in which direction I should reach to find it.

'I knew my researches would never reach a conclusion while I was at the university, so it was agreed I should go on an extended sabbatical. I moved to Kutná Hora, back to where I grew up with my brother.

'I found a place to rent in Sedlec, to the east of the city: a fine house over three floors that had been an artist's home and workplace, with a large double-height studio-cum-conservatory to the back, facing south. Far too big for one person, really.

'Truth is I took the house partly because of the landlady who showed me around. She was a handsome but perpetually sad woman somewhere between forty and forty-five, who lived in a cottage set within the main house's garden. Through time and the incontinent gossip of the grocer who delivered once a week, I learned that Madame Horáčková – Rozálie Horáčková, my landlady, you see – had been mistress of the house and wife to the artist. Following his death, straitened circumstances had compelled her to move into the cottage and rent out the main house.

'I admit to having been somewhat smitten with Madame Horáčková – such a fine-looking woman who held herself with great, if melancholy, dignity. But I seldom had the opportunity to speak to her, except when paying the month's rent, and of course that conversation was always to the point. I did *see* her often, though: she kept the pathetically small strip of garden allotted to the cottage immaculate, filled with as many colours and varieties of plants as its size would allow.

'I'd sometimes watch her from one of the upstairs rooms as she worked methodically in that little garden. It didn't take up too much of her time, so she would most often simply sit in a garden chair in the shade, sitting very, very still, seeming to stare at her slender pale hands – she had extraordinarily beautiful hands – which rested unmoving on her lap.

'I found out from the gossipy grocer that her husband – Oskar Horaček – had been a painter of some repute, who painted, much like Alfons Mucha, characters and tableaux inspired by Slavic mythology. Horaček's gentle character was at odds with his build: the grocer told me Horaček had been a big, burly, fine-looking but unfashionably bearded man.

'According to the grocer, whom I admit encouraging by offering him coffee whenever he made his weekly delivery, Oskar Horaček underwent a sudden change in character. He became dissatisfied with a particular canvas he was working on and his dissatisfaction blossomed into a dark obsession. Particularly disturbing was his fixation with creating the blackest black paint. He experimented continually, mixing black paint with different powders from pitch, charcoal and coal dust to exotic and preposterously expensive inks from sea creatures.'

'What was the subject of this canvas?' asked Viktor.

'Veles. The dark chthonic god of Slavic mythology – more demon than god. Lord of the Dead and Forests. Horaček's obsession with finding the darkest shade of black was for painting the shadows in

Veles's forest. What I later discovered was that Horaček needed it to paint the figure of Veles himself, to do justice to his supreme darkness. Anyway, I'm getting ahead of myself – the house and studio was close to the Cemetery Church of the All Saints in Sedlec, you know it?'

Viktor nodded. 'I've never been there, but I know *of* it. The ossuary. The Bone Church.'

'That's it,' said Dominik. 'A most remarkable place. Apparently Horaček would furiously work and rework the Veles canvas, constantly experimenting with new shades of black – but the only occasions he took time away from his painting was when he visited the church. He'd sit for hours amongst the thousands of bones and make sketches of the church's decorations of skeletons and skulls. As it turned out, he was using these sketches as the background to his painting of Veles. As you know, Veles is the god not just of the forest, but of the Underworld.

'The priest at All Saints became increasingly worried about him, as did many of his neighbours. The focus of their greatest pity was his wife, Madame Horáčková, who was absolutely distraught by her husband's sudden and rapidly deteriorating mental state, and who was now neglected by him to the point of abandonment.

'The artist was to find peace soon enough, sadly. With no word to wife nor neighbour, he took himself off on a particularly rainy morning, going out with neither coat nor hat. He wasn't found until three days later when they dragged him out of a small lake near Ovčáry. He must have walked all the way, knowing all the time he was going to drown himself. So sad.

'Apparently it was only with great difficulty that they got him out of the lake, the big man that he was; added to which he had become all entangled with the branches and mulch and matted grasses that had been floating in the water. He was quite weighted down.

'Poor Madame Horáčková was quite devastated by her loss. Left with no other means of support, she sold her husband's remaining canvases, moved into the garden cottage and rented out the main house.'

'And what about the painting he had been working on?' asked Viktor. 'The one of Veles?'

'Oh she burned that. The story is that the Veles picture wasn't unfinished or poorly painted at all. Those who saw it say it was Horaček's finest work: so good that his representation of Veles filled anyone who saw it with dread. They said even the background of the painting – done from his studies at the Bone Church – seemed to come to life: the black shadows between the bones moving and writhing. That's why Rozálie Horáčková burned it – not just because it had driven her husband mad, but because it terrified her.

'Anyway, two years later, I took on the lease and watched the sad, perennial flowering of her grief and became quite smitten by her.'

'Did you do anything about this attraction?' asked Viktor.

'Good God, no. I'm a quiet man, Dr Kosárek. Really quite shy, reclusive. Anyway, I had no time for romantic foolery – I had my work to focus on. I needed peace to formulate my theory.'

'And what was this theory that had so agitated you?' asked Viktor.

'I believe our whole universe is an infinitely complex structure and that an infinite number of different planes or dimensions all interconnect at a quantum level. These interconnections I call trans-dimensional resonances.'

'Connections to another reality?' asked Viktor.

Dominik Bartoš nodded. 'Mirror worlds. Have you ever looked *past* your reflection in the mirror? Angled your view to see the room and the world your reflection inhabits and wondered if *that* is the real world, and yours is the reflection?'

'No I haven't,' said Viktor. 'But I've treated patients with reduplicative paramnesia who have had a similar delusion.'

'This is no delusion I'm talking about,' said Bartoš. 'In quantum physics, there's nothing insane about believing there's not just one but many realities. I was using mathematics to find the crack in the mirror's glass: the infinitesimally small breach that connects one world with its reflection, one reality to the next. But what I discovered was a form that has to be *intuited* rather than calculated. You see, transdimensional resonances have been known to man since his beginnings. We've always been aware of them, always had an instinctive fear of them – had a name for them all this time.'

'What name?' asked Viktor.

'Ghosts,' said Bartoš matter-of-factly. 'Transdimensional resonances are the ghosts of the dead.'

'Ghosts?' said Viktor. 'How can fictional supernatural beings possibly have any place in scientific thinking?'

Dominik Bartoš smiled. 'When science can't yet explain a phenomenon rationally, superstition explains it irrationally. That doesn't make the phenomenon any less real. Let me tell you how my discovery came about; then you might understand.

'I admit I was working longer and harder than I should. I worked so intensely, and forced myself to stay awake for so long, that eventually my body forgot the mechanism for sleep.

'But the breakthrough – oh, the breakthrough. If I could prove my theory, then our whole understanding of the universe, of physics, of ourselves – of how, why and where we exist – would be changed forever.

'Remember I described looking at the mirror and the mirror looking back? Well, I was so close to proving that the universe really does work that way. Except, instead of one mirror, it would be an infinite hall of mirrors and an infinite number of realities. And one of these dimensions, I realized – I *saw* for myself – is the realm of the dead. The place where human consciousness goes after physical death.'

'You're a man of science, Professor Bartoš,' Viktor protested. 'You can't possibly believe—'

Dominik Bartoš interrupted him. 'Isaac Newton was arguably the most important man of science ever, yet he also practised alchemy. He had ideas so far ahead of the thinking and technologies of his time he sought grains of truth amongst superstitions and magics. I did the same. I opened my mind to other gateways.

'I worked day and night. The only breaks I would take would be to watch the beautiful Madame Horáčková sitting quietly in her garden, or to take short walks to try to waken myself up. One day while taking a walk I passed the Cemetery Church of the All Saints. I remembered what the grocer had said about the artist Oskar Horaček visiting the Bone Church so often – so I decided to go in and look.

'I was instantly awed by its great power, by the overwhelming presence of the dead. Great legions of them. Between forty and fifty thousand corpses, all defleshed, skeletonized; bones disarticulated and reassembled into the strangest, most darkly moving art. Bones and skulls decorate the walls, vaults and arches of the chapels; elaborate chandeliers contain every bone in the human body a hundred times over; huge garlands made from human skulls; door frames, archways, ciboria and friezes fashioned from maxillas, clavicles, sterna and scapulas; radiant monstrances with rays of bleached fibulae and ulnae. A single pyramid alone contains a thousand skulls, simply balanced on each other. It keeps its structure – *adheres* – as if bound by some dark energy.

'Whenever I was in the church I felt *calmer*, as if my overworked mind found some kind of rest. I realized that the artist Horaček must have felt the same. He'd sought a breakthrough in his artistic impasse there amongst the bones; I was seeking a breakthrough in my scientific one.

'Every primitive culture in Europe believed another world co-exists with this one: that at special times and in special places the veil between these contiguous realities was lifted and man, god and demon mingled; the living and the dead were allowed to commune. I realized the Bone Church was one of those places.

'I visited every week. Every week became every second day, then every day. I'd sit in the church and find peace and clarity. Ten-minute visits became twenty, became hours. Then I started to see them.'

'See whom?' asked Viktor.

Dominik frowned. 'Sometimes, sitting there in the bleached-bone quiet with the dead, I'd suddenly become aware of someone next to me – someone who must have come into the church unheard – but when I turned to see who, there'd be no one there.

'Then there were more of them: dark shapes just out of reach – some movement caught on the edge of my vision, like a fleeting shadow, only to disappear when I turned. It started to happen more and more often: dark shadows fluttering just out of the corner of my eye.

'After a while, they were there all the time. I'd come into the church, sit quietly staring at the skull pyramid. After less than a minute I would sense them – the Dark Shifters, I called them – darting around on the edge of my perception, always silent, always darker than night. Much darker. Suddenly I understood Horaček's quest for the blackest hue of paint. You see, I worked out that the Dark Shifters possessed the property of *true* darkness. In our dimension, darkness doesn't exist in its own right – it's nothing more than the absence of light. But whatever it was I caught fleeting glances of, they were composed of true darkness. Darkness as a thing in and of itself. *They* were the transdimensional resonances I'd been seeking.'

'Tell me, Dominik,' asked Viktor, 'at this time, were you sleeping at all?'

The scientist lying restrained on the couch gave a small laugh. 'I had no time for sleep. Little time for food.'

'Then don't you see how these so-called Dark Shifters are typical of the kind of visual disturbances and hallucinations caused by sleep deprivation?'

'Yes – but that's exactly what mystics and seers have done for millennia to get themselves into a state of consciousness where they'd have visions of the godly and the demonic – but what they were really doing was seeing through the quantum veil into other dimensions. I entered the same receptive state but I understood *scientifically* what was happening.

'One day, as I sat before the skull pyramid, I felt a presence. And I mean I *felt* it – like an electrical charge sparking in the air and crackling on my skin. I glimpsed a Dark Shifter at the edge of my field of vision. But this time it was bigger. Huge. And blacker, as if its darkness was even more intense, even denser. For the first time I was afraid. I turned to look and, as always, the Shifter disappeared before I could see it fully. But there was the strangest thing: for a moment there was a stain on the floor where I had sensed the presence, as if the flagstones were wet. Then even that faded.

'There was something about that experience that both frightened and excited me. I'd made a breakthrough of some sort – or something had broken through to me. Things changed.

'I started to glimpse Dark Shifters elsewhere, not just in the church. I'd see them in the street, making me start back from the kerb, thinking a car or a bus was passing. They still vanished when I turned to look, but now they allowed me a glimpse: a fraction of a second to see them. But that was only the start.

'One night, around midnight, I was rerunning some calculations when I was disturbed by noises coming from the conservatory. Fearful that there was an intruder, I armed myself with a fireplace poker and went through. The lights were off but the moon was near full and bright, the sky cloudless. And there I saw him.'

'Who?'

'A great man. Huge and broad. And impossibly dark, like a solid silhouette. I switched on the nearest lamp but even that didn't seem to illuminate him. It was as if his darkness was a thirst, a sponge that soaked up the light of both moon and lamp. I told him to step closer, into the light so that I could see him, and demanded that he explain his presence. He stepped forward, but remained silent. As he moved closer the sight of him filled me with dread.

'He was massive. And I mean he had more *mass* than a man should have: huge, tall, burly – more like a bear than a man – wearing an ankle-length black astrakhan coat, his face almost hidden by a mass of thick, curly hair and great, flowing beard, all the darkest black. And the strangest thing is, he was wet. Soaked through: the dense wool curls of his coat, his hair, the great beard dripping wet. A pool of water had gathered at his feet, yet there was no trail of wet footprints to show where he'd crossed the stone flags of the conservatory. But what frightened me most were his eyes, set deep in the mass of straggled wet hair and beard. Those eyes – red eyes that seemed to *burn*. It was then that I worked out who he was. Why he had come to me.'

'The drowned artist?' asked Viktor. 'The ghost of Oskar Horaček?'

'Oskar Horaček? No, that's not who it was. Whenever I looked at him everything dimmed, his darkness *shone* and banished brightness. I knew right away who he was.

'Veles, the Dark One. The Lord of the Dead.'

'*V*eles had been twice summoned: first by the painter Horaček, then by me. Two voices calling into the void, now answered. *He* was the answer – the great revealing of things, of universes, of dimensions. Veles, the Dark One.

'Veles explained it all to me. His voice was deep, so deep it resonated upwards from the floor beneath me, from the dark earth and rock beneath that. He talked of his dimension and of mine; of all the mysteries I'd struggled with. He explained what I had to do. I was to send travellers to his domain – bridge the gap between the living and the dead. Voyagers through realities who could show one dimension to the other. The greatest achievement in human scientific history. But first I needed to create the Dark Shifters.'

'And how would you create them?' Viktor asked, although he already knew the answer.

Dominik Bartoš frowned, as if puzzled not by the question but by the asking of it. 'I would have to make some of the living into the dead, of course.'

There was a pause, Viktor again aware of the brother sitting behind him in silence and shadow, listening to the raving of his twin.

'How did you choose your victims?' Viktor asked.

'Veles suggested I started with children, and it was difficult to resist his will. He said something strange to me: that this – our time right now – was going to be the darkest of all times for children and they'd be better off shifted. That something worse awaited them here.

'However, I argued that children wouldn't understand the gift I was giving them, their consciousnesses too unformed, too immature. The truth was that I found the idea just too distressing.

'So the first serious attempt at creating a Dark Shifter was when I drove all the way into Prague, to Žižkov – the worst area of the city, full of communists and prostitutes. Red Žižkov they call it. I'd decided to find a street woman for my experiments.

'It was a summer's evening and I drove into Žižkov, parking the car some distance from a public house called the Modrý Bažant. I'd heard years before that it was a place where you could find street women. The evening was pleasant, mellow, the sky and the air warm velvet. It seemed a pity on such a night to be undertaking my mission in such shabby surroundings.

'The bar was a gloomy affair: ill lit, which suited my purposes; the walls clad in oily brown wood and the air fumed with cigarette and cigar smoke. There was a scabrous stuffed, dyed-blue pheasant above the counter, presumably in honour of the bar's name, and the clientele was mostly drunk in the morose, lethargic way of career drinkers. I took a seat in the least populated corner and ordered beer, making an effort not to be conspicuous. My appearance helped in that respect: my brother and I share an eminently forgettable face.

'It was odd sitting there, innocuous and unnoticed: a small forgettable man drinking beer on a warm summer's evening, idly watching the other customers. A mouse in the corner of the room. Yet all the time the mouse was a lion and the women were unknowing prey. They had no idea that I commanded their fates, that I would decide which of them would carry on existing in this dimension and which would leave it for another. It gave me the most incredible feeling of mute power.

'There were three women whom I identified as whores. One was drunk and had a raucous, grating, joyless laugh. I dismissed her right away as unsuitable as an ambassador of dimensions. A younger, quieter, prettier one caught my eye. She was very dark, a gypsy I guessed, but seemed to have some kind of limp, as if crippled. I resolved to follow her from the bar, but a small, vicious-looking young man, also a gypsy, came in from the street and embraced her proprietorially.

'That left only one, who was between the other two in demeanour and age. From a distance she looked like an attractive, healthy, youngish woman. Having done no trade in the bar she left, and I followed her out into the street. It was full velvet night outside, warm and soft. My heart was pounding, not with trepidation but with joy. For the first time in those leaden months I felt the tiredness lift from me. I realized that I didn't find this work distressing: I thrilled at it.

'I blessed my luck that she headed in the direction of my car and made sure I caught up with her before she reached it. I really didn't know what one says to a whore to initiate commerce, but my hello seemed to suffice and she asked me if I was looking for company. I said I was and I indicated my car. She hesitated, saying something about her place being near, and looked up and down the empty street; then looked me up and down. She clearly decided I was no risk to her and when I opened the door she climbed in.

'In the car's cabin light, the from-a-distance semblance of youth and vigour was revealed as heavily applied make-up. Her breath smelled of spirits and cigarettes and the acrid odour of a corrupted soul. Like everything else about her, her smile was artificial and empty, and I regretted having picked her up. As soon as she got into the car she asked me what I wanted, listing the most disgusting acts like a menu of perversions.

'I explained that my purpose was scientific. She laughed and said she didn't care what I called it, so long as I paid her, which I did. I drove out of the city and she started to get anxious, to complain, so I gave her more money, a lot more money, and she stopped complaining, although she still seemed uneasy.

'I chatted to her as we drove. Stupid, empty talk to convince her that I was what I appeared to be: an innocuous, lonely little man who represented no danger. But all the time I felt more alive, more awake than I had in months. At last I was going to make a connection to another dimension. I was going to transform this woman into a Dark Shifter.

'Her journey would begin that night.'

'*O*utside the city I found a quiet road into the forest and parked. She switched on the car's cabin light and un-buttoned her blouse to expose her breasts.

'It turned out that she was a most stupid woman. I told her again I wasn't interested in sex and explained very clearly the opportunity she had: that she would become a traveller across dimensions; that she would experience inconceivable wonders and would be the first ever to come back to tell about them. She didn't understand what I was saying at all, and I realized that I had made a mistake in choos-ing a Shifter of such limited intellect.

'Things went from bad to worse. When I took out the knife and she realized that she would have to change form, to surrender physical life before travelling, she became most unreasonable. She began to scream and claw at me like a harpie, demanding I let her go. Obviously that was impossible. Whether she was willing or suitable to become a Dark Shifter or not, she couldn't be allowed to tell oth-ers of my breakthrough.'

'So you killed her?'

'You've no idea how messy it is to extinguish a human being's physical life; especially when you're not yet experienced at it and you're killing one who won't stay still, as she simply refused to do. She screamed and grappled desperately with the car door handle. Eventually she managed to unlock it and flung the door open. There were open fields all around us and it was by now true dark. A deep, black, moonless night so dark that I wondered if Veles had come to watch my work.

'I knew if she got out and ran I would never catch her. I made a grab for her, forgetting I had the knife in my hand, and it slipped between her ribs. Surprisingly easily, actually. She opened her mouth to scream, but only a wet hissing came from it – I suppose it was the shock, or maybe I'd punctured a lung. So I pulled the knife out and rammed it into her neck. That really was most unpleasant. And messy. I felt the knife jar against bone, her cervical vertebrae I guessed, but I must also have severed the jugular and carotid in her neck, because there came great spouting arcs of blood that splashed all over the inside of the car: onto the windscreen, all over the car's bench seat, all over me. And all the time she shrieked and shrieked – wet, hissing, high-pitched shrieks – and thrashed about wildly. Blood went everywhere, everywhere.'

Dominik gave a vexatious shake of his head.

'Very quickly she stopped screaming and struggling: her cries became small, wheezing gasps and her movement reduced to spasmodic twitches, then shivering as the heat departed her body with the blood. Then it was over: she sat dead and staring through the windscreen into the night and I sat sticky and wet in the copper-smelling damp air of the car.

'Eventually, with quite a struggle I might say, for I am a man designed for mental rather than physical labour, I got her body into the trunk. I wiped down the leather upholstery, the dashboard and the windscreen. I had to put my jacket out of sight too, but it was a sultry night so a driver in shirtsleeves wouldn't be unusual. Although I had cleaned everything up, it wouldn't stand close inspection: the inside of the windscreen was smeared and in the warm night the inside of the car had that cupric smell of blood.

'I drove back to Sedlec and parked close to the rear door of the house. I checked there was no one who could see me – Rozálie

Horáčková must have been in bed for there was no light in the cottage. When I was satisfied I was unobserved, I took the Žižkov woman's body down into the transition chamber. Her transformation into a Dark Shifter was about to begin.'

'The transition chamber?' asked Viktor.

'I'd set it up in the cellar: all the tools and equipment I needed to transform a three-dimensional physical form into a multidimensional Dark Shifter. There was a large, heavy table, extra lamps so I could see what I was doing, vats filled with caustic potash for reducing rendered flesh, butchers' knives and slaughtermen's tools.'

Viktor heard a noise behind him as Kapitán Smolák, having risen from his chair, handed him a note before sinking back into the shadows. Viktor took the note and read it. He sighed.

'Dominik,' he asked. 'Did you wear anything to protect your clothing?'

'Of course.'

'An apron?'

'Yes. And elbow-length gauntlets.'

'The apron – was it made of leather?'

Dominik looked at Viktor, puzzled. He shook his head. 'No, both the apron and the gauntlets were from the same equipment supplier as the vats, and were made of galvanized rubber.'

'Let me be absolutely clear, Dominik,' said Viktor. 'You have confessed to all the murders you committed, including some victims that the police didn't know about, correct?'

'I take exception to the words murders and victims, but yes, I have taken full responsibility for everything I did. Why should a scientist be ashamed of his work?'

'There are no killings that you have hidden. There's nothing we don't know.'

'No. Nothing.' A realization dawned in Dominik Bartoš's expression. 'Oh, I see. Now I understand why you asked about the apron. They do allow us newspapers in here now and again, you know

– you're asking about that killer in Prague, who has the police running around in circles. No, no, dear Dr Kosárek, I am not Leather Apron. How could I be, locked up in here? Anyway, Leather Apron is nothing but a common murderer. I was and remain a seeker after the truth. A scientist.'

'So you worked alone?' he asked. 'In the cellar, defleshing the bones of your victims.'

'Of my *subjects*,' corrected Dominik. 'But I wasn't alone. Veles was there, in the cellar with me. He instructed me on what I was to do and how I was to do it. But his shining *darkness* banished light and I sometimes found it difficult to see, even with the bright lamps I had bought for the purpose. He realized the problem and stood in the furthest corner of the cellar, instructing me as I worked.

'Things didn't go well with the first subject, the Žižkov prostitute. I made all kinds of mistakes excarnating her – I'm a physicist and not an anatomist, after all. It all got very messy, and smelly.

'But Veles talked me through it. The only time he became impatient – and Veles's wrath is something to hold in terror – was when I went to dissolve the flesh from the bone by putting the dismembered limbs into the vats of caustic potash solution. In a voice that rang through me, he commanded me to take the limbs out – the solution I'd prepared would degrade the bone itself. The essence of man, his noble essence, Veles said, lay in his bones. The bones must be respected.

'I begged his forgiveness and snatched the limbs out of the lye. Veles then explained the *mos Teutonicus* – the ancient German custom – where all the flesh is removed and the noble essence of the bone is left. He told me that the *mos Teutonicus* was to be my way, my method, the flesh ablated and disposed of in the lye vats. What remained on the bone wasn't to be removed with caustics or acids, but by boiling the bones overnight in water and wine.

'So I did as he told me. It took a long, long time and Veles stood in the corner, his intense darkness and dampness leaching into the walls, the floor, the cellar ceiling. I asked him about his realm of the Underworld. He told me it was a great, dark, damp, endless forest of intertwined branches and roots. He said the trees in the Forest of the Underworld were so huddled, so tall and full, that it was always twilight, an eternal dusk filled with constantly shifting shadows. Those shadows, he explained, were what I had seen in the Bone Church. They were his heralds, his emissaries: they were the spirits of the dead.

'The souls of others – those who had sinned greatly in life – were bound up in trees. You could tell which because the trees were twisted, rotting, teeming with insects that burrowed endlessly into the flesh without consuming it. Sometimes their souls were tied up in the twists and knots of roots that burrowed deep in the cold, wet soil, and their loneliness drove them to eternal madness. The Forest of the Dead had no end, he said, but it had a heart: a place where the darkness became most intense. That's where Veles has his throne and where he forges his own Dark Shifters to haunt the living and remind them of their vanity and mortality.'

Dominik Bartoš paused but Viktor said nothing. The scientist's description of Veles's forest Underworld had disturbed him. Childhood memories of feeling lost among trees, knowing evil lurked there, haunted him for a moment. He was roused from his thoughts by the sound of movement behind him in the shadows.

'What about the woman? Her body?' Viktor asked.

'Eventually my work was done. Her ablated flesh lay in the vats, slowly – more slowly than I had estimated – turning to thick paste, and her bones lay white and clean on the transformation table. It was then that Veles the Dark One called her forth. That calling forth thrilled and terrified me: his voice resonated in the floor, the walls, in my temples and jaw, in the vault of my skull. My own living bones rang with it. It was the most terrible but magnificent thing to hear.

'And then – oh, it was then I saw her transformation. I felt the air charge with some strange energy. Something intensely dark, darker than obsidian, coalesced in the air above the bones. She was emerging! For a single hopeful moment, she hung there in the air before me. She had no human shape; no face, no gender, no organic form. She had become a small, clustering black sparkle of intense darkness, like a small dark star suspended in the clammy air of the cellar. For that instant her darkness shone from her and I felt elated, overjoyed that I had created a Dark Shifter to travel between dimensions. But it was not to be. There was a single moment of effulgent darkness, then she was gone.'

'But you kept trying?'

'I tried again, and again. I had to travel farther, exploring the lowest parts of our cities to find drunkards, whores or tramps who would not be missed. I gave up my scruples about children and stole them away from their play – but again I chose only from the margins of society, mainly gypsy or street children. There are many today obsessed with "social hygiene" who would laud my efforts.

'Five, ten, then twenty – I became expert in unseen abduction and in extinguishing physical life. I could now excarnate a carcass with the skill of a butcher. The vats in the cellar struggled to keep pace and the whole cellar fumed with the smell of rendered flesh dissolving. I became concerned it was leaching into the main house. Not that I was disturbed by anyone, except for the grocer who still expected his coffee when making his weekly call, and the monthly visit by my landlady, the beautiful Rozálie Horáčková.'

'And all of these victims, these *subjects*,' asked Viktor. 'You never achieved your aim with any of them?'

Dominik shook his head. 'None sustained their Dark Shifter forms for more than a few seconds. Each would manifest above the bones as a brief dark shining, only to flicker and dissolve to nothing. Then I realized where I was going wrong: the consciousnesses I was acquiring were corrupt, morally dissolute, intellectually inferior. I needed to find someone worthy. Someone with the moral and intellectual fortitude to undertake mankind's greatest ever journey and journey across dimensions willingly. Someone who was not attached to this dimension, to their lives.'

'So it was then you decided to murder your landlady?'

'It was then I decided to help Rozálie Horáčková rejoin her husband.'

'I readied everything in the transition chamber. Madame Horáčková's essence, even her ablated flesh, must not be corrupted by contact with the lesser forms that had preceded her, so I filled two fresh vats: one with new lye, the other with fresh water and wine to bleach her fine bones. And as I watched her sitting in her garden, those delicate pale hands folded one upon the other, I imagined her bones, all porcelain white and delicate, and knew she was the right choice. I knew that this time I would achieve my aim.

'Eventually she made her scheduled visit to collect the month's rent. I usually had the money sitting in an envelope on the hall table in the vestibule. I'd hand it to her, first asking her in, even offering coffee, but she always declined. However, that day I pressed her, even sounding a little annoyed, saying I needed to discuss a problem with the house.

'As soon as she entered the house she commented on the smell. I told her that the smell was the problem I wanted to talk to her about; that it seemed to be coming from the basement. I asked her to come down to the cellar with me so I could show her where I thought the smell was coming from.

'She was reluctant at first, but I said I'd have to give up the house if the smell wasn't remedied, so she agreed. As we talked, I watched her beautiful face, so perfectly formed. I studied the bone beneath the flesh, the delicately crafted arches and angles of her skull, the articulation of her mandible in its pivot as she spoke. Just as Veles had told me that the essence, the soul of man, lies in bone, I could see that her bones were the fundament of Rozálie Horáčková's beauty. I wanted to see that beauty unadorned, naked: stripped of the cloth of flesh.

'I allowed her to go first down the stairs into the basement. She recoiled at the smell and complained that she couldn't see where she was going.

'"That's him," I said. "That's his effulgent darkness." "Whose?" she asked me, confused. "What are you talking about?" So I told her. I told her about Veles, about how her husband had struggled so long and hard to capture that ultimate darkness in his canvas of the Dark One. How his frustration with the painting had been that he could never find a paint black enough. I told her that she would soon be at her husband's side. We were by now at the bottom of the stairs, in a little island of light cast down from the door above, and she made to go back up towards it. But I was blocking her way, and when she tried to push past me I pushed back, thrusting her into the dark.

'"You have to understand," I said. "You have to see for yourself." Then I switched on the main lights to show her.

'She became hysterical. Screamed. I think it was when she saw the grocer. You see, he'd made his delivery to me earlier that day. He'd a habit of carrying the groceries directly into the kitchen if I didn't have the door locked. He'd shout out for me and I would come and make the coffee, which was becoming tiresome because he had run out of information to impart. Because of that – and because of the smell in the house – I'd taken to locking the kitchen door when he was due to call, leaving a note instructing him to leave the groceries on the doorstep.

'That day, however, with all the excitement in preparing for Madame Horáčková's transition to a Dark Shifter, I'd quite forgotten about the grocer until I heard him call out from the kitchen. When I went through, he was already sitting at the kitchen table, clearly expecting his customary coffee. He asked me straight away about the smell in the house, rather impolitely referring to it as a "terrible stench". He said it smelled like something had died beneath the floorboards. I told him that it was indeed the smell of corrupting flesh and, while he sat there puzzled, I took a knife from the kitchen drawer and slashed him across the throat. It was a trick I'd learned during my gathering of subjects: if you sever the windpipe, they're incapable of calling for help and become so singularly involved with trying to breathe that you can finish them off without interference. And that's what I did with the grocer.

'Anyway, I hadn't had time to deal properly with his remains, and when I turned on the cellar lights, Rozálie Horáčková saw his severed head on a wall shelf and his body on the stone floor in the corner. I was forced to hit her to stop her screaming. I had to be careful: I didn't want those beautiful porcelain bones of her skull damaged. She stood there shocked for a moment and I tried again to tell her what we were going to do, what we were going to achieve.

'Veles was in the cellar, waiting for us, you see. I introduced him, but Madame Horáčková screamed at me that I was mad, that there was no one there. I told her Veles was indeed there, and had come from the dimension her husband now occupied. But she was hysterical by now and screamed over and over again that there was no one there, that I was mad.

'She was making such a fuss that I had to hit her again, harder. She fell rather heavily and lost consciousness. I was annoyed I had to hit her at all: the whole point of her selection was because she should have been a willing traveller.

'I carried her over to the table and decided it would be less fuss if I cut her throat there and then, before removing her clothes and her flesh to leave the perfect beauty of her naked bones. I set my defleshing knife on the table next to her head and began unbuttoning her blouse. It was a pretty blue silk blouse and I didn't want it to become stained with blood.

'I was disturbed by a noise. Someone was ringing my doorbell and I turned to listen, trying to remember if I had locked all the doors.' Dominik Bartoš paused, shaking his head in vague annoyance, even a little sadly. 'It would have worked, you know. I'm convinced it would have worked. But when I turned back to her, she was awake. Her bright blue eyes were wide and wild, not with fear this time, but with anger, with hate. And she had my defleshing knife in her hand. She slashed at me.' Bartoš paused. In the pale light Viktor saw the deep indentation of the scar that ran from the bridge of his nose diagonally across his cheek to his jawline. 'She caught me in the face and when she slashed again, I held my hand up.' The hand missing its small finger, held in place by the wrist restraint, twitched. 'She stabbed me, leaving the knife in my chest, and I fell to the floor. I could hear her screaming as she ran up the cellar stairs and the banging on the front door grow louder. That was how they caught me. I called on Veles to help me, to save me from capture and take me to the Dark Forest, but he remained silent and unmoving in the shadows. I had failed him.'

Viktor noticed a tear ooze from the corner of the scientist's eye and follow the course of the scar across his cheek.

'You still believe Veles was there with you in the cellar?' asked Viktor.

'Yes.'

'So why didn't Madame Horáčková see him?'

'But she did see him. That's the thing. She kept saying all she could see was the dark. "But don't you understand", I said, "you *do* see Veles. Veles *is* the dark." The Lord of the Dark is there, wherever there is darkness, wherever there are shadows.' Dominik Bartoš looked at Viktor with as much emphasis as the drugs, which were now beginning to fray the edges of his alertness, would allow. 'He's always in the shadows. He's here, now, in the shadows behind you.'

iktor, Smolák and Dr Bartoš dined in the asylum canteen. Professor Románek was waiting there with two men whom he introduced as the head of general medicine, Dr Platner, and his assistant Dr Krakl, and explained both would be joining them for dinner. Smolák noticed that Platner and Krakl both wore Sudetendeutsche Partei pins. The six men had the dining hall to themselves, the patients having had their meal a couple of hours earlier and now confined to quarters.

Two canteen orderlies dressed in white jackets and bow ties brought them *pečená kachna* – baked duck with potato dumplings and red cabbage – served with beer. Smolák was served with a meatless *lečo* stew. As they ate, the Prague detective noticed Krakl pointedly spoke only German to Platner.

As they dined, Románek asked with his customary eagerness if Smolák and Bartoš had found the session interesting, but their muted responses dulled his enthusiasm. 'I'm sorry, Dr Bartoš,' he said. 'That was tactless of me. It must have been distressing for you.'

'You could say that.' Bartoš smiled weakly. 'I don't know what I expected; even with all I know of Dominik's crimes, I didn't expect that.' He turned to Viktor. 'Is there any chance that Veles *was* real? I mean, I know my brother's mad, but do you think there is any chance that there was someone else exploiting his madness?'

'You mean an accomplice who persuaded him he was an ancient Slavic deity?' Viktor's tone indicated his scepticism.

'Actually, that's something I'd like to know too,' said Smolák. 'The same could be said to apply to my gypsy suspect for the Leather Apron killings, particularly as the murders seem to be continuing.'

Viktor shook his head. 'In both cases I'm convinced we're talking about an abstracted, splintered part of the host personality. From what you've told me, your gypsy suspect was giving external form to a part of himself he sought to deny. The same is definitely the case with your brother, Dr Bartoš. Both were acting alone, even if they didn't know they were.'

'Nevertheless,' said Smolák, 'there's something about Tobar Bihari's story that doesn't quite fit with me. And there are the continued murders in Prague to be accounted for. My interview with Macháček has confused rather than clarified.'

'Oh?' said Professor Románek. 'I hoped Macháček would be responsive.'

'He was. Only too happy to tell me what an expert he is. But, like I say, it hasn't helped. I was on a fishing expedition: a detail that may or may not be significant.' Smolák shrugged. 'At least it's allowed me to sample your impressive cuisine here. Is this typical of the kind of meals your patients are served?'

'It is indeed,' Románek replied, proudly. 'We believe a well-balanced, varied diet is important. Although I have to admit one of our patients has such particular dietary requirements that it sometimes makes life difficult – nevertheless we do what we can to accommodate her.'

At the far end of the table, Krakl snorted, and Smolák saw Platner fire a warning look in his subordinate's direction.

'I take it you disapprove, Dr Krakl?' Smolák asked.

'I believe that the state's funding could be much better employed elsewhere, to be frank,' said Krakl. 'All this fancy dining—'

'I'd hardly call it fancy,' interrupted Viktor. 'Or perhaps you'd like to explain to Dr Bartoš here why you feel his brother would benefit from a diet of bread and water.'

'You know damned well that I'm not—'

'Please, gentlemen,' Románek cut off Krakl. 'Let's not have this debate while we have guests.' He turned to Smolák and Bartoš. 'Like all medical institutions, we have a variety of professional opinions on how our work should best be conducted.'

'I understand,' said Smolák. Then, casting a glance in Krakl's direction, 'These seem to be times of varied opinions, and not just in the medical field.'

The night was sharp-edged cold. The witch-hat roofs and spires obsidian black against the cloudless, star-sparkled sky above the castle. Viktor and Professor Románek walked Smolák and Bartoš to their car.

'I hope it wasn't a disappointing trip for you, Kapitán,' said Románek. 'Nor too distressing for you, Dr Bartoš. Please remember to feel free to visit your brother again.'

'I will, thank you,' said Bartoš. It was clear from his tone he had no intention of returning.

'Thanks for making Macháček available to me,' said Smolák. He turned to Viktor. 'And for allowing me to sit in on your session. You were right, it has helped me understand Tobar Bihari's case. I'm sorry about the note I handed you about the apron, but I'm sure you understand.'

Viktor nodded.

Smolák climbed into the car next to a silent Bartoš. 'You've been very helpful, Dr Kosárek,' he said through the rolled-down window. 'Thanks again.'

'Please remember to feel free to phone if I can be of any further help.'

Smolák nodded, resting gloved hands on the steering wheel. 'There was one thing. During the session, when Dr Bartoš's brother said Veles was there in the room, in the shadows – do you think he knew we were there?'

'No,' said Viktor. 'Sadly, the delusional inhabit their own landscape, a different plane from the rest of us.'

'Then he succeeded after all,' said Bartoš from the passenger seat, dully. 'He really has made his connection with a different dimension.'

whispered warning of the imminent arrival of full-blown winter was carried on the chilled breath of a breeze from the east. There had also been sporadic flurries of snow over the preceding days. Viktor suggested to Judita that it might be the last time until spring that they could walk down to the café in the village. By the time they set out, the snow was falling softly from a heavy sky, the thick, fluffy flakes seeming to linger and sway in the air.

As they walked, the snow slowly frosted the shoulders of the castle behind them and the tips and branches of the thick-clustered trees that flanked the road. That morning, Judita had finished typing up the transcript of the Bartoš session and they discussed the case on the way down.

'Professor Románek doesn't know this, but I gave Bartoš less than usual,' he admitted. 'I mean I didn't give him the full dosage of hypnotics.'

'Oh? It sounds as if it was enough from the full and frank description of his crimes you got from him.'

'I didn't like having his brother and that policeman sit in on it,' he said. 'After what happened with Pavel Zelený, I want the conditions to be as controlled as possible. I fully intend to do another session with Dominik Bartoš, on my own. I believe that he's the same as Zelený in many ways. When I was talking to Mr Hobbs, I was speaking to some schismatic, abstract part of Zelený's Unconscious. It's pretty much the same with Dominik Bartoš – he believes that the part of himself that is compelled to kill is actually this other identity: the Slavic god Veles. If I can take Bartoš to the same place I took Zelený, then I believe I'll be able to speak directly with "Veles".'

Judita shuddered from something other than just the cold and gathered the collar of her coat close to her ears. 'It gives me the creeps. It really does. The way he described Veles. When do you plan to have another session with him?'

'I'll have to schedule it in. I'm going to try with Zelený again first. And before either, I'm going to do my first session with Vojtěch Skála, the Demon. That means I'll have done sessions with all of the so-called Devil's Six.'

Viktor and Judita stopped, stepping off the roadway to allow a lorry that had been delivering fuel to the castle to pass on its way back down to the main road. They stood on a carpet of snow so thin it was almost translucent, the green of the roadside grass showing through it. Once the lorry passed, the silence fell around them with the snow. When Viktor made no sign of continuing, Judita turned to him.

'What is it?'

'There's something I have to tell you,' he said. 'About Filip.' He explained about the artist's impression and the description of the man the police were looking for.

'You don't really think it could be Filip?' she asked when he was finished.

'No.' Viktor's brow crowded his eyes in a perplexed frown. 'Maybe. The truth is I don't know. It's just that his behaviour was so – so *hostile* to women. And he said something about having known a woman in the glass trade. Then there's the similarity of the description . . .'

'It wasn't much of a description, Viktor. It could be anyone. But listen, if you have the slightest doubt about Filip, you *must* let this detective—'

'Smolák.'

'You must let this detective Smolák know.'

'And have Filip hauled in, maybe falsely accused?' Viktor sighed and looked up at the sky, as if an answer would fall with the snow. 'Filip is so out of control he would make the police suspect him, even if he's innocent.'

'It's your decision,' said Judita, 'but women's lives are at stake.'

'You're right,' said Viktor gloomily, and they resumed their walk down towards the village.

Something was wrong.

As they drew close to the edge of the village, they became aware of more activity than usual. The downward road took a sharp turn as they reached the outskirts and, as Viktor and Judita made the turn, they were confronted with a knot of people from the village engaged in animated discussion. When they saw Viktor and Judita, their talk stilled and the gazes they directed at the couple were surly, suspicious.

Viktor nodded and wished them *dobré ráno*. None replied but watched them with blank hostility as they passed.

'Something's happened,' said Viktor, leaning in to Judita and speaking in an almost whisper once they were clear of the villagers. 'I don't like it. Maybe we should go back.'

'I'd like to find out,' said Judita. 'Maybe it's just their superstitions about the castle.'

Judita's theory was dispelled as they came closer to the heart of the village, where the inn stood. There were more villagers, more suspicious gazes; but there were also two police cars from Mladá Boleslav parked in the square and several uniformed policemen were gathered around a senior officer giving instructions.

As Judita and Viktor passed, one of the villagers said something to the police commander and he, too, turned to look at them.

'God,' said Judita beneath her breath. 'Why do I feel so guilty when I haven't done anything?'

'Let's get lunch,' said Viktor. 'I'll ask the innkeeper what's going on.'

Their mood darkened further when they entered the café. The moustachioed innkeeper didn't greet them with his usual warmth: dressed in coat, hat, scarf and heavy boots, he was clearly on his way out as they came in.

'We're closed today,' he said without apology. 'I need to go and help with the search.'

'The search?' asked Judita.

'I think it would be best if you returned to the castle,' he said. 'A young girl from the village has gone missing. Little Jolanka . . . It might be an idea to steer clear of the village until she's found.'

'What's that got to do with us?' asked Viktor, indignant. 'I'd like to help if there's a search going on.'

'You know how we are here,' said the innkeeper. 'We're a small and tight-knit community of families that have lived together for generations. When something like this happens, when anything bad happens, then outsiders are the first to be suspected. But it's more than that – there are rumours going around. People are blaming your asylum up there in the castle. They're saying that one of the Devil's Six is using Jan of the Black Heart's old tunnels to get in and out. They think it's somebody from the castle who's taken little Jolanka.'

'But that's absurd,' protested Viktor. 'Our security is impenetrable. There's no way anyone could escape, far less come and go as they please. And these tunnels are folklore – there's absolutely no evidence of any secret doors or passageways.'

'That's maybe all true,' said the innkeeper, 'but that doesn't make it any safer for you here in the village.'

Viktor was about to protest again, but Judita rested a gloved hand on his arm. 'He's right, Viktor. We should go back.'

Viktor sighed and nodded. 'All right.'

They turned and left the café. There was a quieter road through the village that took them a little out of their way before joining up to the road that climbed to the castle, but there were fewer people to encounter. It seemed now that the entire village was in the main square. Viktor guided Judita with a gentle push on the elbow to pick up pace.

As they neared the village boundary, they could see the last of the level ground before the forest-dressed flank of the mountain rose steeply. There was a large flat area devoted to allotments, the winter-naked soil hard and gathering a covering of snow. Nothing was growing there at this time of year, but they saw two dark-clad figures in one of the fields. As they drew close, Viktor could see there was a younger woman, distraught, and an old woman with her white hair hidden by a black headscarf. The old woman was scattering something on the earth, like flour or ash, that clouded the cold air as it was thrown. As she did so her lips moved in silent speech. The younger woman, who seemed oblivious to Viktor and Judita as they passed, had the red eyes and pale face of prolonged weeping, but the old woman paused her ritual as Viktor and Judita passed them, her eyes blazing with hatred. Viktor recognized her as Růžena, the old woman who supplied the café and inn with its vegetables. He noticed that she had a black leather pouch in her hands, containing whatever it was she was scattering on the ground. The weeping woman held a child's doll clutched to her chest.

Judita said hello to the old woman, but again she responded only by glaring at them both. As they passed, she did the strangest thing: she turned her head as far as she could turn it and spat three times over her left shoulder.

She then returned to her voiceless chanting and scattering of ashes onto the ground.

'What the hell was that all about?' asked Viktor.

Judita, when she answered, kept her gaze fixed on the path ahead and the long, cold climb back to the castle.

'It's an old Bohemian peasant belief,' she said. 'You spit three times over your left shoulder to protect yourself from the Devil.'

PART FIVE

THE BUTTERFLY AND THE STONE SUN

CHAPTER ONE

*T*he last time Kapitán Lukáš Smolák had been here, the street had been mantled in night and fog; even now, in the pale grey light of an overcast day, both seemed to linger in the dark staining of the daylight stonework.

However it looked, it certainly sounded different.

There was now a sound like thunderous rain, or a fast-flowing torrent. It was all around him, loud and harsh and urgent. It had started when he first got out of his car: he had turned because he thought someone was trying to attract his attention by tapping a coin against window glass. He could see no one, but turned in the other direction when he heard a second coin against glass, farther down the street. Then a third, then a fourth. Like hot sparks spreading a fire, the sound extended to the windows above him, those on the other side of the street, others he couldn't see from where he stood.

As Smolák crossed the road to where Tobar Bihari's apartment lay, the racket around him continued undimmed, but he ignored it. This was a quarter filled with thieves and prostitutes, Roma and Sinti, Jews and Hungarians, anarchists and communists: a disparate group that had common good reason to mistrust the Prague Municipal Police. The rattling of coin against glass, Smolák knew, was the agreed alarm to alert of police presence.

The dead gypsy's apartment was two flights up. Smolák had the keys the police had found on Bihari, but when he arrived at the door, he found Tsora Mirga, Bihari's club-footed paramour, waiting with the door open and her expression dully hostile. Once again Smolák was struck by her incongruous beauty. Her eyes were large, the irises like black olives, her complexion golden brown and her hair a thick, glossy black. Her red silk blouse and grey skirt clung to her figure, but the skirt was several centimetres longer than the current fashion. She stood with her hips tilted in a pose that seemed provocative, but was merely the effect of her uneven anatomy. He noticed that she hid the corrective-booted foot behind the other.

'Hello Tsora,' Smolák said. 'I'd like to ask you a few questions.'

'What's left to ask?' She stood aside to let him enter the apartment. Tsora Mirga knew that Smolák, sympathetic towards her after Bihari's death, had arranged for the charges against her to be dropped.

'Tobar's story troubled me,' he said honestly. 'I just wanted to ask you about how he was after the burglary and murder. What he said about that night, and what changes you saw in him afterwards.'

She shrugged and led him into the parlour, her narrow shoulders rolling with her limping gait. The apartment was scrupulously clean and Smolák was annoyed by his own expectation that gypsies, even those settled in the city, should be dirty and unhygienic in their living conditions. He had always thought himself uninfected by such prejudices; but, these days, its contagion seemed endemic.

'May I sit?' he asked, and she nodded dully. He sat on a small sofa dressed with a brightly coloured blanket. Like the complexion of its owner, the patterns on the blanket marked it as belonging to some distant time and culture. Smolák wondered what it must be like to be a perpetual stranger, to always be mistrusted.

Tsora sat opposite him, crossing her legs below the knee so that again her good foot sat in front of her clubbed one: an automatic pose born of a lifetime's habit of hiding her defect. There was a modesty in the gesture that made Smolák feel strangely sad. Tsora was a gypsy and a cripple; she had been a pickpocket as a child and had been a prostitute from her teens. Yet another Tsora Mirga lay hidden. He remembered what the psychiatrist Kosárek had said about how everyone had more than one personality, more than one potential self.

'Do you ever go to the Modrý Bažant pub?' Smolák asked.

She nodded. 'Tobar picked me up there after I finished working each night. Why?'

'Nothing, really. Just that I think you may have had a narrow escape a few years back, that's all,' said Smolák, thinking back to Dominik Bartoš's description of the young, limping prostitute he had originally targeted in the bar.

Tsora's silence and lack of curiosity suggested narrow escapes had been commonplace in her life.

'I wanted to ask what Tobar discussed with you in the days after the break-in and murder in Sněmovní Street.'

The small, pretty gypsy again shrugged her narrow shoulders. 'The same as he told you. Mad ravings about Beng and demons in the shadows. But it took me ages to get even that out of him. For days after he sat in here, never daring to go out, just staring at the door. And he never put the lights out either – all of them had to be on day and night. He became obsessed with it and told me to buy in spare bulbs in case they burned out.'

She pointed to where a standard lamp stood incongruously crammed into a corner alcove. 'That corner there never did get much light, and in the evening it would be in shadow. Tobar shoved that lamp in there, saying there must never be shadows in the house. He was like a frightened child – you knew him: Tobar wasn't scared of anything. Whatever he saw in that place changed him for good. And before you ask: no, I don't believe for a minute that he did that to that woman or that he was Leather Apron. I know you'd like to pin it on him and tie everything up all neat, but Tobar would never hurt a woman or a child.'

Smolák nodded as he considered what Tsora had said. 'You admit yourself that he was behaving strangely, maybe even showing signs of mental instability – like him acting paranoid, or his being suddenly afraid of the dark. You don't know what could have been going on inside his head. I've talked to experts about it and it's entirely possible that Tobar didn't know himself what he was doing.'

'But he was fine,' Tsora protested. 'Perfectly normal right up until that night of the break-in. It was what he saw that night that made him act crazy. After, not before. It took me an age to persuade him to go outside. Even longer to go outside at night. That night you caught him, we had to take the long way home, just so we could stay in the streets with most light. That's how come we walked straight past you: Tobar wanted to walk on that side of the street because there were more lights. Did you see his face when you stepped out of that doorway? He was terrified – like he thought you were what he was most scared of. A shadow coming to life.'

*T*he preparations for the next session were even more careful: of the Devil's Six, Vojtěch Skála was by far the darkest, the most dangerous, the most violent.

Before the session, Viktor made a routine call on Leoš Mládek, the former circus clown turned child-murderer. Mládek seemed to have resigned himself to his confinement, even if he remained confused by it and thought it unjust. Viktor had visited him several times since his sessions and they had talked without the use of hypnotic sedatives. Mládek still resolutely refused to believe that Harlequin was simply a hidden, denied part of his personality.

Leoš Mládek's cooperative attitude and absence of aggression had been rewarded with small concessions. One of which had been that Viktor had allowed him his clown's make-up, as well as some scholarly books on the tradition of Commedia dell'arte. Through these small indulgences and their relaxed discussions, Viktor felt he was building a connection with his patient that was perhaps more effective than the drug-induced hypnosis of the narcosynthesis sessions.

Viktor and Mládek would sit for an hour discussing the role of masks and symbols in both Commedia dell'arte and Jungian psychology, often while Mládek made his face up as Pierrot: an act that seemed to bring the Clown some peace.

Today, Viktor found it difficult to focus on his patient. The forthcoming session with Skála hung over his mood like a cloud, and as he stood at the window looking down towards the village, he became more perplexed. Even though he denied it to everyone else, a little girl going missing in a village so close to this much concentrated madness concerned him. The fact that he was engaged in conversation with a convicted child murderer did his mood no good.

'Thank you for allowing me my make-up,' said Mládek, who sat behind Viktor painting his face as Pierrot. 'It makes me feel more *whole*.'

'You're welcome.' Viktor still looked down at the village, which seemed so small and fragile from the dominating height of the castle, as if the crowding forest around it could swallow it up. 'I just wish it would help you remember things more clearly.'

'Oh,' said Mládek. 'What things?'

'We've talked about this so many times, Leoš,' said Viktor absently. He wondered if the girl had been found yet, and in what state. 'Those children. What happened to them.'

'Oh,' said Mládek absently. 'I remember them all right.'

'What?' Viktor, surprised, turned to him. His surprise instantly became shock.

Leoš Mládek was standing in the centre of the room. He had completed his clown make-up. But what Viktor was looking at wasn't Pierrot. Mládek had painted his face blood red. Two black diamonds surrounded his eyes, reaching up into apexes high on his brow and deep onto his cheeks. A grotesque, full-lipped mouth had been painted in black across the whole bottom half of his face, curving malevolently up in a grin on one side, down in a grimace on the other. It was face paint, nothing more, but the effect was terrifying.

'I said I remember them all right. The children. Children's fear is greater, purer, sweeter than anyone else's. I remember drinking their terror and their pain.'

'You're Harlequin?' asked Viktor. He saw that Mládek still had in his hand the brush he'd used to apply his make-up.

'I'm Harlequin. I'm Harlequin and I did it all. I'm the one you tried to find.'

'But you're also Leoš Mládek. You're also Pierrot.'

'I'm more. Much more.' He took a step towards Viktor. As he did so he turned the brush around so the point projected like a dagger in his hand. Viktor cursed his laxity in placing a potential weapon in his hand. Leoš Mládek had transformed from gentle Pierrot into cruel Harlequin: the killer; the sadist who fed on children's fear. And he had a rudimentary weapon. Viktor remembered Professor Románek's warnings about his predecessor's similar permissiveness costing him an eye.

'Give me the brush, Leoš.' Viktor extended his hand. He kept his eyes locked on his patient, but it was difficult to read any expression beneath the demonic face paint.

Mládek the Harlequin looked down at the brush in his hand, as if he had forgotten it was there. He looked up again at Viktor, the painted mask still twisted and demonic, his large eyes bright and manic in their black-painted lozenges, the bared teeth white in the painted twisted smile on the raw red face. This, Viktor realized, had been the face his victims had seen. The last face they had seen.

Without warning, Mládek let out a high-pitched scream and launched himself at Viktor, raising the brush like a dagger. He was a small man but the suddenness and force of his attack unbalanced Viktor, who fell backwards, hitting his head on the stone arch of the window recess. He lay stunned and became aware of Mládek on top of him. Viktor gathered himself just in time to block the downward thrust towards his eye of the brush handle's pointed tip. He punched the Harlequin face, but lying on his back meant he couldn't put any real force behind the blow. Still Harlequin screamed. Viktor grabbed the wrist that held the improvised weapon and twisted it hard.

As he did so, Mládek leaned in close to him and hissed: 'You were too busy looking out of the window, weren't you? You were too busy wondering what's happened to that little girl. You were too busy wondering how I could have got out of the castle and taken her.'

In German. Mládek had spoken to him in *German*. For a split second he tried to work out if it had been the same voice that Zeleny had used when he pretended to be Mr Hobbs. But it couldn't be. It was impossible.

Viktor recovered himself and shoved upwards with all his strength. The smaller man flew from him, landing on his back on the stone floor of his accommodation. There was a large crack, like the sound of stone on stone.

'Help!' yelled Viktor as he struggled to his feet. 'I need help in here right now!'

He rushed over to where Mládek lay, ready to restrain him until the orderlies, whom he could hear running in the corridor towards the door, arrived and secured the patient. But Leoš Mládek made no effort to struggle. To move. He lay perfectly still, staring up at the ceiling with his too-big eyes, while a dark crimson halo formed on the flagstones around the Harlequin-painted face.

When the orderlies came bursting into the room, Viktor held up his hand to halt their urgent advance. There was no rush now. Leoš Mládek, his skull smashed by his fall onto the floor, was dead.

The Devil's Six had become the Devil's Five.

*T*he session with Skála was postponed. Through the shock of what had happened and the pain in his head and neck, Viktor worried that he might never be allowed to use his narcosynthesis method on Skála; that his work at Hrad Orlů was over. That his quest to find the Devil Aspect in human psychology had ended before it had even begun.

The injury to his head was minor, but Viktor had been taken to the infirmary where Krakl tended to him. The Sudeten German passed surprisingly few comments as he put a single stitch in the small laceration in Viktor's scalp. Dr Platner, Krakl explained, was in Mladá Boleslav on pressing hospital business, but had been informed of Mládek's death when he had telephoned, and was now on his way back to the castle.

Professor Románek arrived in the infirmary just as Krakl was finishing up and placing a padded dressing over the stitched wound. He demanded Viktor explain the sequence of events that led up to the patient's attack and subsequent death, leaving out no details. Viktor did so, ignoring the throbbing in his head. It was clear that, having established that Viktor's injuries were minor, the asylum director was angry that Viktor had ignored his caution about allowing patients anything that could be used as a weapon.

Gripping the treatment table's edge to steady himself, Viktor eased into a sitting position and gave his account. As Románek had demanded, Viktor gave every detail. Every detail except two: he didn't mention Mládek's bizarre statement that he had somehow known about events in the village and the girl who had gone missing, nor did Viktor mention that Mládek had spoken to him in perfect, slightly antiquated German.

Viktor knew that telling Románek that single detail could cast his whole testimony in doubt. After all, it made no sense. Viktor's research – his narcosynthesis sessions with the Devil's Six – was in grave danger of being cancelled. There had now been two incidents where Viktor had let down his guard with violent results, and he could sense Románek's enthusiasm for his new assistant waning. But added to that was Viktor's overwhelming feeling that he was on the verge of discovering something truly significant, yet something he could not yet explain. And until he could, it was best not to discuss it with Románek.

When he was about halfway through his account, Judita came into the treatment room looking flustered. She was about to rush across to Viktor but, seeing he was giving a report to Románek, checked her advance. Reassured that Viktor wasn't seriously hurt, she withdrew to the wall by the door and listened.

'You're right that the attack wouldn't have happened if I hadn't given him his face make-up,' Viktor told Románek when he had finished his report. 'But not because the brush amounted to any kind of effective weapon: don't you see that having the make-up allowed him to give a face to his Devil Aspect? The act of painting his face as Harlequin unlocked what I'd been looking for in him. Harlequin was the Devil Aspect in Mládek.'

'And now he's dead,' said Románek bluntly. He paused for a moment. 'Dr Kosárek, I have to ask you something and I hope you understand why. There have been two violent incidents involving previously compliant patients. In both cases there was a trigger – with Mládek it was the face paints you allowed him; with Michal Macháček it was a piece of glassware that didn't come from the canteen. My question is this: did you deliberately give these items to your patients in the hope that they'd stimulate a response like this?'

'What?'

'Let's be frank, your narcosynthesis sessions so far haven't exactly been successes, other than the appearance of some kind of ghostly voice. And we've all been there, Dr Kosárek: frustrated with the lack of progress in proving a theory. The desire to take short-cuts, or to try to stimulate a more dramatic outcome.'

'You don't think the appearance of the Hobbs identity in Zelený is a success?' Viktor strained to keep the anger from his tone. 'But to answer your question, Professor: no, I didn't give Mládek his make-up to trigger a violent episode – and I certainly didn't give Michal Macháček glassware of any kind.'

'Very well.' Románek nodded. Then, after a moment, he said in a tone that didn't invite debate, 'Nevertheless, I think you should take a few days off to recover from that concussion. But, if you're up to it tomorrow, I'd like you to dictate your report to Miss Blochová, so I can submit it to the authorities. But no further sessions, am I clear?'

Viktor nodded.

'I'm afraid you have perhaps placed our entire operation here in jeopardy, Dr Kosárek. Dr Platner is in Mladá Boleslav, talking to the police.'

'The police?'

'The local authorities are under pressure to investigate us in light of the little girl who is missing from the village. The villagers have them all but convinced that her disappearance has something to do with us up here in the castle.'

'Not that again,' said Viktor. He rubbed the back of his neck: what had been a dull ache was blooming into something less easy to ignore. 'All this nonsense about secret tunnels and Jan of the Black Heart.'

'That's as may be,' said Románek, 'but I have the police wanting to inspect our arrangements here and the last thing we need is the death of a patient being investigated. Give me a full written report as soon as you can. Then you and I are going to have a serious discussion about the efficacy of these sessions.'

After Románek had left, Viktor eased himself off the treatment couch. He steadied himself against a bout of dizziness. Krakl ignored him but Judita came and took him by the arm.

'I'll see Dr Kosárek safely back to his quarters,' she said blankly to Krakl.

'I'm sure you will,' said the Sudetener without turning.

When she got him back to his rooms, Judita sat Viktor down at his desk and fetched a glass of water. Placing it on the desk, she leaned in and kissed him gently on the top of his head, sinking her lips into his thick, glossy hair.

'You all right?' she asked.

Viktor sighed. 'No, I'm not all right. I killed a man. A patient.'

'At worst it was self-defence. It was an accident. Tragic, but an accident.'

'I shouldn't have allowed a situation like that to evolve. I shouldn't have created the opportunity. Professor Románek is right.'

'Do you think he'll cancel your Devil Aspect research?' Judita asked. 'Discontinue the narcosynthesis sessions?'

Viktor suddenly became even more agitated. 'He can't. He mustn't.'

'Viktor, what is it? What's wrong?' Judita read something else in his expression.

He sighed. 'This sounds mad – and I'm leaving it out of my report – but Mládek spoke to me in German – and he knew about the missing girl. It didn't make sense.' Viktor drank the water, taking the analgesic tablets Krakl had given him. 'How could he have known about the girl?'

Judita lit a cigarette for Viktor and handed it to him before lighting one for herself. She sat down in the armchair in the corner. 'Most likely he overheard something he wasn't meant to hear: maybe a couple of orderlies discussing the disappearance within earshot.'

'That doesn't explain him speaking in German.'

'Didn't he grow up in Doudlebsko?' asked Judita. 'He'd have German speakers all around him then. For all we know he was fluent.'

'Well, we'll never know now,' said Viktor, gloomily.

'Have you decided what you're going to do about Filip?'

'Do?' Viktor frowned.

'Are you going to tell the police about your concerns?'

'I don't know. Maybe. Professor Románek wants me to take a couple of days off. I think I'll do that, but go back to Prague and look for Filip.'

'Do you want me to come with you?'

'No. The way Filip's been about women—'

'If you think that, then you shouldn't be going to look for him. You should be getting the police involved.'

'Because Filip's been acting misogynistically doesn't make him Leather Apron. I just need a chance to talk things through with him. But first I'll have to get this report done.'

'We'll do that in the morning. I think you should get a good night's sleep.' Judita kissed him once more, gently, on the head.

'*Y*ou're still going to Prague? When?' asked Judita. The next day she and Viktor sat in his office while he dictated his statement about Mládek's attack and subsequent death.

'Tonight, if I can.'

'You shouldn't be travelling with that concussion.'

'I'll be all right.' He smiled weakly. 'Dr Platner has given me a stronger dose of analgesics and I feel fine.' It was a lie: his head still hurt and his neck ached. 'I need to go. I need to find Filip.'

'To find out if he's Leather Apron? God, Viktor, if you think there's even a chance—'

'Don't worry, if I find anything else to suggest he is, I'll go straight to Kapitán Smolák. But I can't go to them now with only the vaguest of suspicions.'

He had just finished dictating his statement to Judita, when there was a knock at the door. Before Viktor had a chance to say 'Come in', Románek and Platner stepped stern-faced into the room. They were followed by a shorter man in uniform wearing the bar-and-star shoulder flashes of a police major.

'This is Major Chromík,' explained Románek. 'He's here to talk about what happened to Leoš Mládek and also to examine our security arrangements.'

Victor recognized the uniformed officer, who looked to be some-where in his late forties, as the one he and Judita had seen in the village; the one who had eyed them suspiciously as they passed. He was short for a policeman, but had a face filled with intelligence and authority: green eyes set in an architecture of broad brow and high cheekbones. To start with Viktor thought the policeman eyed him and his surroundings with the same suspicion he'd shown in the village, but then realized it was an expression of cool assessment.

'You're aware that we've found the girl missing from the village?' Chromík asked. He had a West Bohemian accent; a local accent.

'That's a relief,' said Viktor.

'I didn't say alive and well,' said Chromík, flatly. 'We found her late yesterday. Just about the time you had your altercation with your patient. She was floating, drowned, in the pond behind the village.'

Viktor felt something deep inside tighten and twist. The image of another small girl came to mind – his long-dead sister – her slow, silent sinking; the fading brightness of her dress billowing in the dark water. The distress at the memory must have registered on his face.

'Are you all right, Dr Kosárek?' asked Chromík.

'What? Oh yes. It's just my head and neck hurt. After yesterday, you know?'

'I understand.' Chromík's searchlight stayed on Viktor. 'Anyway, the missing girl had a habit of wandering off, apparently. And she'd been warned so many times about playing too close to the water's edge. For the moment we're treating it as a tragic accident.'

'For the moment?' asked Románek.

'There's nothing yet to suggest foul play, but I'm afraid the vil-lagers are looking in only one direction for an explanation.' Major Chromík shrugged and indicated their stone surroundings with a gesture.

'Not this again,' sighed Platner. 'When will these people—'

'These people are my people,' said Chromík without hostility. 'I was born in the village. Lived here until I was sixteen. These are my people and I understand their fears, how they feel. This place, the castle, has always cast a shadow over them.'

'But the asylum has only been here for three years,' protested Viktor.

'I'm talking about the castle, not just the asylum. The asylum is just – ' he struggled for the right description – 'just its latest *incarnation*, I suppose you'd call it. An inevitable one at that: the confinement of so much evil here is only to be expected.'

'I don't understand.'

'When the locals found out that the castle was going to be converted to an asylum, they protested. Sent letters to the regional and national government, to the ministry of health. But at the same time they were resigned to it. You see, they knew, before anyone ever said, that the Devil's Six would be brought here.'

'How could they possibly have known that?'

'Because they know this place. Generations have lived in the shadow of this castle, knowing evil always comes home to it. Everything bad that's ever happened in this region has had some connection to the castle. It draws evil men to it, evil deeds. That's why everyone here knew, as soon as they heard it was going to be converted into an asylum for the mad, that the Devil's Six would be brought to it. Everyone has been waiting for the suffering to start.'

'But that's all nothing but superstition.'

'Not superstition. Experience. You find it unacceptable that they look to the castle when a girl goes missing, but it's not the first time girls have gone missing and the castle has been involved. When it was an army garrison one of the soldiers became obsessed with a local girl who had no interest in him. He ambushed her, raped her and killed her. When the army tried to arrest him he went berserk and shot his own officers and comrades, then hid in the woods for weeks until they found him.

'The army garrison left at the end of the war and the fall of

Austro-Hungary. From then until the state took it over for use as an asylum it lay empty and neglected. Even then people said it was causing all kinds of things to go wrong. Local girls started to go missing, from the village and the neighbouring hamlets. Of course all the superstitions about Jan of the Black Heart came out again. The locals gathered together and came up to search the castle. They found a tramp had made a bed for himself in the tower room, where no one could see his lamp burning, and which he said was easier to keep warm.'

'Was he known to them?'

'No. He had been wandering through the region, begging or stealing from farms when the opportunity arose. He had passed through the village a month or so before the first girl went missing and no one made the connection. In the meantime he'd set himself up here in the castle.'

'Why did he do that?'

Chromík shrugged dismissively. 'The castle was disused but far from a ruin. Built to last, you see. And because of all of the legends, the locals never came near the castle or its chapel in the forest. So he lived like a lord. He set snares for rabbits in the woods and had made himself very comfortable. He didn't know about the local superstitions and couldn't understand why he had been left alone, but he hadn't questioned his good fortune.'

'And he was blamed for the missing girls?'

'Oh, there was evidence – when the villagers found him they discovered an item of jewellery belonging to one of the missing girls but no sign of the girls themselves.'

'So he was arrested?'

'Unfortunately we – I mean the police – didn't get there in time. You have to understand it was a mob that came looking for him. They were terrified of the castle and they found him in the very part associated with Jan of the Black Heart. I'm afraid they hauled him out to the barbican and threw him from the bridge into the gully before we got a chance to question him. But the jewellery belonged to the girls, all right.'

'But that was sheer murder,' said Viktor. 'He should have stood trial. Then you'd have known what happened to the missing girls. He could have been innocent.'

Chromík shrugged. 'I agree with you and can't condone what the mob did, but we couldn't hold any one person to account. Anyway, they had given him a chance to explain his possession of the jewellery. He claimed he'd heard the sounds of screaming one night but had been too afraid to go to see from where. The next morning he found a secret door had been left open. He said it led into the network of caves beneath the castle but he hadn't dared to go far into it. But he had found the piece of jewellery lying on the floor.'

'What kind of jewellery?'

'I'm not sure. But it was identified by one of the girls' mothers as belonging to her daughter.'

'He didn't confess?'

Chromík shook his head. 'He protested his innocence right up until the end, when he was thrown over into the chasm. Well, he would do, wouldn't he?'

Viktor nodded. He decided not to point out that Chromík seemed very well acquainted with the sequence of events that led to the tramp's death, considering he claimed not to have arrived on the scene until it was too late.

'And everyone was satisfied it had been the tramp who had been taking the girls?' he asked.

'Some claimed it had been Jan of the Black Heart all along. But even they accepted it was the tramp when the abductions stopped. Listen, what I'm trying to get across to you is that people here knew the Devil's Six would be brought to this place – for the same reason a homicidal tramp was drawn to it; the same reason Jan of the Black Heart made this his home. People have lived on this exact spot since the beginning of time. And for as long as they have, something evil has lived here with them. Something in the rock or in the forest. Something that acts as a magnet and draws evil men to it. Some dark energy that gives them the boldness and strength to fulfil their evil.'

'I'm afraid I can't lend any credence to such claims,' said Viktor. 'There is no geography, no geology, to violent madness. The most spectacular evil can arise in the most unexpected places.'

Chromík shrugged. 'All I know is what I know.'

'So this tramp's claims that there was a secret passage – that's why you're here?' he asked instead. 'You think Mládek mysteriously managed to escape his cell and get down to the village?'

'I'm not saying that at all. I just have to examine every possibility. And I thought I made it clear how difficult it is to reassure the local residents. My point is that the locals have good and long-established reasons for viewing anything to do with the castle with mistrust. And the very man who died here yesterday was Central Europe's most notorious abductor and murderer of children. Added to which you've got the rest of the Devil's Six locked up in here.'

'We quite understand,' said Románek, firing a meaningful look at Viktor. 'Why don't we show you around, Major?'

Chromík nodded, then turned back to Viktor. 'Then I'd like to talk to you about Mr Mládek's death, if that's convenient.'

'I'll have the statement typed up in half an hour,' Judita volunteered.

'That would be most useful,' said Chromík with a smile and a bow. 'But I'd also like to hear it from Dr Kosárek directly, if that's not too inconvenient.'

'Not at all,' said Viktor.

CHAPTER FIVE

*H*e didn't take the train this time.

Viktor had taken a taxi into Mladá Boleslav that afternoon to pick up the car he'd bought on hire purchase: a three year-old black Tatra 57. So in the evening, despite Judita's continued misgivings and the snow that still crusted the less-travelled roads, Viktor drove into Prague.

It was a strange experience for him to find his way around a cityscape he knew so well yet had never driven in, added to which was the fact that millennium-old Prague made no concessions to the upstart imperatives of the motor car. But having the car allowed Viktor the freedom to make his way directly to Filip's apartment in Vršovice. Despite the snow-edged streets and pavements being quiet, he had no desire to wander around the quarter on foot, remembering the scuffle Filip had provoked with the German-Bohemians.

Eventually he found the courtyard, recognizing it by the rusting motorcycle and car huddled under shrouds of snow in its corner. The clustering, soot-darkened tenements seemed darker yet in contrast to the moonlight-brightened snow that edged roofs and blanketed its broken cobbles. Viktor parked the Tatra, conspicuous with its polished just-bought gleam, and made his way through the alleyway to Filip's apartment.

His knocking stimulated no answer. He stood for a moment in the snow-muffled silence, the only sound the distant barking of a dog. A grave doubt settled on him: what was he doing there? He had said to Judita that he couldn't afford to be mixed up in Filip's misdeeds, street brawls or other outrages. Viktor had been attacked by two of his patients, Pavel Zelený and Leoš Mládek – and Mládek had ended up dead with a shattered skull. Viktor knew that Professor Románek's enthusiasm for his appointment had waned significantly and just one more scandal could tip the balance against him.

But Filip was his friend. And Viktor suspected that there was more going on with him than simply losing his way. He knocked again: still no answer. No sounds from inside. No lights on.

He stood back from the door and took in the surrounding buildings. There were lights from a handful of the windows, the others blank and dark; nothing to suggest he was being observed. He suddenly remembered how, during his last visit, they had left by the back door and Filip had hidden his key under a loose flagstone. He made his way around to the back of the converted coach-house block. Ringed by a metre-and-a-half-high wooden fence, and with no streetlight at the back of the buildings, the small yard lay in impenetrable moon-cast shadow. There was no light from either Filip's or the neighbouring apartment, and all Viktor could make out in the dark were the jumbled black shapes of refuse bins huddled next to the gate he'd come through.

Quietly closing the gate behind him, he inched forward in the pitch black until he was sure he was close to the door before flicking on his cigarette lighter. He squatted down, using the glow from his lighter to locate the loose flagstone. The key was there and he stood for an indecisive moment with it in his gloved hand. This was not the kind of thing he did, the kind of world he inhabited. All his life Viktor had been cautious, careful. And now he was considering breaking into a home that wasn't his.

He made up his mind. Unlocking the door, he slipped into the silent darkness.

'Filip?' Viktor called out. The streetlamp and moonlight cut ragged geometries across the piles of books and papers cluttering the main room. 'Filip?'

Viktor took a few steps forward and his shin hit a stack of books sitting on the floor by the armchair. He sent them tumbling and cursed as he searched for the main light switch. The sudden flooding of the room with stark light made it seem strangely desolate and, as had been suggested by the presence of the key under the flagstone, it was clear that Filip wasn't at home. Viktor climbed the stair to the gallery where his friend's bed lay unmade, the sheets looking as though they hadn't been changed for some time.

Viktor was at a loss what to do next. He had come all this way to see Filip, to talk with him. He could wait for him to return, but wasn't sure how his friend would react to seeing him sitting uninvited in his home, among his private belongings. Especially if Filip returned drunk and aggressive.

The truth was, he knew, that he was glad Filip wasn't at home. It gave him a chance to look around, to pry into the unseen corners of his friend's life and see what was hidden there. To look for evidence to prove or disprove his darkest suspicions.

He went back down to the main room and through to the kitchen. In contrast to the gallery bedroom with its abandoned, unmade bed, everything in the kitchen was tidy, with only a few washed dishes drying on the sink's draining board. The order and cleanliness of the kitchen cheered Viktor: as a psychiatrist, he knew that mental chaos had a habit of spilling out into people's lives. Any sign that there was a sense of order, or engaging with everyday tasks, was good.

He tried the second door off the living area. From what he could make of the internal layout of the apartment, it was unlikely to be a room, but could have been a sizeable-enough storage cupboard. It was locked, and there was no sign of a key anywhere Viktor searched.

He found Filip's desk. The drawers were locked and the desktop was piled high with papers and books. What appeared at first to be chaos, again on closer inspection revealed itself to have some kind of order. The bulk of the material related to research sources, mainly to do with early Eastern European history or ancient Nordic and Slavic mythologies.

Under a pile of loose papers Viktor uncovered a bulky leather manuscript binder. The rich chestnut leather of the cover had been intricately tooled: carved like an ancient woodcut into delicate bas-relief, the details dyed with vibrant colours and impressed in places with gold leaf. A repeated motif of two figures pursuing each other formed a running frieze around the edge of the leather cover. One figure, highlighted in white, blue and gold leaf, carried a staff in one hand, a golden orb in the other; the other figure carried a sword and a human skull and was rendered in blood-red and black. Repeated in an endless cycle, it was impossible to say who was chasing whom.

The main panel of the cover was a pattern of trees, spun through with an intricate weaving of leaves and vines. The boss in the centre of the panel was a device Viktor recognized instantly: the motif of the Disgorging Head – the Green Man common to all European mythologies – spewing forth vegetation that spilled into the panel to become the intertwining leaves and vines. Except this Green Man wore a headdress made from the head and pelt of a bear. Veles.

Viktor took the manuscript over to the couch. When he opened it he found a thick sheaf of loose pages, hundreds of them, all written out in a small, neat, regular hand, perfect except for the odd underlining and notes added in the margin.

From the first page it was clear that this was the book Filip had talked about, his 'definitive work on Slavic mythology'. As Viktor read through it, selecting pages at random, he was relieved to see that, instead of some wild and raving piece, it was the lucid and scholarly work of an ordered, disciplined intellect. Filip had even illustrated many of the tales, and Viktor was surprised by his friend's skill as an artist – a skill he had had no idea Filip possessed.

As far as Viktor could see, the focus of the book was largely on the West Slavic mythology of the Poles, the Czechs and Slovaks, and the Slavic Kashubian and Wendish tribes of Germany.

Viktor even found a chapter where Filip's interests intersected with his own. Titled *THE MANIFOLD GODS OF THE MIND*, it discussed the psychology of mythology. Set between the handwritten pages was a beautifully executed pen-and-ink illustration, bearing Filip's initials. The caption beneath explained it depicted the three-headed god Triglav who wore the faces of Svarog, Lord of Fire; Perun, the King of Gods and Lord of Thunder; and Dažbog, Lord of the Sun.

Filip, in his small, neat handwriting, had captioned the illustration: *Unlike Svantovit, the four-headed god of war who has but one mind, Triglav is both one god and three: each of his faces a separate aspect, a unique self, yet combined in a single godhead. Triglav represents at the same time a trinity of wills and a unity of will.*

Viktor stared at the illustration for a long time: one will but three. Filip's caption could have been the summary of a psychiatric case file.

He became engrossed in the book. Switching on the small table lamp by the sofa and turning off the main lights, he took off his hat, coat and gloves, lit a cigarette and settled down to read through Filip's work. As he did, he was amazed at how much of what Filip had written matched the drug-induced testimonies of Viktor's patients, particularly those of Pavel Zelený and Dominik Bartoš.

In his strangely neat and flawless handwriting, Filip detailed descriptions of Veles the God of Forests and the Underworld, of Kostěj the Deathless; of the Gods of Light and Dark, Belobog and Chernobog – whom he now identified as the figures chasing each other on the cover's frieze – Viktor became convinced that both Zelený and Bartoš must have studied their subject in depth. And that the supposedly unlettered woodcutter Zelený really was hiding some literate, educated past from the world, perhaps even from himself.

It was odd, thought Viktor, to have come here to find out what was happening in Filip's mind, but to have gained an insight into the cases he was studying at the castle. As the idea settled into his brain it chilled him: what if 'Mr Hobbs' was the commonality? What if this peculiarly specific manifestation of the Devil Aspect had taken hold of Filip? He shook the thought from his head and continued with his reading.

There were hours, days of reading in the manuscript, but Viktor wanted to get as clear a picture of his friend's mind as possible, and tried to find the most revealing sections. There was no doubt that he was reassured by the lucid flow of the writing and scholarly application to the task; but something troubled Viktor about the subject matter. The Slavic pantheon was filled with monsters and demons: mythical articulations of the mind's darkness. It was a concern amplified by the fact that at least two of the Devil's Six were obsessed with this very subject.

One section particularly disturbed him. It related to the creation myth of the Proto-Slavs, in which the giant World Egg of creation was split open to reveal Svarog, God of Fire. Until that moment there had been no light in the world, and when he appeared, Svarog flooded the universe with light and order. However, the fragments of the shell of the World Egg obstructed some of Svarog's great light, and the first ever shadows were formed. These shadows combined to shape the Underworld Realm of the Dead. And the darkest of the shadows clustered together like clay to form the Dark Gods: Veles, Lord of the Dead, and Chernobog, the Slavic Devil.

What troubled Viktor most was how the description of Veles and Chernobog taking form from shadows matched exactly the descriptions given not just by both Zelený and Bartoš, but also what Smolák had told Viktor about the gypsy suspect's fear of shadows.

He looked at his watch. He'd been reading for two hours. Where the hell was Filip? It was now after ten; if Filip didn't return soon, then Viktor reckoned he would come back drunk. He wouldn't want to be found reading the manuscript.

He sifted through the pages to the end of the section.

What are the gods? When one considers Perun, the Overgod and Lord of Thunder, it is clear that he is cognate with the Norse god Thor; Svarog, the blacksmith god of fire and war is clearly the same as the Greek Hephaestus. Why is there this commonality? Why are pantheons in different cultures populated with the same gods under different names? The answer must be that we shared these stories at a time when we were so few on the Earth, and we took them with us when we set out to its distant corners, giving them new names as our languages divided. If not that, then these figures must be embedded in the deepest layers of our memories as a race: gods and demons who return to us in new forms, over and over. Perhaps our rationality and science, our analysis and understanding, will never be strong enough to overcome them. Perhaps the gods not only live within the mind of Man, but are indissoluble from it.

It could have been something Viktor had written himself, discussing archetypes in the collective unconscious.

Another hour. He would read for another hour.

*S*he sat looking out through the window. Evening was falling on Žižkov and the shadows were lengthening, black-etching the stonework of the buildings across the street and casting dark geometries beneath the sills and aprons of their windows. At least, she thought sadly, the shadows won't frighten Tobar any more.

Tsora Mirga had been disturbed and restless ever since that detective had visited her. She had sensed something like sympathy from the police kapitán and had got the idea that in some small way he had actually liked Tobar. That he was genuinely sorry about his death. Until that point, Tsora had suspected her lover might have been murdered by the police. After all, it wouldn't have been the first time a gypsy had not survived an arrest.

But all along she had admitted to herself that Tobar had been acting strangely ever since the night of his last break-in. Since then, she had seen a manic, terrified Tobar who could be capable of anything. What had once been inconceivable – that he could take his own life – had been made credible by his bizarre and desperate behaviour leading up to his arrest.

The policeman's attitude to Tobar, and his kindness towards her, had made her more open, telling him more than she normally would. Of course she hadn't told him anything about the stash of money Tobar had gathered from his crimes and hidden away beneath a loose floorboard. It had almost made her want to laugh when he had sat down on that chair, not knowing that there was several thousand korunas' worth of stolen cash and jewellery right below his feet.

During his spate of break-ins using stolen keys, Tobar had accumulated carefully, taking cash over items; and making sure any items he did steal would be difficult to trace back and could be sold without the need for a fence. It had all gone under the floorboards, along with any surplus from Tsora's earnings. Tobar had told her it would be their golden ticket, their way out of Prague. An escape from a future written for them by hands other than their own.

There was a bright, wide world out there to be explored and enjoyed, he had said, and their blood was that of centuries of wandering, of lives lived under changing skies and over changing ground. They would find their place in the world and be happy, putting their old lives behind them.

They had talked endlessly about it, spinning bright webs from golden threads of hope and imagined futures. On an impulse, Tobar had stolen an atlas of the world from one of the homes he'd burgled. Together, Tobar the Sinti burglar and pimp and Tsora the Roma whore and pickpocket, had become like innocent, wondering children, exploring a boundless world captured on printed pages. Tsora had been bewitched by that atlas, poring over its brightly coloured pages and marvelling at how huge the world was and how small the part they lived in. Small but at the very heart of the world. She had thrilled at the names of places she could not pronounce and had wondered what strange people lived there.

What it would be like for her and Tobar to live there.

Neither ever brought up the fact that no one would ever give them a chance, no one would ever treat them as equals; that the darker tones of complexion and hair would travel with them like a badge to mark them out. She had pushed from her mind that wherever she went, she would be slowed by the dragging weight of her infirmity, the even greater weight of her race.

But how they had dreamed – of having a place somewhere on the edge of Europe, looking out over the sea. Neither of them had ever seen a sea. It had been decided that they would escape to the coast of an until-then-imagined ocean. There, they could spend their days in peace and wonder.

But now Tobar was dead, the dreams they had shared dying with him. And his name had been dragged through the mud – accused of doing those terrible things. Despite what the detective had said, despite what anyone else thought, Tsora knew Tobar couldn't have killed that woman or any of the others. He wouldn't have killed any woman. But no one would believe that now. Another woman had died since, but still they thought Tobar had been the original killer.

Maybe, she thought, there would be yet another murder. Another woman ripped apart. Then they would see it hadn't been Tobar at all. It would be almost worth another woman's suffering to see his name cleared.

She thought again about the treasure beneath the floorboards. She hadn't gone back to work since her lover's death. To do so would mean finding a new protector and she would never find anyone else like Tobar. Pimps took the attitude that they owned you. All pimps did, but Roma or Sinti ones were the worst: once you were in their hands, there was no escape.

Tsora decided she had a duty to Tobar to get out: to find that new life. And when she found it she would do the living of it for them both. There would never be anyone else for her: Tsora Mirga, whose body had been used and abused by countless men, had only ever given her heart to one. In her own way – her own, resolute, uncompromising way – she had been faithful only to Tobar, and that was how she would remain. She would use the treasure to escape the city, escape the pimps and the clammy hands and foul-smelling embraces of their customers. Escape the hatred and suspicion of others.

She might even find somewhere that looked out over the sea. She would see an ocean for the first time for both of them.

When it grew dark that night, she lit the lamp in the alcove, put on the ceiling lights. While she was still there, she would have the apartment the way Tobar had wanted it. If his spirit lingered, she wanted to make sure there would be no shadows for him to fear.

There was a knock at the door. Maybe the policeman was back.

Tsora Mirga had never seen the man who stood framed in the doorway before, but she recognized him immediately. She recognized him from Tobar's description. He wore a long, black, shabby coat with the collar pulled up, and his wide-brimmed black hat was pulled down to cast his features in shadow.

He was, she realized, something that had taken form in the shadows: a coalescing of darkness. Just as Tobar had described the man who had put the idea of stealing rich people's keys in his head.

As he stepped forward, seizing her by the throat and forcing her back into the apartment, his coat gaped open to reveal a leather apron, stained black and crimson and smelling of old blood.

As he silently and steadily pushed her back into the living room, kicking the door shut behind him, Tsora thought how the prophecy had been wrong: her club foot had not confused the Devil. He had found her after all.

Under the bright lights that Tobar had wanted to banish shadows, her attacker seemed to become darker, the only brightness the vicious razor gleam of the blade in his hand, too long for a knife, too short for a sword.

As he pushed her down onto the brightly coloured rug, knocking aside the chair the detective had sat on, she thought of the treasure beneath her, hidden below the floorboards. About a whole imagined world in the printed pages of the atlas that lay hidden there too. Only Tobar and she knew about it. Now no one would know. It would maybe lie there undiscovered for years; maybe until a new century.

She saw his face now, directly above and close to hers while he drank in her fear. She saw the bright, twisted grin and eyes hot with cruelty and knew Tobar had been right all along. It *was* Beng. It had been the Devil after all.

Through her fear, through her terror of what she knew was to come, Tsora felt a faint, inexplicable joy. She would be the proof. She would be the next woman.

Now they would know for sure that Tobar had been innocent.

The universe suddenly became filled with white-hot pain, like an impossibly bright sun exploding. But she knew it wouldn't last for long. She felt the swift and cold-edged cruelty of the blade deep in her flesh; felt hard, dark hands delve into her, twisting and pulling the life from her, Beng's hissing breath cold on her cheek as he worked wordlessly on her.

As her beating heart was being cut from her, Tsora Mirga wondered if, when she was reunited with Tobar in the world of the hidden atlas, she would no longer limp.

If they would walk together with even, bold steps along the shore of an imagined ocean seen for the first time.

When he woke, Viktor's head still hurt and his neck ached. With careful fingertips, he checked the padding taped to his scalp. It took a moment for all the pieces of his memory to fall into place and he sat up with a start.

He was still in his clothes. He was still in Filip's apartment.

Standing up abruptly rewarded him with a wave of pain and nausea, forcing him to sit back down. He looked around the apartment. Still no sign of Filip. Checking his watch he saw it was seven-fifteen. He had slept through the night. If Filip came home now, Viktor's presence would be beyond all reasonable explanation.

Easing himself up more carefully, he gathered the manuscript and rebound it in its ornate leather binding, fastening the leather straps that held it together and put it back on the desk, replacing the pile of papers he had moved on top.

Filip was probably with some woman, or lying drunk in some low dive. A panicked thought seized Viktor as he imagined his friend lying injured in a hospital, or even dead in the morgue. But none of that fitted with the ordered, disciplined mind Viktor had engaged with in the manuscript. Nothing fitted with Filip any more.

Making sure he'd put everything back as it had been, Viktor gathered his hat, gloves and coat and headed out through the back door.

The sun was coming up and it was going to be a bright morning. Checking that there was no one from the next-door apartment in the yard, he stepped out and replaced the key under the flagstone. In the daylight, he could see the yard clearly. The snow had stopped and the chill, cleansing bite in the air had frosted the snow crisp. He saw his footprints from the night before as he had crossed the yard, but there were also other footprints. Someone else had, during the night, crossed the yard to the back door, turned and walked out of the yard. Viktor followed the footsteps around to the front of the coach-house block. Whoever had left them had stood close to the window at the front facing into it and presumably looking in at Viktor as he read or slept on the sofa. Filip? Why would Filip not make himself known to Viktor?

And if it had been Filip, what dark business had he been engaged in until the small hours?

As he made his way through the gathering day back to where he had parked his car, Viktor realized he had come looking for answers but was leaving with more questions.

The biggest question was: where had Filip been all night?

When he walked into the police station that morning, everything was in chaos. The reception and custody halls of the police station bustled with uniformed officers grappling with their arrests, a deafening cacophony of curses and yells ringing in the vaulted ceiling. Every now and then scuffles broke out as captives struggled to be free of captors, only to be subdued by a flurry of batons.

Kapitán Lukáš Smolák, tired and irritable after a night torn by fervent dreaming, pushed his way through the throng and past the custody gate. His deputy, Detektiv-Seržant Mirek Novotný, stood in shirtsleeves behind the gate, smoking, watching the chaos with disinterest.

'What the hell is going on?' Smolák shouted above the din when he reached his subordinate.

'All hell has broken out,' said Novotný. 'There was a march through Wenceslas Square by Gajda's National Fascists mob, licking their wounds after being hammered in the elections. Somehow the communists got wind of it and organized a counter-demonstration. More ambush than counter-demonstration, if you ask me. I don't know why the Reds bother, to be honest, for all Gajda's lot are worth these days.'

'Injuries?' asked Smolák.

'Lots of broken heads but no deaths – or no deaths as yet, anyway. As usual, we got stuck in the middle of it all.'

Smolák nodded. 'Did you gather the statements on the Petrášová case?'

'I did. I also got the full autopsy report, for what it's worth. Like Dr Bartoš said, there was so much missing and so much damage to the body that identifying an exact time and cause of death is impossible.'

'And the glass bead?'

'Nothing yet. I haven't been able to find a secretary who knows English and could translate our request to the British police.'

'Try the president's son,' said Smolák.

'What?'

'Jan Masaryk, the president's son – he's ambassador to Great Britain. Send the request to the embassy in London and get them to liaise with the police there. Tell them it's a matter of great urgency.'

'The bead? You really think it's that significant?'

'I don't know, but it's all we've got. And the best information I have is that it was probably made in England.'

'I'll get on to it.' Novotný turned to head down the hall but checked himself. 'Oh, a parcel arrived for you. I've put it on your desk.'

'Thanks,' said Smolák. 'Is Dr Bartoš in today, do you know?'

'I haven't seen him. I'll check the doctors' duty roster if you like.'

'No, it's fine.'

His office seemed particularly quiet after the chaos downstairs. For a moment Smolák chose to savour the peace, standing by the large window and looking out over Prague. The view couldn't have been more different from the one over village and forest from the mountain fastness of Hrad Orlů castle, yet there was a common language in both cityscape and landscape. There was an instinct that told that both belonged to the same land, the same people, the same deep-ingrained dreams and nightmares.

As he stood smoking and watching the dark geometry of Prague's

roofs and spires jab at a white marble sky, he thought again of Anna
Petrášová. It had been she who had again intruded on his sleep,
insinuating her way into his dreaming. This time the dream had
played out in Prague, not Smolák's childhood village. In this dream
Anna Petrášová had lain naked in his bed, an out-of-place jewel in
the rough setting of his cramped lodgings. They had made love, he
rejoicing in the pale perfection of her body and knowing somehow
that they were man and wife.

Smolák had felt a joy unlike any other he had known. Still dreaming, he had risen from the bed to open the curtains on the brightest of
days, but when he had looked down into the street, there was another
woman standing dark in the morning light, looking up accusingly at
the window-framed Smolák. Despite it being a joyously bright morning, he couldn't make out her face, which seemed cast in shadow. But
when she turned away and headed back down the street, he saw she
walked with the rolling gait of a cripple.

In his dream, Smolák had turned back to Anna Petrášová to ask
her what it meant. But when he did, she stared blankly at him, the
beauty of her face perfect and undamaged, while everything below her
neck was ragged flesh and bone. As he stood screaming, blood began
to pour in vast, smooth red sheets down the walls of his apartment.

When he woke, he had already been sitting up, his mouth gaping
in a silent scream.

Now, standing at his office window smoking and thinking about
the dreams of a man and of a people, Lukáš Smolák tried to smooth
the wrinkles of tired irritation from his mood.

After a while, he turned to his desk and went through his morning mail. He turned his attention to the small package, a brown,
paper-wrapped cube of about twenty-five centimetres in each dimension, that Mirek Novotný had left on his desk. He saw his name and
the police headquarters address typed on a gummed label. When he
unwrapped the brown paper, it revealed a black-lacquered wooden
box of the Russian Palekh type, clearly an expensive piece. The lid

was intricately decorated with a small but vibrantly coloured motif in which a winged figure in white and blue stretched out arms to catch the tail of a demonic figure in red and gold. The motif was cyclical and, as Smolák looked at it, he couldn't decide if the angel was chasing the demon, or the demon trying to catch the wings of the angel. He realized that it was a representation of the Slavic god of light, Belobog, and the god of dark, Chernobog: Night chasing Day chasing Night.

He lifted the lid and saw the box was stuffed with deep red crepe paper, on top of which sat a card. There were three lines typed onto the card, one in Czech, one in German, one in English. All three carried the same meaning:

> *Pozdravy z pekla*
> *Grüße aus der Hölle*
> *Greetings from Hell*

Smolák set the card to one side and eased the crimson, paper-wrapped object from the box, set it on his desk and carefully unwrapped it. He stared at the object for some time before picking up his phone to call Václav Bartoš and then to arrange for a fingerprint expert to come to his office.

Bartoš arrived first and his brow creased in a frown as soon as he saw the pale object sitting wreathed in a crimson paper halo.

'I've still to have the box checked for fingerprints,' cautioned Smolák. 'Not that there'll be any to find.'

Václav Bartoš leaned in closer to examine the human foot, which had been severed about five centimetres above the ankle, exposing a perfectly sheared, flat plane of grey-red flesh and cream-white bone. The foot itself was small and underdeveloped, almost like a child's. It curved in like a small sickle at an unnatural angle to its ankle, and had become slightly deformed by a lifetime of its owner walking on the foot's edge.

'*Talipes equinovarus*,' Bartoš said as he straightened up from his examination. 'You're looking for a victim who has – who *had* – a club foot. But I take it from your expression you already have some idea who this belongs to?'

Smolák nodded. 'I'm afraid I know exactly who it belongs to.'

CHAPTER NINE

Thinking back on it, it all seemed so unreal, like the memory of sleep-imagined events in a fading dream. Mládek's sudden switch of personality, the demonic Harlequin face that had launched itself at Viktor, the viscous crimson halo of blood on stone around his shattered skull. And after that, the trip to Prague, Filip's apartment, the manuscript in its beautifully ornate leather binding talking of dark gods and darker demons.

Judita came to see him in his office. She brought with her the transcript of Viktor's statement, explaining that a copy had already been sent by courier to the policeman Chromík in Mladá Boleslav. Taking the first opportunity they had to be alone, Viktor told Judita what he had found in Filip's apartment – and that he hadn't found Filip there. He told her about his friend's painstaking research, about the fluency of his writing and clarity of his logic.

'What I read weren't the ravings of a madman.' Viktor tried to make his tone emphatic but failed; he was trying to convince himself as much as Judita. 'And that's a professional opinion, not just a personal one. I can't believe he really has anything to do with these killings.'

'To be honest, I think the fact that he attacked someone with a hidden knife he'd been carrying, and that you had a struggle restraining him that night, is much more relevant than an analysis of his literary skills in his absence. And, anyway, for all you know, what you read last night was written months, maybe even years ago.'

'So what do you think I should do?'

'You know what I think,' said Judita. 'You should talk to that policeman from Prague, Smolák. Filip's maybe done nothing wrong, but you can't keep going off to Prague to investigate him yourself. You don't know what you're doing, or what you're dealing with.'

'But that's the thing. As a psychiatrist, I can recognize the presence or absence of serious psychosis. What I saw in Filip's manuscript was an *absence* of it. And if I go to Smolák, then I'd have to tell him about the knife attack. Filip could be locked up just for that—'

'For God's sake, Viktor, listen to what you're saying. Maybe there's a reason he'd be locked up. Listen, I'm not saying that Filip *is* Leather Apron, or even that he's insane. But you must voice your concerns to Smolák. And anyway, where the hell was he all last night?'

'There could be an innocent explanation for that. Anyway, what I discovered in that manuscript has got me thinking about the cases here. Their internal mythologies, as it were. If I can crack those, then I may be closer than ever to understanding and isolating the Devil Aspect. We've dreamed up gods and monsters from common forms that live inside us all. Every religion, every superstition, every folk myth is founded on the same figures. Mr Hobbs is a manifestation of one of those forms. I need to talk to him.'

'That means talking to him through Pavel Zelený?' Judita frowned. 'I think you may experience resistance from Professor Románek if he finds out. Particularly at the moment – I've heard he's having one of his moody periods. I haven't seen him since before you left for Prague.'

'I can deal with the professor. But yes, Zelený is my only route to Hobbs. Zelený *is* Hobbs. But unfortunately both are going to have to wait. Let's say my next session is going to be a challenge.'

'Skála?' Judita's frown deepened, her eyes clouded with concern.

'Vojtěch Skála,' said Viktor. 'The Demon and the last of the Devil's Six with whom I have to do a session.'

*I*t was, he had to admit, a fortuitous turn of events. Viktor had felt a duty to inform Professor Románek about his intention to carry out a session with Skála, but Románek was 'unavailable'. Judita had already told Viktor about Románek's periodic 'moods', during which he would withdraw from the world and into his study. The official line was that the asylum director needed undisturbed peace to deal with pressing administrative matters.

When Viktor tried to arrange an appointment with Románek, he was told that the professor was undertaking administrative duties and was not to be disturbed. He discovered that Románek had shut himself away the day before and would not have been aware of Viktor's trip to Prague. For Viktor, the good news was that the asylum director was unavailable to offer an opinion on whether Viktor's session with Skála should or should not go ahead.

So, as an unseen sun was setting beyond the windowless walls of the tower granary, four orderlies wheeled the Demon into the room on the mediaeval throne of his restraint chair. Skála was not going to be placed on the examination couch. He arrived fastened by metal and leather, bolt and buckle, denied even the slightest movement of hand, arm, leg, neck or head. He would remain bound in the chair throughout the session.

Undimmed by his premedicated state, Vojtěch Skála's eyes burned with a dark, malevolent fury, like hot embers about to burst into flame. He glared at Viktor as he crossed the room and injected the scopolamine and sodium amytal into the intravenous cannula that had been prepared in advance of the session. Despite the movement-stifling restraint chair, two of the orderlies stepped closer until Viktor was finished. After his violent encounters with the Woodcutter Pavel Zelený and the Clown Leoš Mládek, and given the Demon's reputation for extreme violence, Viktor was making sure nothing in this session would be left to chance.

As the drugs began to take effect, Viktor nodded to the orderlies, who stepped out of the room, taking up positions just beyond the closed door. Alone with his patient, Viktor switched on the Magnetophon and ran through the usual formalities, noting the date, time and patient's name.

'I'm going to kill you,' said Skála, matter-of-factly, in his disturbingly high-pitched voice. 'You know that, don't you?'

'And why would you want to do that?' asked Viktor, taking his seat and lighting a cigarette.

'I don't need a reason. It's what I do. I kill. People. Animals. Things. But in your case it's because of who you are, what you are.'

'And what's that?' Viktor asked absently as he prepared for the session.

'A privileged prick. Someone who's had everything handed to them on a plate.'

Viktor laughed. 'That's news to me, Vojtěch. As far as I can see from your notes, you come from a much wealthier and more privileged background than mine. Mine's humble in comparison.'

Skála stared at Viktor for a moment. The heat had gone from his eyes, either as a result of the drugs or because he couldn't be bothered sustaining it. 'Really?' he said dully. 'I always thought you were rich. Had some kind of aristo background – you have that look.' He paused for a moment, struggling to gather together the dissolving shreds of his Ego being dispersed by the drugs. 'But never mind – I'm still going to kill you. That smug handsome face of yours is going to look good when I wear it as a mask. Maybe everyone will think I'm the son of a count when I'm wearing your face.'

'That's not going to happen, Vojtěch, and you know it.'

'Isn't it? All it'll take is for someone to make a mistake – and they *will* make a mistake, sooner or later – and I'll see my chance and take it. You know something? People look at other people and think they're the same as they are, that people they meet think the same, feel the same, follow the same patterns and rules as they do. But you and me, Dr Kosárek, well, we know differently, don't we? Something can have the shape of a man and be something else, something different. Well, that's what I am. Something different. They all made that mistake.'

'They?'

'My toys. The people who misjudged a thing in the shape of a man. That's why they call me the Demon. They see something that looks human but has something else inside, something they can't understand. They call what I do evil and they call me a demon. My toys had to do that because they had to try to make sense of what was happening to them.'

'What do you call what you do?' asked Viktor. 'Don't you see it as evil?'

'Evil is in the eye of the beholder. In the pain of the victim. I worship evil, exult it, perform it at every opportunity – recognize it for its unsurpassed power – but the irony and paradox is I can never truly understand or appreciate it. Only my victims can. So I have to experience it through them. I have to see it through their eyes.

'Take that family in Pezinok – you've read the case files so you know the details. I was on my way to Bratislava when I saw them – it was simple, a passing-by, not even an encounter. I saw them happy and contented, with the sunshine of summer and youth shining on the path ahead of them. They had so much – and, on a whim, I decided to take it all away from them. I called at their house and when the husband opened the door, he saw a man standing there, not the Devil, not a demon. He expected me to behave as a man but I behaved as a demon. I spent a day and a half in that house. That family knew the true nature of Evil.'

'And you have no conscience about that?' asked Viktor. 'What you did to them doesn't trouble you?'

'I have my own ethics, my own morality. For example, I would never ask a married woman to kiss a man who wasn't her husband: so I cut off her husband's face first and wore it as a mask. And I offered choice – a say in how Evil revealed itself. I told that young mother, in great detail, exactly what I was going to do to her child. I told her that if she, the mother, took her child's place, I would leave her child alone. So she agreed and submitted willingly to all the horrors I had described. But just as the last of the mother's life was leaving her, I made her watch as I broke my word. It was that event that earned me the name Demon and my membership of the Devil's Six. I rejoice in both.'

Viktor sat silent for a moment.

'Even knowing all that,' said Skála, 'you will misjudge me too. Sooner or later, you – or someone close to you – are going to underestimate me and I will take my chance. Then you and I – oh, then we're going to dance.'

'All right, Vojtěch, the threats are becoming wearisome.' Viktor drew a breath. 'I'm here to help you. And you're here so we can get to the bottom of all this rage you feel.'

'Oh, I see, you want to get to all my childhood traumas. Let me save us both time. My parents sent me to a religious boarding school when I was ten. The priest there buggered me at least twice a month, when it was my turn. That do?'

'Is that the truth?'

'You know it is. It's in my records. I told Románek about it and he didn't need to dope me up to get it out of me. There you have it, mystery solved: a kiddie-fiddler turned me bad. So why don't you unfasten me from this contraption so I can start work on you? I'll keep you alive long enough for you to watch me try on your face.'

'Let's just focus on what has brought you here. I want you to tell me about your time in the school. What happened to you there,' said Viktor.

Skála regarded Viktor for moment. 'All right, I'll play nice. I'll play along with your game for the moment. But soon you're going to play in mine.'

'The school . . .' urged Viktor.

'My family was a well-established one. All good Slovak Catholics. My father was a pompous, self-righteous man of powerful religious conviction and unshakeable social ideology, neither of which he ever questioned and neither of which were of his own forming.

'We lived in Trnava. You know Trnava? The seat of Catholicism in Slovakia – so much so that it's called *parva Roma*, "little Rome". Both my father and mother were devout Catholics to the point of obsession. My father was also a real clerofascist bigot who saw Czechs as godless Hussites and protestant Slovaks as traitors to blood and tradition. Needless to say, I have been something of a disappointment to my parents.' Skála smiled malevolently.

'I tried to be a good boy, I really did. But you can't change your nature, just like you can't change your height or the colour of your eyes. But it wasn't the colour of my eyes that had to be changed, but the colour of my soul. Mine was a black soul, according to Papa, and he saw it as his duty to try to change the unchangeable.'

'Were you really bad?' asked Viktor. 'I mean, do you think you were a bad boy from the start?'

'I tried to make my father proud, but he never seemed to notice. But when I was bad – oh, when I was bad, well then I got his attention. You taking a note of this, Dr Kosárek? Isn't mine a classic case? Are you going to sit with your colleagues and discuss how poor

Skála is just the product of clerical rape, misdirected filial love and a hunger for paternal approval?'

'What did your father do to try to change you?' Viktor ignored Skála's baiting, but decided to wait only a minute or so before administering a second dose to dissolve his resistance.

'He beat me. He clearly thought a good thrashing could get the bad in me out, like beating dust from an old carpet. But it wasn't like that. It wasn't like that at all. It was more like a band of hot steel inside me and his beatings just tempered it, made it tougher.'

'What happened?' asked Viktor.

'My father gave up on me. I was ten years old – only ten, and he decided I was a case beyond his redemption. So I was sent away. They sent me to this religious boarding school over the border in northwest Hungary. Run by Jesuits and famous for its tough regime and for beating the bad out of errant boys.'

'Were you beaten?'

'Almost every day. To the point that the lighter beatings didn't matter. It's funny, the school was a castle just like this is. I was confined then, at ten years old, just as I am confined now.

'They had crucifixes all over the place. I was used to that, growing up in a house covered with them. But these were different. All the crucifixes in the school showed Jesus emaciated and twisted in death agonies, his eyes always cast down on us, disappointed. I often thought that the school had bought that particular design of crucifix in vast numbers just because of that expression of disappointment. Every day we were told how he had suffered for us, and that we must now suffer for him. He had died for our sins but we were all of us unworthy and still sinners.

'We were taught by monastic Jesuits – a complete education, coloured by an ideology of superstition and enforced with brutality. The Jesuits who administered learning and pain in equal measure were supposed to be the epitome of Good, of Godliness and Right. But to me they just seemed heartless, twisted bullies. There was only one who was kind, a younger monk who took us for science, called Brother Ernő. He never beat us and no one misbehaved in his class because we were just so grateful to have respite from the other monks.

'There were three in particular whom we feared most. There was Brother Lázsló: we called him Stentor, after the Greek herald with a voice more powerful than fifty voices combined. For the smallest infraction Brother Lázsló would make a boy stand before him while he bellowed and screamed into his face. So many soiled themselves, beaten and whipped only by that voice. But he used more than his voice when the occasion called. And sometimes he seemed to feel the occasion called for him to use his fists, particularly with the older boys.

'All the priests had to be feared, but it was Stentor – Brother Lázsló – and two others who were the greatest objects of terror. The other two were Brother István and Brother Ferenc, and while their wrath was to be feared, it couldn't be avoided. Both seemed to seek out reasons to beat us, and both carried these straps, I suppose you'd call them – long strips of leather that had been shortened by being tied into tight, hard-edged knots that would bite into your skin. And oh, how they bit. Of the three, Brother Ferenc was the worse. Generally he was calmer than Brother István, and certainly than Lázlo, but he'd turn into this uncontrollable sadist if he had a drink in him, which was often. Like all the boys, I learned to associate that bitter-sweet apricot smell of pálinka with pain and fear. If Brother Ferenc's breath smelt of pálinka, then you knew it was only a matter of time before he laid into someone on the flimsiest excuse.

'There was one day in catechism class, which Brother Ferenc took, I made the smallest of errors. I jumbled my words, more than anything – and I probably did that only because I was so afraid, having smelt pálinka on his breath. Brother Ferenc went mad. Completely mad. He yanked my shirt halfway up my back and tore into me with his knotted strap. The man had no control: he hit me over and over again with all the strength he had. I was only eleven. Eleven. First there would be the cutting pain of the blow, then the hot burning that seared through my back, stretching hot fingers up my neck and squeezing my brain. Before that pain eased, there would be another blow, another pulse of pain adding to the last and adding to it. I remember that escalation, that accumulating of pain. And, unlike Stentor, Brother Ferenc remained silent through the whole thing, the only sound his breathing, laboured from the effort of beating me.

'The pain kept getting worse and worse, as he hit me and hit me. Over and over again – and all the time pain adding to pain, constantly, exponentially intensifying. I thought I'd pass out or die and I wished for either – anything to stop the accumulating pain. I had no sense any more of where I was, who I was, what was causing the pain. The pain was everything. The pain was all. It became so intense that I could *see* it. A great, searingly white light in my eyes.

'Then the beating stopped. Brother Ferenc hauled me to my feet and hurled me across the classroom and I staggered back to my bench. He went back to teaching as if nothing had happened, as if he had not just nearly beaten an eleven-year-old boy to death. He hadn't changed, but I had. I'd entered some kind of altered state. The searing white light dimmed and I could see again, but the world tilted and swayed; the colours in it shifted and changed. The whole world was both brighter and darker: the light from the windows much sharper and more intense, but the shadows much blacker, harder edged. It felt as though the world was shifting sideways, a new reality sliding into place. I sat there in the same classroom, the pain still burned through my body, the same twisted Christ on his cross looking down at me in silent disappointment and accusation – but it was all in a changed world. And all the time I heard Brother Ferenc lecturing in calm tones, as if nothing had happened, about the Fall of the Angels.

'I recall him reading out loud: "Behind the disobedient choice of our first parents lurks a seductive voice, opposed to God, which makes them fall into death out of envy. Scripture and the Church's Tradition see in this a fallen angel, called 'Satan' or the 'Devil'. The Church teaches that Satan was at first a good angel, made by God: the Devil and the other demons were indeed created naturally good by God, but they became evil by their own doing."

'Even though I was barely conscious, I remember those words clearly. Brother Ferenc read out how the Fall of the Angels was a question of free choice. How Satan and the other Fallen made their own choice to reject God and his reign. As I lay there bleeding and wet from my own soiling, I saw it all with perfect clarity. I realized that Satan wasn't an antithesis, a shadow of God's making; I realized Satan was a revolutionary, a liberator – an overturner of the oppression of God. His revolution wasn't just the rejection of Good, it was a wilful rejoicing in Evil. At that point, Evil was released into the world and liberated Man from God's vassalage.'

'So you turned to evil as a way of life?' asked Viktor.

'More than a way of life: an elemental force unequalled in the universe that had to be let loose at every opportunity. My transformation began that day. It was completed later.'

'How was it completed?' asked Viktor.

'That one good Jesuit I mentioned; that single point of kindness in the cruelty. Brother Ernő. He found out about the beating I'd been given and took me to his cell where he prayed with me and then rubbed salve into the wounds on my back. He had this beautiful polished pebble on his desk: it was small and shiny, seamed like onyx. He handed me the pebble and told me to concentrate on it while he rubbed ointment into the weals on my back. "All things pass," he said. "That pebble was once a mighty boulder in the bed of a river, the waters of which gradually eroded it, smoothed it, polished it, over a great span of time," he said. "Where that pebble was once a ragged rock, the passage of time has soothed the edges, soothed its harshness."

'He then told me that I had to try and understand that Good and Evil coexisted everywhere, that good men sometimes commit evil acts in the pursuit of Good. He told me I had to have understanding and forgiveness for Brother Ferenc. But all the time I could tell he was horrified by what Ferenc had done to me. He told me he was worried that the wounds might become infected and that I was to let him know if the pain got worse, or if I developed a fever, all the time rubbing the soothing salve into my back.

'And then he told me about the butterfly and the stone sun.'

'The butterfly and the stone sun?' asked Viktor.

'He asked me if I remembered what he had taught us in science class: that the sun is so huge; how our world was less than one millionth of the size of the sun. One millionth. He told me to imagine one million, three hundred thousand worlds fitting into the sun. Then he told me to keep my eyes closed and imagine that the sun was not made of fire, but of stone – a huge, solid, unyielding granite mass hanging in God's heavens.

'He said: "Now imagine a butterfly. Imagine this smallest and most delicate of God's creatures, infinitesimally smaller than the Earth, and the Earth less than a millionth of the size of the stone sun. Now imagine that minute, delicate butterfly flying around the entire solar system and once, every thousand years, a single brush of its wing glances off the surface of the stone sun. Can you imagine that?" I lay there, the pain easing from my back, holding the pebble in my hand, and told him I could imagine it. "Now I want you to imagine how long it would take for that once-in-a-millennium brushing of the butterfly's wing against the vast stone sun to wear it down to the size of that polished pebble you hold in your hand. Can you imagine that?" I told him I couldn't, that it was a scale my mind was incapable of grasping. "Exactly," said kindly Brother Ernő. "It is a length of time beyond imagining." Then, suddenly, his voice went hard. "Well, that unimaginable span of time is but a passing second in the eternity that a miserable sinner like you is going to spend in the flames of Hell." I didn't have a chance to say anything, even for the shock to hit me, before the pain came. Pain worse than anything Brother Ferenc had done.'

'He beat you?' asked Viktor.

'He raped me,' said Skála without emotion.

CHAPTER ELEVEN

here was no chatter of coins rapping on windows this time. The Žižkov street outside Tsora Mirga's apartment building was blank and silent in the cold air as a row of police cars lined up: an authoritative sentence punctuated with the full stop of a black mortuary van. No rattled alarms warning of the police presence: word, Smolák realized, must have got around already.

Mirek Novotný was with him – had more or less insisted he came with him. Smolák knew that the coincidences were beginning to pile up: yet another victim of Leather Apron had been recently visited by the kapitán of detectives. Of course, it was clear that the killer was taunting Smolák, defying him to catch him, but nevertheless it presented an opportunity for the fresh-faced, red-haired youth to sow a seed or two of doubt.

Václav Bartoš was with Smolák too, having travelled in the same car as Smolák and his deputy. The journey from the station had been made in silent anticipation of what awaited them.

As they climbed the stairwell to the apartment, Smolák thought back to the last time he had been there, about a crippled gypsy prostitute's quiet strength and dignity, her dark beauty. Remembering the condition Anna Petrášová's body had been found in, he braced himself for seeing Tsora Mirga again, knowing he would have to witness what had been done to her.

Tsora was in the same room, the parlour, in which Smolák had talked to her. She lay on her back, laid out deliberately. Her killer had rearranged her clothes over the devastation of her chest and abdomen, and her blouse was black-red with sodden blood. Her legs were stretched out straight and together. The ankle of the right leg was sheared smoothly, expertly, where her killer had removed her club foot, but there was little blood from the wound. Her hands lay folded on her stomach and her head was angled to look in their direction as they entered. Except her eyes were gone, and Smolák was held in the accusatory gaze of raw, empty sockets. He recognized the brightly coloured and patterned blanket from his last visit, but instead of being draped over the back of the sofa, it had been carefully folded and placed under Tsora's head as a pillow, propping her head up so her eyeless sockets were directed at the door.

Václav Bartoš stepped closer and carried out a quick examination. 'She would have felt none of this,' he said, indicating the caverns where her eyes had been. 'From what I can see, he cut out her heart and that was the cause of death. Everything else – the foot, the eyes – was done post-mortem. That's why there's so little blood. Other than the heart, nothing else has been excised. No internal organs taken as trophies, although there's no sign of her eyes, so presumably he took those with him.' He straightened up. 'This doesn't fit with the last two killings but it's Leather Apron, all right. Same expert knife work.'

'And, of course, he announced this one,' said Smólák. 'His little note said "greetings from Hell". It was an obvious reference to the London murderer, who sent a letter titled "From Hell" to the policeman investigating those cases. And he sent a body part to prove he was genuine. In his case it wasn't a foot.'

'What was it?' asked Novotný, whose pale complexion had turned paler.

'The victim's liver.'

Novotný blanched further. 'Do you think there is some kind of symbolism with the eyes thing?' he asked, studiously avoiding looking again at her face.

'There's symbolism in everything this maniac does,' said Dr Bartoš. 'I just don't know what it's meant to be this time.'

'I do,' said Smolák. He scanned the small room, its order and cleanliness. The only thing that had been moved was the lamp that had been jammed into the corner. It now stood clear of the corner; there was now somewhere for a shadow to gather. 'He's telling us she saw him. He's telling us she could have recognized him.'

CHAPTER TWELVE

'id you tell anyone about this?' asked Viktor. 'Anyone at the school, or your parents?'

'Do you really think anyone would care? It happened all the time. I wasn't the only one who Brother Ernő did that to. Anyway, my parents wouldn't have believed me. They'd have seen it as a slur against their precious, perfect church and faith – and further proof of my mendacity and moral corruption.'

'And this continued?'

'For three years. Once, maybe twice a month. He had other boys as well, you see. We all had our turn.'

'How did you cope?'

'I withdrew into myself, into that new reality of brighter light and darker shadow that had taken form around me. I knew I had to choose between the light or the shadow. I chose the shadow. I chose Satan the revolutionary over God the tyrant. And I planned. In my mind I painted such grand canvases of revenge, of unimaginable suffering wrought by me, instead of against me.

'I grew. Became stronger. I became secretive and scheming. Whenever I got the chance, I explored the boundary of the school, found hidden ways in and out. At night I would slip out and go into the forest. There the darkness was greatest. I found an old wooden building that had been abandoned for years, some kind of old wood shed, and made that my secret home. I would sneak away whenever I could, taking anything I could to make it more my place. I stole from the other boys, you see, but when the Brothers searched our beds and our lockers, there would be nothing to find in mine. On one occasion I actually placed something I'd stolen in another boy's locker, to draw attention away from myself.'

'What happened to the boy?' asked Viktor.

'He was made an example of, flogged, in front of us all, by Brother Ferenc. He nearly killed him. Some of the other boys who watched cried. I had to struggle to contain my emotions, in case it drew the attention I'd tried to deflect.'

'You were upset? Felt guilty?'

Through the drugs, Skála's eyes widened in surprise. 'Upset? God, no – I had to stop myself from laughing.

'After that I stole everything and anything I could. It drove the Jesuits mad trying to find the culprit. I even stole the pebble from Brother Ernő's cell. I had created a real little palace for myself in the wood store in the forest, hidden from the rest of the world. One night I sneaked out and spent the whole night there, making sure I got back to the dormitory before dawn. I tell you, that was a magical night. I lay in the dark and heard the forest alive all around me – more alive at night than during the day. I heard its creaking, its breathing, the screeches of owls, the rustle and scuffle of teeming life beneath its carpet of fallen leaves. There I was free – there in the black of forest night.' Skála seemed lost for a moment of dark reminiscence.

'What about Brother Ernő?' asked Viktor.

'After a while his attention shifted to new boys. Younger boys. I was clearly getting too old for him. A lot of things changed then. I became big, powerfully built even for a fourteen-year-old. It was then that I discovered that, like all bullies, Ferenc, László and István – and Brother Ernő – were cowards. None of them raised his voice, far less his hand to me again and, while I could hold their gaze unflinchingly, they couldn't hold mine. Eventually I left the school, having ironically excelled academically. But I had changed. I changed that day Ferenc beat me and Ernő raped me. I saw everything as it was.'

'And how was that?' asked Viktor.

'That good and evil are one and the same. God and the Devil are the same. The tyrant and the revolutionary are one. All we do is choose our side, but eventually we all do good, we all do bad. What we do to others we do to ourselves. Do you know what panpsychism is?'

'Of course I do.'

'I believe in it. But what I believe – what I *know* – is that while we all think we have individual consciousnesses, we really only have one. One mind. Isn't that kind of what your great Dr Jung thinks?'

'Not really,' Viktor said impatiently. 'So you say you believe in panpsychism – but in your version of it we all share one single consciousness. If that's true, why did you torture your victims so terribly? Doesn't that mean you were torturing yourself?'

Something changed in Skála's expression. Viktor realized that it was simply the absence of hate and fury that was otherwise perpetually there. 'That's the thing, don't you see? When I die, I will simply experience the world through someone else's eyes. Your eyes, my victim's eyes. Everyone's eyes. I'll be the executioner and the executed, the torturer and the tortured, the rapist and the raped. Just as you see the world right now from your perspective, you will eventually see it from mine, from everyone else's. You see, we are all God, we are all the Devil. And everyone, sooner or later, will experience the world as me, see through my eyes. And that is my purpose.'

'I still don't understand,' said Viktor.

'People have called me the Demon, even the Devil. But I'm neither. I'm not a being, I am a *place*. I am the place where you will go, where everyone will go, eventually. Sooner or later, you will experience the world through me and I through you. I'm not the Devil – I am *Hell*. And everything I have done, you will do. I am your punishment and it is my duty to perform as much evil, to fill my experience with as much torment and horror as possible.'

'But, following your logic,' said Viktor, 'you will become your victims. You will become me.'

'But don't you see that was my message? Can't you see that's why, when I'd finished with them all, I cut off their faces and wore them? I wanted to try them out. I wanted to see what it will be like when I come back as them. You see, Dr Kosárek, when I say I will wear your face one day, I really will. One way or another.'

Viktor sat in silence for a moment, watching the dark, malevolent bulk of Skála strapped and steel-fastened into the restraint chair. He thought about whether he should administer a second dose, take his subject deeper, whether it would be worthwhile.

'Incidentally,' said Skála in the silence. 'I went back to the school, years later.'

'Oh?' said Viktor.

'Yes, I crossed the border unchecked and found my way back to the castle there. The school was still there, doing the same things to a new generation of the unworthy. By the time I went back I was already engaged in the Devil's work, creating Hell on Earth, and had to be careful about my movements. I'd already killed more than a dozen people by then, you see.

'The first thing I did was to go into the woods and find my palace of old: the dilapidated wood store I'd converted into my retreat. It was still there, undisturbed, all my little treasures in their place, including Brother Ernő's pebble. No one had set foot in or near it in all of those years. So I made it my base again, just for that week. Just until I accomplished all I had to accomplish.

'I made several visits to the castle over the course of a week. I knew every nook and cranny from my time there and was able to sneak in and out of the school undetected, just as I had done years before. I paid them each a visit: all four Brothers. Reminded them of our time together. As the week went on, I had to be careful, because obviously there was growing concern for their whereabouts as they disappeared one after the other.

'On the last night – the best night – I went to Brother Ernő's cell, the same cell he'd assaulted me in all those years before. It was the strangest thing: when I switched on the light and he saw me standing there, he was terrified. But then he recognized me and there was this – this *look* on his face.'

'What kind of look?' asked Viktor.

'Resignation. Acceptance. Understanding. As if he'd been waiting for me, or one of the others, to come back for revenge. As if he knew what had happened to the others. He didn't move, didn't cry out when I crossed the room, when I put my hands around his throat, when I began to squeeze. There was even forgiveness in his eyes before they bulged and started to dull, and that insulted me the most: that he dared to think *he* could forgive *me*. So I strangled him until his body went limp.'

Skála paused, then a grin defiantly pushed its way through the drugs to the surface.

'If you had seen his face. Oh, if only you could have seen his face after that, when he woke up. There was no gentle resignation, no acceptance, no forgiveness then. You see, I didn't kill him in his cell. I was very careful about that. Like I'd done with the others, I just strangled him long enough for him to lose consciousness and for me to carry him out of the school. Then, when he woke up, he found himself naked and bound in the woodshed in a forest in the middle of nowhere. He didn't recognize me at first, of course, because I was wearing Brother Ferenc's face as a mask. "You didn't think I'd let you off that easily?" I said. "You didn't think your suffering would be so quick?"

'So I started work on him. Slow work. Carefully, delicately, *literally* painstaking work. Cautiously calibrated cuts and burns and torture, all designed to keep dear Brother Ernő in agony but also to keep him conscious. And as I set about my work, I explained the scale his suffering would take. I told him a story.

'A story about a butterfly and a stone sun.'

fter Skála had finished his luridly detailed account of the torture he had inflicted on Brother Ernő, Viktor pressed the button to summon the orderlies.

'Oh, so soon?' said Skála sarcastically, the drugs wearing off, his monstrous Ego reasserting itself. 'Just when I was beginning to enjoy myself. Are you sure you don't want me to stay a while longer? You could unfasten me from this chair, Dr Kosárek, then our exchange could move from the theoretical to the practical.'

Two orderlies came in and made to release the brake on the restraint chair and wheel Skála out. Viktor stopped them with a shake of his head.

'I just need you here while I administer a second dose.' He turned to Skála. 'We need to go deeper, Vojtěch. You're keeping something from me. When you were first admitted here, you talked about the Devil and how he would walk among us. I need to reach that concept of the Devil.'

'Untie me and you'll see for yourself. You don't need drugs to unleash the Devil, just unfasten these straps.'

Viktor loaded the syringe and administered the drug cocktail through the cannula already in Skála's arm. As he did so, Viktor struggled to stop his hands shaking. It wasn't fear of the monster in the chair that made him tremble, but the knowledge that he was taking a risk with the size of the dose. Even on a subject of Skála's size, such a large dose of hypnotics was risky.

'I *will* kill you,' said Skála as the solution entered his veins. 'I will . . .'

Viktor dismissed the orderlies. After making sure he had a syringe charged with the picrotoxin antidote, he sat smoking quietly, soothing his nerves, while the new dose took effect on Skála. The reignited embers of hate and fury faded in the dark eyes, the tension eased in the bound-immobile body. Viktor felt something between bright thrill and dark dread: Pavel Zelený's personal Devil Aspect had taken the form of Mr Hobbs – what form would the Devil Aspect take in the yet more monstrous Vojtěch Skála?

Viktor now knew the Devil hid at the very point of death. That was where he was prepared to take Skála.

Skála's aggression, his hate and his worship of Evil all faded as the drugs again eroded his will. The effect was more pronounced now, and a different Skála was laid bare. Viktor had wanted to get to the frightened small boy who had been denied parental love but had been subjected instead to institutional brutality. If I can get through to him, Viktor thought, then he can describe the moment that the darker, malicious and cruel Skála took form.

Instead, the drugs exposed a cipher: a personality hardly worthy of the name. Without the evil, without the hate and the anger, there was no Vojtěch Skála to speak of left. His personality, whatever that personality had been, had long since been scorched clean by the intense fires of Skála's crimes.

Viktor sighed. Another failure. As Skála became less coherent, began slipping into a sleep Viktor constantly had to stir him from, it became clear there was nothing significant to be learned. Nothing worth risking a patient's life for.

Viktor switched off the recorder and picked up the picrotoxin-filled syringe.

Before he rose from his seat, he was aware of the fire suddenly and fully reignited in Skála's eyes. The same effect as had happened with Pavel Zelený. The place where the Devil hides. Viktor turned the recorder back on, checking that the reels were turning.

He braced himself to confront whatever form Skála's own, personal Devil Aspect would take.

'Are you all right, Vojtěch?'

Skála smiled so coldly, so malevolently, that Viktor was chilled by it.

'Vojtěch?'

'I've told you before,' Skála's voice was suddenly deeper, more resonant; he spoke in a German that was perfectly modulated, if slightly archaic and faintly English-accented. 'You may call me Mr Hobbs.'

PART SIX

MR HOBBS

CHAPTER ONE

*V*iktor checked once more that the recorder was function-
ing. For a moment he was silent, speechless. How could
this be? It made no sense. Hobbs was Pavel Zelený's *personal*
demon. When Mládek the Clown had attacked him, for an irrational
second Viktor had thought he'd spoken with Hobbs's voice, but had
dismissed the thought. But there was no dismissing it now; no doubt:
he was hearing Hobbs's voice – the same voice he'd heard Zelený
speak with – but this time coming from Vojtěch Skála.

It was still Skála steel-clasped into the restraint chair; it was still
Skála who held him in a resolute gaze, the fierceness of which defied
the potent drugs in his system; it was still Skála whose lips formed
the words Viktor heard. But that voice was not Vojtěch Skála's. And
no matter how hard he tried to deny the feeling, Viktor sensed that
something or someone else was in the room with them. Something
yet more malevolent, something even darker.

The appearance of that voice, of that dark personality, was like
some terrible black sun dawning, filling the castle's tower room with
a shining darkness and sinking with malice deep into the dense,
thick stone of its ancient walls. Despite the patient being securely
fastened to the examination couch, Viktor felt isolated, vulnerable.
Afraid. What he was hearing from the patient didn't make sense. It
could not be.

Viktor realized this voice was not simply some fragment of

Skála's splintered personality. This was something else, something other. Something much worse.

'I can sense your fear,' said Mr Hobbs. 'I am attuned to the fear of men. It is the energy which renews me and you renew me now. You have sought me out, and now you have found me. You want to know what I think, what I feel. Well, let me tell you: when I killed them – when I killed all those people, did all those terrible things to them – I enjoyed every second of it. I did what I did because of the dark pleasures it brought. Their pain and their fear were like fine wines to me.

'I especially liked it when, at the end, they begged for their lives: when they did that – and they all did that, eventually – I would pretend to hesitate and see in their eyes the glimmer of a faint, final, desperate hope. I let them have that, for an instant, then I would take it away. It was that – that extinguishing of their very last hope – that I savoured more than anything, more even than the extinguishing of their lives.

'You see, Dr Kosárek, it was at that moment that they would feel the presence of the Devil and beg God to come and deliver them from him. And it was at that moment that I made them see – that they finally realized – that God had already come; that God had been there all along.

'It was then they realized that the Devil is just God in his night attire.'

Silence.

Viktor's mind raced. Make sense of it. Make *sense* of it. He remembered what Judita had said about Skála being isolated because of Románek's fears of psychotic contagion. Maybe that was it: maybe Skála had brought Hobbs like some psychic virus with him into the asylum – or perhaps Hobbs was truly Skála's Devil Aspect and somehow the *idea* of Hobbs spread from one patient to another. Had Pavel Zelený been what he appeared to be all along: a simple, unlettered and suggestible woodsman? All Hobbs's pronouncements, all his sophistication and manner and speech – had it all been impressed on Zelený's mind by Skála's greater will and intellect?

Even that, Viktor admitted to himself, didn't make much sense: Skála's will was so strong as to be able to impress a knowledge of languages on a simple woodcutter? But it was the closest to a logical explanation he could come up with.

'You seem troubled,' said Hobbs-Skála eventually. 'I take it my reappearance has surprised you, even though I told you we would talk again.'

'How do you know that?' Viktor heard his own voice, high and tight, a chord of anxiety stretched through it. 'How can you possibly know what was discussed here with another patient?'

'Another patient to you, another vessel to me. It is with me you speak, Dr Kosárek, not with Vojtěch Skála, just as you spoke to me before, and not to Pavel Zelený. Although I do admit I enjoyed listening to their stories. A strange commonality, don't you think?'

'I don't understand.'

'Of course you don't. Despite Dr Jung's grand theories, despite the philosophies you've tried to weave into your science, you still don't understand. Do you remember how Skála described himself as a place rather than an entity?'

'How *you* described yourself as a place. I'm not buying into this fantasy: you are Vojtěch Skála and this – this *Hobbs* – is all smoke and mirrors. Especially when you managed to plant the germ of it in weaker minds like Zelený and Mládek. I'm not going to fall for some kind of psychical ventriloquist's act, or deep suggestion . . . brainwashing. I don't know how you did it, Vojtěch, but you somehow put your ideas, this façade of a personality into their minds. I'm guessing that you didn't have time or opportunity enough to polish it with Mládek.'

'And that's what you believe?' said Hobbs. His eyes, Skála's eyes, seemed to bore through Viktor. 'That Vojtěch Skála, that most brutal and unsophisticated of butchers, somehow managed to invest a sophisticated consciousness into the minds of a feeble-minded woodcutter and an infanticidal clown? Sometimes the simplest explanation is the easiest. I'll ask again: do you remember how Skála said he was more like a place than a being?'

Viktor nodded.

'Then you'll understand when I say that he is the place I now occupy. Just as Zelený was the place I occupied before and will be again. Just as I have occupied so many over time.'

'So you're some kind of supernatural being?' Viktor said, trying to assert his authority once more, but his sarcasm sounded forced. 'Is that what you're trying to tell me?'

Hobbs laughed. It was the laugh of the indulgent, of the wearily superior. 'There is no such thing as the supernatural. You know that, I know that; anyone with any intelligence knows that. All there is, is all there is – but you know we're a long way from understanding it all. You have a patient here who is a scientist, a quantum physicist . . .'

Viktor ignored the invitation to confirm Hobbs's statement and remained silent. Still his mind raced to make sense of what was happening. He couldn't even explain how Hobbs – how Skála – knew anything of his fellow patients' backgrounds.

'Well,' continued Hobbs, 'you should perhaps talk to him about the countless and untold opportunities the universe offers. Ask him about quantum superposition, where something really can be in two places at one time. Or ask him about Boltzmann Brains – now there's a way to explain me: that consciousness is more likely to spontaneously create itself out of the chaos and disorder of the cosmos, out of a random thermodynamic soup of particles, rather than out of an organized biological system like a human brain. Ever thought about that?'

'Is that what you claim you are? A disembodied space brain?'

'I think you know exactly what I am, Viktor.'

The word formed in Viktor's mouth but he swallowed it. He was not going to be sucked into delusional logic or justify Skála's madness. Was it Skála's madness? Was it Zelený's?

'You doubt me,' said Hobbs. 'I can see that. So let me explain myself a little more clearly. You wonder when I first came into being. When did Skála invent me in the turbid depths of his Unconscious? What dark event in his past formed me? Am I the child of Skála's unholy union with a holy man? I am none of these things. My existence stretches far beyond the span of any one man or woman.'

He paused. Viktor again became aware of the all-enclosing walls of the tower room, of the sound of the Magnetophon's reels turning; of his own breathing.

'I am he who is constant and eternal,' said Hobbs. 'When the first men lit fires to keep the darkness at bay, I was there, because I am that darkness. From me comes all fears, all hatreds, all violence – but also all creativity, all passion, all ambition. I have been known by countless names and countless languages throughout the ages. You say that I dwell in the Unconscious: well, *here am I and I here stay, for this is where Evil resides. Here am I and I here stay, for this is where the Devil hides.* You see, dear Viktor, you really do know who I am. You already know my names.'

CHAPTER TWO

'My last time around I visited as an Englishman,' said the voice of Hobbs. 'They still talk of my visit. They will for a hundred years or more. I have left them with threads of doubt and suspicion to weave together in a thousand patterns, each trying to capture my image.'

'You're saying you were Jack the Ripper?' asked Viktor.

'Just as you enter and leave a room, I come in and out of this world. Whenever I leave it, I take with me servants and playthings to serve and amuse me in the spaces between lives. And that's why I'm here now.'

'So your servants and playthings are Skála's victims?'

'Oh no. Of course it's true to say I influenced him, guided him, even, but his deeds are his affair and his affair alone. Although I admire his faith. His discipular religious zeal. But I make my own companions.'

'But how can you when you're locked up in here?'

Hobbs laughed. 'Do you really believe that I'm confined here? I *choose* to be here. This place was made for me. In one incarnation they even sought to immure me in its walls. And long before that, this castle was built as a stopper on Hell's mouth, a place to shut up evil – but the reality is that the dark, bitter wine they sought to seal has corked: it has soaked into the very fabric that was intended to contain it. It doesn't confine me, it *sustains* me. And as for my between-lives companions, you know very well where I have been choosing them. I wear the leather apron once more, as I did in London.'

'So you claim to be the Prague killer as well?'

'That, and more. I have inflicted pain and death over countless centuries and in countless forms. But yes, I am the shape in the shadows in Prague. I am the shape in the shadows everywhere.'

'So why now? Why here? Why have you revealed yourself to me?'

'Why you? Because you came in search of where the Devil hides. Why now? Because this is a most interesting time – a dark age is dawning, a great tide of blood and torment is coming this way. My kind of dark soul will soon become commonplace among men. Much that will happen here in the coming time will entertain me greatly. So much death, so much suffering, such exquisitely banal evil.' He sighed again. 'And in any case, I have another reason: I lost something.'

'What did you lose?'

Hobbs sighed. 'My most treasured memento from my last visiting. A little glass rose, all white and glistening.'

'How did you lose it?'

'That, my dear Viktor, is a story for another time.' Hobbs frowned. 'This vessel, robust as it is, is failing; your patient is dying. So I must go. And anyway, some news awaits you. You see, I've been busy again . . .'

It was like a light being switched off. In that instant, as his patient slumped in his restraints, Viktor was aware that Hobbs had left the room, that he was now alone with Skála. The nonsense of the feeling added to his confusion.

Rushing across to Skála, he checked the pulse in his neck, then placed his palm in front of his nose and mouth. His pulse was weakening and his respiration dangerously suppressed.

Again, Viktor realized, he had found Hobbs hiding on the very threshold of death. He injected Skála with the picrotoxin and waited anxiously. Within a few seconds his pulse picked up and heavy regular breathing was restored. Skála remained asleep, however, and Viktor decided to leave him in that sedated state. With so many contradictory and confused thoughts buzzing in his head like bees trapped in a jar, Viktor was not disposed to deal with any more of Skála's ranting or joyful confessions.

He needed time to think. He didn't get it.

The door of the tower room opened and Judita entered briskly, only to stop suddenly as she caught sight of Skála bound in the restraint chair. For a moment Viktor was confused – and normally he would have been angry to be disturbed – but what had happened in the session had removed all his certainties, all his convictions about the nature of the Devil Aspect. He switched off the Magnetophon.

'I need you to transcribe this right away,' he said to her. 'You're never going to believe—'

'Forget that just now,' Judita said, and Viktor noticed that her face was pale and drawn, the skin pulled tight, her expression severe. 'I've just heard on the radio. They've discovered another Leather Apron victim. And she was murdered the night Filip didn't come home.'

*J*udita was clearly prepared to argue it out with Viktor, but he could see himself that his suspicions were now too great not to be shared with the police. It could simply be a coincidence that Filip hadn't come home that night, but it was one coincidence too many. And what he had heard from Hobbs during his session with Skála had shaken his view of everything.

They went to Professor Románek's office and insisted that they saw him. Románek's secretary, a cheery, middle-aged woman who travelled in from Mladá Boleslav every day, sat at her desk in the anteroom, standing guard over the professor's privacy with genial indomitability. Eventually Judita and Viktor between them persuaded her of the urgency of their mission and she telephoned through to Románek's study.

When the asylum director emerged from his study, Viktor could see Judita was as shocked as he was by his appearance. Románek, whose dress and grooming were always on the severe side of careful, looked dishevelled, his shirt and trousers crumpled as if slept in. The asylum director hadn't shaved in two days and his face looked drawn and pale. Nor was there any sign of the professor's habitual good humour.

'You'd better come in,' he said brusquely, then turned back into his study.

Viktor scanned the study as they followed Románek in. In

contrast to its usual order, the huge Hungarian desk was heaped with tilting piles of papers and files, the cut-glass ashtrays brim-full. A single blanket lay crumpled on the day cot in the corner, next to which a tray with a half-eaten meal sat abandoned on the floor. The room smelled musty with smoke, stale food, unbroken habitation and unopened windows.

With the vaguely dazed look of a recently awoken sleeper, Románek slumped into his seat behind the desk and waved that they should sit opposite.

'I'm sorry for my condition,' said Románek bluntly, and with no hint that he cared if they accepted his apology or not. 'I am a man of good humours, I like to think. But ever since my wife died I have these periodic episodes.'

'Depression?' asked Viktor. 'There are medications—'

'I'm sure I don't need to remind you that I have considerably more experience of mental health care than you, Dr Kosárek. I am well aware of what is available to me. But this isn't depression. Or at least depression is simply a symptom of the affliction, not the affliction itself. I have absences. Not seizures, but absences with concomitant amnesia. Blackouts in recall. I can tell when an episode is coming on and I sequester myself for its duration. I've only agreed to see you because I'm emerging from this one. I think you can understand my desire for diplomacy.'

'Of course,' said Viktor. Románek rang through and asked his secretary to bring in coffee.

'What can I do for you?' he asked, straightening himself in his chair.

Viktor told him everything he knew about his friend Filip, including the fact that he hadn't returned home the night of the latest Leather Apron killing. Because of Románek's frankness with them about his condition, Viktor felt emboldened to also tell him about what had happened in his session with Skála. As he did so, he could sense Judita's alarm: it was the first she had heard of what had transpired.

Románek seemed to be trying to shake off the shreds of his ailment, irritated by the confusion Viktor was causing him. 'So you're saying you have two contradictory suspicions? That your friend is maybe this killer, yet Skála has confessed to the murders through his invented identity of Hobbs?'

'But that's the thing,' said Viktor. 'This Hobbs identity doesn't belong just to Skála. The same voice has appeared in Pavel Zelený, as you know – and I suspect I heard him speak through Mládek.'

'But that's impossible. You really think your Devil Aspect could manifest itself in the same form – as Hobbs – in wildly different minds? I find that unlikely, to say the least.'

'So do I, but that's what's happening.' Viktor sighed in frustration at his own inability to give his argument credible form. 'Maybe there's no such thing as the Devil Aspect – maybe what's happening is proof of your theory of a psychotic contagion. A physical virus behaves the same way in different hosts, why not a mental one?'

Románek thought for a moment. His hand rasped on stubble as he rubbed his cheek. 'Miss Blochová, please transcribe the tape of this latest session as soon as possible – I need to see it for myself. Dr Kosárek, it is imperative you contact Kapitán Smolák and tell him about your friend. In the meantime, I think it best if you suspend all narcosynthesis sessions.'

'With Skála?' asked Viktor.

'With all patients.' When Viktor began to protest, Románek raised a hand as if halting traffic. 'I'm afraid I must insist. I don't know what we're dealing with here. What kind of psychosis or syndrome is causing different patients to manifest this same identity, but until I have read this latest transcription – and gone through the others again – I feel it's too dangerous to carry on with your research. I'm sorry, Viktor.'

'But don't you see, Professor? The only way I can get to the bottom of this is to make contact with this Hobbs identity, or the

Devil Aspect, or whatever it is that manifests itself. Only Hobbs can explain what is going on.'

'For God's sake, man,' said Románek abruptly. 'Are you listening to yourself? You're talking about a delusion, about a fragment of a sick mind, as if it were a real person. No, I have to insist you carry out no more sessions. Your focus now should be on helping the police locate your friend.'

*L*ukáš Smolák stared at the telephone on his desk after he had replaced the receiver, as if it would offer further explanation. He thought it unlikely too that Dr Kosárek's friend was Leather Apron and, after all, the phones rang constantly with people accusing neighbours, employees or employers, relatives and friends of being the maniacal Prague killer. Nonetheless, the psychiatrist's reticence to inform the police of his suspicions had irritated Smolák, and he had left the doctor in no doubt about his annoyance.

Yet something troubled him. When most people reported a suspect there was usually a hint of malice, or of dark excitement. Viktor Kosárek had been reluctant to implicate his friend, suggesting he took the possibility seriously. Whatever the truth of the matter, it was clear that Starosta was unhinged and violent. Leather Apron or not, he was well worth a look.

Prague was grey-greased with winter. The snow had turned to rain and the streets were edged with soot-freckled, gelatinous slush and punctuated with the oily black mirrors of puddled rainwater and melted snow. Kosárek took Mirek Novotný with him and the detektiv-seržant sat mute in the passenger seat as they drove to the address in Vršovice that Viktor Kosárek had given him.

It took them a while to find the apartment, the location and appearance of which surprised Smolák. Filip Starosta lived in one half of a converted stable block or coach house, and Smolák realized it spoke of a time when the quarter had been much more prosperous. He sent Novotný around to the back of the property while he tried the front. There was no answer when he rang the doorbell and he could see no signs of life when he peered in through the windows. Novotný reappeared and confirmed that the back was locked up too.

'Hold on,' said Smolák, remembering something Kosárek had told him on the phone. 'Come with me.' He led his junior officer around to the rear and searched for a loose flagstone near the door. He found it and, when it was lifted, it yielded the key Kosárek had told him about. As he turned the key in the lock he looked over his shoulder at his junior. 'The door was unlocked and ajar when we arrived, got it?'

Novotný nodded.

There was something you picked up over the years: Smolák didn't like to call it instinct, because it was more than that. It was like a shattered fragment of knowledge had been picked up at each murder scene, in each interrogation of a subject, with each success or failure with a case. Sometimes, for some unknown reason and by some unknown power, those fragments came together and you got, for a passing instant, a clarity of vision. He had it here. As soon as Kapitán Lukáš Smolák set foot in Filip Starosta's apartment, he knew he had found Leather Apron. A quiet jangling of nerves when he first entered picked up pace and intensity as he made his way through the apartment.

On the desk he found the ornate leather binding wrapped around the manuscript, just as Kosárek had described it.

'Take a look around,' he said to Novotný. 'But careful what you touch. I have an odd feeling we've found our boy.'

Once Novotný started searching, Smolák sat in the leather chair and began leafing through the manuscript's meticulously handwritten pages. He saw in those pages that which had eluded the psychiatrist. Kosárek hadn't heard Tobar Bihari's descriptions of monsters taking shape in the shadows – Smolák had. And here in the careful sentences and dark illustrations he saw the same monsters, the same shadows. Bihari had called him Beng, the manuscript called him Veles. Smolák knew his real name. Filip Starosta.

'Find a phone,' he said to Novotný. 'I want four men in here with us searching, another four on door-to-door. And I want a man on every corner of every block to warn us if Starosta is on his way back.'

'You really think it's him?' said Novotný. 'Then you might want to look at this – I've got a locked door here.'

Smolák's deputy stood where a second door led off the living area, locked with no sign of a key. Bringing a fire iron from the fireplace, Smolák gave Novotný a knowing look as he jammed the iron into the gap and levered the door open, wood splintering as it yielded to his weight.

It was too small to be called a room and too large to be called a cupboard. Windowless, a single naked bulb was suspended from the centre of the ceiling. Smolák tugged on the pendant cord and the walk-in closet was flooded with bright, bleaching light.

'Oh fuck . . .' Novotný stretched the curse out, wonder and shock spun through it.

Two walls were lined with shelves; the third, to Smolák's right, was empty except for a single, heavy coat hook screwed into it. Nothing hung from the hook, and it was age-tarnished except for the bulb-like tip, the brass of which had been burnished bright by something heavy having been repeatedly hung on it and removed, over a very long time.

It wasn't there, but Smolák could imagine a dark-stained leather apron hanging from it.

Behind him he could hear Novotný controlling his breathing, as if fighting back nausea. The shelves on the other two walls were stacked with pickle jars filled with what Smolák guessed was preserving fluid. Glossy black-red or grey-brown masses pressed sleekly against the glass of the jars, each jar containing a different human organ. One jar, the one facing them from the centre of its shelf, contained what at first looked like a mask, but Smolák recognized it as the sheared-off face of the Prager Kleinseite victim, Maria Lehmann, who gazed accusingly at them from eyeless black gapes.

'Yes,' he said without looking at Novotný, 'I really think it's him.'

*V*iktor was in his office when the call came in from Smolák. He stood at his desk, the heavy receiver held to his ear, and felt frozen, as if the chill of his worst fears being confirmed had spread through muscle and bone, transforming him into a statue. Judita stood opposite him, her expression grave and intense. Beyond his windows the snow was now falling as an impenetrable curtain of focus-less grey, a premature darkening and enclosing.

The weather was the excuse Smolák had used to dissuade Viktor from coming to Prague. Viktor guessed he simply didn't want him under his feet. Smolák explained that there was no sign that Filip would return to his apartment, but they had left a couple of men there just in case.

'In fact,' Smolák had said, 'I don't believe your friend has been there since before you were in the apartment. The neighbours say they haven't seen him since – my guess is he has a new lair some-where. He probably decided to clear out after that incident in the street with the German-Bohemians – which would be the night after he had murdered Anna Petrášová, the glass-store owner. He maybe guessed you might act on your concerns and get in touch with us.' Smolák paused at the other end of the line. 'I have to say I wish you had, Dr Kosárek. Another young woman has died in the meantime. Anyway, I've circulated the description you gave me and we'll get his records from the state registry and the university in the morning.

I'll be in touch. In the meantime, you stay at Hrad Orlů where I can reach you.'

The first thing Viktor did after hanging up was to read again what Judita had noted down from the radio news broadcast. A young woman with a strange name, Tsora Mirga, had been found murdered, and the police had reason to believe it was yet another case of the Prague murderer, informally known as 'Leather Apron'.

'It's my fault,' he said disconsolately. 'What that poor girl went through – it's all my fault.'

'You didn't know,' said Judita, coming around the desk and laying her hand on his shoulder, her touch comforting him. 'Even I didn't think Filip would really be this – this *monster*. What did Smolák say?'

Viktor ran through the conversation with her.

'I think he's right that you're safer here. Filip might blame you for being detected and want revenge. In any case, this snow's getting heavier. The road up from the village will become impassable if this keeps up.' She turned to the window and, reading his expression, frowned. 'What is it?'

'The session with Skála. What he said. What he *knew*. There's more to this than meets the eye. There's something that links "Mr Hobbs" with Filip and these killings. I've got to find out what it is.'

'But you can't. Professor Románek has forbidden any more sessions.'

Viktor turned to Judita and took hold of her by the shoulders. 'There *is* something I'm missing. Some piece of the puzzle that Hobbs holds—'

'Viktor, you're talking about him as if he were a real person—'

'He's not a person, I know that, but he is real. And he has something to do with the killings – I need to understand how he knows all he does.' Viktor paused, still holding Judita in his hands and in his urgent gaze. 'I'm going to carry out another session. I'm going to carry it out tonight. While Smolák hunts down his Devil in Prague, I'm going to hunt mine here.'

'You can't Viktor. It's forbidden. And it's dangerous.'

'I have to do it. I must find out.' He leaned even closer to her. 'But I can't do it without your help.'

*S*molák revisited Magda Tůmová, the sales assistant who had worked for Anna Petrášová at Petráš Sklo a Skleněná Bižuterie. He again called around to her apartment but, it being the evening and her two flatmates being at home, they conducted their conversation in the hallway, Magda gathering her knitted cardigan tight around her and folding her arms against the cold. Smolák had brought with him one of the Bohemian drinking glasses he had found at Starosta's apartment. She recognized it as soon as he unfolded it from the newspaper he had wrapped it in.

'It's part of a set of six,' she said, nodding. 'I remember them clearly.'

'Do you remember who bought them?' asked Smolák.

'Oh nobody bought them. Madame Petrášová took them home. They were her personal pieces. Sometimes she would do that. Glass wasn't just her trade, you see, it was her life. Poor Madame Petrášová.'

'You're sure she took them home? There's no chance she brought them back to the shop and someone bought them?'

'I'm sure,' said Magda. 'Did someone take them from her house?'

Smolák smiled. 'Thank you, Miss Tůmová, you've been very helpful.'

It was beginning to get dark by the time he left Magda Tůmová's apartment, but the snow had eased a little, although his car radio advised him that there were still heavy falls to the north of the city. He had been right to tell Dr Kosárek to stay put: he would only have been stranded in Prague, and Smolák didn't want some amateur tripping him up every step of the way. Added to that was the image that haunted him of young, darkly pretty Tsora Mirga lying dead in her colourful but neat apartment. Another life, another universe of experiences, hopes and emotions, brought to a premature end. And Smolák couldn't ignore his anger that if Kosárek hadn't been playing amateur detective, Tsora would still be alive. Perhaps.

He picked up Mirek Novotný on his way to Vršovice. Novotný had his hat pulled down and his coat collar pulled up over his ears, but the red-haired detektiv-seržant's pale nose and cheeks had been pinched florid by the cold of the street corner where he'd waited.

'Anything?' Smolák asked.

'It took longer than I thought,' said Novotný, hunching his shoulders against the cold. 'I spent an age waiting for the bloody elevator to come down, but it's busted. Anyway, the apartment's been rented by an electrician and his wife for the last four months. They're outsiders – Ruthenians, I think. They did everything through a letting agent and had no contact with the previous tenant, but they know his name was Filip Starosta. Only one person ever came asking for Starosta and they gave him his new address.'

Smolák nodded. 'That was when Kosárek came looking for him.'

'Anyway,' continued Novotný, 'I did a door-to-door and the neighbours all said the same thing that his new neighbours said: they couldn't describe Starosta because they hardly ever saw him and, when they did, he was always dressed in that scruffy long coat and wide-brimmed hat pulled down over his eyes. The only thing I got was one woman thought he had blond hair, but she couldn't be sure.'

'He knew what he was about – making sure no one could give an accurate description.' Smolák sighed. 'Maybe our German chums can help.'

* * *

It was early evening and it was snowing, so the German bar a few blocks distant from Starosta's apartment was empty of all but the most determined drinkers. The barman knew exactly what Smolák was talking about when he mentioned the attack in the street. He had been on duty that night and remembered the trouble-maker mouthing off before leaving. Smolák left the bar with the name – Anton Sauer – and address of the man who had been injured in the scuffle.

'But Anton works until seven,' the barman explained. 'He won't be home till then.'

'Where does he work?' asked Smolák. 'We can see him there.'

'You'll be lucky. He works out of Strašnice tram depot. He's a driver. He's out on route until finishing time.'

'What about the friends he was with?' asked Novotný.

The barman shrugged. 'I see them in here with Anton sometimes, but they're not regulars. Don't know their names, sorry.'

CHAPTER SEVEN

*I*f he had believed in such a thing, Viktor would have ascribed it to fate.

Professor Románek had travelled to Mladá Boleslav on business and the weather there was even worse than the near blizzard falling on the castle. The professor had phoned his secretary to tell her he would stay the night in town but return the following morning. It had been the last phone call the asylum had received before the lines went dead, presumably brought down by the weather, which was not an uncommon experience.

He waited until Platner had completed his rounds and retired to his rooms before meeting with Judita in the equipment storeroom. He ran through his plans to carry out another narcosynthesis session, his tone determined and urgent.

'I won't help you do this with Skála,' she said. 'He's far too dangerous.'

'But that's who Hobbs manifested himself through.'

'He also manifested himself through Pavel Zelený – and more often.' Judita bit her lip and frowned. 'You should go with Zelený. God knows he's dangerous enough, but Skála is in a perpetual state of homicidal rage.'

Viktor thought for a moment then shook his head. 'It has to be Skála. Don't ask me why, but Hobbs was more – more *convincing* when he spoke through Skála. And anyway, I'm not ready to believe that Hobbs exists independently and flits from host to host. He's some kind of, I don't know, psychiatric infection. When Hobbs spoke through Skála, his knowledge of the murders had to be Skála's. That's the lead I have to follow.'

'I won't do it,' said Judita decisively. 'The first chance he gets he'll kill us both.'

'Then I'll make sure he doesn't get a chance. I'll sedate him to the maximum and have him in a straitjacket. You've got to trust me, Judita. It's the only way. I *have* to find out what's going on.'

She stared at him with that uniquely intent look she adopted when thinking something through. It made her look stern and appealing at the same time.

'He'll be doped from the start? And straitjacketed?'

'I promise.'

She nodded abruptly. 'What do you need me to do?'

'I need you to wait until the duty orderly is doing his rounds, then slip into the porters' office and switch off the magnetic locks and alarms for patient suite six. Then I'll get Skála out and into the tower room.'

'Why not just do the session in his patient suite? I could transcribe everything that he says without the need of the Magnetophon. It just seems getting him all the way to the tower is an unnecessary risk.'

'Don't ask me to explain – and I know this is less than scientific – but it's as if the tower room is essential to Hobbs. Like some kind of receiver.'

'You're right, it is less than scientific – and not strictly true: you said you thought Mládek also spoke as Hobbs, and that was in his rooms, not the tower. And I still think it's an unnecessary risk.'

'You have to trust me on this, Judita. I've thought it all through.'

'How will you administer the sedative? As soon as you step into his room without orderlies he'll tear you apart.'

'I've already told the duty manager I'll need two orderlies to help me administer an injection to him. I said Skála's been suffering from disturbed sleeping patterns and the injection's something to help regulate them. By the time I sneak back an hour or so later, Skála'll be unconscious. I'll straitjacket him and transport him to the tower room in a wheelchair.'

Judita held him in her frank gaze for a moment. 'All right. When do we do it?'

Viktor smiled. 'There's a shift change at seven. The duty porter will do his rounds shortly after, meaning you can get into the porters' office and switch off the magnetic locks. I'll meet you in the tower room as soon after as I can manage. My main problem is I have to get past the infirmary, and Krakl will be on duty. He's a lazy swine, though, and never leaves the infirmary, just sits on his backside reading *Völkischer Beobachter*, or some crap like that.'

'You know this will cost you your job?'

Viktor nodded grimly. 'It has to be done. I have to get to the bottom of all this insanity. What if Hobbs really is some kind of psychiatric contagion? All I know is that multiple patients are exhibiting a shared symptom – a shared personality – and somehow, I don't know how, it's all got something to do with what's going on with these murders. And whatever is going on with Filip.'

'You're sure there's a connection?' asked Judita.

'I know it doesn't make sense, and God knows what kind of connection it could be, but yes, I am sure.'

Viktor knew the secret was not to look guilty, shifty. He was a physician in the asylum and had a right to be anywhere he needed to be, so when he made his way back towards patient suite six, he walked with purpose and authority.

Judita, on the other hand, had no reason to be where she was. Particularly in the porters' office, she would have no credible excuse for her presence. At the seven p.m. shift change, with all the patients confined to their quarters for the night, the lighting in the asylum was dimmed. Every second ceiling lamp in the hallways was switched off and Judita hugged the many shadows the castle afforded as she made her way along the main halls to the arch nearest the porters' office.

She took a moment to breathe, to think about the insanity of what she was doing. But insanity was the stock-in-trade of this place; insanity was becoming the stock-in-trade of the world beyond its walls. Maybe, she thought, madness would soon become so commonplace it wouldn't be recognized as madness any more. She looked back along the corridor: she could go back now, put it all behind her. But Viktor was depending on her. Viktor was convinced he had to do this.

She turned back to check the porters' office: there was no sign of life. Taking off her shoes and carrying them in her hand so she would make no sound as she crossed the flagstones, she made her way to the office and slipped in through the door.

She almost gasped when she saw the duty manager still sitting at his desk, next to the array of switches that controlled the locks and lighting for the patient accommodation wing. He had his back to her but he must have heard something, because he began to swivel around in his chair. Judita didn't take the time to turn, instead taking three backward strides, swinging back around the open door and out of sight behind the wall.

'Hello?'

At the sound of the duty porter's voice, Judita scanned the arched hallway for somewhere to hide. She heard the scratch of wood on stone as the porter pushed his chair back. The only place to hide was back behind the ridge of the arch, and she ran to it, dodging behind the meagre cover of the arch's abutment, pressing her back to the cold stonework. The porter appeared at the doorway of the office and Judita shrank further back. If he started his rounds in her direction, there was no way he could avoid seeing her. She held her breath for a moment, scanning the hallway. After what seemed an age, the porter went back into the office to collect his keys for his rounds. When he re-emerged, he turned and headed in the opposite direction. Judita waited until he was some distance down the hall before moving swiftly to the office.

It took her a moment to work out which of the switches applied to patient suite six. But once she did, her hand hovered over the switch. This was mad, she again told herself. What they were doing was reckless, dangerous. Once more she forced herself to think of Viktor. Of his certainty. Of his resolve in wanting to help others.

She pulled the switch.

Viktor forced his focus onto the task at hand – a task that would be difficult to complete undetected and demanded his full concentration. Yet ever since Hobbs had spoken through Skála, ever since Smolák had confirmed his worst suspicions about Filip, so much crowded in on his thoughts: so many questions awaited answers. It all came back to him forcing the truth from Hobbs. But first he had to force Hobbs from Skála.

He reached the storeroom closest to the gate leading to the patient suites and hoped the wheelchair and straitjacket would be undisturbed where he had left them. Everything so far had gone to plan: the duty manager and the orderlies hadn't questioned his need to sedate Skála. The policy of rotating orderlies assigned to the Demon's care meant they were unaware whether Skála had had trouble sleeping or not, and they had placed him in the restraint chair for Viktor to inject with the sedative. All he needed to do was to get his patient to the tower room where, like some mediaeval necromancer, he could summon Mr Hobbs to life.

The straitjacket and chair were there. He eased them out, unlocked the gate to the patient accommodation and headed towards patient suite six, relocking the gate behind him.

He was relieved to see Judita had succeeded in her part of the mission: when he got to the patient wing he found the magnetic locks had been deactivated and he gained access to Skála's accommodations. Viktor had come this far without hesitation, but found himself pausing before he unlocked the heavy door of the Demon's room, peering in through the inspection window. The room was in darkness and Viktor felt his pulse quicken: if he had miscalculated and Skála wasn't unconscious, then stepping into his room would be stepping into hell. And it wouldn't end there: with the magnetic door system deactivated, Skála would be able to gain access to the rest of the asylum. The castle would become his toy-box and everyone in it his playthings. The idea of it chilled him, especially when he imagined Skála free to torture, maim and kill while wearing Viktor's face as a mask.

He swung the door open.

'Vojtěch?' Viktor called into the silence and darkness. His desperate fingers scrabbled across the cold stone of the wall, seeking out the light switch. He fought down the panic rising and the phantom shapes and sounds his imagination shaped in the dark.. After what seemed an age, he found the light switch and the room flooded with light. Skála was slumped on the couch.

Viktor realized he had been holding his breath and let it go slowly before crossing the room quickly and checking Skála: the Demon was unconscious but breathing deeply and regularly. As he tried to get him first into the straitjacket and then into the wheelchair, Viktor struggled with his patient's bulk, and he found himself panting with the effort, his face becoming sleeked with sweat. And it was taking too long. Viktor had timed everything perfectly and, if he wasn't out of the patient accommodation wing soon, there was a real danger of him running into the duty porter doing his rounds.

Eventually Skála was secured in the straitjacket and loaded into the wheelchair. Locking Skála's door behind him, Viktor pushed the wheelchair and its cargo at as close to a trot as he could manage. Twice he had to stop because he thought he heard footsteps; a third time to unlock and relock behind him the main door into the hallway.

He turned the corner at the end of the hall and started down the incline towards the door of the tower room. Judita was waiting for him at the grain-store door, beckoning urgently. From behind, Viktor could hear the porter's footsteps in the main hall as he made his rounds, heading in their direction. The angle of the incline and Skála's weight made the wheelchair difficult to steer, and for a moment he thought it would career out of control, crashing into the wall and spilling its straitjacketed contents.

Judita, seeing Viktor struggle, ran forward, and between them they managed to steer the wheelchair in through the tower-room door just as the porter rounded the corner.

Using both hands, Judita eased the door closed behind them and dropped the latch as quietly as she could.

It felt like another world. The darkness in the tower granary was total, complete, absolute, as if painted in the elusive shade of perfect black sought by the obsessed painter in Dominik Bartoš's insane tale. Judita became aware of her and Viktor's confinement in a total darkness with a maniac who had murdered countless innocent victims. The panic began to rise and she drew a long, slow, calming breath.

The sudden luminance of the flame from Viktor's cigarette lighter lit the room, casting writhing shadows on the walls. He found his desk lamp and switched it on.

'Help me get him onto the couch. I need to strap him in.'

'What about the straitjacket? You're not going to take that off, are you?'

Viktor looked at his patient, who was beginning to stir from the depths of his sedation. 'We'll leave the straitjacket on but fasten his ankles to the couch. He won't be able to do us any harm. Bear in mind he's going to be heavily medicated throughout.'

Judita taking his legs and Viktor taking his shoulders, they managed to wrestle Skála out of the wheelchair and onto the couch. They were both breathless from the effort and, once he was on the couch, Judita fastened the straps around his ankles.

They stood catching their breaths, holding each other's gaze with the determination of people committed to a perilous course. After a while Viktor prepared a small dose of stimulant to rouse Skála sufficiently to be able to talk. He stood with the syringe raised in his hand.

'Are you ready?'

'Are you sure you want to go through with this?' she asked, laying her hand on his holding the syringe.

'I have to know,' he said. 'I have to find out.'

With grim resolution, Judita nodded and switched on the Magnetophon recorder.

Viktor injected the stimulant: just enough to bring Skála back to the threshold of consciousness.

'Vojtěch,' said Viktor. 'Vojtěch, can you hear me?'

Skála murmured, mumbled. His eyes half opened, closed again; his head lolled. As she watched him, Judita could not imagine how, in such a drugged state, he could articulate anything as himself, far less as Hobbs.

'He's too drugged,' she said. 'He's incapable—'

Viktor silenced her with an impatient shake of his head, then turned to his patient.

'Vojtěch,' he pressed again. 'I need to speak to Mr Hobbs. I need Mr Hobbs to come back, do you understand?'

There was a moment's silence. Then it was broken by two sounds. The first was the voice Judita recognized from the recordings: deep, resonant, terrifying.

'I am here, Viktor. I promised you I would be back,' said Mr Hobbs. 'I told you I had unfinished business to conclude.'

The second sound was shrill, ragged, piercing. It rang jarringly against the circular walls of the tower room.

It was the sound of Judita screaming.

CHAPTER EIGHT

he snow had turned to a chill, sleety rain, and the forecourt of the Strašnice tram depot was an oily black shield
shining sleekly under the suspended lamps. Soiled snow sat in shov-
elled heaps around its edges, and intersecting tram lines weaved
across across it like silver tracery.

Anton Sauer was a big, burly man, who would have looked more
at home in farm overalls than in his municipal tram driver's uniform.
When he emerged from the depot's tram sheds, his foreman pointed
across the forecourt to where Smolák and Novotný stood waiting for
him.

Lukáš Smolák showed Sauer his brass shield emblazoned with
the words, Služba Kriminální Policie.

'What's the problem?' Sauer's Czech was heavily German
accented. His eyes narrowed in the shadow cast by the peak of his
driver's cap.

Smolák explained that they wanted to talk to him about the incident in the street near the German pub.

'It's not me you should be after for that, it's the other guy,' he said
emphatically, gingerly pulling up the sleeve of his uniform jacket
to reveal a white bandage wrapped around his forearm. 'Twelve
stitches it took. I'll be scarred for life, the doctor said. So it's not me
you should be looking for, it's the bastard—'

Smolák halted Sauer's protest with a held-up hand. 'It *is* the other man we're looking for. I'm not interested in you other than as a witness.'

Sauer's eyes widened. 'I knew it! I knew there was something more to him. If you'd seen him, if you'd seen his eyes. He would have killed all of us. I can describe him for you. I seen him good and there's no way I'd ever forget him.'

'We already have a description of him,' said Novotný, who read it out from his notebook. Smolák watched Sauer's face, his expression changing as Novotný read and he felt a cold electricity course through him.

'What's wrong?' Smolák asked when his junior officer had finished. 'Doesn't that sound right to you?'

'Not right? It's nothing like him. That's not the guy who slashed me. Where did you get that description?'

'From his friend,' said Novotný.

'What friend?' Sauer's thick features reassembled in a coarse frown.

'The friend who was with him that night in the bar, then in the street,' said Smolák. 'The friend who tried to stop him – calm him down.'

Sauer shook his head, his expression one of confused annoyance. 'What are you talking about? There was no friend. There was no one with him that night. He was on his own.'

'What about in the bar? Did you see his friend with him then?' asked Smolák.

'He was in the bar on his own. We threw him out onto the street because he was talking away to himself, ranting and calling us Krauts and *Skopčáci* and all that crap. Bloody madman he was. That's why he attacked us – because we chucked him out. He was waiting for us outside, in the shadows. Then he just launched himself at me.'

Smolák fixed Sauer with a searchlight gaze. 'And you're sure he was alone?'

'Absolutely sure. There was no one with him, and I got a good look at him. And he looked nothing like you said.'

Smolák exchanged a look with Novotný. The detektiv-seržant hadn't caught up with him yet and still looked confused.

'In that case,' he said, 'maybe you should describe your assailant to us after all, Herr Sauer.'

And he did.

Standing there in the chill rain on the blank, cheerless shield of a tram depot forecourt, listening to the tram driver give the true description of his assailant, Lukáš Smolák felt someone turn up the dark current running through the nape of his neck. He grabbed Novotný by the elbow and steered him towards the depot gates where his car was parked.

'We've got to get to Hrad Orlů asylum,' he said as he half ran towards the car. 'Now.'

*J*udita stifled her scream with the hand she clamped to her mouth. She was frozen for a crucial moment, her ability to move, to reason, to think, stripped from her by that voice. Hobbs's voice. The voice she had heard before on the tapes, and the madness and cruelty of which she had transcribed into measured, typewritten sheets. She looked at Skála in disbelief: he lay on the patient couch with his eyes closed, his mouth slightly agape but unmoving. Unconscious.

Silent.

'I don't know why you're so surprised,' said Hobbs. She turned in the direction of the voice. She turned to Viktor. He was grinning malevolently. What she had always seen as a vaguely imperious and cruel handsomeness was now just cruelty. A dark, fathomless, time-less cruelty. 'How could the same voice appear in different patients? How could a personality exist in separate bodies? Are you really so stupid? Even that old fool Románek started to believe in psychiatric viruses to explain it. Didn't any of you ever think that the one constant – the only person to have been present every time I spoke was Viktor Kosárek? No one *saw* me appear, only heard me on those tapes.'

'Viktor . . .' Judita said pleadingly. 'Viktor, you have to get help. Let me go and get help.'

'I'm not Viktor,' he said matter-of-factly. 'You know who I am. *What* I am. I'm not a pretence, I'm not a superstition, I'm a reality.

Viktor Kosárek is my host. He has been for almost all of his life. None of you saw me for who I truly am; none of you recognized me. But there were those who did. That fool in Masaryk Railway Station, the one who was shot – he recognized me. He had been given the wisdom, the sight, to see me and my kind, but he didn't have the wit to conceal his gift, so they called him mad and shot him. But he saw me all right. And that old witch in the village – Růžena – she saw me for what I truly was. Even Leoš Mládek the Clown saw through my mask. He told me he knew who I was and I made him paint his face as Harlequin. I made him bear my mark. But the rest of you were too stupid to see what was in front of you all the time.'

Judita scanned the room for a way to escape, a weapon, a hope. There was none. 'You killed Mládek on purpose?' she asked, her mind racing. She had to keep Viktor – keep Hobbs – talking. She had to keep him talking until she worked out how to get away from him. 'He didn't really attack you, did he?'

'He saw me for who I am. And he bored me with his tedious innocence. He blamed me for what he did to those children, not realizing he has his own demon locked up inside him. He saw me and he feared me and when I commanded him to become Harlequin once more he did as I bade. Then I smashed his head on the floor.

'No, Mládek didn't attack me. But your lover thinks he did: poor, confused Viktor remembers it that way. He remembers everything the way I make him remember. Now, for example – he'll remember being helpless, being beaten down by Skála and having to watch while the Demon lives up to his name. He'll remember seeing all the terrible things done to you – they'll be seared into his retinas and branded into his recall forever – but he won't know I used his body to do them. He'll remember Skála doing them, not him.'

Judita looked across at the Magnetophon. The reels were turning. At least they would know. At least, after she was dead, after they found her body and what had been done to it, they would know the truth.

'I don't understand,' she said. Still trying to keep him talking. Her shock at hearing Hobbs's voice come from Viktor had robbed her of the chance to make for the door, and he had now placed himself between her and it. An opportunity to escape, a chance for life lost. 'How long have you been part of Viktor?'

'The superstitions have one thing right: the Devil has to be invited to cross the threshold. Viktor invited me in. He found me after I had been asleep for a long time. I can't remember too clearly – I may have been resting between lives deep in the waters at the bottom of Čertovo Jezero. That would be appropriate, wouldn't it? That Viktor and I encountered each other at the Devil's Lake?'

'The accident?' Judita asked, her eyes wild as they again scanned the room for some escape, for some weapon to protect herself. There was nothing. This had been a nobleman's thick-walled prison. A tomb. 'You mean the day your sister Ella drowned?'

'Not my sister, his. But yes. Since then.'

Judita tried to slow her thoughts, make sense of her situation. The trauma of losing his sister had been the catalyst for the splitting of Viktor's personality. His loss and pain an axe-blow through his sense of self. She remembered her breakdown, how it had been her own will, her own rationality, not the treatment given, that had brought her through it. She needed to reach that same part in Viktor. 'Listen, I want to help you Viktor. I want to see you get out of this.'

'You really are a stupid Jew bitch, aren't you?' The voice was deeper, angrier. 'Are you so incapable of understanding that I am not Viktor Kosárek? I'm not some *Devil Aspect*, I'm not some splinter of a madman's mind. I am Mr Hobbs, whom they call Jack the Ripper, I am Peter Stumpp, I am Gilles de Rais, I am Peter Niers. I am Christman Genipperteinga – the cave-dwelling presser of children's necks, the keeper and spoiler of women, the killer of a thousand. I am Jan Černé Srdce – Jan of the Black Heart. And I *am* Leather Apron. I am all the names for evil and pain. I am eternal and I am constant.' Viktor stepped forward, closer to her, leaning his face close to hers. 'But I know what *you* are – you're a bitch. A German. A Jewess. A *Fotze*. And it's time for you to be prepared. What is going to happen to you now will be exquisitely painful and terrifying – but it will be nothing compared to the horrors that await you as one of my companions, one of my amusements, in the endless space between lives.'

'Wait . . .' Judita held up a hand. She needed to keep him talking, humour him into losing himself in delusional ravings so that she could work out how to get away. 'I still don't understand. What about Filip Starosta? What have you done with him? You made it look like he was the killer and the police are looking for him now – that was clever, Mr Hobbs. Very clever. Did you kill him?'

Viktor shook his head, as if disappointed in Judita. 'My God, you really *are* stupid. Filip Starosta doesn't exist. He never has, other than as a convenience to allow me to carry out my work, to provide places to base myself. He is one of the memories I have placed in Viktor Kosárek's mind. He really does believe Starosta exists. One of the explanations to divert him from suspicion of himself. Filip Starosta is a ghost in Viktor's mind and by the time the police realize it you'll be dead.'

Unfolding the leather wrap on his desk, he picked up an already charged syringe and stepped back towards her.

Judita shrank back but he seized hold of her wrist and yanked her towards him. She kicked at him, hard, stamped her heel down on his foot, but it was as if he truly was disconnected from his body. He pulled her towards him and instead of resisting she thrust forward into him, their combined impetus sending them crashing onto the small desk. She put out a hand to steady herself and it found the ashtray. With every ounce of force she could muster she arced the ashtray up. It slammed into Viktor's temple and his grip on her slipped. Struggling free of him, Judita screamed in fury and slammed the ashtray into his head again and again until the side of his face was crimson with blood and the fierce intensity faded from his eyes. For a moment, for nothing more than a sliver of a second, she saw confusion and hurt in his eyes. She saw Viktor, not Hobbs.

His eyes closed and he slid off the desk and landed heavily on the stone flags. He lay motionless. The smash of the ashtray on the ground as it fell from her hands galvanized Judita and she sprinted for the door, screaming for help.

She struggled with the door, rattling and tugging the handle without effect. The door was locked. She'd have to go back and take the keys from Viktor.

When she turned he was there, standing behind her, the gash on his temple streaming blood but the fire in his eyes – Hobbs's eyes – fully rekindled.

Before she could act there was a sting in her neck and she felt the chill rush of the injected solution. The dim light in the tower room grew dimmer. She could have sworn she saw the shadows become darker, swell, move, come to life.

'Before you die,' he said coldly as she drifted towards unconsciousness, 'there are many glories to be discovered, a lot of suffering to be done. You will wonder at the pain and fear I will bring you.

'But first, I'm going to show you why we're here, in this place. I'm going to show you the Gate to Hell.'

*S*molák cursed as he slammed the receiver back onto its cradle. He and Novotný had headed directly from the tram depot to the nearest police station, the Vršovice Police Inspektorát, where he had tried unsuccessfully to phone the asylum at Hrad Orlů. The lines, he was told by the operator, had been reported down.

'We're going to have to drive up there ourselves,' he said to Novotný. 'It'll take us an hour. Longer in this weather.'

'If the roads are open all the way.'

'It's all we can do.' Smolák shook his head, as if its weight was a sudden burden. 'It's my fault . . .'

'What?' Novotný frowned. 'What's your fault?'

'Tsora Mirga. When I visited Hrad Orlů asylum and spoke with Kosárek, I mentioned I was going to see her. Kosárek was the one who put the idea of the key-theft burglaries in Tobar Bihari's mind. Viktor Kosárek was Beng, the demon who made Bihari watch what he did to Maria Lehmann and, God forgive me, I sent him back to Tsora. And I was too stupid to work out that Kosárek spent the night in Prague that same night. He was in Starosta's apartment all right, because he was Starosta.'

'You couldn't have known,' said Novotný, shaking his head as if in wonder. 'It's all beyond knowing, beyond understanding.'

Smolák didn't say anything but turned to the duty detective. 'I need you to phone Major Chromík at Mladá Boleslav Police

Inspektorát. If he's not on duty, I don't care if they have to drag him out of bed, they have to get him in. Tell them we're on our way and we'll meet Major Chromík at the Inspektorát in an hour or so. And make sure they know we'll need some kind of transport that's good in snow to make it through to Hrad Orlů castle.'

The duty detective nodded.

Smolák turned to Novotný. 'Let's go.'

*W*hen it started to return, Judita's consciousness didn't come to her intact, it came in stages: slowly gathering pieces of a broken world. The first thing she became aware of was the taste in her mouth: harsh, metallic. The rest of her assembling memory had not yet formed enough for her to realize it was an effect of the narcotic she'd been injected with. For a few moments she was without knowledge or memory, didn't know who she was, what her name was, what this place was. Yet there was no mercy in the amnesia, because some primal instinct drove her to panic, telling her her life depended on how fast she could put everything back together again. How quickly she could remember.

In relentless bursts, like an artillery onslaught against her senses, she remembered who, where and what. She remembered about Viktor, the man she loved, then remembered that someone else had stepped into the clothes of his flesh. She remembered about Hobbs.

She remembered what was going to happen to her.

This wasn't the tower room. It felt cold and dank, the air stale. She looked around and saw the place she found herself in was rough-hewn from rock and dimly lit by three oil lamps sitting in the corners. The floor beneath her was damp and paved with slick, uneven cobbles that she had never seen before in the castle. If this was still the castle.

Judita tried to get to her feet but her legs gave way beneath her, the effect of the narcotic compromising her motor control. Taking several deep breaths, she willed herself back into her body, forcing her limbs to acknowledge her control. It surprised her to find she hadn't been tied up, but she realized when she struggled to her feet that the room she was in was doorless and windowless. There had been no need to tie her up, because her bonds were hewn from solid rock. She had the sense of an incline, the cobbles folding away from her, before yielding to total dark. She was in a gradually descending tunnel, she realized, and considered taking one of the lamps and seeing what lay beyond in the dark; but some instinct told her that wherever it led, there was no escape, no redemption in that direction.

There was a noise from over by the far corner, where the meagre light of the lamps hadn't penetrated. Something was there, in the shadows. Something slow and quiet and dark. She remembered on the recordings she'd transcribed how patients described seeing shadows coalesce and take solid form, and she feared that she too was losing her mind.

Viktor. The thought struck her suddenly that it could be Viktor hiding in the shadows, watching her, making his plans for her: the twisted, deviant personality of Mr Hobbs the architect of her torture and death.

She picked up the oil lamp nearest her and edged towards the sound, ready to throw the lamp at whatever was there. Its pool of light advanced, rippling over the cobbles. Feet: the feet of someone lying or sitting on the floor, trousered legs, the sand-coloured canvas of an asylum straitjacket. Skála. He lay on the ground, his back against the stone wall. His eyes were wide with terror, despite the drugs that were still slowing his movements.

'The Devil,' he said through his stupor. 'Don't you see, he really *is* the Devil. The Devil is coming for us. He's coming back. You've got to help me.'

Judita ignored him, her mind trying to make sense of it all.

'You can't leave me to the Devil!' Skála implored. 'You've got to help me. We've got to help each other. You have to set me free.'

Judita's mind still raced. She had transcribed the sessions with Skála, heard all about his cruelty, his tortures, his crimes. But nothing was clear to her any more. She had listened to his monstrosity on the tape and heard when he had become Hobbs. Except it hadn't been Hobbs. It had been Viktor.

'Please!'

She went over to him and looked into Skála's eyes. She thought about how many had looked into those eyes as their lives had left them. Now, as she looked at them, they were empty of hate. Skála was afraid.

'Where did he go?' she asked. 'Where is Doctor Kosárek?' She half expected Skála to indicate the darkness of the tunnel; instead he nodded towards the solid stone behind her.

'The wall. He went through the wall.'

She sighed and shook her head. It was useless: Skála was hallucinating.

'A door,' he said. 'There's a door.'

'How did he open it?' she asked urgently.

Skála's eyes dimmed and she grabbed his shoulders and attempted to shake him violently, but his bulk dissolved her efforts. She slapped him hard across the face. 'The door, Vojtěch, how did he open the door?'

Skála shook his head. 'I didn't see.'

She looked in the opposite direction. Into the darkness of the tunnel.

'Can you get to your feet?' she asked. 'We can try heading into—'

'No!' Skála's eyes became wide again. 'Not that way. That's the Gate to Hell.'

'It's better than waiting to die here,' she said, but she felt the same instinctive dread.

'You've got to free me,' said Skála. 'Please, you have to get me out of this straitjacket.'

Again she hesitated. If she unfastened Skála's straitjacket, there was nothing to stop him killing her there and then. But what awaited her – awaited them – if she didn't?

'Hurry!' Skála urged through the drugs. Judita looked into the dark fire in Skála's eyes, then into the swallowing darkness of the tunnel. She was going to stay in control. She wasn't going to be a victim. She was a woman and she was Jewish and someone, somewhere had decided that those were qualifications to be a victim. Judita Blochová would not, she told herself, be anyone's victim. She made her decision and started to unbuckle the brass and leather fastenings on the straitjacket. She was unleashing one evil to aid her against another, greater evil. She was letting loose a homicidal maniac – but, if he killed her, then at least it would be because of her decision, her own choices, her own actions. If he didn't, she would have a powerful ally in the battle to come. If she stayed in control.

But she had only got one brass buckle unfastened and loosened a second when there was a grinding sound behind her: stone against stone.

The journey to Mladá Boleslav had been quicker than Smolák had estimated: the main road had been clear of snow and there had been no fresh falls. As soon as he and Novotný arrived at the Police Inspektorát in Mladá Boleslav, he tried phoning the Hrad Orlů asylum. The lines were still down.

Major Chromík arrived at the Inspektorát a few minutes after them, explaining he had been arranging suitable transport for them. Shorter than Smolák had expected, Chromík had penetrating, intelligent green eyes in which there was no hint of annoyance at being called upon. However, when he briefed Major Chromík on what his suspicions were, he noticed the local police chief hadn't looked at all surprised.

'I'm not a superstitious man,' said Chromík. 'But I grew up in the shadow of that place – and anyone who has will tell you the same thing: for us the Castle of the Eagles is the Castle of the Witches. Hrad Orlů draws evil like a magnet. Some instinct seems to attract evil men to it. I wish they'd shut down that bloody asylum and dynamite the castle.'

'All I know is I have to get there,' said Smolák. 'You say you have transport for us?'

Chromík nodded. 'I've borrowed a military half-track from the local garrison. It should make short work of the drive up to the castle. I've also got three men standing by to come with us.'

'The sooner we get there the better.' Smolák looked at his watch impatiently, measuring out a distance between himself and his goal.

'We can head off now,' said Chromík. 'I wouldn't worry too much about time – from what you say your suspect doesn't know we're on to him and the weather works as much in our favour as his. He won't be able to make any kind of run for it. We'll get your man, Kapitán Smolák. Don't worry.'

*V*ictor stood framed in the opening created by the stone door, blocking any escape. Before he closed the door again, Judita had just enough time to register what lay beyond Viktor. She saw the tower room with the patient couch, the desk with the Magnetophon recorder, the wheelchair he used to bring Skála into the tower treatment room.

It had been there all along, she realized. And Viktor had known that it was there. This was an access to the tunnels and he had been using it to come and go from the castle. But *how* did he know?

Viktor saw her hands working at the second buckle of Skála's straitjacket and strode over to her purposefully. She saw the vicious arc of his fist but didn't have time to dodge it. The dark world of the cave flashed suddenly bright as the blow hit her temple, sending her sideways and sprawling onto the sleek black cobbles. She lay stunned and watched helplessly as, with a single fluid movement, he bent down over Skála, who gazed up at him in awe.

'It's all right, Vojtěch,' Viktor said in Hobbs's voice, and rammed a syringe into Skála's neck. 'You have nothing to fear.' Judita could see the fire leave Skála's eyes, the tension leave his body. Viktor had left the concealed door open and Judita scrambled to her feet, her shoes scrabbling for purchase on the cobbles as she lunged towards the tower room and freedom. Viktor's carefully aimed sweeping kick caught her across the shins and brought her back down onto the cobbles before she was halfway there. She could hear him sigh, as if irritated by the misbehaviour of a child, then felt his grip tight around her ankle as he dragged her, face down on the cobbles, away from the ragged doorway.

'I found the entrance soon after I arrived here.' The most terrifying thing was the matter-of-fact way he spoke. He was dragging her like a predator dragging its kill, preparing to butcher her like he had all the others, and he was talking as if they were passing the time of day at a bus stop. 'Of all the generations to search for it, it was I who found the door. Then I realized, *I always knew it was there*. Odd that, isn't it?'

He paused to stoop and pick up one of the oil lamps, then continued to drag her. The cobbles gave way to a rougher floor: grit and loose stones. They were heading into the tunnel.

'For a while the castle was used as a prison,' he said. 'Not just for Jan of the Black Heart, but for prisoners in the Thirty Years War. They knew about the caves then, about the tunnels that go down and down. They would offer prisoners their freedom if they agreed to be lowered on a rope into the Gate of Hell and tell what they saw when they came back. Most preferred imprisonment to jeopardizing their souls.' He paused, letting her ankle go, then grabbing her above the elbow and hoisting her to her feet. The rough ground was making her too much of a burden to drag. He held her roughly by the upper arm, his fingers digging painfully into her flesh, pushing her onwards, downwards, into the intensifying darkness. 'But some agreed. And all who did came back completely insane and impossibly aged. You see, Judita, this really is the gateway to Hell. That's why I was brought here: it takes me closer to my natural environment. My domain.'

Judita gasped for breath. The tunnel had narrowed around them and the air had become strangely dry. 'Viktor . . . Viktor, please . . . remember who you are. Come back to me. I can help you. I *want* to help you.'

He stopped abruptly and spun her around to face him. In the upward-cast light from the oil lamp, his features looked sharp: a face all angles. Again the face she had once thought cruelly handsome just looked cruel. Looked like the Devil.

'Viktor isn't here,' he said in a voice that was not his, and for a moment she believed totally in Hobbs. 'Viktor was never here. Viktor was just a pretence, a sham. A cloak I threw around myself, like so many others.'

'I don't believe you. *You* don't believe you – deep down you must know this is a delusion. You *are* Viktor. All Hobbs is is a damaged part of Viktor. You're not real. You're a broken part of a good man. You don't have to do this.'

He laughed. Quietly, which terrified Judita even more.

'I have to do this. It's what I am. What I *truly* am. I'm going to deconstruct you, like I did the others. I am going to separate body and mind, body and soul, so that you can serve me in the spaces between lives.' He drew his face even nearer. 'You will understand, Judita. When I cut pieces out of you and hold them in front of your eyes for you to see, you will understand what connects the flesh with the mind, and what separates it.'

Viktor pushed her forward again. Suddenly the tunnel opened out into a second cave, larger this time. He shoved her violently and she fell, painfully crashing into the ground. The floor here was different: neither cobbled nor rough, it was finished in large flagstones. While she caught her breath, she heard Viktor move from one corner to another, each time more light adding to that of the oil lamp he had set on the floor. She eased herself up. The corner facing her was still in shadow, but again she could perceive something in the shadow as Viktor set more wall-mounted fire-torches alight. She screamed. The face of the Devil gazed at her from the shadow, taking shape as the light flickered across it. It had thick, curling horns bursting from a hairless head, its eyes empty sockets, its mouth twisted in a grotesque grin of long, sharp teeth.

A Perchten mask.

As more light was cast in the corner, she realized the Devil she thought she'd seen was a Krampus-type Perchten mask hanging on the wall in the corner. Her relief was short lived for beneath it hung a long leather apron, dark with bloodstains, old and new. This was his killing outfit. It had been that mask and apron he had hidden behind as he had lurked in shadows before lurching forth and visiting horror on his victims. There was something else there: the flickering light glittered coldly on the blade of a long, pendant knife.

She got to her feet and looked around. More horror.

There was a huge mediaeval chair, almost like a throne, raised on a podium, as if the cave was some kind of imperial receiving hall. Above the chair, fastened to the wall, was an ancient wooden shield, bearing a coat-of-arms. In one quadrant was the heraldic figure of a thick-set man with the head of a bear.

And there was someone in the chair: a man sat staring at Judita, except his eyes hadn't seen anything in centuries. Partly skeletonized, the dead man must have been mummified by the strangely dry, desiccating air in the cave. His clothes were still intact, but time-faded and dust-covered. His hands sat on the pommels of the armrests and his booted legs were crossed at the ankle.

Jan Černé Srdce – Jan of the Black Heart.

'He's magnificent, isn't he?' said Viktor in Hobbs's voice. 'My former vessel. The shape I took so long ago. Long before this time, long before my walking through the fogbound streets of London. He waved a hand in a sweep to indicate the cave. 'This is where they sought to confine me. This is where they immured me all those centuries ago, not understanding that this isn't my confinement – it's my hiding place.'

'Viktor,' said Judita, imploringly, 'none of that is true. That's a story I told you about the castle. These are all just stories you are telling yourself.' If he heard her, he showed no signs of it. She glanced over to where the Perchten mask hung with the leather apron. Where the knife hung, keen-edged and bright, waiting for its next victim. I will not be a victim, she told herself again. I will not give in to my nightmares. She measured the distance to the knife, but Viktor anticipated her and placed himself between her and it.

'This will be glorious,' he said to her. 'You will be more than my servant in the spaces between, you will be my bride. Your shaping will be the most elaborate. Your pain will be the most exquisite. It has to be that way, you understand that, don't you?'

'You're mad.' Judita was surprised at her own calm, measured tone. 'You're mad and a pervert. All you are is just another twisted deviant who gets his thrills out of hurting women. The psychiatrist in you knows it's true. All this crap – it's all conflation and confabulation: the dressing up of all the banal, sick shit you do in some kind of mythology, some kind of glorious mission. You need help, Viktor. You need to be stopped. You know that.'

He looked at her blankly, without anger. Then, without warning, he launched himself at her. She saw his first blow coming and dodged it, but the second hit her full on, just below the eye, and sent her crashing to the floor. She lay dazed.

'You're spoiling it,' he said without anger, without heat, still with the voice of Mr Hobbs. 'You're spoiling it all.' He went over to the corner and unhooked the leather apron and put it on. He carefully placed the Perchten mask over his head and face; took the long knife from its place. There was no Viktor any more: only Hobbs, only Leather Apron. His transformation, she had to admit, was complete. He *had* become the Devil.

The flickering light of the wall torches glittered and gleamed on the long blade of the knife as he advanced towards her.

*J*udita got up and ran. She turned from Viktor and headed towards the mouth of the tunnel, back in the direction of the tower room

'It's no use, I'll catch you,' he called out, casually.

It's no use, he'll catch me, she thought. She ran towards the lampless ink darkness of the tunnel and the glimmer of light beyond, falling several times. Each time she got up and ran on again. Judita was focused solely on her survival, on escape, and didn't notice that the emotion that drove her on wasn't fear but anger: a deep-burning fury that fuelled her onwards. There was some light ahead: the slice of dim illumination from the secret door back into the tower treatment room and the oil lamp still burning on the floor beside it. It was still too far.

Behind her in the hall she heard Viktor's footsteps as he ran, closing the distance between them. She looked over her shoulder and saw him: a Devil emerging from the dark, the evil twisted grin of the horned Perchten mask. She let out a roar as she thrust forward for the tunnel. She wouldn't make it, she knew that. When she reached the door she'd have to pause to push it open enough to pass through. That was where he would catch her. Where he would snatch away her last hope.

She reached where the hall joined the tunnel back up to the tower. But instead of running on, she spun around, turning on her heel.

As she did so, she hoisted up the oil lamp from where Viktor had left it on the floor. With another defiant roar and all her strength she threw it at him. It arced through the air and for a moment fully illuminated his mask, his apron, the knife. With that vision Judita's fear came flooding back. The oil lamp hit him in the centre of his leather-aproned chest before falling to his feet and smashing. There was a burst of flame that surged upwards and ignited the oil on his apron. The Perchten mask too began to blossom with flame, making it look even more demonic.

Viktor was burning. Yet he stood still, calm, watching her from the black sockets of the mask. She couldn't tear her eyes away. She saw Mr Hobbs in his mask and apron calmly burning in the centre of an underground hall in which a centuries-old monster held court in mummified dignity. It was true: he really was the Devil and this really was Hell.

She snapped herself out of it, turned and ran. She heard Hobbs's inhuman scream – of anger, not pain – as he ran after her. She was now in the tunnel and when she looked over her shoulder she saw him, enough oil still burning on the mask and apron to light up the tunnel walls, enough flame to still convince he was the Devil.

She reached the first cave and saw the hidden door still open and the tower room beyond. If she could get into the tower. If she could get the door open and scream for help.

Her feet skidded and slipped on the cobbles. Just a metre and a half from the door, she fell.

Viktor threw himself on top of her, holding her down. The flames were out but smoke curled from the apron, from his mask. He smelled of the earth, of burned blood, of death. It isn't Viktor, she told herself as he raised the knife. It isn't Viktor who's killing me. She hung on to the thought desperately as she waited for the first cut.

Something massive emerged from the shadows. A huge shape barrelled into Viktor and knocked him off her. The impact winded her and she rolled with the two bodies.

She heard Vojtěch Skála screaming in fury as he rolled over and over with the demon-masked figure of Viktor. She hoped that she had unfastened his straitjacket enough for him to struggle free, but when she looked over at the two bodies, she saw he was still bound. Skála had depended on his sheer bulk and strength, but now Viktor straddled him. He gave a bizarrely high-pitched, inhuman scream and the knife arced through the air over and over again: through the thick canvas straitjacket and into Skála's body, into his face, his eyes, his mouth. Skála's screams turned to a wet gargle, then silence.

Judita got to her feet and ran towards the tower room, shouldering the slab of rock that served as a door wide enough to squeeze through. Once she was in the tower room she looked to see if there was some way she could close the heavy stone door behind her, but it would take too long. He would have hold of her by then. She ran straight for the door out of the tower room and into the asylum, but it jammed, the latch still in place. She heard Hobbs scream: an inhuman bellow of rage. He burst into the tower room, blackened from burnt oil and stained dark with Skála's blood. Only the long, sharp teeth of the Perchten mask shone bright.

He strode across the room, shoving aside the desk in his way and sending the Magnetophon crashing to the floor.

Judita unlatched the door, but Viktor had her now. His fingers dug into her shoulders and he wrenched her from the door and across the room. She stumbled backwards and fell and he was on her, straddling her as he had Skála. The weight of him robbed her of breath. He held the knife to her face and she saw the blade sleek with blood. Skála's blood.

'Now,' he said calmly from behind the scorched mask. 'Now I'll show you the true gates of Hell. Now I'll show you where the Devil truly hides.'

She felt as if she'd been punched in the side, what breath that was left in her forced out. But when a white-hot pain seared through her body, she realized he had stabbed her. Judita's hand scrabbled across the floor, her fingers desperately seeking some weapon, something, anything. They found nothing.

Another searing pain and he pulled the knife from her side and pushed the tip into the skin of her forehead, just below the hairline.

Judita grabbed his wrist with both hands. He was too strong for her, but she would do all she could to make his killing of her hard work. He might kill her, but she would *not* be a victim.

'You have such a pretty face,' he said. 'I think I'll cut it off and keep it in my collection.'

Judita felt the knife move: the intense focus of new pain as the blade sliced through her skin.

As Judita Blochová prepared to die, the dreams she'd had came back to her. Dreams of a path taken by her and her kind into a dark forest, and a darker, unseen fate. At least she would be saved that.

There was a crashing sound, as if the door had been thrown wide. Then a second, deafeningly loud. A gunshot. Viktor toppled to one side and the knife fell from Judita's brow.

She felt blood running down her temple, into her hair. The weight gone from her chest, she drew a deep breath. But it didn't seem to fill her lungs.

There were faces over her. Urgent faces with concerned expressions. Mouths moving. Professor Románek. The policeman from Mladá Boleslav. The other policeman from Prague, Smolák. Platner appeared and set to work on stemming the flow of blood from her side.

She wanted to smile, to thank them, but found she couldn't move, couldn't speak, couldn't breathe. Things dimmed and she saw the shadows on the high vaulted ceiling move, writhe, gather around her. Eventually they coalesced into a warm, black darkness that swallowed her up.

EPILOGUE

here were days that were peaceful, days that were confused, days that were sad, and days that were terrifying.

Thankfully, most days were peaceful, spent in silent, pleasant contemplation of the forest below his barred window. Viktor found he had a deep love of that forest, warmed by the glow that radiated gold and amber from its broadleaved trees, soothed by the deep velvet green of its firs. Forests were the soul of the world, he thought; ancient and living their lives on a scale that transcended the short, meaningless spans of men. Forests were the repositories of all memories; the accumulation of dreams and nightmares; of all that was thought to be forgotten. There was deep, eternal comfort in forests.

He even occasionally got to spend time among the trees. When Viktor was judged calm and lucid enough, and had been soothed with a sedative, Dr Platner would take him out of the castle and for walks through the surrounding woods. These excursions were always undertaken with two burly orderlies who walked behind the two men, but close enough to grab Viktor should some delusion or overpowering emotion suddenly seized him.

He grew to like Platner. On their walks the two men would converse mainly in German, but Viktor was surprised at how often the Sudetener now switched to Czech. Much of the time Platner seemed preoccupied, but always managed to dress whatever concerns he had with cheerfulness. Viktor had been tempted to ask Platner if he had lost his Sudetendeutsche Partei lapel pin, for he never saw him wearing it these days, but decided to keep quiet.

Occasionally, as he spent hours at his castle window watching the slow dance of sun and shadow in the trees, he would frown at some vague and implausible memory that he had once been afraid of forests. That something bad had happened amongst the trees, some time long ago. And another equally unlikely memory would sometimes trouble him: that he had once felt uncomfortable in this suite of rooms, which sat apart from the others and had at one time been used as a storeroom for equipment.

He seemed to remember being a student; he remembered a Viennese hospital, bright with large windows and whitewashed walls, where he had been so young and the future had shined and he had been so keen to soak up the light and knowledge and the world. He remembered sitting listening to his mentor.

'Everyone,' Dr Jung had told his eager student, 'sees him- or herself as a statement: a declaration to the world. *This is what I am. This is who I am.*" The truth, however, is that every human being, every consciousness, is not a statement at all. It is a question.

'Your task, once you have qualified, my dear Viktor, is to seek the answer to each of these questions. And sometimes the most difficult question to answer is your own.'

Now his question puzzled him, confused him.

A lot of the time it was difficult to remember; difficult to think clearly. All Viktor's thoughts seemed unfixed, impermanent, his mind tending to move unbidden from one certainty to another, leaving him stumbling to make sense of things. And it was when this happened, when a landslide of memories and impressions would tumble into his mind, that he lost his peace. These would be the agitated days of confusion.

On such days, he struggled to sort out the conflicting thoughts and memories that would suddenly materialize in his mind, work out what was real, what was false; which memories were his and which had been placed there by others. He seemed to remember he had been a doctor here once, a psychiatrist.

At other times he was convinced he had been confined as a patient in the castle for decades. Occasionally the thought even occurred to him that he had been held in the stone embrace of its walls for centuries. He recalled a desperate encounter between a doctor and a madman in some distant station, at some distant time, discussing demons of fire and the ocean of the mind – but he was unsure whether he had been the doctor or the madman.

One thing Viktor remembered clearly was an interesting discussion on a train with an archaeologist from Hamburg called Pedersen, who told him all about the castle and the area around it. But Platner tried to assure him that he had seen no one else disembark the train in Mladá Boleslav. Platner even claimed he had contacted Hamburg University who had reassured him there was no Gunnar Pedersen there.

When the confusion got too much and Viktor became too agitated, Dr Platner would give him something to calm him, but it was like the volume being turned down on radio static: the confusion became diffuse, unfocused, but it was still there.

And, of course, there were the frightening days.

Those were the days when *he* came. There was what Viktor called the 'advent': a confusion of strange sensations, fleeting shadows seen out of the corner of his eye, that would herald *his* arrival.

Mr Hobbs.

Those were the worst days.

It always began the same way, with the darkness gathering in the corner. More malevolent than mere gloom, the shadows that had fleeted on the edge of his vision would coalesce in the corner like congealing blood, slowly taking form and shape. Blacker yet than black, darker yet than dark, it would gather there and reach forth with a scrabble of ink fingers, seeking out that which it claimed to itself. Reaching out to Viktor.

And then *he* would be there.

When he came, Mr Hobbs would most often appear as a lean, giant jangle of black limbs hunched over in the corner of the room, for he was much taller than any mortal man could be and his height was increased by the black silk tile hat he wore to conceal his horns. When he took this form, Mr Hobbs dressed as a Victorian English gentleman, his fine black attire protected by a leather apron stained dark crimson.

Sometimes he would take another form, like that of Krampus, when he would make no effort to hide his horns, instead displaying them proudly, and glare at Viktor with eyes like hot embers. Or he would appear as a giant, bearded, bear-like man in an astrakhan coat of tight wool curls, sodden heavy from unseen rain and smelling of a dark, dank forest.

But there were other times, and these were the times he dreaded most, when Viktor would turn from the window and his study of the forest below to see Mr Hobbs sitting silently watching him – bigger yet and hunched over even more – in the form of Kostěj the Deathless: the Grey Man with a face that was all angles, diamond-hard eyes, and a mouth forced into an overlarge, grotesque grin by a hundred teeth like long, thin, sharp needles that the pulled-taut pale lips could not cover.

But whatever form he took, Mr Hobbs always spoke with the same voice and German he had used when he had spoken through Viktor's patients: deep, resonant, cultured and faintly archaic. Viktor, cowering with terror, was forced to listen as Hobbs told him of all his misdeeds over centuries of pain and suffering, of depravity, cruelty and horror; and of how his true time was coming and he would bathe in the blood of innocents.

Those were the worst days.

But the peaceful, forgetful days outnumbered the troubled or the confused ones. The fleeting focus of Viktor's mind meant he often forgot Hobbs's visits.

He was disappointed that his friend, Filip Starosta, had never come to visit him; disappointed, but not surprised. After all, Viktor had taken on the guilt that was truly Filip's. Somewhere, out there beyond the castle's stone embrace, Filip was leading his life a free man. It was a thought that comforted Viktor, yet he sometimes felt confused as to whether it really had been Filip or Mr Hobbs who had committed the crimes for which Viktor had been blamed.

He had been allowed books and, until six months before, a radio. In his three years of confinement, however, he had never been permitted to mix with the other patients. So much so that he had begun to doubt they were still in the castle. When the radio had been taken away without explanation, Viktor suspected it had something to do with the increasingly desperate tones of the announcers, the playing of patriotic music.

The reports of the Sudetenland crisis.

When Viktor had first been confined, Professor Románek had visited him. The asylum director had seemed older and sadder, and Viktor remembered how the professor had on occasion to withdraw from the world, to lose himself to forgetfulness and melancholy. He sensed Románek was preparing for some longer, greater withdrawal. He also seemed deeply remorseful, as if he had let Viktor down. Viktor had wanted to tell the kindly psychiatrist that he shouldn't feel that way, that he was just pretending and taking the blame for what Filip had done. But he couldn't. That was all a secret.

Eventually Professor Románek stopped coming.

Dr Platner started to spend more time with Viktor, and after a while explained that Professor Románek had retired and he, Platner, was now in charge of the asylum. He spoke kindly to Viktor, sometimes in the same sad manner Románek had. Viktor was puzzled that a general physician had been placed in charge of a psychiatric institution and he got the strange idea that his promotion gave Platner no pleasure.

Other than a clouded, confused remembrance of him treating Viktor's gunshot wound and burns, Viktor hardly ever saw Krakl, but he got the impression that he too had been promoted. The oddest thing was that sometimes the tall, stooped Krakl frightened Viktor with his similarity to Mr Hobbs. Krakl's last visit to Viktor had been a brusque affair, the doctor hardly speaking to him except in sharp commands while he took measurements of Viktor's skull with callipers, barking the findings to an orderly who noted them down. Viktor had noticed that Krakl, beneath his white surgical coat, had been wearing some kind of uniform with polished black boots.

The days after were quiet. More quiet than he could remember the castle being before. One day, as he watched the forest from his barred window, he saw two military vehicles – an open Kübelwagen with two German officers and a canvas-covered troop transport – make their way up towards the castle. The sunlight flashed on the steel sliver of a Tatra 77 saloon that followed them. The vehicles drove up the sweep of the road and out of sight as they headed towards the stone-bridged chasm and castle gatehouses. Viktor wondered if the castle was now under military control. Now that he had no radio, he had little idea of what was happening in the world, but he could guess. The darkness through the trees had finally reached Czechoslovakia.

And that was why Judita had left.

Shortly before they had taken his radio and he still knew what was happening in the world beyond the castle's walls, she had come to see him. He had been so happy to see her, so very happy; but Judita had wept as she had talked to him. Viktor had been annoyed that Dr Platner and an orderly had remained within earshot, but at least they had allowed him to sit with Judita in the castle's dining room and drink coffee as they spoke.

She had reached over the table top and held his hand in both of hers and Viktor had felt good. The years of his confinement had seemed to fall away and it became like the earlier times, the happier times. She had been so beautiful when she came to see him, but her beauty was a sad beauty, a melancholy beauty, and it reminded him of a story he'd heard once, but couldn't fully recall. He told her that he liked the way she wore her hair now – looser and over her forehead – but that seemed to make her sadder.

He had talked to her about his plans for the future, for their future, and explained how wrong she had been when she said there was none for them. But his bright optimism just seemed to make Judita sadder still.

'I'm leaving Czechoslovakia,' she had explained tearfully. 'I wanted to say goodbye.'

The news had stung Viktor. 'But why? Where are you going?' he asked. 'Why won't you stay here with me? I need you here with me.'

'I can't stay.' Judita had glanced over his shoulder at Platner, then back to Viktor. 'Dr Platner has helped me get the necessary papers. I'm leaving Europe. Do you remember we talked about it? I'm going to America. There's nothing left for me here and I'm going to start fresh over there.'

Viktor lowered his voice to a desperate whisper. 'But *I'm* here. I need you to stay. Please stay and help me. I need you to help me. They won't let me leave here and I don't understand why. They say I did terrible things but it wasn't me. You know that, don't you? It was Hobbs. It was Hobbs who did all of those terrible things.' He frowned as if clarifying the thought to himself. 'Hobbs or Filip.'

By now he had her hands clasped desperately in his, and Platner and the orderly stepped forward, but Judita stopped them with a shake of her head.

'I have to go now, Viktor.' She leaned forward, her beautiful, pale face streaked with tears, and kissed him on the cheek. 'Dr Platner will look after you.'

A sudden realization dawned on Viktor. He smiled and nodded. 'Yes, yes, I see. I understand. It's best. You go to America now and I'll follow later. You can find out where would be best for me to carry out my work. Like you said, the Americans are more likely to support my research. No, no – the more I think about it, you're right. You go on first and I'll follow.'

Judita broke into deep sobs and Platner came over, took her by the shoulders and guided her away.

'Don't be sad,' Viktor called to her as she was guided from the canteen. 'It won't be long. I'll come to America too. I promise you Judita: I'm coming to America. I swear I *will* come to America – '

After Judita was gone, after Viktor had been taken back to his rooms, something heavy and dull had sat in his chest as he'd watched a taxi make its way down the ribbon of road through the trees towards the village and the world beyond. When he had turned back from the window he jumped, his sadness transformed to terror in an instant. He had turned to see Mr Hobbs, in his high tile hat, black silk cravat and bloodstained leather apron filling the corner of the room, his thin shoulders hunched, his neck bent at an impossible angle and his head twisted sideways so he could fit into the space.

Viktor screamed, but no sound came from his mouth, and Hobbs laughed at him, derided him in the same voice that he had used when he had spoken through Viktor's patients.

'I heard you,' he had said. He had sneered at Viktor and the sneering changed him for a moment into Kostěj the Deathless, his mouth stretching wide and deep and filling with a hundred thin, sharp teeth. 'I heard you say you'll go to America. That will never happen. You're never leaving here, don't you see that? You'll never go to America or anywhere else, so why don't you find some way of killing yourself? Then I would be free again and not stuck with you. You're pathetic. You failed me in every way possible.'

'I'm sorry . . .' Viktor sobbed, terrified. 'I'm sorry.'

'Do you remember when we first met?' said Hobbs. 'Do you remember the day your mother took you and your sister Ella to Čertovo Jezero – the Devil's Lake – deep in the forest, for a picnic.

You were visiting your grandparents, your German grandparents, remember? You all went for a picnic and you and Ella played in the forest?'

'I don't want to talk about it,' said Viktor, distressed by the memory and terrified by the monster in the corner. 'That was the day of the accident.'

'Yes, the accident.'

'Ella fell in the water,' Viktor had explained. 'I tried so hard, so hard to save her, but I was tiny. I couldn't swim. I nearly drowned trying. I ran to get my grandfather and mother but . . .' Viktor had broken off, the memory biting into him of a small body, so small, floating face down like a dropped doll, a white dress billowing in the dark water.

'But that's not really how it happened, is it Viktor?' Hobbs had sneered and again, for a second, his mouth distorted into Kostěj the Deathless's grin. 'That's not what happened at all.

'And your mother. She didn't kill herself just because your sister drowned, did she? She killed herself because she found out what a monster her son was. It wasn't your sister who was her favourite, was it? That's why she felt so guilty when your sister drowned: because she was heartbroken but still so glad it hadn't been her precious Viktor. But then she found out. She found out what had happened to all those cats that had gone missing in the village. She followed you into the woods and saw what you did. Saw the terrible things you did to please me. Saw you for the monster you were.' There was a great spider-scuttling of limbs as Hobbs-Kostěj-Veles sought out a shadowed place closer to Viktor.

'Of course, I hid from her,' said Hobbs into Viktor's ear. 'She didn't see me, see my part in it all, see that it was I who had been awakened in Devil's Lake. I've been with you ever since, Viktor. Every day. And when your mother got the truth out of you about what happened at the lake that day, she couldn't live with it. She told you you were a monster. You were twelve years old and your mother called you a monster so you called her a German cunt. She couldn't live with it and hanged herself there in the forest – she took the belt from her coat, looped it around a branch of one of the trees and hanged herself while you watched.'

'It's not true!' Viktor had yelled. 'It was you. It was you!' He thought back, forced the memories to the surface of his mind. The movie that had played so many times in his head: Ella in the water, yelling, struggling. Viktor running into the water, desperately reaching out to her, his fingertips brushing against her but not getting a grip. But the memory changed, the perspective altered. Little Ella was pleading with him, begging him. He saw his hands on her small, weak shoulders, pushing her down, her blonde hair billowing green-gold in Devil's Lake. Again there was a moment of confusion and he couldn't be sure if he was remembering his sister or another small, drowned body, or another closer to the castle. In the small lake behind the village that had reminded him—

'It's not true!' Viktor yelled again, but more images came to him, more memories came to him. Horrors. So much blood. Blood on *his* hands, on his lips, in his mouth. Red flesh rendered from white bone. Women screaming. 'It's not true!'

Viktor screamed his denials over and over to the monster in the corner. The true monster. The real killer. But he just scuttled back into the most shadowed corner and sat there, laughing at Viktor.

The door burst open and Krakl came in with two orderlies. They followed Viktor's gaze to the corner of the room – the empty corner of the room. Rough hands fell on Viktor and there was the sharp jab of a hypodermic needle in his forearm. His will and his strength faded as he was wrestled into a restraint jacket and thrown onto his sofa.

In the weeks that followed Judita's visit, things quietened down. Viktor entered one of his remissions: lucid, rational periods in which he became again the conscientious psychiatrist bemused by his own confinement. During such times, the hallucinations not only ceased but were forgotten. Mr Hobbs's visitations became unremembered or only vaguely recalled as something that happened in a nightmare. All he remembered with any clarity was that Judita was gone and he would never see her again.

At times like these, Dr Platner would visit Viktor more often. Viktor found it difficult to assess the Sudetener's mood: there was a weariness, a worriedness, about him that hadn't been there before, and Viktor wondered if current events were weighing on the doctor. But whenever he pushed Platner about what was happening in the wider world, the doctor would say simply, 'It's best for you not to worry yourself about such things, Viktor.'

Platner came to his rooms early one morning, not long after sunrise. Viktor was already up and had washed, shaved with the electric razor they had allowed him, and was dressed. When Platner came into his room, Viktor was bent over a book, a dense tome that was his favourite non-medical book: a text on Slavic mythology and its origins.

'I wondered if you wanted to take a walk in the forest before breakfast,' said Platner, smiling. Behind him was a soldier in black uniform. Of late, whenever they went for a walk, their escort had been armed soldiers rather than orderlies.

'I should like that,' said Viktor. 'Very much.'

'It's all right,' said Platner, when Viktor made to put the text he'd been reading back on its shelf, 'you can take your book with you. We'll find a nice spot to sit.'

It was good to get out of the castle. As they passed through it on the way out, Viktor noticed that all the staff now seemed to be military, and the place was full of crates being unpacked, equipment being installed. Viktor was disappointed that Platner didn't say to him that it was 'nothing but the very latest thing'. He also noticed that some of the halls had been converted into open wards, tight-packed with narrow beds.

'Are we taking in more patients?' he asked, but Platner either didn't hear the question or chose to ignore it.

It was a fine day outside. The autumn sun was low and gold but winter was taking its first tentative chill bite at the bright air. As Viktor pulled his coat collar up to his ears, he turned and looked up at the castle, which was as it always had been, except for the red and white banner, the crooked black cross of a swastika at its heart, that danced in the breeze from the top of the main tower. They must have found a way up, he thought to himself; they must have found Jan of the Black Heart's resting place.

As they made their way down the road to the village, the uniformed soldier following them with his rifle slung over his shoulder, Platner chatted to Viktor, talking of changing seasons, changing times. When they were halfway down to the village, Platner steered Viktor into the side path that led to the old forest chapel.

'Oh I know this place,' said Viktor with sudden brightness when they reached the chapel. 'Oh yes, yes – I remember this place. I used to come here with Judita. Yes, Judita . . .' Viktor frowned, trying to catch and fasten a fleeting memory, and looked round to where the forest chapel stood dark and strong and ancient. The soldier in the black uniform stood silently smoking a cigarette in the chapel's portico and the furrows of Viktor's frown deepened as some other memory, vague and rough formed, took shape in his mind. He seemed to remember the ancient wood yielding to a knife in his hand as he carved something into it.

'Would you like to sit here and read your book for a while, Viktor?' suggested Platner. 'It's peaceful here. Quiet. Then on the way back up to the castle you can tell me more about Slavic mythology.'

'I'd like that.' Viktor opened his book and set it on his lap, but before reading, he turned to Platner. 'Thank you for bringing me here. It makes me feel happy. Sometimes I get so sad,' he said. 'Sometimes I feel this great sadness. Tell me, Doctor, am I really mad?'

Platner sighed and smiled sadly; so sadly it troubled Viktor. 'All things are relative, Viktor; I'm very much afraid an even greater sadness – a greater madness – is coming to us all.'

As Platner walked off to give him peace, Viktor started to read his book about the ancient gods and demons of the Slavic woods, aware of how perfect this location was and how grateful he was to Dr Platner for bringing him here. He was content – and so engrossed in his book that he took no notice of the sounds behind him as the soldier came down the wooden chapel steps, of metal sliding on metal, of the mechanical snapping sound of a bolt mechanism.

He barely had time to register the cold kiss of the soldier's rifle barrel on the nape of his neck before Viktor Kosárek's great sadness ended.

*I*t was the blooming of a fine late autumn day. The morning sky was a blue, cloudless shield over San Francisco, so John Harvester had the roof down on his Mercedes convertible as he drove through the city to his downtown office. It was a fresh, bright day to feel good, all right, and Harvester had a lot to feel good about: life was a gift – life was *great* – when you were young, attractive, successful and rich.

Harvester didn't even allow the news on the radio to dampen his mood. San Francisco was a city twice shaken: shaken by the Earth and shaken by the dark will of a single man. The first report on the radio was about the escalating repair bill for the Santa Rosa earthquake of two weeks before; the second was about San Franciscans' continually escalating terror of the so-called Zodiac Killer.

The radio reported in solemn tones that the killer had sent another letter to the *San Francisco Chronicle* – this time accompanied by a blood-soaked piece of shirt from his most recent victim to prove its authenticity. In this latest letter, the Zodiac Killer had announced he was considering ambushing a school bus and killing all the children on board. It was a threatened act of evil that everyone knew he was capable of, and the already frightened city fell victim to a new, pervasive paranoia. As a psychiatrist, John Harvester found fascinating the way the mind of one man, the will of a single individual, could infect a population of nearly three quarters of a million with terror.

Parking in the basement car park of his office building, Harvester took the elevator to his eighth-floor suite of offices. He smiled at his reflection in the elevator's smoked glass: his Italian-tailored suit, shirt, silk tie were all the best quality; the dark hair above a handsome, tanned face was expensively barbered. Everything about him spoke of early success, of a life not yet half lived, yet a promise already fulfilled.

He was greeted as he left the elevator by his receptionist and secretary, Jodi. Tall, lithe and blonde, Jodi had been hired as much for her looks as her administrative abilities – although those had fortunately turned out to be formidable. Everything about Dr John Harvester, about his elegant offices populated with Eames furniture and Pollock canvases, about Jodi, made a statement that his was an exceptional success. That his were exceptional patients. And they were.

Just as he was now, when John Harvester had first qualified as a doctor, he had been driven by great ambition. At that time that great ambition had been to make a real difference in the world: to find new ways of treating the sicknesses of the mind. But as opportunities had presented, as less lofty aims had insinuated themselves, the ambition remained, but the focus had moved. His patient list had become a clientele; his treatment had shifted from the psychoses of the desperate to the neuroses of the rich – of California's wealthy elite, including several Hollywood stars.

Harvester had everything – except the one thing he craved most: to be taken seriously by his peers. But there would be the book. When his book and his theory came out – then they would take him seriously.

'Morning Jodi.' He smiled at her. 'A beautiful morning.'

'It is, Dr Harvester,' said Jodi. 'But that's terrible news this morning. That letter in the *Chronicle*. Do you think he'll do it? The school bus, I mean.'

'I think this guy's capable of anything,' said Harvester.

'They say he's smart. Like super-intelligent. Did you read that some people out in Salinas have decoded the cryptogram he sent the last time? Or at least most of it.'

'No I didn't. What did it say?'

'It was really creepy. The Zodiac Killer says he's killing all these people so that they can serve him after he's dead – they'll be his "slaves and playmates in paradise", he said. *Really* creepy. How can he get away with it for so long? Even with him being so smart. I mean, there's no sign of them catching him.'

Harvester considered what she had said for a moment. 'I have this theory,' he said, 'that there's a chance he hasn't been caught because even the Zodiac Killer doesn't know who he is.'

'I don't get you.'

'I think he's hidden himself well – even from himself. Come on Jodi, you've transcribed enough of my notes to understand the concept of multiple personalities. Maybe the reason the Zodiac Killer hasn't been caught is because he's an identity – an alter – hiding deep inside an unknowing host.'

'What?' Jodi frowned prettily. 'You really think that someone could be the Zodiac Killer and not know it?'

'It's entirely possible. You know that from the notes for my book.' A thought suddenly occurred to him: *maybe I can discuss the Zodiac Killer in my book as well.*

Harvester's book, as well as offering another opportunity to enrich himself, was his big project: his attempt to be taken seriously by the larger psychiatric community. He had formulated a theory that multiple personality disorder was much more prevalent than currently believed – maybe even, to varying degrees, an element in everyone's psychology. There were all kinds of angels and demons in all of us, and Harvester was determined to prove it.

He had taken a huge risk in using his rich and celebrity patients as test cases, without their knowledge. But the data he had gathered would only ever be presented as relating to anonymous subjects.

And anyway, the thiopental or lorazepam he used in the sessions had an amnesiac effect: they remembered nothing, and only he knew the full content of their discussions. And, of course, there were the tape recordings he made for reference.

Whatever it took, Harvester was determined to prove the validity of his thesis.

It was shortly after ten when Jodi brought through his first patient. Alice Sterling smiled shyly as she entered Harvester's office and lay down on the Corbusier couch. It was the oddest thing about many of these Hollywood types, Harvester had often thought, that they made their livings from being professional show-offs, yet often were afflicted by shyness – sometimes crippling shyness – when not in front of the camera. There again, we were all just actors playing out roles.

'How are you today, Alice?' Harvester asked. He made an effort not to let his excitement show. The last session with this patient had yielded spectacular results. Unbelievable results.

'Not too good,' she said sadly – the studio polish was rubbing off her Midwest accent. 'Pretty low, if I'm honest. I can't seem to shake off this – I dunno – this depressed feeling I've got all the time.'

'Let's see what we can do about that,' Harvester said. Alice Sterling was a slim, elegant and exceptionally beautiful twenty-four-year-old. But her flawless complexion, bone structure and figure were all she shared with Alice Silberstein, the girl she had grown up as in a blue-collar mill town in Missouri, where jobs, money and all kinds of opportunity had been scarce. And therein lay the seeds of her discontent: a kind of reverse adjustment disorder where her sudden wealth and freedom from all material and financial worries had, paradoxically, resulted in depression and feelings of diminished self-esteem. 'Are you ready to begin?' he asked.

She nodded and Harvester administered the same dose of thiopental and lorazepam he had the last time. As the tension eased from her, he reached across to his desk and pressed the button to start the tape recording.

Remembering the events of the last session, Harvester felt the thrill of anticipation as he waited for the drug to take full effect and place his patient in a hypnotic state. Eventually he asked his first question:

'I want to talk to the person I talked to before.'

She didn't respond.

'I want to speak to the person who is looking for something. The person who said they had lost something precious.'

And then it came. Harvester felt his heart pick up pace as he heard his slender, delicate female patient begin to speak.

'I've lost it,' she said in a voice that was not hers. Deep, masculine, hard-edged and English-accented. 'My most treasured memento. My little glass rose, all white and glistening.'

'Who are you?' asked Harvester.

There was a pause, then:

'You may call me Mr Hobbs.'

Behind the Devil:
the research and development of *The Devil Aspect*

I am, I suppose, a method writer. In much the same way as a method actor immerses him- or herself completely in a part, remaining 'in character' throughout the time they are involved with the role, I immerse myself totally in the time, the culture and the world my characters inhabit. It is something I have done in my previous novels and is an experience that I feel has enriched me. To see the world through another's eyes is to change and enhance one's own personal perspective. It is also a lot of fun. With this book, it was a lot of dark fun.

People often ask me if the research for my novels – dealing as they do with other times and places, and often involving specialist scientific or historical detail – is not incredibly onerous. The truth is that, for me, the research isn't hard work: it is so indissolubly inter-woven into the writing process that I cannot separate the two, and I find the process of learning and immersion a joyful one.

It may seem strange, given that *The Devil Aspect* is such a dark and menacing tale, that I derived so much pleasure from not just its telling, but the process of immersing myself in the rich folklore, myth and culture of Central and Eastern Europe, as well as the more shadowed regions of the human Unconscious. But these are the things that fascinate me, and the great joy of writing for a living is that you are free to follow the paths that call to you most. In the case of *The Devil Aspect*, those paths led to some very dark places indeed.

The main engines that drive the story are Jungian psychology, Central European myths and legends, the history of Czechoslovakia immediately before the Second World War and the ethnic tensions that existed within the country at that time. What I enjoyed in the research and writing of the book was how all of these themes came together, interconnected and intertwined. My choice of Czechoslovakia was informed by the country's place at the very heart of Europe – geographically, ethnically, culturally, psychologically. The Bohemians particularly are a people of intricate psychology. Here is a place shaped by the fusion of Celtic, Slavic, Germanic and Jewish cultures. It is no coincidence that that most unique of creative voices, Franz Kafka, with all of its absurdism, surrealism and dark humour, was a product of this time and place.

I spent a great deal of time in Prague and the wider Czech Republic researching this book. What emerges in any novel is only the very tip of the research iceberg: much of the research is familiarization with a people, a culture and a history and never reveals itself in a written sentence, but is manifest in the confidence and authority with which you write about a place, a time and a people. For example, knowing that Moravians mock Prague Bohemians for their sing-song accents is something that never comes out in the book – but it is a cool fact to know!

I find it odd the way different elements must come together for a novel to take its true form. I had the broad idea for *The Devil Aspect* for some time, but it was during a trip to Bohemia that it all came together for me. I was visiting Hrad Karlštejn – it was off-season and it was a dull day, the castle sitting under a dramatic, dark-clouded sky. Hrad Karlštejn, it has to be said, is one of the spookiest places on the planet, even on a sunny day, and would probably be rejected by a house-hunting Dracula for 'having a bad vibe'. I was in the main hall used by Karel IV when the whole idea fell into place. I was standing where the Emperor would hold audiences, his throne placed between two large windows so that, while those who addressed him were cast in light, his demeanour and expression were so in shadow his audience could not read them. (This is mentioned in the novel and reflected in the policeman Smolák's office). As I stood there, I imagined the dark events and even darker secrets that must have been confined in the castle's walls over the centuries. It was then that it all came together for me: I saw the castle as an asylum, imagined it in the period immediately before the war as both a place where the individual madness of killers was confined, yet which paradoxically was a refuge and asylum from the greater madness of Nazism beyond its walls, creeping inexorably closer.

I had the place, I had the time. My story was almost ready; but the key ingredients to be added were the myths and legends, the presence of which one can almost feel in the Bohemian Forest, and the psychological theories of Carl Jung. These two elements were the most closely interwoven: Jung's theories revolved around the creation of myths and legends as an externalization of the collective Unconscious. Jung's theory of Archetypes gives us the common characters in mythology – and in literature, for that matter. Jung fascinates me: a scientist whose father was a village pastor who didn't believe in God, and whose paternal grandfather was rumoured to be the illegitimate son of Goethe. On his mother's side, his grandfather was a well-known theologian who experienced visions, learned biblical Hebrew because he became convinced it was the language spoken in heaven, and, just like Dominik Bartoš in the novel, believed he could commune directly with the dead. Until Jung's mother married his father, his grandfather would make her sit behind him as he composed sermons – just to make sure the Devil wasn't at his shoulder, reading what he wrote.

Researching the Slavic mythology that pervades the stories in *The Devil Aspect* took me into my favourite place. The Bohemians owe their name to the ancient Celtic tribe, the Boii, who were the founder population (also the founder population in south-east Germany, where their local name Baiovarii, gave its name to Bavaria/Bayern). On top of this substrate of Celts, came Germanic tribes, principally the Suebi, followed by the invasion and dominance of the Slavic Czechs. Throughout history, this rich mix was further enhanced by German and Jewish settlement. This admixture of cultures, legends and beliefs led to an exceptionally rich mythology. Slavic mythology itself is so very closely related to Norse mythology, probably revealing the influence of the Kievan Rus. All of this deep, dark and intertwining mythology offered me the perfect parallel to Jung's theories.

The more I researched, the more dark wealth I found, such as the Bone Church – the Church of the All Saints in Sedlec – with František Rint's bizarre deathly artwork. The deeper I got into the history and the culture, the more ideas sparked in my brain. Added to this was, of course, the cataclysm that befell Bohemia's Jewish population. The Holocaust, its brutality, its scale and the impoverishment of European culture that resulted from it, is something that has haunted me since I first became aware of it. Through Judita's eyes, I tried to see its foreshadowing in those dark days immediately before the Nazi invasion. That research offered no joy, and indeed added to my sense of unease, even astonishment, at what seems to be the re-emergence in our society of fervent nationalisms and anti-Semitism.

I had two particularly strange experiences when writing *The Devil Aspect*: the first was an experience I had when I was more than three-quarters of the way through the manuscript. I had created the castle of Hrad Orlů, using an amalgam of real Bohemian, Moravian and Slovakian castles, and given it this dark history of a castle built not to be lived in, but to stop up the gateway to Hell. All of this I invented freely, without reference to any real location. However, one evening, when I was doing further research into Czech castles,

I discovered the real Hrad Houska, which actually had been built without kitchens or accommodation, but with massive, impenetrable foundations to stop up what was believed at the time to be the mouth of Hell. The second such experience was when a friend, an academic who specializes in the Gothic, told me he had a copy of Carl Jung's *Red Book*. I had, of course, heard of *The Red Book* – which the Jung family forbade being published until 2009 in case it damaged Carl Jung's reputation – but I had never seen a copy. I was absolutely astounded at how similar *The Red Book* was to my description of Filip Starosta's illustrated manuscript in *The Devil Aspect*. Two fictional creations that, unknown to me, were paralleled in reality.

If Carl Jung were still around, he'd call it synchronicity.

ACKNOWLEDGEMENTS

I owe huge thanks to my wife Wendy, for her unfailing support, belief and enthusiasm; to my wonderful UK publisher Krystyna Green for the sheer energy and passion of her championship of my writing and belief in this book; likewise to my US publisher Jason Kaufman, for his enthusiasm and commitment. I greatly appreciate Martin Fletcher's excellent and sympathetic editing suggestions and Penny Isaac's superb copyedit. Thanks to Eleanor Russell for her great care and attention, and to designer Sean Garrehy, who put so much thought and creativity into the cover. Thanks also to Dr Matt Foley for our chats about the Gothic and Carl Jung. I am hugely grateful to Sabina Sakařová for helping me with my Czech, similarly to my Czech translator, Jan Kozák, who was a huge help and went above and beyond the call of duty.

Thanks too to my literary agents Andrew Gordon and Esmond Harmsworth, to Alice Howe and the foreign rights team, and to my film agents Georgina Ruffhead and Joel Gotler. For their friendship and support, I'd like to thank my fellow authors Jens Østergaard, Nick Elliot, Michael Ridpath, Graham Smith, Shona Maclean, Neil Broadfoot, Theresa Talbot and Douglas Skelton.